Daddy's Little Matchmaker

Roz Denny Fox

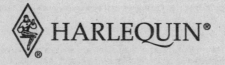

ISBN 0-373-71220-0

DADDY'S LITTLE MATCHMAKER

Copyright © 2004 by Rosaline Fox.

www.eHarlequin.com

Printed in U.S.A.

This book is for John Wisecarver,
high school English teacher extraordinaire.
With his gift for teaching,
and because of his enthusiasm for all books,
he opened new worlds to us
and inspired all who passed through his classes
to reach higher and dream bigger.
He will be missed.

Books by Roz Denny Fox

HARLEQUIN SUPERROMANCE

649—MAJOR ATTRACTION
672—CHRISTMAS STAR
686—THE WATER BABY
716—TROUBLE AT LONE SPUR
746—SWEET TIBBY MACK
776—ANYTHING YOU CAN DO
800—HAVING IT ALL
821—MAD ABOUT THE MAJOR
847—THE LYON LEGACY
      "Silver Anniversary"
859—FAMILY FORTUNE
885—WELCOME TO MY FAMILY
902—BABY, BABY
926—MOM'S THE WORD
984—WHO IS EMERALD MONDAY?
999—THE BABY COP
1013—LOST BUT NOT FORGOTTEN
1046—WIDE OPEN SPACES
1069—THE SEVEN YEAR SECRET
1108—SOMEONE TO WATCH OVER ME
1128—THE SECRET DAUGHTER
1148—MARRIED IN HASTE
1184—A COWBOY AT HEART

CHAPTER ONE

A NOISE AT THE DOOR made Laurel Ashline glance up. She was working with Donald Baird, an elderly stroke victim, teaching him to operate a hand loom. The woman who stood in the doorway was someone Laurel didn't know. Laurel was fairly new to Ridge City, Kentucky, and had recently become a volunteer occupational therapist here at the local hospital.

The white-haired woman wore a dusty-rose chenille robe and matching slippers. She seemed unsure about crossing the threshold.

"Hello." Laurel offered a warm smile. "Are you here for weaving therapy? I wasn't told to expect a new student, but if you'll take a seat I'll run out to my car to get another loom. I'm sure your chart will catch up eventually. They always do."

"Oh, I'm not here for therapy. I'm practically recovered from a touch of pneumonia, although my doctor and I don't see eye to eye about my going home today." The woman sighed. "In fact, he ordered me to spend the afternoon in the sunroom. Said he'll decide later if I have to eat hospital food again tonight." Her droll expression spoke eloquently about her opinion of hospital fare.

"I see. Well, the sunroom is at the end of this hall." Laurel pointed.

"I know, dear. I just couldn't help noticing how you have my friend pulling that bar toward him with both hands."

The man in question stopped a painstaking quest to thread

the shuttle in and out between thick rag strips. "Vestal? Howdy." He had to peer around Laurel to see the woman. "It's sad when a tough old duck like me is reduced to making pot holders. This is woman's work," he said, although his disgust seemed exaggerated.

"Nothing of the sort," Laurel quickly interjected. "Weaving's a time-honored craft anyone can feel good about. All the better if working a loom allows you greater arm and wrist mobility. Isn't getting well your primary goal?"

"You tell that old coot—uh—sorry, I don't know your name," the patient lingering by the door said, gazing at Laurel from faded blue eyes.

"It's Laurel. Laurel Ashline. And you're—?"

Her gaze still on what Donald Baird was doing, the elderly woman moved in for a closer look. "Is this type of therapy successful for all upper-body disabilities?"

Laurel hesitated. At twenty-nine, she was a master weaver, not a certified occupational therapist. "I don't know about *all* disabilities. But it's an old technique, one that gained respect and popularity with orthopedic physicians after World War Two. Lou Tate, a weaver from Louisville, was the first to use desktop looms to help partial amputees and other maimed soldiers. There's a wonderfully soothing quality connected to the repetitive motion of working a beater bar. The exercise develops tone in atrophied muscles." Laurel might have expounded further on a subject near to her heart, but a nurse appeared to escort the inquisitive stranger away.

"Goodbye," Laurel called belatedly. "Good luck getting sprung by suppertime." Her conspiratorial grin was answered in kind as the departing woman glanced back over one shoulder.

Laurel set to work again shuffling between the three people currently in her program. During the course of the day, the stranger faded from mind. Laurel maintained a hectic schedule. As well as volunteering at the hospital, she wove in cotton, wool and chenille. But her specialty was fine linen table-cloths and napkins.

When she'd first come to Ridge City, she'd been reclusive, hiding out to nurse her deep wounds from a bad marriage—until she decided it was time to take back her life. Now she had an ever-widening circle of private clients, plus she'd renewed a project her grandmother had begun—the collection and preservation of old mountain weaving patterns. Laurel found it was an endeavor that was both worthwhile and enjoyable; it was also a way to honor her grandmother's memory. Added to that, she taught weaving at a community college two days a week. And a few weeks ago, she'd been approached to demonstrate at local clubs. Her schedule kept her almost constantly busy. Laurel needed that, because it meant she had fewer hours at home where Dennis Shaw, her alcoholic ex, might call and harass her. He paid no attention to restraining orders issued in Vermont and in Kentucky.

As Laurel finished up at the hospital and loaded her car, her thoughts were already on her next project.

ALAN RIDGE, current CEO of the once wholly family-owned Windridge Distillery, stood and quickly closed out a spreadsheet displayed on his home-office computer. He smiled faintly as he listened over the speakerphone to his grandmother, who ordered him to drop everything and come get her from the hospital. She'd vehemently resisted going there at all.

Vestal still spoke to him in the autocratic manner she had when he was a boy. But though he was thirty now, Alan didn't mind. He was deeply concerned about his grandmother's failing health. He didn't think he could bear yet another loss.

Ending the call, Alan snatched a jacket from the hall coat-rack. Spring evenings in Kentucky could be quite chilly after the sun set. "Birdie, Grandmother's coming home. Louemma's napping," Alan called, by way of requesting that Birdie Jepson, the Ridge family's cook and housekeeper, keep an eye on his nine-year-old daughter.

She came out of the kitchen as Alan gathered up a lap robe to tuck around his grandmother.

"I do declare, Mr. Alan, that child's gonna sleep her life away. What did that new doctor have to say yesterday? Did he have any good ideas?"

"She. Dr. Meyers is a female neuro-orthopedic specialist." Alan felt his smile disappear altogether. "All the specialists say the same thing, Birdie. Medically, Louemma's back surgery was a success. Every doctor I've consulted believes her problems are psychological. Except the psychiatrists haven't helped. The last one claimed she's just spoiled. I do indulge her. But…for pity's sake, she lost her mother in a car wreck that's left her…" Alan hated to say the damning word—*paralyzed.* "I know she'd move her arms if she could."

"There, there. I reckon the good Lord will heal the poor baby in time. We're all just so anxious to see her bouncing around like she did before the accident."

"God's certainly taking his time, Birdie. Come March fifteenth, which is next Monday, it'll be a full year." Alan rubbed a hand over a perpetually haggard face.

"That long? I guess it's been at that. Doesn't seem but yesterday I moved in, instead of popping in and out to cook for Miss Emily's parties. You and Miss Vestal must feel like it's been eons since that hellish phone call from the state police."

Alan felt the pain always. Life at Windridge had been topsy-turvy since that call telling him his wife had been killed and his daughter injured in a senseless crash. Everything had changed then.

"Well, you'd best go collect Miss Vestal. If I know her, she'll be pacing at the hospital door. Tell her I made buttermilk pie. For Miss Louemma, but Miss Vestal don't need to know that."

Alan's smile returned briefly. "Talk about spoiling, Birdie. I'm pointing Louemma's next psychiatrist straight at you. And Grandmother. That last shrink said we were all enablers."

"We don't know how to be anything else, Mr. Alan. Just tell that grouchy old doctor it's 'cause we all love Louemma to bits."

He laughed outright at her comment. Laughter seemed to be the only way they could deal with the parade of doctors, most spouting either useless or contradictory diagnoses, who'd become commonplace in their lives.

Out of habit, Alan detoured past his daughter's room. Tiptoeing into the shuttered bedroom, he gazed lovingly down on sleep-flushed cheeks and pillow-tousled curls. The poor kid had a cowlick just like his, at the hairline above her left eyebrow. His wife had cursed that cowlick—and Alan for passing it on to Louemma.

Alan's fingers gently skimmed the dark-blond hair. Backing quietly from the pink room that lacked nothing in the way of girlish accoutrements, he sighed and shifted the lap robe to his other arm as he dug out the keys to the car Vestal preferred over his more serviceable Jeep. Her baby-blue Chrysler New Yorker wasn't Alan's kind of car, and it rarely got driven. In her late seventies, Vestal Ridge had been so shaken by Emily's accident she rarely drove now. Only on occasion, and then only back and forth to town.

Alan liked his four-wheel drive. Outside of visiting a myriad of doctors, his trips, consisted mainly of dashing between the house and the distillery, built a mile uphill on the vast family estate. The road was often muddy, especially in spring. Since 1860, a Ridge had owned the three hundred and sixty acres that made up Windridge. In all that time, the estate had remained virtually unchanged. With the exception of forty acres, Alan recalled with a scowl. Lord knew he wished he could forget the pie-shaped wedge sliced from their eastern border. Jason Ridge, Alan's grandfather, had let that parcel slip out of the family's hands before his death. And no one apparently knew how or why.

On the way to the hospital, Alan thought about the fact that his plant manager and board of directors wanted that wedge back. Considering how much work had piled up while Alan was taking Louemma to the most recent doctor, he hadn't yet found time to delve into old county records to determine any options regarding Bell Hill. In the distillery safe, he'd found the land grant that deeded the entire parcel to the first Ridge to settle there. Written on parchment and signed by Daniel Boone himself, the document ought to prove ownership. Although Boone's fort and settlement, rebuilt and now run by local artisans, had long since been incorporated into Fort Boonesborough State Park. So many local families had sold and moved out. Alan liked that sense of permanence. If it'd been up to him, he wouldn't have incorporated Windridge Distillery, but kept it strictly a family-owned company.

Not wanting to think about that, Alan lowered the electric windows on both sides of the Chrysler. Settling his wide shoulders against the leather seat, he inhaled the relaxing scent of wet limestone and loamy soil refreshed by a recent shower. He shoved in a CD of mountain music. Alan's preferences ran toward bluegrass played on fiddles, dulcimers, harmonicas and other old-time instruments.

Turning off the main road, he drove through the small town his ancestors had founded. In five minutes he reached the hospital he and Vestal had been influential in getting built. Granted, the town hadn't yet floated a bond to install the newest equipment available. But it was a well-maintained facility, boasting a fine staff.

Birdie had been right. His grandmother was pacing in front of the door. Alan entered the hospital and, crossing the lobby, picked up her suitcase before greeting Vestal with a kiss on her soft, powdered cheek. For as far back as he could remember, she'd smelled like the wild roses that grew up the stone walls ringing the distillery. During certain times of the year they warred with overpowering odors of rye and barley mash used to produce Windridge's high-grade bourbon.

"Why aren't you waiting in your room?" he scolded gently. "Doc Fulton wouldn't be happy to see you standing in a draft."

"What does that twerp know? I diapered his behind when that boy was knee-high to a chigger."

Alan grinned. "It'd serve you right if I phoned Marv right now and told him you said that. But if I did, he'd turn you over to Randy Wexler. Then I'd never get you to see a doctor again."

Vestal latched on to Alan's arm and maneuvered him out. "Randy Wexler has chickpeas for brains. I'm not trusting my body, old though it may be, to a kid who failed fifth grade. Marvin at least was an A student."

"Randy knuckled down. According to his credentials from Duke University Med School, he graduated magna cum laude." Alan opened the heavy car door and helped her in. Before Vestal could object, he wrapped the lap robe around her legs, then tossed her bag in the voluminous trunk. He'd barely slid under the steering wheel when she fixed him with a look Alan knew from experience usually meant trouble.

"I met someone today who can help Louemma."

Alan jabbed his key in the vicinity of the ignition twice, missing both times. "A doctor? Here?" he asked, clearly excited. "A consultant?"

"Not a doctor. What good have a host of sawbones done my great-granddaughter? No good, that's what."

Alan felt the bubble of hope burst. "Oh, not an M.D." He clung to the belief that a doctor on the cutting edge of a new discovery about muscles and nerves would one day solve Louemma's inability to raise her arms.

"Hear me out, Alan. I've lived many years and I'm not without common sense, you know."

"I know you're a dear, smart lady. And you love Louemma. Up to now, though, all the doctors we've seen—and these are the very best—claim her dysfunction isn't physical. That it's beyond the scope of their expertise."

"I think the woman I met is an occupational therapist. She's got Donald Baird using his left arm and moving his fingers. What do you say to that?"

Alan turned his head. "Roy said his dad had severe, permanent damage to his entire left side, because of the stroke."

"Uh-huh. And today I watched him weave a rag pot holder."

"Weaving?" Alan snorted. This time he started the car easily.

"Don't be making pig noises at me, Alan Ridge. Laurel Ashline said doctors recruited weavers during the Second World War to help injured soldiers regain the use of their limbs through learning to operate hand looms. Can it hurt to talk with her? Invite her to Windridge to evaluate Louemma? Short of voodoo, Alan, you've hauled that child around the state to every other kind of expert—and quack."

"Never quacks! Every man or woman I've made an appointment with, in or out of the state, has been a licensed practitioner."

"A ward nurse gave me Ms. Ashline's business card. She apparently has a studio in the area. Her phone number has our local exchange." Vestal waved the card under Alan's nose.

He snatched it out of her hand and shoved it in his shirt pocket. "I'll think about it," he muttered. "I'll ask about her program around town. You say she's an occupational therapist?"

"I'm not sure of that. She volunteers at the hospital. Dory referred to her as a master weaver."

"Right…" Alan half snarled under his breath.

"Just phone her is all I ask. If not for Louemma, then to humor me. You know I won't stop badgering you until you do."

"Tell me something new, Grandmother." Alan sighed heavily. "Fine. Tomorrow I'll put out feelers. That's my best offer. I'm not about to hand Louemma over to some dingbat. What brought this weaver to Ridge City? Do you know the name Ashline? Who would move here unless they already have roots in the valley?"

"Would you listen to yourself? You're always telling me times are changing." Vestal sank back and fell silent for a minute or two. "I have to admit, when she first said her name I had a notion I'd heard it before. But for the life of me, I can't recall where." Closing her eyes, Vestal rubbed a creased forehead. "These bouts of senility are the main thing I detest about aging. You just wait, Alan. It's no fun."

He immediately picked up a blue-veined hand. "Your dad lived to be ninety. If you take care of yourself, you'll have a lot of good years left. And you're far from senile."

"You're a good boy. A caring father, too. I've got no doubt that you'll explore every avenue to help Louemma. Including contacting Ms. Ashline."

"Enough." Alan dropped her hand. "Flattery won't work, you know. And I'm hardly a boy. But…it's no secret I'd step in front of a train if I thought it would help Louemma be normal and happy again. I'll look into this weaver when I get time."

Vestal twiddled her thumbs and continued to frown.

ALTHOUGH LOUEMMA HAD missed her great-grandmother, it seemed to Alan that during their first meal together again, the child was especially withdrawn. One reason he didn't believe her problem was only psychosomatic was that she detested having to be fed like a baby. Their family doctor worried about her weight loss, and she did look terribly thin to Alan. "Honeybee, you love Birdie's potato soup. Please take a few more sips."

The child turned her pixie face away from the spoon. "I'm not hungry. You eat, Daddy. Otherwise yours will get cold."

"With all the times I've been called away from the table to handle problems at the distillery, I've grown to like cold soup, honey. Hot or cold, it has the same nutritional value." He waggled the spoon again to coax her.

Vestal adjusted a red bow Birdie had tied in Louemma's dark hair. "You want to eat, child, otherwise you'll end up in the hospital like I did. I can tell you from experience that no one lines up for their tasteless meals. Hospital cooks have never heard of spice." Vestal launched into a funny story about patients on her floor who hid or traded food. She'd always been able to wheedle smiles from Louemma. Tonight, she only managed a tiny one. Eventually the girl ate a bit more, but by then they were all exhausted.

Louemma yawned hugely as Birdie collected the plates. "Daddy, please carry me to bed before you and Nana have dessert."

It broke Alan's heart to see his formerly energetic child so listless. The accident had caused too many noticeable changes in her personality. It wasn't normal for a kid her age to sleep as many hours as she did. No wonder her muscles had lost their tone.

Birdie, who'd come back with the coffeepot and one of her famous buttermilk pies, shook her head. "Your daddy had better take your temperature, missy, if you be turning down this delicious pie I baked special for you and Miss Vestal." The cook passed it under Louemma's nose. A fresh scent of vanilla, mixed with the cinnamon dusted lightly on the rich custard filling, wafted through the air.

"I'm sorry, Birdie. I'm just too full." Louemma turned helpless eyes toward Alan. "And I'm really, really sleepy." She failed to stifle another yawn.

Vestal yawned as well.

The dinner hour at Windridge had always been set late to allow the men of the house time to tidy up at the end of long workdays. He glanced at his watch and saw it was just ten. Not particularly late by Southern dining standards.

As if Vestal had tapped into his thoughts, she murmured, "If you're going to continue working from home, Alan, and if it's agreeable with Birdie, we could move our dinner hour to seven, or even six."

"We've never…" Alan crumpled his snowy linen napkin. Nine had been the tradition as far back as he could remember. But really, what did time matter? The Windridge family hadn't entertained since…Emily's death.

"Can we discuss this later?" He shoved back his chair, unclear as to why he hated the idea of altering yet another routine. Since the accident, so many practices had gone by the wayside. His hands-on grasp of the business, for one. The loss of old friends, although these were couples he and Emily had known forever. Even simple laughter seemed a thing of the past. Childish giggles for sure, as no children ran in and out of the big house anymore; playing tag with Louemma. Male-female banter was nonexistent, too. Windridge had become a virtual tomb.

And whose fault is that? a little voice nagged Alan.

His. He hadn't wanted any overt reminders of Emily's absence. And somehow, around other kids her age, Louemma's handicap seemed magnified.

"I'm sorry, Birdie. Unless Grandmother wants pie and coffee, I'm going to pass. I'll take Louemma to her room," Alan said, carefully lifting the girl. Louemma suffered intermittent muscle spasms, because of which her doctor had suggested using a wheelchair. "Afterward, I'm going back to the spreadsheets I left unfinished when Grandmother phoned."

Vestal folded her napkin neatly and set it aside before unhooking an ornate cane from the back of her chair.

Birdie faced them all, hands on her broad hips. "Pie'll be in the fridge," she snapped. "I'll leave a thermos of coffee on the counter. In case that spreadsheet threatens to put you to sleep, Mr. Alan."

"Birdie, I'm truly sorry. We all appreciate how hard you work."

"We do indeed," Vestal assured her. "And the pie will keep. You know, Alan," she said, "there's something I missed more than pie during my hospital stay. Our catching up over a nightcap. I believe I'll wait in your office."

The reigning Ridge matriarch patted Louemma's thin face. "Good night, sweet pea. Sleep tight and don't let the bedbugs bite."

Alan smiled in spite of everything. Vestal had sent him off to bed as a boy with that same admonition. His father had said it'd been their ritual, as well. One thing was different—the way Louemma used to throw her arms around Vestal's neck, and how girl and woman used to giggle delightedly. That ritual, too, was gone.

Alan escaped then, because it hurt deep inside his chest to be holding his precious child, and feeling her slip away from him in body and spirit, with apparently nothing he nothing he could do to change that.

Hiding the tears stinging his eyes, he dragged out the routine of tucking his daughter in for the night. He was aware, from Vestal's insistence, that she had something more than a nightcap in mind. Eventually, Alan trudged slowly and heavily down the hall.

Bracing for whatever awaited him, he wiped away all traces of anxiety before entering the room he'd usurped for his office. On top of a desk crafted from local hardwood, aged and polished to a glossy shine, two old-fashioned glasses sat, each holding a splash of Windridge bourbon.

When Vestal picked up one glass and handed him the other, it struck Alan that it'd been she, not his father, who'd taught him how to appreciate the taste of bourbon. His dad had been

struck and killed by lightning up at the distillery the year
Alan turned thirteen. His grandfather Jason's health had gone
downhill after the loss of his only son. It'd been Vestal, and
Alan's mother, Carolee, who'd plunged him into the business
of producing top-grade bourbon.

Their lives had seemed smooth until Alan was twenty or
so and Carolee met and married a wine maker from California. At that point she turned her back on Windridge and her
only child. She'd looked back once—when she'd signed over
to Alan her shares in the corporation she'd set up. She'd sold
forty-nine percent of overall shares, pulling the wool over
Vestal's eyes. And Carolee's brash move had sparked the
business with a new influx of cash.

Alan clinked his glass to the rim of Vestal's, smiling fondly
at her as they waited for the chime of the crystal to fade. That
was another of her mantras. *Fine bourbon should be served
in the finest crystal.*

"You seem restless tonight, Grandmother. This being your
first day home after a lengthy illness, shouldn't you trundle
off to bed?"

The woman sipped the amber liquid with her eyes closed,
ignoring his nudge. "I love the barest hint of a woody taste. I
assume I can thank our new, ungodly expensive aging barrels.
I hope you don't mind that I broke the seal on a new bottle."

"Not at all." The bottles were all carefully filled and corked
by hand in a manner that made Windridge a constant favorite of a discerning liquor market.

"Did you want an update on expenses, Grandmother? I can
run you a cost analysis worksheet tomorrow."

"Don't rush me, Alan. Ever since you were a little boy,
you've rushed through life hell-bent for election."

He smiled again at her longstanding version of the cliché,
then cleared his throat "I'm just wondering what this is about.
Monday, as I pulled into the hospital parking lot, I saw Hardy

Duff driving off. You didn't mention his visit. I figure he must've decided the fastest way to get me to move on reacquiring Bell Hill was to go through you."

"Hardy brought me violets. His neighbor grows them." Vestal took another sip. "Very well, Alan. But I'm telling you the same thing I told Hardy. Ted Bell saved your grandfather's life in Korea, and Jason meant for Ted and Hazel to live out their days on the hill. Still, Hazel had no call to go behind our backs and file squatter's rights. Granted, she and I had a falling out. Didn't mean I'd ever have tossed her off our land."

"You, Grandfather and the Bells were once best friends."

"Yes." Vestal stared into space. "Relationships can crumble. Hazel had…hobbies that obsessed her. Then she… we…well, we argued after her daughter, Lucy, ran off with that no-account transient tobacco picker your grandfather hired. We hired a lot of transient laborers then. Hazel had no say in hiring or firing."

"It's late. Talking about this upsets you. Let's save it for tomorrow."

She polished off her drink and set the glass on the tray with a thump. Stretching out slightly arthritic fingers, she pried the business card she'd given Alan earlier out of his shirt pocket. "Bell Hill will solve itself. Louemma, however, is wasting away before our eyes. I want you to promise you'll call Ms. Ashline first thing in the morning. If it wasn't so late, I'd insist you phone her now."

Alan snatched back the card, dropping it next to his phone. "Even though I fail to see how a stranger who doesn't have a medical degree can be any help, I'll call the damn woman. Scout's honor," he added, seeing Vestal's arched eyebrow.

"Call it meddling if you will, Alan. Or call it intuition. I saw what she did for Donald Baird and…a feeling swept over me. I'm sure Ms. Ashline's the one who can help our sweet girl get back to her old self."

Alan downed the rest of his drink and set his glass beside hers. After walking his grandmother to the door and kissing her cheek, he muttered, "Unless Laurel Ashline is a magician or a witch, I sincerely doubt she can make a difference in Louemma." He sighed. "Why can't you knit or travel abroad like other women your age?" But Vestal just gave him one of her famous looks.

Still brooding, he shut the door and picked up a family photo sitting on a bookshelf. A picture of him, Emily and Louemma, the shot had been taken three years ago, on Louemma's sixth birthday. Alan suspected she'd one day match her mother's beauty. Maintaining a tight grip on the silver frame, he splashed another three fingers of bourbon into his empty glass, although he'd learned a year ago that drowning his sorrows in whiskey never worked. Not even drowning them in the world's finest bourbon. Holding the glass to the lamp, he assessed the color and clarity. It was perfect. His daughter wasn't.

Grimacing, he drank half in one swallow. Still, the subtle burn sliding down his throat couldn't compare to the constant fire consuming his heart. He gently returned the photo to where he kept it for Louemma's sake. After draining the glass, Alan stared at his former wife through a sheen of tears brought on by the fiery drink. "Dammit, Emily, I wish you'd reach out from the grave and tell me why in hell you were on a mountain road going to Louisville. Why were you driving on such an icy night? And why did you have Louemma with you?"

In the silence following his questions, Alan knew he couldn't work on spreadsheets, after all. Not that bed was an answer to his restlessness. As had become habit since the accident, he grabbed a flashlight and an old jacket off a rack in the mudroom near the kitchen. Exiting the house, he tramped up the long hill to the distillery. The solidity of the building's mossy stone walls had withstood generations of storms worse than the one raging inside him.

Finding that thought vaguely calming, Alan went into the vault and checked alcohol levels in two current batches of yeast-laden mash. Every batch fermented naturally for three to five days. On a chart, Alan made notations under Day Four. Their night watchman was used to his midnight prowling. The two men exchanged waves as Drake Crosby made his rounds.

Roaming familiar floors eventually brought about the desired exhaustion. By the time Alan left the building, again waving to Drake, he thought maybe he could fall into bed and manage two hours of dreamless sleep.

But at seven-thirty, he sat at his desk again.

Laurel Ashline's business card still lay where he'd tossed it last night, taunting him. He passed a hand over his jaw, rehearsing possible openings in his mind. A prickly jaw reminded him that he hadn't shaved. Vestal and Louemma were habitually late risers, which gave him plenty of time to get presentable.

Birdie popped into his office carrying a tray. "Mercy, if you don't look like something dragged in from the woods. Have you been working all night?"

Alan accepted his usual juice and coffee. "No. I'm debating what's the proper time to phone a lady."

The cook's eyes sparked with uncommon interest as she poured the coffee.

"Not that kind of call, Birdie," he declared dryly, pulling the cup of rich, chicory-laced coffee toward him. "It's a woman Grandmother met at the hospital. She apparently uses weaving for therapy, or some such nonsense—" Stopping suddenly, Alan vigorously shook his head. "It even sounds far-fetched."

"I don't know. Miss Vestal mentioned that weaver while I was fixing supper. Way I look at it, the Almighty arranges for people's paths to cross for a reason. I'm just gonna scoot on out so you can make that call. Yell if you need the pot refilled."

"Thanks." Alan shut his eyes and rubbed the bridge of his

nose. Why was he thanking her? This household was blessed with stubborn women.

Twice he lifted the receiver and set it down again. The third time he hurriedly punched in the number on the card.

A sleepy female voice ventured a wary "Hello…?"

Something in the low, husky timbre sent shock waves to Alan's toes. *Damn, this wasn't her office.* Clearly, he'd called too early. But now that he had her on the line, Alan was determined to state his case, set an appointment and be done with it. "I apologize for calling before eight," he said. "This is Alan Ridge. Yesterday, at the hospital, you met my grandmother. Vestal," he added. Despite the silence, he forged on. "She was impressed by how you've helped a friend of hers— Don Baird. Vestal thinks you can do the same for my daughter, Louemma." Nothing Alan had said thus far had produced so much as an iota of response from the other end.

"So I'm phoning to arrange a consultation with you, Ms. Ashline. What day can you come to my home to evaluate her? My daughter," he added hastily.

"Ms. Ashline?" he said a long moment later. For all Alan knew she'd dropped the phone and fallen back asleep.

"Yes. I'm here, but… I'm, ah, afraid you…have me at a disadvantage. I was up all night finishing a commissioned weaving. And I suspect your grandmother misjudged my role. Oh, I'm probably not coherent enough to be making any sense."

A fellow night owl, he thought. "You're making perfect sense, considering. Look, I'm quite sure you're right about my grandmother's incorrect assessment. However, if you knew her, you'd know she won't stop pestering me until you see my daughter. We're easy to locate. If you need a personal reference, ask anyone. Our family's been in Ridge City for years. Drive west along Windy Creek Road, and you can't miss Windridge. The distillery's on the knoll, but our house sits closer to the highway. Just name a time and day."

Laurel had finally managed to sit up and shrug off her stupor enough to process most of what her caller had said. She now knew exactly who he was. Obviously, neither he nor his grandmother had placed her. They couldn't know she was Hazel Bell's granddaughter, or else Laurel was certain Alan Ridge wouldn't have been this pleasant. In any event, his very association with making and selling a product responsible for the ruin of countless people, including her ex-husband, precluded her from getting involved with his family. Besides, it was unlikely she had anything to offer his child.

"No, I won't come upon your house first," Laurel said bluntly. "I won't come to your house at all."

Hearing the shock in his indrawn breath, she wasn't quite sure how to end the call. But what else needed saying? *Nothing,* she decided, and she hung up with a quick but definite goodbye. A solid smack of the phone in the cradle should send him a clear message.

Alan heard the sound, and also the resulting dial tone. Anger ripped through him. "Who in hell does she think she is?" he muttered, belatedly slamming down his receiver.

Vestal poked her head into her grandson's office. "The news must be bad if you've resorted to talking to yourself in that tone of voice, Alan."

"I just spoke with your Ms. Ashline," he said with an annoyance. "She refused to come see Louemma. But it's just as well. I knew she was so much smoke and mirrors."

"No, she's not. Phone her again, and be nicer this time."

"She hung up on me! Not the other way around."

"Honestly! You do take after your grandfather. Ridge men can be so abrasive. And dense. Mercy, will you look at the time? Who calls a lady at this hour? It's only quarter of eight!" Vestal tapped the clock on his desk. She sent Alan a look of the type that always left him stumbling to apologize.

"Run into town later and send her flowers or fruit from Saxon's. Include a business card, and write Ms. Ashline a nice apology on the back. Ask her to phone at *her* convenience."

Alan clamped down on the *hell, no* leaping to the tip of his tongue. Instead, he grumbled, "Can't, Grandmother. No address on her card."

"A lack of address has never stopped Eva Saxon from making a delivery. Oh, for pity's sake. I'll do it."

"No, you won't. The subject of Ms. Ashline is finished."

But Vestal Ridge had her own stubborn streak. Alan knew he wouldn't have a moment's peace unless he appeased her. More than that, he loved her. Still…it felt like groveling. "Give me a week to rethink this, Grandmother. Right now I need to shave before breakfast, and roust Louemma." And with that, he left the room.

Vestal stared after him for only a moment, then picked up the phone and punched in Eva's number at the flower shop from memory.

CHAPTER TWO

LAUREL TRIED TO GO BACK to sleep, but the early call had left her stomach feeling jittery. At first she'd thought the caller was her ex, Dennis Shaw, phoning again to either insult her or beg money, as was his pattern. He never held a job for long, even though he had the charisma to get a new one each time he sobered up. It was that charm she'd fallen for, even thought she should've learned from her mom's bad experience with men.

Stifling a yawn, Laurel wandered into the kitchen and bent to pat the big German shepherd she'd rescued from the animal shelter. Living alone, so far back in the woods, she'd decided it would be wise to have a fierce companion. At the time she got him, she'd had no heart for loving man or beast. Her intention was to keep the dog at arm's length, using him strictly as a bodyguard, not a friend. For that reason, she'd simply named him Dog. While the name stuck, little by little he'd worked his way past her defenses—until Laurel couldn't imagine life without him. Dog *looked* fierce. She hoped if push came to shove, he could scare off an intruder. But like her, he was a marshmallow inside. And like her, he was both lonely and a loner. Well, less lonely now that they had each other for company.

She missed corresponding with her grandmother. The letters had been her lifeline though tough times. Living here in Hazel's house, surrounded by her things, Laurel wished now that she hadn't been cursed with her own mother's stubborn pride. A pride that had kept them both from coming home to this safe haven for far too many lonely years.

She washed her hands and face, then put water in the kettle for her favorite herb tea. Whenever old memories closed in too tightly, the ritual of making tea generally staved them off.

Today, however, she allowed a few of those memories to seep in. She'd grown up fatherless, taking charge of a chronically ill mother at an early age. Just before her death, Lucy Ashline had sworn to haunt Laurel if she ever dared phone her grandparents. From ages fifteen to eighteen, Laurel had lived like a rabbit in a hole. She'd struggled to make ends meet, and she'd lived on her own, deceiving social workers, going to school.

Then one rainy day she woke up and broke her word to Lucy. Laurel wrote a letter to Hazel Bell, introducing herself—even sending a graduation photo. She'd let Hazel believe her life was rosy.

At first Laurel didn't tell her grandmother that Lucy had died. Eventually, through letters, she'd gradually opened up. It was also through these letters that Laurel developed an interest in her grandmother's passion for weaving. Hazel sent money from time to time. Laurel used the funds to apply for an apprenticeship in a weaving program. The instructor said she had a knack, and within a year had recommended her for a master weaver's apprenticeship in Vermont. Only after Laurel left the last apartment she'd shared with her mother, did she invite Hazel to visit her.

Hazel made excuses. First, she said her husband was ill. Then he died and she didn't feel like traveling. All the while Hazel begged Laurel to continue corresponding.

Looking back, Laurel knew she'd let Dennis Shaw slip past her defenses because she was so lonely. Lonely, living in a new city in a too-empty little studio apartment.

Dennis was selling yarn when she met him. At the time,

Laurel had no idea it was just one in a string of jobs he held on to until he went on a bender and got fired. Sober, he was funny and charming. He'd traveled places Laurel only dreamed of seeing. In the early days of their courtship, he used to sprawl on her couch, easing the emptiness in her life. Dennis had said he loved watching Laurel create the items she sold on consignment. And maybe it was true—then.

They began discussing a future together. They made plans. That was one thing she could say about Dennis: he always made big plans. Not until after she consented to marriage did she slowly learn he was all talk. Any plans they implemented used money *she* earned. Dennis's plans all ended in losses Laurel bailed him out of.

Her grandmother sensed her unhappiness, although Laurel never meant to spill it into the pages of her letters. Hazel suggested on more than one occasion that Laurel leave Dennis and come to Kentucky. She'd even offered plane fare, but the same foolish pride that had kept Laurel's mother from hightailing it home, a failure, also kept Laurel in her mistake of a marriage. Until it was too late.

Unfortunately, it had taken seven years of living in hell, and Hazel's sudden, surprising death, to pound sense into Laurel, enabling her to overcome that stiff pride of hers. She regretted that it was her grandmother's last letter, delivered through her attorney, that finally kicked her hard enough in the backside and gave her the funds to divorce Dennis.

Refilling her cup, Laurel called Dog. The two of them went out to enjoy the sun warming the front porch. Here, and in the upper cottage where she did her weaving, the past always faded into obscurity.

A row of window boxes on the porch spilled over with violets and fragrant pinks. Their perfume filled the air with the promise of spring. Winter rains had subsided, and the creek had once again receded below its banks. Laurel loved everything about the cottages, including the fact that no one could drive up and surprise her. A footbridge crossed the creek. Visitors had to park in a clearing on the other side—not that she had any visitors.

Laurel also owned two horses she'd bought about the time she adopted Dog. That was because her grandmother had once written about how she carried on the laudable work begun by another Kentucky weaver. Lou Tate Bousman had devoted her latter years to keeping the art of hand-weaving alive. Both women, during different decades, had traveled the hollows of the Kentucky hill country, collecting and preserving patterns that would otherwise have been lost.

As she went back inside, Laurel reflected on her efforts to carry on the tradition. Last fall, she and Dog had roamed those same hills, she on horseback, he loping beside her. Laurel had met some fantastically talented women, although uneducated by most standards. The beauty of the hollows, and the strength of women who survived under mostly primitive conditions, had helped heal Laurel's shattered life.

Sort of. She and Dog both tensed at hearing a car heading toward the clearing.

Actually, it was a panel van. Squinting through an ivy-covered lattice that framed one end of the screened porch, Laurel made out the lettering on the side: Saxon's Flower Shop. Was the driver lost? Unless Dennis had suddenly gotten flush again… But his flush times were growing fewer and further between, and his ability to bounce from job to job lessening. Besides, he'd never waste money on flowers.

A chubby woman with flame-red hair piled high atop her head crawled out of the vehicle. "Hello, the house," she called. "I have a delivery for Laurel Ashline. Am I in the right place?"

Dog sensed Laurel's uneasiness. He barked and lunged at the screen door. Silencing him with a word, Laurel ordered him to stay as she stepped outside. Tightening the sash on her robe, she walked to her side of the bridge. How should she respond? She'd never received a flower delivery before. Never. Would the driver expect a tip? Nervously, Laurel smoothed a hand over her shoulder-length, wheat-blond hair. Goodness, she must look a fright, judging by the scrutiny she was getting.

The driver, puffing a bit, crossed the rickety bridge. She lugged a wicker basket wrapped in cellophane.

Wryly, Laurel saw she still wasn't getting flowers, but rather a fruit basket the woman plopped at her feet.

"Thank you," Laurel said softly. "I'm sorry to greet you in my robe. I worked all night on a weaving I need to deliver for a bridal shower today. Are, uh, you positive this is mine?"

Bending, the woman unpinned the attached card. "I'm Eva Saxon, owner of the flower shop in Ridge City. If you're Laurel Ashline, it's yours." Eva slid the card out of the envelope and held it up for her to read. "Came from Alan Ridge himself, I'm told—which makes you special. Alan keeps to home these days. Has since his wife died last year in a car crash. Emily was a beauty, she was. A born prom queen. 'Course, she was a lot younger than me. You're a lucky woman." Eva nodded sagely. "Alan Ridge is a good catch."

Laurel stiffened. "I'm sure he is, should a woman be fishing for a man. I am not," she said loudly. So loudly that Dog began to bark again, throwing himself against the screen. Laurel worried that he'd get hurt or come through the mesh. "Excuse me, my dog is very protective. Thank you again for the delivery. Really, it's not personal. Mr. Ridge contacted me regarding business. Very early in the morning. It's totally unnecessary, but he probably sent this by way of an apology for waking me."

The shorter woman under the mountain of hair nodded as if she understood. As Laurel turned and left the bridge, she, too, retreated.

Once the van had driven off, Laurel let Dog out. He continued to growl so she let him sniff the basket filled with rare fruit—mangos, guavas, pineapples and grapes. Laurel let the van's dust settle, then marched across the bridge to where she had to keep her garbage can if she wanted the city to empty it. Collectors wouldn't come until Friday, and it was only Wednesday. Her receptacle was full. Nevertheless, because she didn't wish to accept anything from a man who made his money off whiskey, she jammed the basket as far into the can as possible. As a result, she had to hang the lid sideways on the basket handle.

"Come, Dog. With luck, that's the last we'll hear from Mr. Ridge."

IT WAS THREE DAYS before Alan made it into town. He had to run by the elementary school to pick up the quarterly lesson packets that Louemma's tutor used. They'd tried having his daughter attend classes after she'd healed from the initial surgeries, but she'd gotten so upset that in the end he'd decided to have her taught at home—for a while, anyway.

From there, he stopped to pick up groceries for Birdie. He dragged out the trip because he wanted to avoid hearing Vestal fuss at him to apologize to the Ashline woman.

As well as that aggravation, Hardy Duff, his distillery manager, had been pressuring Alan to do something about Bell Hill. So he swung by the courthouse to have a clerk trace its history—to figure out how they'd lost what had once been part and parcel of Ridge land. Everything seemed to be in order, up to when Hazel filed squatter's rights. Alan didn't know what else to do. He'd left a note to that effect in Dale Patton's office, even though Dale, the company attorney, was on vacation.

Following that, Alan decided to get his hair cut prior to moseying over to Saxon's Flowers. Finally, when he hit the very end of his to-do list, the only thing left was to order a damn bouquet for the disagreeable Ms. Ashline.

Even worse, Eva Saxon was like the town crier. Alan suspected that seconds after he walked out of her shop, everyone in town would know he'd sent a strange woman flowers. As he approached the store, he had a brilliant idea. He'd send a bouquet in Vestal's name.

Eva Saxon, nearly as wide as she was tall, glanced up as the bell over the door sounded. She was ten years older than Alan's thirty, and used to baby-sit him. Smiling, she greeted him with the snap-snap-snap of her ever-present Cloves gum.

"Hi." Alan fumbled Laurel Ashline's wrinkled business card out of his jeans pocket, along with a fifty-dollar bill. "This is all the information my grandmother has on the woman. She said you shouldn't have any problem finding her and delivering a plant or something. Enclose a note saying that Vestal invites Ms. Ashline to drop by Windridge at her convenience, or something to that effect. Oh, you'd better include our address. I believe she's new in town." He shoved the money across the counter.

Eva dug a pencil out of her beehive hairdo. For as long as Alan could remember, she'd worn her hair in the exact same style, and yet it still astonished him. As he gaped at her big hair, he noticed Eva eyeing him oddly. "Is something wrong?"

Crack went the gum. "Uh, no. 'Cept Vestal phoned a few days ago and ordered a deluxe basket of fruit sent to Ms. Ashline on your behalf. I helped her compose a real sincere apology. If you haven't heard back by now, hon, I've gotta say you must've really done the lady wrong." She stuffed the fifty in her cash register and counted out change. "The basket cost twenty-five dollars."

"What?" Alan saw red, and it wasn't just Eva's hair color.

"I suggested a dozen roses instead of fruit. Or a box of chocolates displayed prominently on top of the fruit. Vestal nixed both." Eva shoved Alan's change toward him. "It's probably not too late for roses. 'Course, I don't know what you did to the woman. But I got some nice pink buds in today. Shall I carry Laurel out a dozen this afternoon? Is she worth another twenty-five bucks?" Eva kept a hand on the last bill.

"I haven't got the foggiest idea what she's worth. I've never met her." Alan wadded up the change and stuffed it in his pants pocket. He retrieved Laurel's business card, then started for the door. Then he hesitated and pivoted back. "Hell, Eva, stick a few of those roses in a nice vase. Write her address on the back of this card. I'll deliver the flowers myself."

"Uh-huh. You made her mad, but you don't even know where she lives?" Reaching into the cooler that sat behind the counter, she hauled out an already made up arrangement. "That'll be six ninety-five. A bargain, even for self-delivery. These buds are beauties. Out of curiosity, what did you do to the lady that requires flowers?"

Alan flung down a ten, muttering, "Keep the change." He snatched up the vase. "For the record, I never have met Ms. Ashline, so don't be spreading rumors, okay?"

The pale blue eyes regarded him frostily. "But Vestal said—"

"Yes, she's got a bee in her bonnet. This need for me to apologize is due to a mess of Grandmother's creation. I'm caught in the middle. You know Vestal's been ill? Ms. Ashline's someone she met at the hospital."

Eva frowned slightly. "Vestal didn't *sound* dotty. But I s'pose she is gettin' on in years. Ralph's mama's not as old as your grandma, and that woman's plumb gone off the deep end." Launching a diatribe against her mother-in-law, Eva followed Alan to the door.

"Thanks," he said, all but running from the shop. Alan didn't stop to study the address until he was in the Jeep and had the motor running. Then his jaw dropped.

Laurel Ashline lived in Hazel Bell's old cottage. The first of two tucked deep in a grove of sycamore and red maple trees—a scant few miles from the source of the spring gushing down Bell Hill. That spring was at the core of Alan's current problem. Hardy Duff insisted they had to tap into it in order to expand Windridge; he wanted to add a hundred new mash barrels per each milling process.

Alan was well aware that the water they used, rich with essential minerals and naturally filtered through Kentucky limestone, made Windridge bourbon one of the most sought-after whiskeys in the world. What he didn't know was how Laurel Ashline had ended up living next to a coveted stream that really belonged to him and his family.

Alan might not know, but he intended to find out. With or without an offering of fruit or roses, he thought, wedging the vase between the passenger seat and his center console.

He fumed to himself all the way from town, taking a shortcut fire road that bisected his property from the Bells' land. What they claimed was their land. He made the mental correction as he got out to open a gate posted with a Private Property—Keep Out sign. For the first time, he wondered if his grandmother knew the Ashline woman had settled in quarters they owned. Well, maybe owned. He revised that thought, too. According to the clerk he'd spoken with earlier, Hazel Bell hadn't done anything illegal.

Hazel and Ted had met the state statute for filing squatter's rights. Jason Ridge, Alan's grandfather, had issued a temporary deed, which gave Ted the right to erect two dwellings. The couple had resided in one cottage long enough to qualify them as land claimants, otherwise known as squatters, according to a historic act that had apparently never been removed from the county statutes. Such folks had the right to petition for ownership of land they'd improved and occupied for twenty years. Clearly, no Ridge had suspected the Bells would ever file.

Alan didn't understand all the legal mumbo jumbo. And Windridge's business attorney was in Europe on vacation.

There was little Alan could do until Dale Patton returned. Except…he could determine who'd let Laurel Ashline move in. Hazel had been dead and buried for over a year. Alan could attest to that, as he and Vestal had attended her funeral. It was then that they'd learned of her treachery. Hazel's lawyer, an upstart from Lexington, had paid her outstanding bills and practically thumbed his nose at locals over the squatting.

Now Alan wracked his brain and tried to recall who else had been at the service. A van filled with mostly middle-aged women had shown up at the last minute, making a total of maybe fifteen. Sad for someone who'd lived her entire life in Ridge City. But as Vestal had pointed out, Hazel had cut herself off from neighbors.

Alan supposed Laurel Ashline must've been in the van. He knew Hazel was involved in local craft fairs. Ted had complained often enough that his wife spent more time with her "artsy-fartsy friends" than she did at home doing what he figured wives should do. Alan guessed that meant cooking, cleaning and the like.

He never commiserated, because he didn't share Ted's belief, and because his wife had acted in a similar fashion. Not that Emily ran with an arts crowd. She'd spent her days—and nights—with the horsey set. Racehorses. Down in Louisville. Alan had rarely seen her during the months leading up to the Kentucky Derby. But race season was long over when Emily had had her accident, which was why Alan had such a hard time understanding why she'd been on that particular road. He knew what people whispered, though.

Even now his stomach pitched at the memory of the call from the state police. He forced his mind onto other subjects. Such as what questions he ought to ask when he arrived at Laurel Ashline's door—about two minutes from now.

Pulling up, Alan parked on the west side of the stream near the footbridge leading to the largest of the Bell cottages. Ted had built the second, smaller place for Hazel's crafts. Down-home items sold like hotcakes to summer tourists.

If he'd hoped to find the structures in major disrepair, he was sadly disappointed. The oiled-wood siding on both buildings looked to be in pristine shape. Slate-blue trim gleamed as if newly painted. All around the cottage, a profusion of crocuses and daffodils created a riot of color against the bright green of trees just beginning to burst with spring leaves.

Absently, Alan reached back to retrieve the vase with its pale-pink rosebuds. They seemed puny compared to the Ashline woman's garden.

Not for the first time, Alan considered forgetting about this stupid mission. Except, it had never been said of Ridge men that they were cowardly. Hitching up the belt of his well-worn jeans, he thrust a hand through his freshly cut hair, which still bore a cowlick. Alan slammed the Jeep door and set out across the footbridge. He'd taken two steps onto the spongy wooden slats when a huge, snarling dog flew from around the left corner of the cottage, running straight at him. Black ears laid flat spoke of the animal's displeasure at seeing a stranger. A second look at the black muzzle, lips curled over gleaming white incisors, had Alan edging back the way he'd come.

He tried softly cajoling, muttering, "Good dog," several times, to no avail. After which he resorted to shouting for the dog's owner. "Ms. Ashline! Laurel? Hey, could you come out and call off your watchdog?"

He got no response. But Alan would swear the white lace curtains covering the largest window moved. And wasn't that the shadow of a human form appearing briefly behind a rip in the lace?

Maybe that was wishful thinking. Gripping the neck of the vase, Alan scanned the hill behind the cottage. Between the upper and lower dwellings, two horses poked their heads over a split rail corral.

Alan had assumed, maybe wrongly, that someone was home, based on the battered pickup beside which he'd parked his Jeep. It occurred to him now that she could be out riding. Although… He glared suspiciously at the window again. Was it logical to leave her monster dog to watch the house instead of taking him along for protection? Hell, maybe her bite was worse than her dog's.

He knew absolutely nothing about Laurel Ashline, except that she had a sexy voice. He probably should've gleaned more details from his grandmother. Or from Eva Saxon, who loved sharing gossip more than anything else on earth.

He felt like a fool standing here, clutching a vase of pink rosebuds, squared off with a snarling dog. Yet it was obvious the German shepherd wasn't going to let him cross.

Hitting on a new plan, Alan dug out his cell phone and punched in the number written on the crumpled business card. She might be working in the upper cottage. He had no idea whether looms made more noise than that fool dog. He frankly doubted it, but then he knew nothing about weaving.

The phone rang and rang. If he took the cell away from his ear, he could hear it ring in the cottage across the way. Listening through at least twenty rings, he finally swore again, closed the phone, and stowed it away. That was when he noticed the garbage can sitting near his Jeep. Damned if sticking out of it wasn't a still-wrapped basket of fruit.

"Phew! Stinko!" Striding up to the container, Alan waved away a swarm of flies and saw that the fruit had rotted. He would bet ten to one that Ms. Ashline had read the card Vestal had composed in his name and then tossed the whole thing in the trash. Hell, the proof was staring at him. She *had* tossed away a kind gesture, lock, stock and basket. The card lay on top of the torn cellophane.

Alan moved away from the odor and the flies, wondering what kind of person could do that—throw away an apology, judging a man she didn't know. Unless she just hated men, period.

That notion raised his hackles. It made him want to lob the damn vase at her front window. But, no, that'd probably be the type of macho jerk action she'd *expect* him to pull.

Instead, baring his own teeth at the dog, Alan stalked across the bridge and roared, "Hush up!" The animal backed off with a surprised whimper, just long enough to give Alan a chance to set the vase on the porch. "Pitch those in the trash," he yelled at her tightly closed door. "You can't hide forever. We have unfinished business, you and I. One day we'll meet. Bank on it!"

Because the shepherd had recovered from the onslaught, and now raced at him again, barking furiously, Alan lost no time hotfooting it back to his Jeep. Though he was sweating like a pig and panting like a man twice his age, he felt a measure of satisfaction at accomplishing his mission.

And oddly, he hadn't felt so alive in months. Not—he realized with shock—since the accident. As he started the Jeep and made a sweeping turn, aiming the vehicle downhill to the highway, he thought about the hermit he'd become in recent months. And he didn't like the picture. Didn't like it at all.

FLATTENED AGAINST THE WALL between the window and the door, Laurel waited several long minutes following her visitor's last diatribe. She wished she'd had a clearer look at him. Framed against the trees, with the backdrop of brilliant sunlight, he'd been little more than a shadow.

She'd apparently out-waited him at last. Dog had stopped his incessant barking. Venturing another glance through a gap in the curtain, she saw that the pesky man had indeed gone.

Laurel opened the door just a little, and Dog trotted up, shaking his shaggy coat. "Good boy," she said, praising his efforts as she stepped out and rubbed his ears. He seemed to grin at her, slobbering on her jeans when he rose on hind legs to lick her face. Dropping again, the dog lowered his head to sniff at something behind the screen. A low growl alerted Laurel and she went to investigate.

A cut-glass vase holding several rosebuds of a delicate pink winked at her in the flickering light. Laurel's breath caught in her throat. He'd left her flowers? Roses. Store-bought roses.

Kneeling, she fingered the soft, fragrant petals. She had to shove Dog's nose aside as she hesitantly picked up the vase. Breathing in the light, sweet scent, she smiled through suddenly teary eyes. This must be what he'd shouted at her to pitch. She thought he'd retrieved his earlier offering of fruit from the garbage can. Why on earth would the man brave being bitten by Dog to leave flowers for an ungrateful wretch who'd disposed of his first gift? Fruit baskets weren't cheap. Nor were roses in cut-glass vases. Too bad they'd been purchased with the profits from whiskey, she thought with a sigh.

She nudged open the screen door, letting Dog lead the way inside. Despite everything, she couldn't help being touched. Laurel tried the vase in three separate locations before finally carrying it up the hill to her loom cottage. Shabbily though she'd treated him, Laurel reasoned it didn't mean she shouldn't enjoy the first bouquet anyone had ever given her. Well, technically she supposed, three rosebuds, some fronds of fern and a stalk of baby's breath wasn't a bona fide bouquet. Nevertheless, they were lovely.

Gazing at them, she felt more…more…well, *more* for the giver than she'd wanted to. Guilt cloaked her as she took a seat at one of her floor looms, which she'd set up for weaving a commissioned rose-patterned bedspread.

Alan Ridge's roses sat on the windowsill, reminding her how abominably she'd acted.

Whether he was aware of it or not, Mr. Ridge had made a favorable impression, and she should probably revise her earlier opinion. She was sorry she hadn't gone out to see him. Maybe she should call him—just to say thank-you.

Humming a tuneless melody, Laurel kept time alternately with the foot pedals and the beater bar of her giant loom. The double-rose pattern her client had selected for this piece dated back to the late seventeen hundreds. An elderly weaver who'd given Laurel the pattern had painstakingly written directions with a stubby pencil on tablet paper. The old weaver called the entwined roses "Bachelor Among the Girls." Did that describe Alan Ridge? Laurel supposed not. Eva Saxon from the flower shop had said Ridge's wife had died in an auto accident. That made him a widower.

So Laurel could call this version of the pattern "Widower among the Ladies." Given his stature in the community, if he handed out roses willy-nilly, Alan Ridge had to be a hit with every unattached female for miles around.

A hit with everyone except her. The kindness of his gesture aside, Laurel still disliked the man's business. Did he know or care how many potentially good people had problems with whiskey? How many lives had been destroyed by liquor? On second thought, she wouldn't be phoning the whiskey baron of Ridge City to say thank-you anytime soon. Laurel had made one monstrous mistake when it came to letting a man's charm sway her. She'd do well to remember that flowers faded, and so did romance.

But he didn't have to bring you flowers, insisted a nagging voice inside her head—a voice she was determined to ignore.

ALAN STOPPED IN TOWN for the second time that day on the pretext of picking up a few groceries for Birdie and checking on a grain order for Windridge. His visit didn't go unnoticed, since he so rarely got to town these days. So when he asked questions about Laurel Ashline he couldn't really blame the shopkeepers who were reluctant to give much away.

At the granary he was told Eva Saxon had described Laurel as a tall, willowy blonde. Peg Moore, waitress at the corner café eyed Alan as she wiped off the counter and poured his coffee. "Laurel Ashline is…rather plain, I'd say. And she's either really shy or exceptionally quiet."

"About how old, would you guess?" Alan asked casually.

"Um, late twenties or early thirties," Peg ventured.

That surprised him, and pretty much ruled out the possibility that she'd been one of the women who'd attended Hazel Bell's funeral. They'd all been matronly.

He could see that everyone in the café was curious. But, typical of folks in this part of Kentucky, no one pressed Alan to say why he wanted to learn more about the stranger in their midst.

"It's later than I thought. I should be getting home. Louemma will be finishing her lessons, and I have a message for her tutor from the school." Depositing a tip next to his coffee cup, Alan stood up.

"Is Louemma improving at all?" Peg asked what few ever did of Alan.

"Not really," he admitted reluctantly.

"I thought that was probably the case. Yesterday Charity Madison brought her Camp Fire troop in for ice cream. Used to be you never saw Sarah Madison without Louemma. Peg shook her head. "That Sarah's getting a mouth on her, and Charity doesn't seem to know how to curb it. If it was me, I'd be giving that little miss some chores, and I'd take away privileges."

Alan didn't respond. Charity and Pete Madison had been his and Emily's best friends. To their credit, the couple had tried to include him and Louemma in their social events after the accident. But there was no denying the dynamics were different now. Maybe Charity couldn't bring herself to discipline Sarah, he mused. Because Louemma's experience showed how quickly life could change for the worse. Could be Charity was plain glad Sarah hadn't been with Louemma at the time Emily's car spun out of control.

At home again, Alan carried the groceries he'd bought in the back door. He'd missed Louemma's tutor, so he'd have to call her later. He sat down beside his daughter on the couch in front of the TV and kissed the top of her head.

"Hi, Daddy. Where've you been?"

"Nowhere. I just ran some errands in town."

Birdie bustled into the room bearing a plate of oatmeal-raisin cookies and a tall glass of milk. Vestal appeared out of nowhere, clearly wanting to nab Alan.

As Birdie sat down to help Louemma drink and eat, Vestal yanked him out of the living room, into the hall. "What happened when you went to see Laurel Ashline? When's she coming to see Louemma?"

He scowled. "Who said I even went to see Ms. Ashline?"

"Eva. She phoned right after you left her shop. Trying her best to learn why you followed up a basket of fruit with a vaseful of roses for a woman who apparently told Eva she hadn't even met you. You know Eva can't stand to think that anyone in town is keeping secrets from her."

"Three roses, Grandmother, not a vaseful." Alan wiggled three fingers. "She wasn't home, by the way. And speaking of secrets, why didn't you tell me you sent her that fruit basket in my name?"

Vestal did have the grace to look guilty.

"Also, were you aware she's living in Hazel Bell's cottage? Her cottage, on our land. It is, you know. Ours." He narrowed his eyes and watched his grandmother clasp a fist to her thin chest.

"*That's* why her name sounded familiar. Ashline—that was the transient workman Lucy Bell ran off with. Oh, my. Laurel must be Lucy's daughter."

"What? Ted never mentioned having a granddaughter."

"No. But it has to be. In that case, you have your answer as to why she settled here. Laurel Ashline has roots in Ridge City."

"No way! Her mother ran off how many years ago?"

"At least thirty. But you said it yourself, Alan. Strangers never move here. Only people who have roots. She does."

Alan turned and stomped toward his office. At the door, he stopped. "She may *think* she has roots here," he said. "Obviously Hazel or her lawyer led the woman to believe Bell Hill belongs to her. But that forty acres is Ridge land—always has been and always will be. Hardy needs the water from that spring to expand Windridge. We're paying him big bucks to ensure Louemma's legacy and her children's legacy long after you and I are gone, Grandmother. Isn't that reason enough not to get chummy with Laurel Ashline?" He started to slam the door, but Vestal blocked it with a toe.

"Now you listen to me. Way back before Lucy Bell went wild, her mother and I dreamed about our son and her daughter forging an unbreakable bond between our two families. That didn't happen. But maybe…"

"Uh-huh. No, ma'am. Don't even think it!" Alan's voice rose sharply. "You're not pairing me up with…that woman. Not with any woman."

"Grouchy as you are, no woman in her right mind would have you, Alan Ridge. Chew on this—if you don't get help for her, the Ridge bloodline ends with Louemma. I tell you, I have a feeling about Laurel. You know Jason and your father both respected my intuition. I can't imagine why you're in such a state over someone you've never met. Quit being an ass and make peace with the woman, for Louemma's sake."

Squaring her shoulders, Vestal withdrew her foot from the door, then slammed it shut herself.

Behind the door, Alan rubbed his eyes. Obviously he had to do *something*. If this battle between them continued, Vestal could work herself into a heart attack. Or he would, considering how furiously the blood pounded through his veins. No, he couldn't let this go on. Somewhere there had to be a doctor able to cure whatever ailed Louemma.

CHAPTER THREE

ALAN THOUGHT HE HEARD faint sounds of someone crying as he stood braced against the door. He gave himself a mental shake and opened it a crack.

It wasn't like Vestal to give way to tears. And it wasn't like him to push a confrontation to the brink of tears, either. That had been part of his and Emily's problem. She'd spoiled for a fight over the least little thing and had been adept at employing tears to get her way. Alan had realized early in their marriage that she'd manipulated her parents in pretty much the same manner. He'd been determined not to fall into the same trap. When the hysterics began, his response was usually to walk away, which only made Emily more furious.

Someone was definitely crying, he decided. But it wasn't coming from his grandmother's wing. Setting off to investigate, Alan found Louemma still in front of the TV. Her face was wet. Tears dripped off her chin, as she couldn't lift a hand to wipe them away.

He dashed to her side and whipped a clean handkerchief out of his pocket. On his knees beside her, Alan gently blotted her face. "Louemma, honey, what's wrong? Are you in pain? Tell me where so I can call Dr. Fulton."

"Why were you and Nana yelling? It…it reminded me of you and Mama."

"We never yell—" Stunned, Alan let the hand holding the handkerchief fall away. "Baby, I never raised my voice to your mother." Emily, though, had screamed loudly enough for ten people.

Again the dark eyes studying him glistened with tears. "But…Mama yelled at you. And sometimes stuff hit my bedroom wall."

Alan's stomach lurched. Good grief, had Louemma somehow picked up on the fact that he'd been thinking about Emily's tantrums? Vestal swore her side of the family was clairvoyant—could Louemma sense other people's thoughts? No. If anything, it was the strain they were all under.

"Honeybee, your mother had a…a temper. But never doubt that she loved you more than anything in the world. I love you, the same way. Please don't cry." Alan felt an urgent need to reassure her. Yes, he and Emily had had their spats. But one thing they'd agreed on was that their child came first in both their lives.

"In reruns of *The Brady Bunch,* they got a new mom. She's nice."

"We do okay, don't we? Look, I made Nana mad a minute ago. Even before I heard you crying, I was about to go and apologize. I'll go see her right now if you promise not to cry another tear."

Louemma lowered her lashes. Her lips trembled. Finally, in a small voice, she sighed, "Okay, Daddy."

He kissed the tip of her nose. "You didn't drink much milk. Remember, Dr. Fulton said you need milk to strengthen your bones." Alan got up and moved the TV tray closer, adjusting the bendable straw that allowed Louemma to drink without using her hands. "Did Birdie help you eat a cookie?"

"I'm not hungry or thirsty. Daddy, will Miss Robinson always have to give me my lessons at home?"

"I thought you liked Miss Robinson."

"I do. But…sometimes I miss going to school. I could try walking more."

Again Alan felt at a loss for words. Louemma had obviously forgotten how frustrated she'd become when they'd sent her back to her regular classroom. Shunned by former friends, she'd felt left out. Alan had ached as he'd held her through those first horrible crying jags. "Honey, the doctors all agree that for the time being, until someone figures out what's causing your muscle weakness, leg cramps and balance problems, home-schooling is best."

"When will the doctors find out what's wrong? When, Daddy?"

"Soon, baby. Soon," he said, with conviction enough to make it so. "Oh, your program's over. Shall I put in the *Space Kids* DVD? I need to go find Grandmother."

"Sure," the girl agreed listlessly, sliding down until she lay cradled in the pillows.

Alan discovered his hands weren't steady when he removed the DVD from its plastic case. He let his mind drift to the various doctors and clinics they'd visited since the accident. So far, all were in Kentucky. Maybe they should try New York or Chicago? Dammit, someone somewhere had to have answers.

"After you see Nana, do you have to work? Or can you watch the movie with me?"

Running his fingers through her tangled bangs, Alan tried not to think about the paperwork piling up on his desk. Hardy had pressured him this morning to calculate the end costs on the imported virgin white-oak barrels he wanted to install in the new warehouse they planned to build. None of which would do Windridge an iota of good until they solved the matter of diverting water from the Bell Hill spring.

Everything on his list seemed to circle back to that forty acres, where he now had an unwanted tenant dug in. A tenant who had at least two horses and a bloodthirsty dog. What other creatures was Laurel Ashline harboring? he wondered.

"Louemma, if you finish your milk, as soon as I clear the air with Nana, I'll come straight back and watch the movie with you." Alan decided that if his lot in life was to negotiate and strike bargains, he may as well start with one he had a chance of winning.

Without a word, Louemma wriggled closer to the TV tray. As he headed for the door, he noted with satisfaction that the straw was white and the level in the glass was on the decline.

Striding down a side hall, he tapped on the door to his grandmother's suite. He waited for her "Come in, it's unlocked," before entering.

There was a fire going in her sitting-room fireplace. Vestal reclined in an overstuffed chair with her feet propped up on a matching ottoman, book in hand. She sat up straight as Alan approached, and closed the medical thriller she'd been reading.

From the way she refused to meet his eyes, Alan knew she was still annoyed. He edged her ankles aside and perched on the ottoman. "Did you ever see Emily throwing things any of the times she got mad at me?"

"What? I thought you'd come to gripe some more about Laurel Ashline."

He shook his head and set a hand lightly on her knee. "No more arguments. Louemma heard us. It frightened her. She told me it brought back memories of some of my less than happy encounters with her mother. Louemma all but accused us of throwing things at each other. I never—" He shut his eyes and rubbed a thumb between his brows. "Maybe I was wrong to walk off when Emily started a tirade."

"No good ever comes from talking about the dead, Alan."

"You know our friends in town think Emily was having an affair." He said it haltingly. "Our troubles began after Grandfather died. Even more so when my mom up and married Royce and left us. I couldn't let you run the business alone. Emily hated my working long hours."

"Those were tough times until you promoted Hardy. But even with all his experience in making bourbon, he needed to learn the business end. We all did our best," she said quietly. "I hope you're not feeling guilty. You have nothing to regret, Alan. Emily was headstrong. Payton and Joleen spoiled her rotten, and they would've done the same with Louemma."

He smiled at that. "Yes, I can't say I was sorry to see my in-laws retire to Arizona. I didn't relish the prospect of having to limit their contact with their only grandchild."

Vestal picked up her book again and prepared to open it. Then she hesitated, marking her place with one finger. "I forgive you for being so stubbornly resistant to seeking help from Ms. Ashline, Alan. Louemma is your daughter. I shouldn't be an interfering old busybody."

Alan's eyebrow shot up to meet the lock of hair that perpetually fell over his brow. "If I thought you honestly meant that, I'd leave now, a happy man. But I'm betting tomorrow you'll find another way to bring up her name in a flank attack. So I'll capitulate. If I can ever get an audience with her, I will speak to Ms. Ashline about Louemma."

"Really?" Vestal removed her reading glasses and gazed at her grandson with a hopeful expression. "It so happens I have the perfect plan, Alan." Setting her book aside again, she swung her feet off the ottoman and stood. Walking over to her small cherrywood rolltop desk, she picked up a section of the Ridge City weekly newspaper. "According to this article, Laurel's giving a weaving demonstration to Charity Madison's Camp Fire troop tomorrow. It's no coincidence. It's synchronicity, Alan. Louemma still belongs, doesn't she?"

"Yes, but…she hasn't attended since the accident. What are you suggesting? That I barge in on one of their meetings?"

"No. Well, yes. Louemma's been cut off from her little pals long enough. Call Charity. Say you're bringing Louemma to the meeting. Those kids are all her friends. She used to look forward to seeing them."

"I know, but…" It struck Alan that these were his fears welling up. He'd quit visiting Pete and Charity because they were among the people who, after the accident, had first alluded to his wife's possible infidelity. "Give me the article. I'll go out right now and talk to Louemma. If she wants to attend, I'll contact Charity. Only…aren't you forgetting that some of those kids are the same ones who treated her so badly at school?"

"That's the way of kids. Especially girls. Trust me, Alan, I saw it all during the years I taught third grade."

Releasing a breath trapped deep in his lungs, Alan pushed to his feet. "I'm not going to *force* her to interact with her former friends. Whatever her response might be, will you take my word for it? Or do you want to come along and see that I actually throw out the possibility and let her choose?"

"I trust you, Alan. I've questioned your hardheadedness, but never your integrity."

He laughed at that and walked toward the door. "I'll give you the verdict at dinner. Oh, by the way, are we eating earlier tonight?"

"I asked Birdie to move up lunch and dinner by an hour or two starting tomorrow. I know you said we'd discuss it, but I thought it had probably slipped your mind."

"It had until now. If it works for everyone else, I'll make it work for me."

Alan went straight back to the living room. Louemma was engrossed in her movie, so he dropped the paper and sat down to watch it with her as promised. He had to lift her up and settle her against his side. At times like this, more than any other, Alan longed for the return of the active boisterous girl she'd been before the accident. For that reason, it seemed churlish of him to have argued with Vestal over the Ashline woman.

He ought to grab at any chance of helping Louemma, no matter how unlikely or bizarre it might seem.

The minute the credits started to roll at the end of the movie, Alan sat Louemma up. He grabbed the section of the newspaper and turned off the movie with the remote. "Nana found something interesting in today's paper. Your old Camp Fire group has someone coming to the meeting tomorrow to demonstrate weaving."

The little girl glanced up with interest. "What is weaving?"

"Uh…well, all cloth is woven. There are different kinds of thread, and various types of weaving. The article mentions pot holders. Woven on a hand-operated loom."

"Oh." The spark died in her dark-brown eyes. "I couldn't do it, then."

Alan hated to raise her hopes, only to dash them again. On the other hand, he'd promised Vestal. "Nana saw this weaver working with patients at the hospital. A friend of hers who'd had a stroke and used to be paralyzed on one side can apparently operate the loom now. I'm not saying you can do it, baby, but it's worth trying. Plus you haven't seen Sarah Madison in a while. I thought I could knock off work early and take you to the meeting, and let you see what weaving's all about."

She pursed her lips. "Sarah called me a spoiled brat. But I miss Jenny, Maggie and Brenna. I guess it'd be okay to go."

Alan had hoped for more overt enthusiasm, or else a flat refusal. He supposed he'd have to live with her tepid response. "Fine," he said, clasping sweating palms over his knees. "I'll phone Mrs. Madison and tell her to plan on two more at the meeting. Oh," he added as he stood, "I understand we're eating earlier beginning tomorrow. Did Birdie tell you?"

"Birdie and Nana discussed it with Miss Robinson. She said it didn't matter to my lesson schedule."

"Good, that's what we'll do."

He realized he was stalling, not wanting to make that call to Charity. Alan removed that DVD disc and found another appropriate program for Louemma to watch before he decided he could stall no longer.

AT THREE-THIRTY the next afternoon, Alan found himself sitting in front of the Madison home. Louemma wore an anxious expression. Her Camp Fire uniform hung on her, emphasizing her weight loss.

"Sure you're still okay with your decision, honey? It's not too late to change your mind."

"I want to go."

Alan heard a *but* in there. "But…?"

"I don't like riding in the wheelchair. And I'm nine, so when you carry me, I look like a baby."

"Don't you remember how you woke up crying every night with terrible muscle aches? That's why Dr. Fulton got you the chair."

She dragged her lip between her teeth.

Allowing her to make up her own mind, Alan remained silent. He and Charity already thought the meeting, added to the demonstration and the social half hour, might be too much for Louemma's first outing. They'd settled on skipping the meeting portion, at that time Charity would prepare the other girls for Louemma's eventual appearance. As he waited, staring out the car window, he saw a pickup cruising slowly toward them on the opposite side of the street. He recognized it as the one he'd seen parked near the footbridge at Laurel Ashline's cottage. It galled him to think of it as her cottage. If she was related to Hazel Bell, then she was kin to a woman who had scammed his family.

Well, maybe *scammed* was too harsh a term. But Hazel had certainly deceived them.

"What's the verdict, Louemma? I think that's the weaver

across the street. We'll want to go inside and get settled so we're not interrupting her."

"I'll use the chair, Daddy. The other girls sit on the floor."

Since the last thing Alan wanted was to encounter Laurel Ashline on the porch, he jumped from the Jeep, pulled out the wheelchair and flipped it open. He unbuckled Louemma and lifted her down, placing her in the chair. It became apparent that their demonstrator had things to collect, too. He saw her leaning into the pickup bed—and he couldn't help admiring her backside. Forcing his eyes away, he managed to maneuver his daughter and himself into the house, greeting Charity and the other girls, all before Laurel knocked at the door.

Alan took a seat in the far corner of the Madisons' family room. It was a good place from which to evaluate the weaver without attracting her attention. Apparently, Eva Saxon's assessment of Laurel as a tall, willowy blonde was fairly accurate. Peg Moore, though, had called her plain. And shy. Alan wouldn't attach either of those labels to this woman, whose skin was flawless. After putting down a loom and a large quilted bag, she talked animatedly with Charity, all the while flashing brilliant smiles at the small circle of girls.

Alan wasn't close enough to get a good look at her eyes, but if he had to guess, he'd say they were hazel, more aqua and gold than brown. She didn't wear a speck of jewelry. Perhaps that was why Peg considered her plain. In his experience, southern women tended to drape themselves in gold necklaces, with charms, crosses and other things hanging at varying lengths. Like the ones Charity had on and Emily had worn. Plus gemstone rings on every finger. Alan hadn't thought much about the practice until now, following the graceful sweep of Laurel Ashline's bare, slender hand through the air.

He suffered yet another guilty start and sat up fast. He had absolutely no reason at all to compare her with other women

of his acquaintance—especially not in an interested fashion.
A romantic…

More to the point, Alan needed to observe her reaction
when Charity introduced her to Louemma. Or when they got
around to him.

He didn't have long to wait. Alan saw the woman take in
Louemma's full name, and thought he saw a narrowing of her
eyes. Just as quickly, she pasted on another smile. But when
Charity pointed to him, the smile disappeared and her mouth
dropped open.

He got to his feet and ambled over, acknowledging the in-
troduction with a brief nod of his head. Then he casually tucked
his thumbs under his belt and resumed his seat. He couldn't
help gloating that his nemesis seemed so obviously rattled.

And rattled she was. Although she'd kept his pink roses
long after another woman would have thrown them out, Laurel had built a less than flattering picture in her mind of Alan
Ridge. She'd imagined him fortyish, slightly paunchy, possibly even with receding hair, but definitely with a ruddy complexion from partaking of the product that had made him a
wealthy man. Her stomach fell suddenly as she realized she'd
attached to Alan Ridge attributes her ex-husband had developed over their seven-year marriage.

Ridge was melt-in-a-puddle-at-his-feet gorgeous.

Belatedly, Laurel realized that she was standing there gaping at him, and had completely missed what the hostess, Charity Madison, had said next.

"I'm sorry? What?"

Charity darted a sharp glance between her visitor and her
husband's former best friend. "I asked if you needed a card table
for your demonstration. But perhaps I should've explained why
a man is sitting in on what is normally an all-girl event. I assumed, from talk around town, that you and Alan were ac-
quainted." Charity discreetly murmured the last few words.

"Ah, no. We've never met." Laurel hauled in a deep breath. The infusion of oxygen to her lungs and brain had the desired effect. "A card table will work just fine," she said briskly. "I'll talk a bit about the history of weaving in Kentucky, then start a pot holder I've set up on a hand loom. While you prepare refreshments for the girls, I'll take them individually and let them weave four or so lines apiece on the mat. By the time they finish, they'll have a fair idea of how a weaving comes together."

"Oh, that sounds marvelous. Exactly the kind of program I'm always searching for. In a small town it's hard to find things year after year to interest kids who have the attention span of gnats." Both women laughed at that.

"Sarah and Brenna," Charity called. "Ms. Ashline needs the card table. It's your turn to set up for our speaker."

Laurel saw two girls jump up. Both were pretty and gangly like colts. One had long golden hair and the other was a freckled redhead. The golden girl appeared somewhat bossy. But it wasn't until the group leader spoke sharply to her that Laurel gathered the bossy one was her daughter.

Charity followed Laurel to where she'd left her loom and bag. Kneeling, she helped collect the various things, although that clearly wasn't her primary goal. It became obvious that she had something to say to Laurel that she didn't want the girls to hear.

"Come into the kitchen for a minute, will you please, Ms. Ashline?" Charity kept her voice low and her eyes shuttered. Laurel couldn't determine exactly why she wanted a private consultation. Like it or not, she was about to find out.

Charity announced, "Girls, we're going to grab the adults some coffee. Finish preparing the table and return to your circle. Ms. Ashline and I will be right back."

"Call me Laurel," she murmured, dutifully falling in behind the other woman.

In the homey country kitchen, Charity filled cups already set out on a tray.

"What's this about?" Laurel asked, getting straight to the point. "I can't drink coffee while I demonstrate."

"I know." Charity bit her lip. "I assumed you were aware of Louemma Ridge's disability, or I'd have advised Alan not to bring her today."

"Are we speaking about the child in the wheelchair?" Suddenly it all began to fall into place.

"Louemma is Alan's daughter." Charity tucked a stray curl behind one ear. "It's too long a story to give you details, but the short version is that she was injured in the accident that killed his wife, uh, Louemma's mother. Since then, the poor child hasn't been able to, or refuses to, move her arms. As a result, she also has difficulty with balance and therefore walking, and her legs are withering from disuse. Frankly, there are so many…rumors flying around.…" She paused, frowning. "My Sarah and Louemma used to be best friends. After the accident, well… Alan and Louemma have dropped out of everything. I was shocked when he phoned and asked to bring her today. To be honest, I'm not sure why they're here. I assume, since his grandmother suggested I invite you to do a program, that she's the instigator." Shrugging, Charity broke off and picked up the tray. "Oh, I've probably only confused you, Ms. Ashline…uh, Laurel," she said, as Laurel opened her mouth to correct her. "I thought you'd want to know so you won't expect Louemma to participate in trying to weave like the other girls."

"Thanks. I do appreciate knowing." Laurel grabbed a mug off the tray and even though she'd denied wanting coffee, took a sip. It gave her an excuse to be in the kitchen while she tried to make some sense out of the information Charity Madison had so unceremoniously dumped on her.

As she returned to the family room a minute later, Laurel

didn't even glance in Alan Ridge's direction. She went straight to the table and began unloading her kit. From everything that had been said in the kitchen she deduced two things. Vestal Ridge, the pleasant woman she'd met quite by accident at the hospital, had a purpose in mind when she'd asked if weaving therapy always helped patients regain use of injured limbs. And the elfin child huddled in the wheelchair was the reason for Alan Ridge's initial phone call, and his subsequent attempts to contact her by plying her with goodies.

That much Laurel had straight. Now she was even more furious that the man would place her or his poor, sweet child in a situation doomed for failure.

But here they were. She had an audience that expected to be taught weaving. And there was nothing she could do except muddle through. Afterward, however, Mr. Ridge of the Ridges for whom the town was named was going to get a piece of her mind. And he wouldn't like it.

The eager faces of the girls wiped away the frown Laurel felt between her eyebrows merely thinking about Alan Ridge. Laurel and the waif in the chair connected with a brief meeting of their eyes.

Laurel began stringing the loom. "Hand-weaving is an art brought to this country from Europe by women who had dreams of raising their families in a society free of religious oppression. The women, the pioneers who settled the state of Kentucky, wove cloth out of necessity. For clothes, bedding, curtains…well, for everything. Back then there were no stores. No malls. Sheep provided wool, and the women spun it into yarn. If you've never seen a spinning wheel, maybe Mrs. Madison can bring you to my loom cottage on a field trip."

One child's hand shot up. "Is that sheep's wool you're using?"

"Good question. No. It's cotton. The first Kentucky weaver to use cotton probably bartered for as little as four pounds of cotton seed from a Virginia farmer. Records are sketchy, but that's the recollection of early settlers. Again, your great-great-great-grandmothers spun the thread and dyed it with native bark and berries. It was expensive to buy indigo-blue or cochineal-red coloring. Which is why, if you see early Kentucky weavings in museums, they're true natural colors."

Sarah Madison tossed her head saucily. "Why go to so much work, Ms. Ashline, when we can drive to the mall to buy clothes, pot holders, bedspreads and stuff?"

"Not so many years ago, women helped supplement the family income, or filled their kitchen cupboards, by bartering and trading their weavings. And believe it or not, there are still families who live too far from a town to have ready access to the things you mentioned. My grandmother and others before her traveled on foot or horseback in remote sites to collect and preserve weaving patterns that might otherwise be lost."

"Why do you weave?" asked a bored-looking girl. "I mean, you live in Ridge City, right? You could just go to the mall."

"Ah. Another good question. I discovered I have a strong urge to create. I enjoy seeing an ancient pattern come to life under my hands. Like many other women, I gain satisfaction from making such pieces and using them in my home." She laughed. "Fortunately for me, Maggie," she said, reading the name off the last questioner's badge, "a lot of busy women think like me but feel like you. They want handmade items on their tables, beds and windows, but lack the time, desire or knowledge to produce cloth themselves."

Another reed-thin girl straightened to peer at her friends through thick cocoa-colored bangs. "I think it'd be cool to weave. Look what Ms. Ashline's done just since she started talking. I'll bet if we tried, we could all make our moms Christmas gifts."

"You could," Laurel agreed, and at once saw that the interest she'd noticed in Louemma Ridge's expressive eyes had been extinguished. "I see disbelief written on a few faces. Making things like pot holders or place mats is much easier than you obviously think. Maggie," she said, choosing the girl who, other than Louemma Ridge, least wanted to participate. "Come here and I'll show you how to work the shuttle. I'll show each of you while Mrs. Madison prepares your snack."

The children jumped to their feet and crowded around. Without fanfare, Laurel left the table. She gave the child seated in the wheelchair a warm smile, then wheeled her into position near the table so she could watch what the others were doing.

"Louemma can't do this," Sarah Madison said snippily. "She can't do anything the rest of us can. I don't even know why she's here."

Laurel sent her a stern look. "A highly respected Kentucky weaver by the name of Lou Tate Bousman had more faith in our craft than you do, Sarah. Thanks to her and some of the weavers she taught, a lot of people with hand, arm and back injuries learned to successfully operate a loom."

"Right," Sarah drawled. "I guess Louemma could move that bar back and forth with her feet."

Most of the children tittered. Except for Brenna, who darted a sympathetic glance toward Louemma before scowling at Sarah.

Laurel wouldn't let Sarah's remark go. "Girls, there are artists who paint holding a brush in their mouth or with their toes. *Everything* is possible."

Charity Madison and Alan Ridge, who'd gone into the kitchen, arrived back in time to hear Sarah's rude statement.

"Sarah Michelle Madison!" Her mother set down a tray of juice and cookies, and grabbed her daughter's arm. "If I hear you speak in that manner again, you won't go to the new Disney movie tonight."

The child jerked out of her mom's grip, but although her

expression was one of stormy resistance, she bit back any response that may have run through her mind.

Charity paused behind Louemma. "Pay Sarah no mind, hon. Her daddy says she's going through another phase. Oh, my! Look what you all have made in the few minutes I've been gone." Charity leaned across the table to admire the weaving, which had grown several inches under Laurel's tutelage.

"I did the most," Jenny said, dancing back and forth. "For our program next week, Mrs. Madison, can we all go out to Ms. Ashline's place and see the spinning wheel and stuff?"

"Oh, I don't know." Charity, who was now being pressured by all the girls except Sarah, turned to gaze helplessly at Laurel.

"I'll have to check my calendar," Laurel said, not wanting to make those arrangements in front of Louemma, which would surely add to her discomfort.

Charity pointed to a day planner peeking out of Laurel's quilted handbag. "Isn't that where you'd write down your appointments?"

Flushing, Laurel snatched up the book and flipped to the proper page. Unfortunately, the children had crowded around her, and they all saw that the page was blank.

"Yay!" Jenny flung her arms in the air and squealed at the top of her lungs. "She hasn't got anything at three o'clock. We can go, we can go!"

Since there was nothing to do but block out the time, Laurel grabbed a pen and drew a big X through the hour from three to four. "Will you bring treats?" she asked Charity. "Or do I need to provide a snack for the children?"

"Mercy, I wouldn't expect you to feed the girls. It's kind enough of you to extend your program to include a session on spinning. Thank you so much. It's been quite a while since I've seen them this excited over a project. Well, some are," she added, dolefully eyeing her daughter.

Laurel figured she'd have to suffer through Sarah's cattiness and probably even Maggie's indifference for one more day. She quickly dismissed the idea of seeing Louemma Ridge at the next gathering. Her father was already preparing to leave. As Laurel still wanted to tell him how insensitive she thought he was in subjecting his daughter to this demonstration without adequate preparation, she rushed to gather her things, and started after him.

"Thank you for giving me an opportunity to explain the art of weaving," Laurel remembered to tell Charity as she moved toward the door. "Which reminds me, you'll need my address." Taking out a business card, she scribbled on the back.

Charity gave it a cursory glance. "I turn at Vining Mill Road?" She looked up. "Are you living at Hazel Bell's old place? Goodness, you probably don't even know who that is. I guess you're renting from Alan."

"Renting from—?" Laurel paused, pulling her eyes away from his broad back as he disappeared out the door. "Hazel willed me the property when she died."

"*Willed* it to you? But I, uh, gosh…didn't realize she and Ted had bought Bell Hill. Last week I thought Hardy Duff told Pete—Pete's my husband… Oh, never mind. Pete only listens with half an ear to what's being said." Charity was called away from the door by her daughter, who demanded her immediate attention. With a shrug, Charity grinned at Laurel. "At times I envy you single women."

"It does have its benefits," Laurel agreed. "But I do have responsibilities. Two saddle horses and a dog. By the way, are any of the girls allergic to dogs? Mine is underfoot all the time." She said it almost hopefully.

"I don't think anyone in the group has allergies. Unless Louemma's developed some since her accident. Maybe you'd better catch Alan and ask him."

"Oh, I'm sure he won't bring her all that way. The area

around my cottage is still quite primitive. Visitors park west of the stream and cross on a footbridge to reach my place. The cabin where my spinning room and looms are located is quite a trek up a gravel path, if you can even call it a path."

"Well, then you definitely should speak with Alan. I just assumed Louemma would participate in our regular meetings, starting today."

Laurel flew out the door then and called to Alan, who'd already placed his daughter in the Jeep. He closed her wheelchair and set it in the back before answering Laurel's summons. He waited beside the open driver's door, jingling his keys, clearly indicating his desire to get underway.

But Laurel really didn't want to talk to him where Louemma might overhear, so she stopped by the Madisons' front gate.

"Are you stuck, or what?" Alan demanded, sounding annoyed at her intrusion into his planned escape.

It was plain to Laurel that the man didn't intend to budge. Reluctantly she started toward him. "Mrs. Madison suggested I remind you of the undeveloped condition of the walkway leading up to my loom cottage."

He ignored that. "So, you really weren't home when I came out to your place?" he inquired instead. "Doesn't matter. I fulfilled my grandmother's request today. It was even worse than I expected. Of course Louemma won't be at next week's meeting."

Laurel was at a loss to explain why her relief was mixed with a twinge of sorrow when she heard his curt words.

"Daddy," Louemma called plaintively from inside the dusty blue vehicle. "I want to see the spinning wheel. Can't I please go with the others?"

From the frown that instantly crossed his face, throwing the angles of his cheeks into sharp relief, Laurel fully expected him to deny the child. But as he half turned to peer at her through the door, the lines softened measurably. "You want to go, honey? Are you positive?"

"I want to see how to get yarn out of sheep's wool. And I like Ms. Ashline."

"Is that what you're going to do?" Alan practically barked at Laurel, blaming her with his eyes for the fact that Louemma thought she was nice.

She could have ended it then and there. But the eagerness on Louemma's face wouldn't let her. "I plan exactly that," she mumbled at last. "I'll demonstrate washing, carding and spinning yarn from sheep's wool, and thread from raw cotton bolls." The stab of guilt she felt over her testiness toward him also came with an unexpected reward in the slow smile that lit the girl's dark eyes.

"Uh, so I'll see you next week, Louemma," Laurel said. "I'm glad Mrs. Madison has a van big enough to transport all of you girls." She abruptly sidestepped the Ridge Jeep, waved to the girl and ran across the street to where she'd parked. As she felt Alan Ridge's smoldering gaze tracking every inch of her progress.

CHAPTER FOUR

THE OUTING TOOK A TOLL on Louemma; she fell asleep on the drive home. Still furious about the way Laurel Ashline had fouled his attempt to stonewall a second meeting, Alan carried his sleeping child into the house. It galled him that Laurel had sashayed off in that sugar-wouldn't-melt-in-her-mouth manner after setting him up.

She'd planted the suggestion in Louemma's mind by mentioning she could ride there with Charity. As if he'd entrust his daughter's transportation to anyone else! Her own mother had disregarded something as basic as weather warnings.

The house was silent, so he walked quietly along the hall. Entering Louemma's room, he placed her gently on her bed, then removed her jacket and shoes. Finding a lightweight coverlet, he settled it over her, thinking he'd let her nap until dinner. Then he might ask if she'd like to go see the Disney movie that Charity had mentioned. He wanted their lives back to normal. Wanted Louemma to have friends again.

Alan knew he was guilty of hovering. Marv Fulton, their family physician, said to quit treating Louemma like an invalid. He said they should plunge back into their pre-accident routines. Ha! Marv obviously didn't understand how hard that was.

Finding Louemma's favorite stuffed animal, a plush brown bear she'd had since birth, Alan propped it on the pillow where she could readily see it if she woke suddenly. She was still prone to nightmares, although she never said what they were about. The accident, everyone assumed. Marv thought maybe they'd never know. He hoped in time they'd fade. So did Alan.

He left the bedroom and bumped into Vestal.

"Oh, you're back from the weaving demonstration." She peered past him, into Louemma's bedroom. "How'd it go?" she whispered.

Pursing his lips, Alan left the door ajar. With a slight shake of his head, he led the way to his office. Leaving his grandmother to choose a seat, he rummaged in the small fridge and extracted a bottle of water. "Can I get you something to drink?" he asked, not looking at her, but rather out the window at the budding tulip trees.

"Nothing, thanks. I take it from your evasiveness that things didn't go well. I'm so disappointed. I'd hoped—"

"What?" he snapped, whirling. "Did you think a weaver would have some magic potion? That she'd succeed where the very best medical talent has failed?"

"Maybe," Vestal admitted wearily, sinking onto a high-backed leather chair, which had been her husband's favorite. She rubbed the brass studs on the rich green armrests. "I'm sorry if Louemma hated the demonstration, or if being there made her feel worse. What's next, Alan? Find a new bone doctor? Or another psychiatrist?"

He took a deep swig from the icy, sweating bottle. "I didn't say Louemma hated the demonstration. It…just opened a can of worms. She's begged to go to the woman's cottage next week. She'll be spinning thread like some damn black widow spider."

The old woman leaned forward eagerly, adjusting her trifocals over her myopic eyes. "Why didn't you say so right off the bat? That's good! Think how long it's been since Louemma took an interest in anything outside the house."

"I'm afraid I don't agree it's good to foster an interest in something she'll never be able to do, Grandmother. Is it wise to throw her in with peers who only make her feel more inept? Sarah Madison was such a pain today. According to Charity, it's only a phase. All I know is that Sarah caused Louemma's problems at school, too. I thought those two were best friends. Was I so blind and naive before the accident?"

"Girls are fickle, Alan. Sarah may not know how to handle what's happened to Louemma. Maybe its her way of coping. Your friends haven't all known how to act, either. Shoot, most of them don't know what to say or whether to even mention Emily. These are just kids. Go a little easy on them."

"I'll try. But I'm not letting Louemma ride out to Bell Hill next week with Charity, and that's final. It's not that I think she's a bad driver. She's probably fine. But Emily drove fine, too." He brooded for a minute, staring into his water bottle. "Anyway, hauling Louemma and her wheelchair across the footbridge needs a man's strength. Did I tell you that Ms. Ashline has a ferocious watchdog? Oh, and horses. You know how hysterical Louemma got over our horses when she came home from the hospital. How will she react to a yapping dog?"

Vestal rose. "It sounds as if you're making a laundry list of excuses so you can avoid the next Camp Fire meeting yourself. Is this really about all the things you just brought up? Or do you plain dislike Laurel Ashline?"

"She's pushy. And takes independence to extremes."

"Hmm. I thought she was attractive and quite gracious. With a smoky voice that reminded me of a young Lauren Bacall. But you know how I love Bogie and Bacall's old movies," she said, absently straightening papers on Alan's cluttered desk.

"Don't organize my controlled mess," he said testily, setting his plastic bottle atop a particularly precarious stack of shipping orders.

"Laurel or something else really rattled you today. It isn't like you to snap, Alan. I've always said you were the most even-tempered of all the Ridge men. Unless…" She paused. "Unless it wasn't her at all. Maybe it had to do with being in Charity and Pete's house again—without Emily."

"Vestal, why are you bent on giving me a hard time?"

"I'm not. I know what's it's like to lose the other half of your heart."

As if noting how Alan stiffened, Vestal sighed, stood and glided quietly from the room. Over her shoulder, she called, "Dinner's at seven, remember? Birdie's fixed chicken and dumplings."

Alan grunted a reply, crushing the thin plastic of the water bottle. Instead of getting straight to work as he'd planned, he moved restlessly back to the picture window and stood silently evaluating empty rows of paddocks and bluegrass growing too tall inside unused corrals.

Perhaps his grandmother was unaware of the strains within his and Emily's marriage. Probably just as well. He never wanted Vestal or Louemma to know the full extent of the questions raised by the police who'd investigated the accident. The note Emily had left on their dresser for him to find had said she and Louemma were spending a week in Louisville shopping for school clothes.

The police had asked a million times why, if Emily had gone on a shopping spree, so many suitcases brimming with clothes were packed in the trunk of her Mercedes. And why she had left Alan a note instead of simply calling the distillery to apprise him of her plans. There'd been plenty of whispers floating around at the funeral, too. Thankfully, Louemma hadn't been well enough to attend. Alan wished he really knew why a woman he'd known all his life and lived with for a lot of years would ruthlessly run off with the one thing they both loved more than life itself. Except he knew, deep down, that Emily felt they were in competition for Louemma's affections.

Was he afraid of the truth? Was that the real reason he hadn't wanted to rekindle old friendships, like the one he and Emily had shared with the Madisons? Alan didn't want Louemma's memories of her mother ever to be marred by unsubstantiated hearsay. And if that meant forgoing social pleasures, so be it.

JUST BEFORE THE SECOND Camp Fire meeting, Laurel had to ready the loom cottage for the invasion of children. A long bench set with hand looms and plenty of chairs were already in place. Her grandmother had given lessons, but not to women from Ridge City. Laurel was unsure why.

She'd been prevented from attending Hazel's funeral by the most serious of Dennis's drinking binges. An attorney had sent her the sympathy cards collected by the funeral home. Several women from a nearby town had spoken fondly of the hours they'd spent at Hazel's, learning how to weave.

If anything had given Laurel the impetus to sever the bonds of a marriage she'd tried so hard to hold together, it was the fact that Dennis had found and destroyed those cards, plus a letter from the attorney saying Hazel had wanted Laurel to attend her funeral without her husband. That had sent Dennis into an uncontrolled rage. He'd been drinking a lot in the weeks before. But the cards and the letter had set him off. His anger had apparently made him crazy—so crazy he'd smashed her loom and her spinning wheel and cut up finished products that would've kept a roof over their heads for another month. For the first time in their marriage, Dennis had raised his hand and struck Laurel, so hard she fell, bruising her cheek and her shoulder.

That was the end. Up to then she'd maintained the marriage. She'd kept a spotless house. Had paid bills on the sly so he wouldn't feel emasculated. And she'd accepted his hat-in-hand apologies time after time. But he'd never hit her before.

She was just sorry that it took her grandmother's death to give her the strength and the means to stand up and walk away. Hazel had offered a ticket out more than once, and Laurel had always refused. Not a day passed that she didn't wish she'd come sooner. Now she could only hope her grandmother was looking down to see how much this place meant to her. "Well, Dog, we're as ready for them as I guess we'll ever be."

He raised his head from his paws. Then he jumped up and loped to the door, running back to Laurel, then to the door again, barking loudly.

"It's okay, boy. There's no one in this group I need protecting from." But because she wasn't sure how he might act around noisy kids, Laurel snapped a leash to his collar. Together they followed the winding creek down to the footbridge.

She stopped short of the bridge, realizing Charity Madison hadn't brought all five girls. Alan Ridge's Jeep had pulled in behind.

"Maybe I do need protecting," she murmured to her pet. But even as the words left her lips, she chided herself for such silliness. She hadn't met a soul in town who didn't speak highly of the man. She didn't need twenty-twenty vision to see he was a doting father. And by all reports, cared for his grandmother.

So why did she get squirmy merely watching him climb from his Jeep? Maybe because she liked the way he looked in his tight blue jeans and open-throated white shirt. Laurel frowned. It wasn't like her to swoon over a man's looks. Yet there was a definite shift in her equilibrium.

Dog growled deep in his chest and didn't let up.

"Hush. I know you recognize him. He's not bringing flowers this time, but he will be carrying his little girl. She's fragile, Dog, so if you don't want to be shut in the house for the next hour, start making them feel welcome."

As if he understood, the animal dropped to his belly at Laurel's feet. And as the children trooped across the wooden bridge, he woofed softly, letting his tongue loll out the side of his mouth as the girls gathered around, lavishing attention on him.

"Big change in that animal between now and the last time we met," Alan said in a husky voice. He held Louemma aloft and pushed her empty wheelchair.

Laurel, who kept an eye out for any adverse reaction from his child, ignored Alan's remarks. "This is Dog," she announced. "Don't let his size or bark fool you into thinking he's mean. He might look fierce, but he's a big gooey marshmallow inside."

All the girls laughed.

"Hey, you have horses," Jenny exclaimed excitedly. She'd raced ahead up the trail on her own. "Cool. After you show us how to spin thread, can we take turns riding the horses around the yard?"

Laurel caught the panicked expression on Louemma's face. The girl's thin chest rose and fell fast, as though her heart might leap out through her flowered T-shirt. Laurel recalled hearing someone in town say that before her accident, Emily Ridge had been an accomplished rider who owned a stableful of Thoroughbreds. Then, shortly after Alan had brought Louemma home from the hospital, he'd sold every one of his wife's prize horses.

At the time, Laurel supposed an anguished man had no time to bother with the care and feeding of high-strung animals. Now she wondered if Louemma's obvious panic had been the catalyst for Alan's behavior.

Not that it was any of her business. "The horses are penned," she told the frightened girl.

Charity Madison solved the dilemma, saying, "Jenny, you kids aren't here to ride but to observe spinning. Head on up the path. Look, you can see the cottage roof peeking through the oak leaves."

Four jabbering girls raced away, all wanting to reach the cottage first. Their noisy departure scattered the horses and sent them galloping for the far side of the corral. Once they were out of sight, Louemma relaxed again.

Charity kept pace with Alan. Laurel took care to stay between him and the fence. She forgot to tighten her hold on Dog's leash until she heard a giggle.

"Daddy, the dog licked my ankle," Louemma said, trying to bend so she could see. It was impossible, as she couldn't move her shoulders.

"Oops, sorry, Louemma. Dog didn't hurt you, did he?" Laurel shortened the leash enough to pull her pet away.

"Last year my teacher said dogs only lick people they like. I think he likes me. Why do you call him Dog, Ms. Ashline? Doesn't he have a name?"

Laurel wasn't about to admit in front of Alan, the reservations she'd felt about ever again becoming more than superficially attached to any living thing. That left an awkward, empty minute. "Dog *is* his name."

Alan observed the range of emotions that skipped across Laurel's face. Up close, he found her undeniably attractive. Well-acquainted with pain, he recognized the stark emotion visible only for an instant, and it prompted him to say, "Honey, we've talked about strays that get left at shelters. Folks who work there don't name them, so they won't feel bad when someone adopts them and they have to say goodbye."

"Oh. But he's found a home. He should have a real name now, shouldn't he?"

"Louemma, it's not for us to decide." Alan set her in the chair and proceeded up the path at a slower pace, letting the two women lead the way.

Laurel was happy to see he'd effectively put an end to the

topic. However, she'd never have guessed a child's silent accusation would bring her so much guilt. After all, Dog answered to his name.

Midway up the rocky incline, Alan saw where they were headed. He forged ahead to better view the cabin. It was smaller and more weathered than the one below. A narrow porch had wisteria vines crawling up and over the roof. He liked how the cottage blended with the treed hillside.

Laurel brushed past Charity, Alan and the chattering girls to go unlock the door. She created a small breeze that carried a fresh scent. Apple blossom, Alan thought, feeling an unexpected punch to his gut. It wasn't until then that he realized how much he missed smelling traces of Emily's bath powder or perfumes in their bedroom. Friends had come in while he was at the hospital with Louemma and cleaned out Emily's closet and dresser. He'd been thankful—then.

Laurel waited at the door, directing everyone to chairs as they came in. Alan took a good look at her as he wheeled Louemma inside the cool room. Today, her hair was pulled back from her oval face and tied with a colorful band she'd probably woven herself. It required a huge effort on his part not to lean closer to her and take another whiff.

He almost smiled, imagining what her reaction would be if he followed up on his desire. She'd probably coldcock him with one of the two paddle things she'd just picked up. Both had wire teeth on one side, and either would make a good weapon.

"These are wool cards," she announced, wasting no time beginning the day's lesson. "Living in farm country, you girls have probably seen sheepshearing." Laurel held up a box filled with piles of dirty wool. "This is newly sheared wool. Here's what it looks like after washing. Washing removes all the natural oils, so before carding and spinning, I have to add enough oil to make the fibers cling together." She demonstrated the process. And she let each girl try the carding paddles.

"Ooh, this is harder than it looks," Jenny exclaimed. "Wool is sticky."

While the other girls were making similar exclamations, Laurel rounded the long table and knelt beside Louemma.

Alan tensed and started to leave the chair he'd taken at the back of the room. Then he heard Laurel say, "I'm going to put your hand in mine so you can feel how soft washed wool is, Louemma. Will that be all right?"

"Yes, please, I'd like that," the girl murmured in wonderment.

Dog rose from where he'd flopped in front of the door. He trotted up to Laurel, and Alan's nerves jerked spasmodically. But she handled the animal's approach in the same quiet manner she handled everything else.

"Look who's come to investigate," she told Louemma. "Dog's fur is even softer. Here, feel." For just a second, Laurel cupped Louemma's hand and let their joined fingers rest between the shepherd's pointed ears.

Alan couldn't see his daughter's response, but Laurel smiled and a pleased light flickered in her hazel eyes. That alone lessened his mounting tension. He settled back in the wicker chair, his attitude markedly warmer.

Laurel repeated the process with cotton bolls, moving along the table to show each girl the black seeds that had to be removed before the cotton could be turned into thread.

"I have three sizes of spinning wheels. Anyone who'd like to may try each one. Notice that a spinner has to stand all the time to operate the big wheel. Watch how I walk three steps forward and three steps back, developing a rhythmic motion."

"I'm next after Jenny," Sarah announced, shoving her way between Jenny and Brenna. "Louemma," the girl said, looking down at her former friend. "Cripples like you can forget about the spinning wheel."

Sarah's mother looked aghast but also helpless. Alan rose immediately, intent on defending his child.

Laurel waved him away. "Sarah," she said mildly, "one of my teachers, an award-winning weaver, I might add, was a victim of polio. She had the use of only one arm, and her upper body was quite twisted. I'd like everyone to look at this sampler of hers I have hanging on the wall. It's 'Wheels of the Western World.'" Laurel went to stand next to an intricate piece woven in blue, tan and creamy thread. The circles within patterned squares were perfectly round and evenly spaced.

"Did my friend face more challenges than I can even imagine to complete such a weaving? Yes. But the point is, she overcame her handicap."

Sarah got the message, but she clearly didn't like it. Tossing her light golden curls, she pulled Maggie out of the circle to go look at work hung on the opposite wall. Charity joined the girls, and Laurel soon heard her low, urgent voice laying down the law.

Laurel moved on with the class, showing her students how to operate each wheel. Jenny and Brenna both learned quickly. Maggie would've done better if Sarah hadn't kept distracting her.

"I'm bored," Sarah whined for the fifth time in an hour.

"Ms. Ashline, my mom said I could ask what you charge for lessons," Jenny said to Laurel, who was inspecting Jenny's finished mug mat.

Before they arrived, Laurel had laced a loom for each child. She'd included one for Louemma, hoping to see some interest. But after Sarah's unkind remarks, the injured girl had understandably withdrawn.

Feeling terrible, Laurel made a point of going to sit next to Louemma. She included the girl in dialogue as she wove her a mat. It seemed only fair that each girl have something tangible to take home. But now Laurel was faced with the possibility of repeating this tension-filled day.

"Jenny, I haven't scheduled private lessons. Nothing beyond my volunteer therapy at the hospital, that is. Next month I'll be demonstrating for the first week of the trade and craft fair at Boonesborough."

"Brenna and I want lessons. We wanna make stuff. Christmas gifts."

"I have brochures from the Little Loom House in Louisville. They offer lessons. It's a drive, I know, but perhaps they have Saturday classes."

Getting up, Charity came to the table. "You have so many desktop looms, Laurel. Couldn't you spare an hour a week to teach the girls? At least between now and Christmas?" she added, gently pressuring her with a winsome smile.

"It's barely April. That's a lot of time to commit." Frankly, the undercurrents running through this particular group gave Laurel pause.

Charity solved one big issue. "Weaving doesn't seem to be Sarah's forte. And probably not Maggie's. But Jenny and Brenna are certainly serious." It didn't seem to occur to Charity that she'd thoughtlessly left Louemma out of the equation. However, Alan Ridge and his daughter were very much on Laurel's mind. She aimed a worried glance his way. He appeared fully prepared to pack Louemma up this minute and take her home.

"That cuts your class by three-fifths," he said firmly, leaving little doubt as to the likelihood that he'd let Louemma join a class.

Laurel would hate to say she was relieved, but in a way she was. Not because she didn't want to expend time and energy to help Louemma, but because Alan made her nervous. Nervous and off-kilter.

As she'd done after the previous session, Louemma spoke up. "I want to have lessons, too, Daddy."

Sarah glanced over, laughed and started to comment. A pointed nudge from her mother brought an abrupt silence.

Laurel decided there was no sense widening the rift between the girls, especially when she could tell that Alan would deny Louemma's wishes.

It didn't happen. He looked exasperated, and damn the man, he caved in again. "I guess you can set up a class for three," he said gruffly, apparently assuming his decision on the matter automatically made the class a done deal.

Laurel discovered she hadn't the heart to disappoint three pairs of pleading eyes. "Let me get my calendar," she mumbled. Unfortunately, she found she had Wednesday afternoons free for at least six months.

Thumbing through his pocket calendar, Alan jotted down the times. He handed his cell phone to Jenny and then Brenna. Their moms were quick to promise they'd carpool the two girls from school.

With the session at end, Charity led her flock along the path toward the footbridge. Alan hung back, waiting for Laurel to lock the cottage.

When Louemma's attention was focused on Dog, he lowered his voice and edged Laurel aside. "The fee you're charging is more than reasonable. I'll pay for the whole package, regardless of whether or not we continue. We'll give next week a try, then decide if we'll continue."

"We?" Laurel arched a brow. "Shall I prepare a loom for you as well, Mr. Ridge?"

"Call me Alan," he growled. "You know damn well I'm referring to Louemma."

"I don't know how you'll take this, Mr…er, Alan," Laurel began.

Alan found himself bristling immediately, not from her mild tone but from a sudden wash of heat created by her nearness. Their hips brushed accidentally, and he stopped short.

Laurel continued with her sentence. "I predict Louemma will do better coming here with her friends."

"That's not going to happen, Ms. Ashline."

"I'm supposed to call you Alan. I insist you call me Laurel."

"Fine. That's not going to happen, *Laurel.*"

Thrown off stride by the fact that he'd suddenly thrust his face closer than she was comfortable with, Laurel stumbled backward. His hand shot out to keep her from falling. She cringed, and as a result, caught her heel on a root. She fell, and try as he might, Alan couldn't hang on to her and maintain his grip on Louemma's wheelchair. Laurel slipped through his fingers, and he heard her land hard.

Dog raced up, growling and baring his teeth the minute Alan stretched out a hand to aid her. "I'm sorry," he said, feeling his neck and face heat.

"Daddy, why did you push Ms. Ashline down?" Louemma demanded in a shocked voice.

"I didn't!" Alan's eyes flew to his daughter. "As if I'd do such a thing. Honestly, Louemma." This time, deciding he'd fend off the dog if need be, Alan set the brake on the chair, and he did haul Laurel to her feet.

"I stepped sideways on a tree root, and your dad couldn't quite catch me, that's all," Laurel told the anxious child, feeling more than a little embarrassed.

"You tripped, but you yanked your hand out of mine as if you thought I was planning to hit you or something."

Guilt tightened her features. She offered no further explanation. "Would you like some juice or water before you leave?" Laurel asked as she put more distance between them.

"That's not necessary," he said. But he still pondered her odd reaction as he climbed into his Jeep. Once he'd turned the vehicle around, he gave his full attention to driving.

"I wanted to stay and pet Dog some more, Daddy. I don't see why we had to leave. Ms. Ashline asked if we wanted something to drink. I think that's because Mrs. Madison said they were having snacks on the way home."

"Pet the dog…more? You mean you actually touched his fur with your hand?"

Louemma's smile faded. "No. Dog moved. But I liked how he felt, Daddy. He's soft. Softer than my bear Scrappy. Isn't Ms. Ashline cool? She's nice and she's pretty, don't you think?"

The hope that flared in Alan's chest shriveled. Skipping over her comment about Laurel, he returned to their earlier discussion. "I know the doctors have all asked if you can feel hot and cold in your fingers, Louemma. Have any of them asked if you could detect soft, hard or sticky?"

"They all do." A frown lodged between her delicate eyebrows. "That's why Dr. Meyers, the last doctor we saw, brought you in the room and told you I might be faking. Before you came in, she said I have sen…sen something all over my back and arms."

"Sensation?"

"Yes. What's that, Daddy? I'm not faking. I…want to be like I was before. I…just…can't." Huge tears drenched her big brown eyes.

"Baby, baby, please don't cry." A knife twisted in the center of Alan's chest, and something the size of a boulder threatened to choke him. He'd never been good with tears. Not his mother's. Not Emily's. And he was even less able to handle Louemma's. He was the one who'd always walked the floor with her when she was ill. Emily had needed eight-plus hours of sleep every night. At times, Alan had thought she'd have let their baby cry for hours. But then, Emily had known he would crawl out of bed.

"Louemma," he pleaded now, awkwardly trying to wipe her eyes with his handkerchief. "Daddy needs to keep two hands on the wheel, especially now that we're driving through town. Dr. Fulton, Nana, Birdie and I know you aren't faking. If we see Dr. Meyers again, I promise I'll tell her that. Sensation means feeling. The doctors think if you can feel things, honeybee—things like the dog's fur—you ought to be able to lift your arms. They're frustrated because they don't know how to help. We're all frustrated."

"Yesterday, Nana told Birdie Ms. Ashline's going to do that."

"What?" he said distractedly.

"Help me move my arms. With weaving."

Alan's foot hit the brake hard at the stoplight. He and Louemma flew forward and back again. "Sorry," he muttered, brushing aside the hair that had flown into her face. "Louemma, your nana's like a pit bull once she sets her teeth into an idea. Remember when she made millions of little bonnets to cover her tomato plants because she'd read in some magazine that they'd keep birds from pecking holes? Or this past winter when she stripped all the electric blankets from our beds after Ruthie Pittman's chiropractor said they might cause everything from allergies to heart attacks?"

"So?"

"So, I'm saying we indulge her because we love her. But not all the notions she gets in her head are the gospel truth."

"Then you don't think Ms. Ashline can help me?" Her lips quivered.

Alan was positive no man had ever been happier to reach the end of his driveway than he was at that precise moment. Louemma was a lot like Vestal in certain ways—like the fact that she could harp on a subject until the cows came home. Today he was saved from revealing his honest-to-God doubts about Laurel Ashline when Birdie greeted them at the door, announcing she'd just frosted a chocolate layer cake. Few things could have broken his daughter's single-minded concentration, but chocolate in any form was one.

"Birdie, will you help Louemma with her snack? If I don't enter the new case-lot prices on our Web site today, Hardy Duff will have my head on a pike. The weaving lesson ran longer than last week's and I promised Hardy the quotes would be on the site by four o'clock. It's after that now."

"Did you have a good time?" Birdie asked, aiming the question at him.

Alan dragged a hand over his downturned lips to hide his true feelings. "I'll let Louemma tell you all about our afternoon."

As he handed the wheelchair over to his housekeeper and started down the hall, the first words out of Louemma's mouth had him grinding to a halt.

"Daddy shoved Ms. Ashline down on the trail and she fell right on her bottom. And I got to—"

Rushing back, Alan interrupted her midsentence. "Louemma Ridge," he declared, drawling her first name. "I did *not* shove Laurel—er, Ms. Ashline down." He spread imploring hands toward Birdie. "Ms. Ashline slipped. I grabbed for her, missed, and she fell. She wasn't hurt. At least, I don't think she was." He blinked, trying to recall if he'd even asked. He remembered how startled he'd been by the look that crossed her face. *Fear.* Now that he was further removed from the incident, he knew that was the only way to describe Laurel's reaction to him.

Birdie laughed the way large, jolly women did—the sound welling all the way up from her toes. "Louemma, love, you're teasing Daddy. Why, he doesn't have a mean bone in his body. Oh, but speaking of falls…" Birdie's grin dissolved into concern. "Miss Vestal took one today."

"What happened? How bad? She's not back in the hospital again, is she?"

"No. She's resting. She's shook up and bruised a bit. As for what happened, I tried to tell her the ground's still too wet from the last rain to ask Neil Murdock to plow. You know how she is once she's got something in her head. Next thing I know, I'm looking out the kitchen window and there she is, hauling rakes and such from the toolshed. Sure 'nough, her feet hit a patch of wet grass, and then she's down, sliding toward the house."

"I can picture it, Birdie. Louemma and I were just discussing what she's like when she gets her teeth into an idea."

"Uh-huh," Louemma agreed. "Daddy, will you go see how she feels before you start work?"

"I will. Right now, honeybee. If I don't come straight back, you'll know Nana's okay. Then you can have your milk and cake and finish telling Birdie about your day. Just get the story straight this time," Alan cautioned, tweaking his daughter's nose.

"Okay. Like Birdie said, I was teasing. I know you wouldn't push Ms. Ashline down. Next time we see her, I'll tell her, okay?" Louemma frowned. "The way she looked, I think maybe she's afraid of you. Why, Daddy?"

Birdie scoffed. "I'm sure that's not the case, child. Everybody in the county knows your daddy's a big old teddy bear."

Brushing a thumb thoughtfully over his lips, Alan watched the two disappear into the kitchen. For some reason he'd never made more than superficial inquiries about Laurel Ashline. What was her background? Old-timers certainly had plenty to say about her mother, Lucy.

After checking on Vestal, and updating the Windridge Web site for Hardy, Alan decided to run back into town. It shouldn't be hard to engage some of Ridge City's most reliable gossips in conversation at the café. The problem wasn't so much engaging gossips as knowing how to keep his name from being part of the subsequent rumors if he asked questions—for the second time—about Ridge City's newest resident.

He could stress, however, that he needed to know more about her before signing up his daughter for those weekly weaving lessons.

Satisfied he'd hit on a solution, Alan set off to tell Birdie he'd be home before dinner.

CHAPTER FIVE

THE MONDAY BEFORE the girls' first paid lesson, Laurel drove to town to pick up two bags of oats she'd ordered for her horses. At the feed store, the clerk ringing up her purchase said, as she handed Laurel a receipt, "You're causing quite a stir around town."

Laurel stuffed the slip in her jeans pocket and puckered her brow.

The apple-cheeked woman—Laurel knew her name was Ethel Jamison—smiled and continued talking. "Yep, Alan Ridge is conducting a pretty thorough background check. You haven't robbed any banks back where you're from, have you? Come to think of it, no one knows where you're from. Is it a secret?"

"Does Mr. Ridge investigate everyone who moves to Ridge City?"

"Aren't too many," Ethel said noncommittally.

"Oh. So the fact that I'm a Yankee is the reason for his nosiness?"

"I 'spect it's more the fact that you're living in his hip pocket—on Ridge land."

Laurel was growing more upset with each step of this conversation. "There you go. He's mistaken on both counts. His home is at least twenty miles from mine. And I live on land that belonged to Hazel Bell. Since I possess a deed, I believe that makes it mine."

"Hmm. There's some around here who'd argue that point. I still didn't catch where you came from, Ms. Ashline."

Grasping the handle on the hand truck holding her bags of oats, Laurel made it halfway to the door before she retorted, "Nice try. Tell Sherlock Ridge to do his own sleuthing."

Her temper simmered all the way home. Who did that man think he was, investigating her? And why was he instilling doubt about her in the minds of people she had to deal with in town?

Parked across from the cottage again, she let Dog out to run while she took the oats from her pickup to the shed inside the corral. All the while, Laurel pondered what Ethel had said about there being people besides Alan Ridge who questioned her owning this place. Besides him, who else might think that? Furthermore, why would anyone care?

Laurel supposed she could pick up the phone, call Alan and ask him point-blank what in hell he thought he was doing. But she wouldn't give him the satisfaction of knowing he'd spooked her.

She fed the horses, relishing the task. She'd dreamed of having her own horses ever since the seventh grade, when a caring counselor used to take Laurel to her farm to ride. Those weekends had been her salvation that year. She gave Dog and the horses fresh water, then went inside and brewed a cup of peppermint tea. The ritual of making tea and the comfort of drinking it brought everything into perspective for her, she thought as she carried the sweet-smelling tea into her bedroom.

As she sipped, she stared at a small trunk she'd found in the attic. A cursory peek had told her it was where her grandparents had stored tax records. The trunk was old and ornate, and went well with Laurel's antique decor.

Until now Laurel hadn't seen any need to paw through their private belongings. She had every letter Hazel had written her in a small cedar box. Luckily, Dennis hadn't found those during his last tirade. It was obvious—from the occasional comment Hazel had made and from Lucy's complete unwillingness to talk about her parents—that her mom had hurt Hazel and Ted badly. Laurel's own history with Lucy Bell Ashline had been rocky, another reason she wasn't anxious to delve deeper into the background of what was most likely a dysfunctional family.

Now was the time, though, she decided with a sigh, and gingerly let the trunk lid fall back on her handwoven bedspread. She set her teacup on the nightstand, on a mug mat she'd made to match the curtains and the spread. She loved the double Irish chain pattern, done in off-white and sky-blue for a light airy touch to counter the room's dark wood paneling. The whole cottage had been dark as a mole hole, with dark furniture, forest-green carpets and dark brown paneling. Laurel's first few months in the house had been taken up with lightening the rooms. She honestly wondered how her grandmother could have spent a lifetime in darkness. But then, people were different, and they certainly had different tastes.

The top layer in the trunk held five years' worth of tax returns, as she'd thought. Next came a ledger listing income and expenditures. In the last year of Hazel's life, the majority of money had come from social security, plus a monthly direct deposit from Windridge Distillery. That stopped Laurel short. Her finger paused at the figure before moving on to a less substantial amount—income derived from her grandmother's sale of her weavings.

Laurel flipped to the start of the ledger, curious to see how far back the deposits from Windridge went.

"Ah!" The first page described the sum as Ted Bell's pension payments. So her grandfather had helped make bourbon. The mere thought of liquor evoked a smell that was all too familiar, and brought back other unpleasant memories. She shut the book abruptly, having lost any desire to look further into her grandparents' finances.

Uncovering the layer below the ledger, Laurel found it offered up an old photo album. Settling against the pillows, she picked up her cup before opening the book. Its pages were yellowed by age and tattered from use, but neatly arranged and labeled.

At first Laurel didn't recognize the jumble of names. Gradually it became clear that the oldest photos were of her grandmother as an infant, then a girl. There were faded black-and-white prints of Hazel's grandparents, her parents and their siblings. Then came Hazel's elementary-school chums, and on to high school.

Hazel and a taller girl were together in more than half the pictures. Were they friends? Cousins, perhaps? Vestal was an unusual name.

Laurel sipped the minty tea. She'd heard the name somewhere. But where? Had she met someone named Ward since moving to Ridge City? Not that she could recall, she thought, quickly running down the meager list of her acquaintances.

Anxious to see if the latter half of the album might reveal early photos of her mother, Laurel started to skip ahead. But the book fell open to sepia-toned shots of two weddings, the photos held in place by white corners. The church, flowers, attendants and bridal gowns were identical; the brides and grooms were different. *A double ceremony,* Laurel realized. With the friends or cousins all grown up.

She set her cup aside as Dog trotted into the room, his tags clinking. He lay his muzzle on the bed next to her thigh. "Hi, boy," she said, reading the names of the wedding parties while she ruffled his fur. Ted Bell and Hazel Hopewell were the bride and groom in the picture on the left, Jason Ridge and Vestal Ward on the right.

"Holy cow, Dog!" Laurel lurched, letting the album fall shut. Her pet gave a start. Laurel picked up the album with shaking hands. If the brides were cousins or otherwise related, did that mean she and Alan Ridge were… "No," she said abruptly. "No way! It can't be."

She fanned the pages until she got back to the wedding shots. Wedding invitations wedged behind the pictures indicated the grooms had both been in the military. The ceremony coincided with the end of the Korean conflict.

Although she wanted to rush, Laurel flipped through the remaining pages. A story grew in pictures. Young happy wives. Their husbands—buddies—shown working, barbecuing and drinking together. Windridge bourbon, Laurel bet. It seemed she couldn't escape the stuff.

Vestal, it appeared, lived in an elegant home. Hazel and Ted, with the help of Vestal and Jason Ridge and others, had built the cottage that was now Laurel's. Also the one up the hill, which housed her spinning wheels and looms. The men holding hammers and saws clowned for the camera.

Next came babies. First, Hazel's friend and her husband proudly showed off a boy. Dates indicated Mark Ridge was six or eight months old at the time Hazel brought her own baby home—Lucy, swaddled in pink. Though faded, those pictures were all in color. Laurel ran a finger over one old photograph, studying what was probably the first picture ever taken of her mother.

"My stars, Dog. My mom and Alan Ridge's father grew up like twins. Look!" She shoved the album under the shepherd's black muzzle, then yanked it back before he could drool on it. "They played together, ate together, were even bathed together." She flipped page after page, pausing now and again to note how little she resembled the early photos of her mother. The Lucy in these pictures looked nothing like in her later years. Hard living had stolen her mother's youthful beauty.

Lucy and Mark must have remained close throughout middle and high school. There were pictures of them at a lake wearing swimsuits, and later in school clothes. Even a few in formal attire. Then, all at once, even though the album still had empty pages, the photographs ended. Laurel felt vaguely cheated. The last one was a group portrait of a high-school graduation. The date stamped on the pictures was June 1974.

Two months after her birth.

Laurel moved the book closer to the lamp. She identified Mark Ridge, grinning and waving a diploma. It dawned on Laurel that he'd graduated the same year her mother must have dropped out of school to get married. By the time this picture was taken, Lucy Bell was Lucy Ashline. *Or maybe not.* Laurel had always suspected she'd been born prior to her parents' marriage. She had no proof except for her mom's lifelong bitterness toward a father Laurel had few memories of. She could conjure up shadowy images of a tall, skinny man sharing her mother's bed. Of loud shouting and slamming doors. Of him dragging suitcases out of an almost empty apartment; a dingy, grim place. And soon after, things had gotten worse.

How old had she been when Lucy started moving from shelter to shelter? Three?

Laurel reached blindly for her cooling cup of tea. Brooding, she stared into the murky depths, for so long that Dog began pacing. He whined to go outside.

Closing the album, Laurel swung her legs off the bed. She carried her cup to the kitchen and collected a jacket. She and Dog slipped out the back door and headed down the hill at a run.

They ran until Dog's tongue was hanging out and Laurel was panting. Something had crossed her mind, but that she wouldn't, *couldn't,* allow herself to think about it. Had her mother and Mark Ridge been lovers as well as pals? Might the man she'd always thought was her father have been a convenient husband? Was Laurel, instead, a Ridge?

That might account for the irreparable split between Lucy Bell and her parents. And between Hazel and her onetime friend. The album told their story. Was that why Alan Ridge had dug into her background? What if they hadn't even known she existed? Could that be why Vestal Ridge had sent her grandson to invade Laurel's quiet life?

She dropped down on a log and absently pulled out the dog treats she always kept in her pocket. Then she threw back her head and laughed. One of the Ridges. Wouldn't that be a hoot?

She considered a host of possibilities, giggling as she wondered what the current bourbon king was thinking. That she and her grandmother had plotted for Laurel to lay claim to a portion of the Ridge fortune, ill-gotten though it probably was? After all, a plaque in the city park indicated Windridge had started before prohibition.

"Even if we share blood, Dog—and perish the thought…" Laurel shuddered. "Any funds from the sale of whiskey is the very last money I'd want."

Dog raced around her in circles, chasing first a butterfly, then a bee. Laurel caught him before his latest quarry stung his nose. "Ooh, that would hurt, you silly thing," she scolded, rubbing his neck and sides.

The sound of an engine and tires crunching on gravel across the creek grabbed their attention. Laurel shaded her eyes against the glare of a sinking sun reflected in the swift-running stream. Only someone headed for her cottage would have ventured this far up the road.

The vehicle slowed and stopped opposite her. Laurel stiffened the instant she identified her late-afternoon visitor. *Alan Ridge.*

"Are you hurt?" he called, cupping his hands around his mouth.

His voice carried easily across the distance, although he might not realize, since the creek widened considerably at this point.

"I'm fine," Laurel shouted back. "Dog and I were out for a run. We're catching our breath and watching butterflies."

"I didn't picture you as the type who'd waste time watching butterflies."

Resentment rushed through Laurel. "Really, Mr. Ridge. You don't know *anything* about me."

Alan broke off a piece of tall grass that slapped his knee. "I know we'd settled on being Alan and Laurel, at least."

"Well, I believe that's a mistake."

"Why are you always so prickly?" Alan set a booted foot on an outcrop of limestone and jammed the stem of grass between his teeth.

With the sun sliding ever lower, Laurel no longer had to shade her eyes to see him. In fact, he made an imposing picture standing in such a typically arrogant male fashion. Worn jeans molded to muscular legs were stuffed into ankle-high boots. An open navy windbreaker casually covered a plaid shirt. His jaw looked dark, yet not as dark as his hair, which was ruffled appealingly by the breeze.

"What do you want?" Laurel demanded. She refused to respond to his masculinity, no matter how many feminine chords he struck in her. Thankfully, the music was faint, and better left that way.

"Meet me at the footbridge," he said, tossing aside the piece of grass. "Something's come up that I need to discuss with you."

Laurel opened her mouth to decline, but the protest stuck in her throat. He'd already jumped back in his Jeep and slammed the door, driving toward her cottage.

"Damn, Dog. What now?" She kicked a few rocks off the bank and watched them plop in the happily murmuring creek. It was several minutes before she clipped on the dog's leash and they began the jog home.

Alan hadn't waited on the other side of the bridge. Fingertips tucked in his back pockets, he ambled toward the woman moving in his direction at a fast clip. She presented a lovely vision framed against the last rays of the sun. There was a halo of gold around her shoulder-length hair, which had fallen out of the woven band meant to restrain it. Her lithe body moved with grace. A stab of—what? lust?—suddenly checked Alan's forward motion. For a minute he didn't know what had hit him, so unfamiliar was he with that particular hunger.

In the early days of his marriage, he and Emily couldn't keep their hands off each other. Then had come a pregnancy that had been rough on her, followed by hectic months of learning to deal with a new baby, which had changed them both. Or maybe that difficult period had only changed him. Because right after Louemma's birth, his grandfather Ridge passed away. Shock and grief had taken a big toll, to say nothing of the fact that Alan was forced to learn everything about a family business in which he'd merely dabbled during summers and college breaks.

He hadn't quite pulled himself together by the time Laurel and her bodyguard stopped and stood panting several yards away.

"I have horses to feed and dinner to fix," she announced as soon as she'd stopped huffing and puffing.

"That clearly isn't an invitation to join you. In these parts, people are more hospitable."

"I'm not from these parts. Is that what this unexpected visit is about? Did your inquiries about me hit a brick wall?" She couldn't keep her feelings from showing.

Frown lines tracked across Alan's smooth brow. He raised a hand to rake back his hair. The move caused the ever-alert shepherd to lunge at his leash and growl ferociously. "Whoa. I mean no harm. These days it's good policy to know the background of anyone who'll be working with your kids."

"And that's the only reason for your cloak-and-dagger capers? That's why you've spread doubt about me in the minds of businesspeople in Ridge City? Why didn't you ask me for references, for heaven's sake?"

He shrugged, glanced down at his toes and rammed his hands in his back pockets again. "Would you have provided them?"

"Certainly. For your information, I have a secondary-school teaching certificate. I taught weaving in high-school classes, as well as in the college continuing-education program in Burlington, Vermont. I paid my bills." She didn't add that her ex had run up so many that at times she'd had to work far into the night on private projects she could sell. That was personal and embarrassing.

"Hmm. But not under the name Ashline. A friend of mine, a P.I., learned that you went to court to change your name back to Ashline from Laurel Shaw. Why, might I ask?"

"That, Mr. Ridge, is none of your business," she said coldly. "Alan."

Laurel fiddled with Dog's leash. Gnawing on the inside of her cheek, she grumbled, "Would you rush to be on a first-name basis with someone who'd hired a P.I. to dig into your past?"

"I've lived here since the day I was born. *My* past is an open book. Not even an interesting one," he said in a teasing tone.

His ability to poke fun at his own expense loosened a slab of ice Laurel had felt building higher and higher inside her. She relaxed her stiff stance and managed a smile. "Mine reads like bad fiction. I prefer to leave it at that. I can, however, give you the names of former co-workers. I'll even call them if you'll hand over your cell phone. I assure you…Alan, the bad chapters in my life story have no bearing on my ability to teach Louemma, Jenny or Brenna."

His right hand flew to the phone attached to his belt, yet he didn't remove it. "I've maintained a successful business by knowing when to accept someone's word—and when not to. I didn't come here to challenge you on that score."

"No? Then why?"

"My grandmother had a fall the other day, the time I left her alone while I brought Louemma here for the spinning demonstration. Vestal's still recovering from pneumonia, and she's insisting on planting a big vegetable garden," he said, shaking his head.

"I'm sorry she's not well," Laurel said, "but how does this affect me?"

"Birdie Jepson, our housekeeper, says she can't keep my stubborn grandmother from overextending herself. And it's not her job. Frankly, I can't seem to convince Grandmother to hire someone to put in the garden for her. She's determined to plant every seed, and she's chosen Wednesday to start. I want to make sure I'm there. However, that's the day of Louemma's first weaving lesson."

"Yes, I know when lessons begin."

"Right. So since your looms are portable, I thought you could give the first one at Windridge as easily as here. Our dining table seats twenty. The light in the room is good. If you agree, the other girls' mothers have no objections. Jenny's mom said it'd actually be a relief, because she'd for-gotten an after-school dental appointment for Jenny's younger sister."

Laurel started to walk around Alan. "Jenny's mother should've called me. I have no problem postponing the les-sons for a week. That solves both problems."

He scowled at her slender back. It appeared she was leav-ing. "That won't work," he said, raising his voice. "The girls are excited about the class. Postponing is out of the question. How can you suggest disappointing them at this late date?"

Turning, Laurel arched a skeptical brow. "I'm not the one with a scheduling problem, Alan. You and Jenny's mother have the issue with Wednesday. Not me."

"But...but if it's a matter of wrestling with three desk

looms and all the paraphernalia, I'll come to the cottage now and haul the stuff to my place."

"No."

"What's with you?"

"I don't wish to go to your home."

Alan gaped. Darkness was falling fast now. He couldn't read her expression, so he took two steps closer, but was brought up short by Dog. "What do you have against Wind-ridge? It's a nice house."

"I shouldn't have to explain my reasons, but I will. Quite simply, you make and sell whiskey."

"Not at the house." Hesitating, Alan moved nearer in spite of the dog's escalating objections. "Are you a Quaker?"

"No. My objection has nothing to do with religion."

"Good. I'm not too popular with Baptists, either." He grinned.

"My feelings are not a joking matter."

"I can see that. I'm sorry." Alan stepped directly in front of Laurel, silencing the dog by putting out a hand and letting the animal sniff his fingers. "Hey, we're not talking moon-shine. My family has distilled and sold gold-medal bourbon since 1852, except for a brief hiatus during prohibition. You can taste the difference between our bourbon and others. Ours is better. Smoother. Richer. Bourbon's a gentleman's liquor, served in fine restaurants, clubs and boardrooms. So how about you satisfy my curiosity and tell me what you have against it?"

"I hate the color, the taste and the smell of booze, includ-ing whiskey, Scotch, rum, brandy, tequila and vodka. If I've left any out, I dislike them, too."

"There's no smell to vodka." Alan didn't know what made him toss that out.

Laurel started for the house.

"Okay, you've made your point," he said loudly. He'd met

people who were against even social drinking. However, Laurel Ashline was the first to attack him for making liquor and selling it to those who chose to buy. Alan wanted to get to the bottom of her strong feelings. But he hadn't lived for most of his life with outspoken, opinionated women without learning when it was smarter to shut up and withdraw. There were times, like in poker, when it was a good plan to hold, and others when it made sense to fold and walk away. Alan sensed this was the latter time.

Only he didn't want Laurel to postpone the next lesson and disappoint the girls. And it was patently clear she intended to enter her house without another word.

"Hey!" he called. "I'll make other arrangements for my grandmother. Plan on having the girls as scheduled."

She turned in surprise. "As I explained last week, there's no need for you to be here for Louemma's lesson. Does this mean you'll send her with Jenny's mother?"

"In a word, no."

"Why?" she exclaimed, her irritation visible in every tense line of her body.

"To steal a phrase from you, Laurel, I shouldn't have to explain."

"But I *did* explain my reasons."

"Not really!" Turning his back, he strode across the swaying bridge.

Laurel's temper flared, too late for him to hear the blistering remarks she might've made had he not leaped into his Jeep and peeled out in a haze of blue smoke. She thought it was blue, anyway. It was too dark to see much across the stream except for the bobbing of flame-red taillights as his vehicle disappeared around a bend.

Mentally she calculated the number of weeks between now and Christmas, which seemed to be the date Jenny had in mind for the end of her lessons. She'd quit in June, Laurel decided; waiting until December left too many weeks to be nice to that man.

No wonder Hazel had severed her relationship with the Ridge clan. One member, at least, was insufferable. Laurel stomped into the cottage and poured kibble in a dish for Dog. Then she banged pans around on the stove. When she'd finished her solitary supper, she was left with the same questions she'd had prior to going out for her run. Why had two women who'd apparently been as close as sisters become so estranged? The Ridge name never appeared once in the many letters Hazel had written.

Clearing the table, she washed dishes and at the same time pondered various possibilities. None had a concrete basis. Perhaps the answer lay in the trunk lying open on her bed.

Two cups of tea later, she still hadn't unraveled the mystery—if it was that. And yet she'd uncovered some sad pieces of her grandmother's life. Wrapped in tissue and carefully preserved were four handmade christening gowns. The first had Lucy Elizabeth Bell's birth certificate pinned to it. The next two had death certificates attached. Stillborns. Theodore James, named for his father. And Frederick Jason. A note indicated that this son bore the name of Hazel's father and of her husband's best friend. But Laurel already knew from the album that when her mom was five, at the time of Frederick Bell's stillbirth, the two families had been close.

A fourth little gown, unfinished this time, told an even sadder tale. A note in shaky script simply stated, "Another failure. A girl. According to Dr. Baker, there'll be no more babies."

Laurel knew now why she had no aunts or uncles. She'd been curious, but the relationship she'd developed with Hazel, a little at a time via letters, had never run to a tell-all exchange of information. Looking back, she saw they'd both avoided personal issues. Laurel had sensed her grandmother led a lonely existence. In the same way, Hazel had known Laurel's marriage was troubled.

Surrounded by sad mementoes, hopes for a future that could never be, of the babies Hazel had lost, sad memories of the one Lucy had had, but never wanted, Laurel cried. The tears kept flowing and she didn't know why. She wasn't prone to the futility of weeping. But oh, how she wished she hadn't waited so long to come to Kentucky, where there were more questions than answers about her past.

Dog whined and bumped her knee repeatedly with his paw. For the first time, Laurel wasn't able to relieve her pet's anxiety.

She hugged the tiny dress her mother had worn. All those years, Laurel had vowed that she'd never wreck he life the way Lucy had wrecked hers. And here she sat, alone and sobbing among the remnants of another woman's hopes and dreams. Dreams were once Laurel's lifeline. If she shut her eyes tight, she could still see the perfect marriage and family she used to imagine. The one she'd desperately wanted as far back as she could remember.

Awkwardly wiping her cheeks, she sniffed and, one by one, refolded the little gowns, returning them to the trunk. If Hazel's keepsakes did nothing else, they'd proved how silly and sentimental it was to waste productive hours on foolish dreams.

ALAN ARRIVED HOME just in time for the evening meal.

"I thought you'd gone up to the distillery," Vestal said. "Hardy phoned here looking for you." She passed Alan the pork chops Birdie had marinated and baked in the juice from homemade bread-and-butter pickles. That, together with mashed potatoes, was another of Louemma's favorite meals. Alan glanced up from feeding the girl a small bite he'd cut.

"What did Hardy want? There's no problem with the new bottles, is there? I know the crew planned on bottling today."

"No problem. He called to say he liked what you did with the Web site. If you weren't at the distillery, where did you go?"

"I went to see Laurel Ashline. Since you persist in planting a garden we don't need rather than taking care of your health, I decided to see if she'd hold the girls weaving classes here."

"And?"

"And if a more uncooperative female exists, I don't know where."

"So she turned you down?"

Scowling, Alan fed Louemma several more bites without replying. His daughter choked before he realized he'd fed her too much, too fast. "Sorry, sweet pea." He dabbed her mouth with a napkin.

Louemma swallowed, then said, "I like Ms. Ashline. I don't want lessons here, Daddy. You wouldn't let her bring Dog into the house."

"I don't recall saying he wasn't welcome."

Louemma's eyes widened. "But…you always said I couldn't have a puppy or a kitty, 'cause pets mess up a house."

"That was Emily's—er, I went along…" He sucked in an unsteady breath. "Listen, it doesn't matter. Laurel refused to come here, with or without Dog."

"Perhaps if I invited her…" Vestal ventured.

"Don't waste your breath. If this were 1860, she'd be banging her drum, heading up the local temperance league."

"What's a temperance league?" Louemma asked after chewing and swallowing another forkful of meat and potatoes.

"Ask Miss Robinson. Temperance leaguers were the bane of your great-great-great-grandfather."

Vestal wagged a finger. "Not true. If a temperance-preaching woman hadn't forced Dan Call to sell his small-scale whiskey-making business to Jasper Daniel, and if he hadn't moved it from Lynchburg to the limestone quarry at Cave Spring Hollow, Jim Ridge would never have apprenticed under the famous Jack Daniel. His unique distilling process was a forerunner to the one we still use at Windridge. History lecture finished," she said. "Maybe you should treat Laurel a bit more charitably, Alan."

He snorted. "I've heard the story about Dan Call. He was a Lutheran minister, and that was the big beef against him by the temperance league ladies." He hesitated. "Laurel said her reasons for disliking our business aren't religious. But she didn't tell me what they are."

"Did you ask her?"

He cast a nervous glance at Louemma. "Uh, she more or less said her reasons weren't my business."

"Hmm. Maybe I should phone and extend the olive branch. She isn't to blame for the fact that Hazel and I parted ways."

"Please, Daddy, may I be excused? I'm full, and Miss Robinson set up some voice-activated story problems for me today on the new computer. I want to surprise her and finish the whole set by tomorrow."

"Sure." Alan offered a sad smile as he stood and helped her slide off the chair. "One of these days, I wish you'd surprise me by eating everything on your plate."

"I will if you stop fighting with Ms. Ashline. How come you do, Daddy? You're never cross with Miss Robinson."

"Yes," Vestal noted, also pushing back from the table. "That is curious, Alan. I mean, we hardly know her."

Alan had no answer, so he didn't attempt to give one. He only said, "Are you finished, too, Grandmother? If so, will you have a second cup of coffee? I'll be back as soon as I settle Louemma. There's some business I need to discuss with you."

She sank back into her chair again, and was still toying with her cup when Alan returned. "What business?" she asked abruptly. "You know I'm happy leaving company matters to you and Hardy these days."

"I know. But something you said a moment ago reminded me." Resuming his seat, Alan set aside his untouched meal. "Hardy and the board are adamant about needing the water from the spring on Bell Hill in order to expand. He's had the spring water tested and its mineral makeup is perfect for mixing mash."

Vestal turned to gaze out of the dining room window, into the darkness beyond. "Do we need to expand, Alan? I've studied our profit sheets. We're making money—for ourselves and our shareholders."

He contemplated her question for a time. "What if I decide to take Louemma out of state to see other doctors? I've been considering Sloan-Kettering in New York. It's costly, plus we'd have to hire someone to do the accounting while I'm gone. I've looked into it. They'd want to run their own independent tests. It'd take three to four weeks, minimum."

"Shouldn't you give Laurel a chance to see what she can do with Louemma first, before you run off to New York?"

Alan dropped his chin to his chest. "You and I just don't agree on this weaving stuff, Grandmother. And…I'm worried that Louemma may grow too attached to Laurel. You heard her say she likes the woman—*and* her dog."

"Is that so bad? I believe there's a lot to be said for trust in the healing process."

"The thing is, if Louemma's not healed, I've got to expand Windridge in order to sell more the expense. That means laying claim to the natural spring on Bell Hill." Noting Vestal's obvious discomfort, Alan gritted his teeth and added, "It's our land, you know."

She rose regally if a bit unsteadily. "I agree. I just can't bear to think of what your grandfather would say. If Ted Bell hadn't knocked Jason aside and shot the man holding a rifle on him, Windridge would've been sold. There'd be no Ridge males to carry on. For all we have, we owed Ted so much more than forty acres. It's just…what Hazel did, and how. It was so sneaky and underhanded. I don't want to discuss it, Alan."

Alan watched his grandmother walk stiffly away, leaving a chasm between them. Ordinarily he'd have smoothed over their disagreement. At what cost, though? Ted Bell and Grandfather Ridge were dead, but Alan had his child's welfare at stake. Dammit, he wished Laurel Ashline had stayed the hell in Vermont.

CHAPTER SIX

LAUREL HAD SPENT Wednesday in a remote hollow with a woman purported to be a hundred and one years old. Though her face was lined and she was toothless, her weathered hands worked a loom with a speed Laurel doubted she'd achieve if she lived twice as long. She discussed weaving with the old woman for three hours, and stayed longer than she'd intended. However, she'd come away with three jars of persimmon jelly and two weaving patterns she'd never seen before. Patterns Laurel didn't recall having seen in her grandmother's scrapbook, either. In weaving circles they'd be considered a great find.

She cantered home, loving every chance to ride again. Working her way over the hills and through the forest, she thought about what a good day it'd been. As the roan mare trotted into her yard, Dog kept pace. Glancing up, she saw her students crossing the footbridge.

Laurel hadn't heard a word from Alan Ridge after their last shouting match. Until this minute, she hadn't known whether to expect Louemma. But there she was, with her father, trailing the others. So it was a good thing Laurel had set up three looms, she thought, swinging out of the saddle. She waved to the girls before leading her horse past them, toward the corral.

Brenna and Jenny turned to wave at their departing driver, then ran to catch up with their teacher.

Louemma, seated in her wheelchair, shrieked and begged

her father not to go anywhere near the horse. Her fuss attracted Dog, but also made the roan edgy. The mare, already winded, snorted and blew more than normal, which Laurel thought might have added to Louemma's fright.

"It's all right, honey," she called. "The horse isn't hurt, if that's what you're worried about. Horses snort to help cool themselves down after a ride." Her calm voice had no effect on the distraught girl, who seemed not to hear her explanations. At a loss as to what to do next, Laurel attempted to rush the mare out of sight.

"Jenny, the cottage is locked. I'll unsaddle Cinnabar and give her a quick rubdown, if you'll take this key to Mr. Ridge. Ask him to open the door. The looms are laced, so you and Brenna can start. Rather than mug mats, I decided you could do scarves. You did say you wanted to make gifts for Christmas. Scarves are easy to weave, and practical."

"Can Brenna and me help brush your horse first? Why did you call her Cinnabar?"

"She was already named when I bought her. Cinnabar is a reddish-brown color—like her coat. The man I purchased the horses from was a painter. The black gelding, Cinnabar's son, is named Coal Fire. I was told it's because his black coat occasionally has a red cast when he's standing in the sun. Uh, Jenny, why is Louemma afraid of horses?" They could hear her crying.

The energetic girl, who never stood still as far as Laurel could tell, shrugged and continued hopping from foot to foot. "I dunno. Louemma's way different since she was in that car wreck. Sarah says she's weirded out. I'm glad it wasn't me. I feel sorry for her," Jenny added, darting a troubled glance toward her former classmate. "She doesn't sound glad to be here, does she, Ms. Ashline?"

"No, she doesn't. I'll have a word with her dad later. Hurry and take him the key." Louemma's sobs were unnerving Laurel. She'd thought the girl wanted lessons, but if she was somehow being coerced into coming, either by her dad or her grandmother, well, Laurel didn't want any part of that.

From inside the corral, she kept one eye on the group, all the while unsaddling the mare. The horse stood quietly, nuzzling Laurel's shirt pocket, looking for treats. This was a docile mare, not intimidating in the least. Louemma's discomfort couldn't be over all animals, either. Last week she'd reacted favorably to Dog.

Laurel hung the bridle on a peg before removing the precious patterns from her saddlebags. She set them on a box and turned to look for a curry brush. She yelped as she bumped into someone.

"This what you're looking for?" Alan Ridge dangled the brush between his thumb and forefinger.

"Thanks." She grabbed it from his hand and began to brush the muddy horse in long strokes. "Did you let the children into the cottage?" She peered around him, but couldn't see all the way up the path.

"The kids'll be fine for a few minutes. Jenny and Brenna are excited about starting a new project. Louemma's content for now being in the company of the dog."

"I don't like leaving them unsupervised."

"Then you shouldn't have been late for their lesson."

Laurel felt her mouth gape like that of a landed fish. She drew back, astonished by his nerve, then saw him sifting through her stack of patterns. "Leave those alone, please. They represent three hours and a lifetime of work."

"That doesn't make a lot of sense."

She noticed that he set the papers carefully back on a stand inside the shed. "Sorry. I spent three hours filling in detailed reed charts on each of those patterns. A reed chart shows the number of threads per inch needed to form the design. The woman I got them from has used variations of these same patterns for ninety years. She and her daughters make nearly all of what their families wear on a loom her great-grandfather carried up the mountain on a mule. Six generations have lived miles from civilization in a place called Little Rose Hollow. Their only record of family births or deaths is handwritten in a worn Bible. Yet they're a talented, fascinating family. Proud and independent. Oh, you don't care about any of this, do you?"

"You're wrong," Alan said, crossing his ankles and casually propping an elbow on the casing of the shed door as he studied her. "In all our encounters, this is the most passionate I've seen you get over anything—with the exception of when you're taking a strip off my hide."

"That's a blatant exaggeration." Changing the subject, she said, "Are you forcing Louemma to attend my weaving class?"

"What?" Alan sprang away from the casing. "You heard me try and talk her out of coming. I have a business to run, after all."

"Yes." Laurel pursed her lips. "Let's not discuss your business. Maybe your grandmother's subtly pressuring Louemma. You said she thinks I can create some miracle with her."

"My grandmother might pressure me, and does regularly. Never Louemma. She's the light of Vestal's life. It's the horse." He shook back the hair that fell stubbornly over his forehead. "None of us, doctors included, can figure out why she suddenly became scared to death of horses. She used to own a pony that she loved. Her mother taught her to ride. Shortly before the crash, I gather they passed one of the largest horse farms in the state." Pausing again, he took a deep breath. "Louemma has no memory of the accident. The theory of one psychiatrist is that maybe a rider heading in from an evening jaunt startled Emily—uh, my wife—causing her to go into a spin as she reached the crest of an icy hill. From the tracks, they know her car spun out of control at that point and slid right over the cliff."

"Wouldn't a rider have heard the crash and gone to investigate?"

"You'd think." Alan kicked at a clod, falling silent when Laurel led the roan mare to a water trough.

"If you're sure she's reacting to seeing my two horses, there's a simple fix. I'll keep them out of sight during lessons. I truly didn't intend to be late today," she added. "Sometimes the directions I'm given to locate these hill families are pretty sketchy. I swear their kids, whom I generally meet through the college, have no grasp of how far out of the mainstream their families are."

"You ride the ridges a lot? That's risky. The majority of our hill folk don't like or trust outsiders."

"In my experience, they're down to earth, delightful men, women and children. Anyway, just in case you're right, I always take Dog along. He looks like a guard dog, even if he's a pussycat under all that bluster." She gave Alan a sideways smile.

The change that came over her face when she smiled tapped into a yearning Alan thought he'd suppressed. And she was the last woman he wanted stoking his long-banked fires. Deliberately putting distance between them, he changed his tone from friendly to businesslike. "Another thing before we go in. I've got a proposition to offer you. A business proposition."

"For me?" His sudden stillness brought out her wariness, as well.

"Don't look so alarmed. I'm not going to ask you to partner in the bourbon trade. I'd like to buy the upper twenty acres of your land, that's all."

"Why?"

"For water. You have a headwater spring up there that bubbles out through several feet of limestone. I need access to it."

Laurel frowned. "You intend to divert this beautiful creek?" She flung out an arm.

"Not divert it. Siphon off some of it. He rubbed a hand over his chin. "I'm making a mess of this, although last night it sounded fine. I only need one tributary coming out of the spring. Have you ever ridden to the top?" When she shook her head, he knelt and, with a stick, drew some lines in the dirt. "The original spring feeds two branches of the creek. It splits around a large boulder and runs for several hundred yards, and then the two loop back together. At most, I'd divert half your flow. You have my word on that." Alan raised his right hand. "Frankly, come next spring, if we get a big snow runoff, you'll thank me. Otherwise you could be stuck here, unable to cross until the water recedes. Sometimes for weeks at a stretch."

"Really?"

"Of course, really. I wouldn't lie. We're currently enjoying a mild spring after an unusually mild winter. Most years, that footbridge is under water, by now. Occasionally in the fall, too, if our neighboring states to the south get hit with hurricanes. According to Grandmother, Ted and Hazel rebuilt the footbridge every other year. I can't think why they never built something more permanent. I mean, to cut themselves off from help for days at a time seems foolish, if you ask me." He rose, dusting his hands on his jeans.

Heading toward the cottage, Laurel said, "I hope you don't mind if I take my chances with Mother Nature. My land's not for sale. I'll deal with runoff if and when it proves to be a problem."

It was on the tip of his tongue to tell her this was Ridge land. But they'd already reached the steps. As Laurel grasped the knob, Alan's hand shot out and circled her wrist.

"I can't believe you'd turn me down without first visiting the headwaters and weighing the paltry difference it'll make to your creek against the money I'm prepared to offer. Look, before you say no, let me ride with you up to the top of the hill. Tomorrow. I can carve out time to go while Louemma's with her tutor."

Laurel felt her pulse leap at the warmth created by his palm. She ought to refuse to even consider his outlandish proposal. But she'd never explored her property fully. Alan Ridge probably knew the best, safest route up there. Maybe she should see how difficult it was for someone to trek across her land. She'd felt safe here. Had never imagined that anyone—Dennis, for example, if he came looking for her—might sneak in on her from above.

Indecision played across her face. Alan saw it, and kicked up the wattage of his smile. "A two-hour ride is all I'm requesting. According to the weatherman, tomorrow's supposed to be nicer than today. The wild rhododendrons might even be starting to bloom. If nothing else, they're worth the trip."

"I have a lecture at the college scheduled for ten. I can be home by noon. I need time to change and eat. I could be ready to go by one o'clock."

"Forget about eating. I'll have Birdie pack us a lunch. Nothing fancy. We can break up our round-trip ride by stopping to eat. There's a table rock that's perfect for enjoying the view at the top."

"I guess that's okay. Why not let me fix sandwiches and soft drinks? That way we're not giving your housekeeper extra work."

"Birdie loves to cook. Oh, do you have any food allergies I need to tell her about?"

"None. At least none I know of. So, we're saying closer to noon, then?"

"Make it half past twelve. You'll have a chance to change into jeans. Take a jacket and wear boots. Part of the trail winds through thick timber. It may be chilly there, with patches of snow. And you need boots because it's really spongy around the headwaters."

"Got it. Now will you let go of me, so we can go inside?"

He uncurled his fingers slowly. "One other thing. I hate to ask, but it might be better not to mention our outing to Louemma. I'll have to borrow a horse from a friend. Because she's become so fearful, I sold ours. I don't make a habit of lying to her, but I'm not sure how she might react to my going off on a horse."

"I understand. There's no reason to mention our outing to anyone." In fact, Laurel would rather they did keep it to themselves. She could imagine people in town having a field day if that news leaked. "Rather than borrow a horse, Alan, you can ride my gelding. He needs exercise. I bought two saddles and tack with the horses. He's solid. Strong enough for you. I've just ridden him twice. He has a nice gait."

"Good, then it's..." Alan had started to say *a date*. But the way his heart skidded in anticipation stopped him. Or maybe it had more to do with his reaction to being so near her. As their hands accidentally collided on the doorknob, he changed his words to a simple, "It's set."

She said nothing, just hunching her shoulders to avoid touching him further. She breezed into the room, giving the students a cheery and rather breathless smile. "Hi! Putting away my horse took longer than I'd planned."

Louemma looked unhappy, even though Dog had his head on her lap. "Daddy, when you didn't come back, I was worried. Where did you go?"

"I said I'd be back in a minute, that I'd be right outside. I'm sorry if you were worried. There was no need." He dropped to his knees and gave her a hug.

Her lower lip trembled. "Brenna and Jenny wouldn't leave their weaving to go see where you were. They've already started their projects. Daddy, this isn't going to work. I can't do what they're doing. Besides, they're giggling together and leaving me out. Will you please take me home?"

Wondering if she and Alan had caused the injured girl added stress by staying outside talking about personal matters for so long, Laurel gave father and daughter some space. After all, maybe Alan needed to see for himself what Laurel had insisted all along—that bringing Louemma to this class wouldn't work.

Climbing to his feet, Alan approached Laurel. "I'll refund your money," she said quickly.

"It's not the money, it's the situation. Louemma needs individual attention. How much more to set up private lessons?"

Laurel bit her upper lip. "I'm sorry, Alan," she murmured, lowering her voice. "After this week, I simply have no other time available. And her case is so special. *She's* special. Maybe we can consider arranging something when she's completed all her physical therapy."

"She's not in therapy. The orthopedic doctor who operated on her leg fractures and pinned her hip after the accident arranged for eight weeks at the sports medicine clinic in Lexington once the casts came off. She can walk. But she eats so little, her muscles are giving out. She hates the fortified drinks we've tried. As far as the clinic is concerned, their program was a success."

"But…no one's exercising her hands and arms?"

He shook his head. "We have a masseuse. For Grandmother, really. The woman comes to the house once a week. She occasionally gives Louemma deep-heat treatments to keep her muscles from atrophying totally."

"I should think so." Laurel frowned. "I…have a full schedule."

"What about early evening? Any early evening?"

"That's when I work on commissioned projects. Those are what pay my bills."

"What about directly after Jenny and Brenna's lesson? They come from three-thirty to four-thirty. Or maybe an hour's too long for Louemma. What if I brought Louemma twice a week on the dot of four-thirty? Could you work with her until five?"

Laurel sighed. This man wouldn't take no for an answer. "I suppose we could try. Not today, though. She's already too tense and I won't risk harming muscles that haven't been warmed up. Next week. Bring her and I'll assess whether or not there's any profit for her in continuing."

"Good. That's all we can ask. Thank you. I'll see you to-morrow at twelve-thirty for our ride."

Wishing she could take back her agreement, Laurel gave a brief nod, then trailed Alan and Louemma to the door. "Bye, Louemma. Next week we're letting you come by yourself."

"Without Daddy? Where will he go?"

"No," Alan interjected quickly. "She means a private les-son for you. Without your school friends."

"But I'm not in school with them anymore. And I don't think they're my friends anyway," she said, her chin quivering.

Alan seemed so disturbed by his daughter's words, Laurel almost didn't issue her next edict. But after a brief tug-of-war with herself, she decided it would be best to get everything out in the open.

"Alan, I've said from the beginning that your staying for her lesson won't be beneficial. And it may be a hindrance. You're welcome to sit in next week, but if we continue, you'll have to go elsewhere while Louemma and I work."

"For half an hour? That's ridiculous. It'd take me that long to drive from here to town. Out of the question."

"That's the only way I'll agree to go forward. Take it or leave it."

He seemed so torn, and Louemma so hopeful, that Laurel was moved to offer a solution. "Bring your laptop or a book to read. You can sit on my porch. The back porch at my cottage is shaded and screened. I've put a table and chairs and a wicker settee back there. For thirty minutes a week, I should think it will do."

"That's very generous, Laurel. Thanks. So what do you say, Louemma? Shall we give this a whirl?"

"Yes, please. Dog can be inside the cottage with me, can't he?"

The big dog, who'd padded beside the girl to the door, wagged his tail as if he knew they were talking about him.

Laurel marveled at how the pair had bonded in such a short time. She thought it was a good sign. Animals were being used more and more in therapy programs. "Louemma, honey, I think Dog will be most happy to sit in on your lessons. He's content to watch me weave. Has been from the first day I brought him home from the shelter. So…it's settled. You both take care. Dog and I will see you about this time next week."

Once they departed, she closed the door and went back to see how the other girls were doing. "Jenny, I think you're trying to rush. See how loose these last three rows are? That means you aren't being careful to pull the beater bar forward enough."

Jenny's face fell. "Oops. Do I have to rip it out? That means Brenna will get ahead of me."

"Weaving isn't a race, girls. The object is to have a product you can be proud of when you finish. I'm going to show you how to untie the shuttle, rip this back and retie it. Brenna, you come and watch. There'll be times you'll have problems and be forced to rip out, too."

"Ms. Ashline, we weren't giggling at Louemma," Jenny said, sliding out of her seat to trade places with Laurel. "Me and Brenna were talking about stuff at school. Louemma wasn't close enough to hear what we were saying. She jumped to conclusions. That's right, isn't it? I think that's what my mama says."

"That's the proper term. However, one of you might've

moved Louemma's wheelchair closer so she could hear. She can't operate the chair by herself, you know."

Brenna leaned an elbow on the table. "She doesn't go to our school anymore. So she wouldn't understand stuff we were talking about, 'cause it was something that happened yesterday at recess."

"To a new person at school? Someone she wouldn't know because she hasn't attended classes since the accident?"

Jenny and Brenna exchanged a guilty look. "Louemma knows Robbie Hendricks. Last year he used to pester the life out of her. She knows everyone in third grade. We've all been together since kindergarten."

"Well, then, I think you realize she must've been feeling quite left out."

"I'm sorry, Ms. Ashline." Brenna wriggled uncomfortably.

Jenny nodded. "Me, too. I'm sorry for not 'cluding her," she mumbled.

"Don't think I'm scolding you, girls. I'm not. It's that we all need to be more aware of our actions when we're dealing with a disabled person."

"That's what our teacher said. She said a kid can't know when something might happen to put them in the same spot."

"You have a wise teacher. Okay, enough about Louemma. Watch how I remove the shuttle. And we have to pull the thread back out very carefully so as not to get tufts in the middle or break the yarn. Trying to pull it through the warp too fast can damage the threads making up the yarn. You could break strands. One of these days, I'll show you how to make a variety of knots. For today, it's enough to learn how to back out and restart a piece of work."

"When we came in, me and Brenna stopped to look at the cloth you're weaving on your big loom. Those looms are so cool. But they look hard. Will we ever learn how to use them?"

"Like everything, Jenny, it takes practice. You work up to tackling more intricate projects. I think both of you show real aptitude. So I guess the answer to your question is yes, in time, if you keep at it."

"Awesome," they exclaimed in unison.

Laurel laughed. It felt good to be able to be spontaneous about something." It struck her how long she'd spent in the shadow of her ex-husband, afraid to laugh, afraid to express any emotion lest it set him off. Every day she was getting stronger, feeling freer.

A horn honked outside, and Dog ran barking to the door. "Girls, I think your lesson is over and your chariot awaits. Leave your looms as they are. Next week we'll take up where you left off. At the rate you two are working, I predict several people will be the lucky recipients of your Christmas crafts."

The girls seemed reluctant to go. Laurel walked them to the bridge to make sure they crossed okay and that the person honking was indeed their chauffeur, Jenny's mom. The women exchanged waves. They'd never been introduced, but Laurel saw that the other woman had her hands full with a group of younger girls. "If your parents have any questions," Laurel said, "have them call me."

Brenna hung back as Jenny dashed away. "I feel bad about Louemma. If I phoned her, do you think she might come back and be in our class again?"

Laurel smiled. "Phoning her is a wonderful idea, Brenna. I know it's hard being cut off from friends. As for rejoining the class, she needs more one-on-one attention. I'll be instructing her right after your class ends. So you'll probably meet coming and going until we see how things develop."

The girl beamed and scurried off, seeming relieved that she and Jenny hadn't totally lost their friendship with Louemma.

HARDY DUFF, general manager of the distillery and a Wind-ridge shareholder, was climbing out of his pickup at the Ridge house when Alan and Louemma drove in.

"Good timing on my part," Hardy said, greeting his boss. "Howdy, Louemma, you're looking fine today. Just getting home from the doctor's?"

"I've been to weaving class," the girl told him without any particular inflection.

"Weaving?" The older, stockier man paused in the middle of removing a tube of architectural blueprints from his vehi-cle. He sent Alan a pointed stare. "Weaving as in terms of our nemesis?"

Alan returned a dark look. "Go on in and have a seat in my office, Hardy. I'll join you as soon as I get Louemma settled at the TV or in her room with a talking book."

The house was quiet inside, but there was a pleasant odor of something spicy cooking. Alan called out to let Vestal and Birdie know they were home.

Birdie poked her head out of the kitchen. "Miss Vestal's resting. She probably overdid out in that garden, like you and I knew she would. Oh, Mr. Duff, hello. I didn't know Mr. Alan brought company home. I'll go right now and add another place setting. Supper will be ready in two shakes of a lamb's tail. Miss Vestal thought we should try eating a bit earlier today."

Alan started to say Hardy wasn't staying. Vestal and he tended to keep family meals private, especially since Louemma felt self-conscious about having to be fed. Hardy, though, almost tripped over his tongue accepting.

"Why, thank y'all, Birdie. An old bachelor like me leaps at any and every opportunity to eat home-cooked meals. I knew there was a dang good reason I didn't rush over here earlier with Dave Bentley's drawings." He tapped the tube he carried against Alan's shoulder. "I think Dave's got a winner this time, Alan. Soon as you've got clear title to our hill, his construction crew is ready to roll."

"You're always welcome to sit and eat a bite with us, isn't he, Mr. Alan?" Birdie, who loved nothing so much as cooking for a crowd, let her pleasure at having company show. It was no secret how much she missed Emily's frequent teas, luncheons and cocktail parties. Vestal had virtually given up entertaining after Jason died. And these days, Alan shied away from the responsibility of entertaining friends, neighbors and business associates. Windridge used to be known for its lavish parties, but not since the accident.

Alan couldn't say why he resented the intrusion of a man who'd become vital to the running of the family business. Or—he did know. Alan resented the way Hardy was pressuring him to acquire Bell Hill. He wanted the land yesterday. Alan wasn't one to rush, and he sure didn't intend to reveal the idea he'd dreamed up last night about personally buying back the land. Not until he knew for sure that Laurel would accept his offer. If her reaction earlier was any indicator, it'd be a cold day in hell before she went for his plan. Then he'd have to think of something else.

Hardy, the board of directors and Vestal probably wouldn't see it his way. They'd think he'd gone nuts, paying for land they actually owned.

"Hardy, I make it a point not to discuss business matters during meals. Vestal gets more stressed over things than she used to. Right now, Louemma and I will go wash up after our outing. Dump the blueprints in my office. You and I will take our coffee and go in there to look at the drawings later."

"Sure." Hardy's brow puckered. "Aren't you champing at the bit to see what Dave's proposed? Damn, man, this could well mean a fifty percent increase in our exports."

"Hardy, are you happy working for Windridge?"

"What do you mean? Of course," he said, a worried look crossing his face.

"Are the workers happy? With their hours and the benefit package we offer?"

"Far as I know. I haven't heard anyone complaining."

Alan lifted Louemma out of the chair and stood a moment, supporting her. "If everyone's happy, why do we have to lay out money on a new facility? Can't it wait?"

"Didn't you look at the industry studies I had done? Nine of our closest competitors, all from this state, have increased their production by a third over the last year. If Windridge doesn't keep pace, Alan, buyers will begin to bypass us. Shareholders, no matter how limited, will dump their stock. They'll look at our competition as being more up-to-date and forward-thinking."

"I suppose." Still hugging Louemma, Alan walked down the hall.

Hardy called after him, "If you've got some kind of history with the woman standing in our way, I'll do the dirty work for you."

"There's no history." Alan threw the denial over his shoulder.

Vestal emerged from her quarters. "What woman? Hello, Hardy," she said, covering a yawn. "Is it any wonder my grandson has no history with a woman? He's practically become a hermit. Listening to him stomp down the hall when someone's trying to rest—well, it's plain to see he's taken leave of his manners."

Alan wished he'd never started the conversation with Hardy. Now they'd upset his grandmother. Loud enough for Hardy to hear, Alan said, "Birdie says it's almost time for dinner. Louemma and I are going to wash up. And where are *your* manners?" he teased. "You should be playing hostess and serving Hardy a before-dinner drink."

"That'd be nice, Alan. Shall I pour you one, too?"

He started to automatically say yes, but had a sudden vision of Laurel Ashline all but accusing him of being his own best customer. "A short one."

"I was thinking of uncorking a bottle from our last gold medal private reserve."

"Do," Alan called from inside the hall bathroom. "That batch came from the malt barley we bought from a grower in South Dakota. A flag I put in the computer program on that order came up yesterday, saying it's time to renew for fall if we like the flavor."

"Then you'd better have a tall glass," Hardy said as Alan set Louemma down to walk. "You're the dean of tasters."

"Tasting takes only a couple of fingers."

Vestal sniffed the cork, poured some of the dark gold liquid into two glasses and paused, studying her grandson. "Aren't you feeling well, Alan?"

"I feel fine."

Louemma, who stood halfway between her great-grandmother and her father, piped up. "Ms. Ashline thinks drinking is bad. And he likes her, don't you, Daddy? We *both* like her."

For ten seconds it was as if all sound in the room, even breathing, stopped.

Hardy Duff choked on his first swig. "Tell me she's not referring to our public enemy number one."

Louemma's face clouded. "She's nice. She's not our enemy. Daddy's taking her on a picnic. Tomorrow. And I'm glad," she said shyly.

"Who told you that?" Alan demanded.

Meekly, the girl confessed. "Jenny listened at the door when you guys were talking on the porch. That's why she and Brenna were acting silly and giggly when you came in. They said—Jenny did—that Ms. Ashline's only being nice to me 'cause she's got her eye on you." Louemma frowned. "Is that the only reason, Daddy?"

"That is simply not true, Louemma." Alan wished this whole day hadn't happened. Vestal gazed at him over the rim of her old-fashioned glass, a calculating gleam in her eyes.

Hardy's disdain told him that after they closed themselves into the office after dinner, his manager was going to give him hell. *And why? For nothing.* Alan's hope for a compromise that would give them the land and allow Laurel to stay on in the cottage was doomed to failure from the start. She wouldn't give up without a fight. Damn, he hated that prospect. As Louemma said, Laurel was nice—except for some unrealistic feelings about his occupation. But he didn't want to fight with her. In general, he preferred to avoid conflict. Life with his mother and with Emily had resulted in one clash followed by another, reason enough not to get involved with another woman. With Laurel, though, it wasn't personal, and maybe the situation was salvageable without lawyers.

"Hardy, back off on the expansion for now. Stall Bentley. I'll handle this water crisis, my way."

Hardy downed the rest of his drink in one swallow. "I hope you don't screw around too long, Alan. Remember, our competition marches on. Plus, we have Dave's crew on retainer. It's costing us big bucks."

Birdie called them to come and eat, saving Alan from saying something he might later regret. He already imagined he felt an ill wind blowing down the back of his neck.

CHAPTER SEVEN

As LAUREL LEFT the college where she'd been lecturing on historic Kentucky weavings for the home economics program, she looked forward to the upcoming ride with Alan Ridge. An oddity for her. It'd been years since she'd eagerly anticipated a leisure activity other than weaving. That was something else she had to thank her ex-husband for. It wasn't that Dennis hadn't made exciting plans, but more that he'd rarely followed through—like her mom. Lucy's circumstances and a constant shortage of money had prevented her from keeping promises. Excessive drinking not only interfered with Dennis's ability to keep his word, but touched off other problems. Laurel sometimes found herself trying to talk him *out* of his plans. The result was an unpleasant kind of dance that ended in bitter arguments.

Probably that was why her stomach began cramping in an old familiar way as she drove home. Laurel couldn't help it. All the what ifs... What if Alan forgot? What if he just plain didn't show up? Or worse, what if he did and she threw up on his boots or something out of sheer nervousness?

"Idiot," she muttered, licking dry lips as she checked her pale reflection in the sideview mirror. Laurel reminded herself that she was a grown woman who at long last didn't answer to anyone. She had plenty of things to do if the man didn't put in an appearance, for heaven's sake.

It'd been a groundless fear, she saw when she noticed Alan's blue Jeep parked in her clearing. Interestingly, he didn't seem any more relaxed than she felt. He stood on the bridge skipping rock after rock in nervous succession across the stream. Laurel automatically checked her watch to be sure she wasn't late. Nothing made Dennis explode as quickly as being kept waiting. But that was silly; Alan had no say in her schedule. And he didn't strike her as a man who'd be unnerved by a simple afternoon outing with a woman.

Except that she was a woman he wanted something from—namely access to the creek—and he already knew where she stood on *that* subject.

Power. She had some for a change. Delicious, she thought, her butterflies abating enough to free up a smile. "You're early," she said mildly, stopping to remove her briefcase and lecture boards from the bed of her pickup.

"Yeah." Alan skipped a last rock. "Right after Louemma's tutor showed up, I went in to ask Birdie to make us sandwiches. I shouldn't have used the word *picnic*. That started her probing. It doesn't take long for Birdie or Grandmother to turn a request for a couple of PB & J sandwiches into a candlelit dinner à deux."

If that hadn't shaken Laurel, Alan's disgusted expression would've been laughable. "I hope you set them straight about our ride today being strictly business. I mean, otherwise it could easily be misconstrued in your town of eleven hundred and fifty-two gossips."

Alan relieved her of her gear. "Eleven hundred and fifty-two must be the whole town."

"I know. That's the population listed on the Welcome, You Are Entering Ridge City sign. I think every person in this town gossips."

"I suppose. Maybe I shouldn't have offered to bring lunch," he said, appearing more flustered. "But it's too late to backtrack now. I threatened those two schemers at my house with dire consequences if they blabbed. At dinner Louemma mentioned that we were doing this—in front of my general manager. But he won't say anything. Anyway, if you'd like to go change, I'll saddle the horses. Is all the tack in the shed?" Alan set her things on the porch.

She brushed past him to unlock the door, and felt a shiver run down to her toes. "Oh, watch the mare—she bites. I'd show you her handiwork, but she nailed me in an unmentionable spot. What the heck." Laurel gave a nervous laugh. "I'll mention it. I probably have the only rainbow-colored posterior in the county."

"Ouch. Would you rather not ride today?"

"And let that little turkey get the upper hand? Uh-uh. I make it a point to saddle and ride her every day. It's really my only retribution."

Alan laughed. "Thanks for the warning. You could've kept quiet and let me find out the hard way."

"Why would I?" Laurel's gazed at him curiously.

"I don't know," he said, hiking a shoulder negligently. "For starters, you might consider me a bigger turkey."

She tossed her head to one side in a way that sent her unfettered hair rippling across her shoulders. Reddish strands, mixed in with the blond, glittered in the sun. Alan had noticed before that she had a direct way of observing a man, which suggested an honesty and lack of artifice that was very different from his experience with Emily and her friends.

His fingers itched to touch Laurel's hair. It looked so shiny and soft. He slowly released his breath and slapped his palms against his thighs. "If you have to think on it that long in order to decide if I'm the bigger turkey, I'll take it as a yes. Well, forewarned is forearmed," he said, stumbling down the steps to make a beeline for the shed. With luck she wouldn't have read his mind.

Him developing an itch for Laurel Ashline didn't serve

Windridge's purpose—or his own. His intent was to win her over to their side through logic and sincerity, not by *wooing* her. "Jeez," he muttered, grasping one-handed the first saddle he came to. He flung it up on the gelding's back with enough energy to surprise them both.

Engrossed in tightening the cinch, he found himself considering reasons he might hanker after such an unsuitable woman.

Alan forgot to watch the mare. Her teeth snapped near his shoulder, and he dodged in the nick of time. Damn, maybe a good bite on the butt would get his mind back on business where it belonged, and off…other things.

If only he hadn't glanced up to see Laurel and Dog running up the hill. She looked beautiful, sexy as hell…and happy. As if this outing with him wasn't *only* about business. For the second time in as many minutes, Alan barely avoided the mare's teeth. Deciding it was anything but smart, and probably the result of not being with any woman for a long time, he gave in to the reckless pleasure of watching Laurel's shapely body moving toward him.

She stopped some distance away and bent, placing her hands on her knees until she caught her breath. "You…uh…were right yesterday when you said this would be a beautiful day for a ride," she said. "Dog agrees."

"You asked him, did you?" Alan gave her a teasing grin as he untied both horses and handed her one set of reins.

"Give me a minute. I need to throw a plastic bowl in a saddlebag and fill some water bottles for Dog and the horses."

"Why? We'll follow the creek most of the way. We won't lack for water on this trip."

"I didn't realize the creek went to the top of the hill. By the way, I thought of something in the middle of the night that I want to ask you. What supplies the water? Does it come from a well?"

"All around this valley, the hills are honeycombed with wet and dry caves. Old timers spin yarns about the bald crest of the hill being a gathering place for Southern Choctaw and Eastern Cherokee powwows during the Civil War." Alan held her stirrup steady and boosted her up into the saddle. Then he vaulted into his with ease.

"Are you saying there may be native artifacts on my land?"

Alan, who'd cantered out of the corral first, swore succinctly under his breath. That was a stupid move on his part, raving on about Indian campgrounds when he wanted to buy that section of terrain. Now she'd think he'd discovered something worthwhile up there. "They're old men's tales, Laurel. I've never found so much as an arrowhead. Nor did my dad, far as I know. And he roamed all over this area as a boy."

"Hmm. I found one of my grandmother's photo albums. It's filled with pictures of my mother and your dad as kids. There are two photographs of them as teens, in formal wear. Like they went to a prom together. We're almost the same age, you and I. When did our parents stop being an item?"

"I didn't know they ever were. But I just remembered I need to stop at my Jeep and grab the lunch knapsack."

As they'd already splashed across the creek and were abreast of the parked vehicles, Alan slid from the saddle and reached behind the driver's seat. He drew out a canvas bag and quickly secured it to his saddle. Coal Fire stood patiently, even though it was clear the roan and Dog were anxious to charge ahead.

Laurel expected Alan to resume discussing their parents. He didn't. Instead, he nudged the black with his heels and shot off. Dog, sensing an adventure, bounded forward, too. The shepherd seemed determined to stick with their leader. Every so often, though, he loped back to make sure his mistress followed.

About ten minutes into the ride, Dog dived into the underbrush. He flushed fifteen or twenty big birds that squawked and flew in different directions.

Laurel reined in the mare, then moved up beside Alan. "Wow, are those wild turkeys?" she whispered.

"Yep. The first of many we'll see today, I imagine."

"How fantastic! To think they're here on my property. I've seen one or two in the distance on previous rides. But these are...mine."

"Yes, I suppose. If you're still here at Thanksgiving, you can sneak up here and bag yourself a nice fat hen to roast for dinner."

"As if I would! Look at them, so beautiful and free. They were here first." She gave him a thoughtful look. "I *will* be here for Thanksgiving. Where else would I go?"

"I don't know. To see your mom? Thanksgiving is reportedly the biggest holiday of the year."

"She's dead. I'm all that's left of my family."

She looked and sounded so forlorn, Alan was moved to cover her hand, which rested on the saddle horn, with his own.

Shaken out of her reverie by his unexpected touch, Laurel tensed. Seeing nothing in his expression but genuine sympathy, she remained as they were. "My mom died fifteen years ago. I only ever met my grandmother through letters. I found an address when I was packing up Mom's things. I thought Hazel and Ted should know about Lucy's death—and, well, know I existed. I had hoped they'd provide a link to an extended family, but my grandmother was only interested in the present." Laurel's voice caught. She breathed deeply, and let the mare shift to the side, which disconnected her hand from Alan's. "I imagine you knew Hazel far better than I did. Maybe someday when we're not jaunting through the woods, you'll share your memories of her."

Alan found himself wishing Laurel hadn't let go. "I knew Ted pretty well. Hazel cut herself off from neighbors long ago. My grandmother's the one to ask about her. Vestal, Jason, Hazel and Ted were once best friends. Our grandfathers worked together, and from my earliest recollection, Ted always came to Windridge alone. He did most everything alone."

"How old are you?" Laurel asked abruptly.

Alan laughed. "Now, wouldn't you be offended if I asked you that question?"

"No. I'm thirty. Well, and a half."

"Me, too. So, you were right about us being near in age. I feel older, though. Comes from having a nine-year-old daughter," he said with another laugh.

Laurel made some rough calculations. "There's a picture in Hazel's album of your father at what I'd guess was his high-school graduation. You must've been born before he graduated." She frowned, doing the calculation in her head.

"My parents were both sixteen when I came along. Dad finished high school and college. Mom quit. It was a sore spot between them until he died. Carolee actually took correspondence courses and got her GED. She went to college when I was in elementary school. What's the matter?"

"Nothing. It's sad, don't you think? They were so young. My mom wasn't quite sixteen when I was born. She didn't go back to school. That made it almost impossible for her to support us."

"It seems young to us because times have changed." Alan nudged his horse forward, and as the path widened, Laurel kept pace. "Kentucky history will tell you that until recently, our marriage laws were pretty lax." He turned to study her. "You've never mentioned your dad. Is he…dead, too?"

"I never knew him. Well, I have vague memories of a man I think might've been him. What about your mom? Someone in town said your father was killed by lightning. I find it hard to believe, but I hear it's still common."

"Yes. As for Mother—Mark's death released her. She never got along with her in-laws. I was raised by Grandmother and a nanny. I can't say for sure, but I suspect that if my father hadn't died, my parents would've divorced. Or maybe not. Divorce isn't prevalent here. People tend to stick with their mistakes."

"I don't recommend it."

"You sound like the voice of experience."

"Unfortunately, but we're not talking about me. I'm working hard to close the door on my past." She let a scant moment go by. "Getting back to your mom. She just ran off and left you with your grandmother?"

"No. She talked my grieving grandparents into hiring her to be a sales rep for Windridge. For all her failure as a mother, Carolee had great business sense. A week before I announced my engagement, though, she married a California wine grower. Within days she'd moved on and forgotten all about us. They didn't attend my wedding, and she's never seen her grandchild. Her loss, not Louemma's."

Laurel was aware of the longing behind his resentment. Despite everything she'd seen on the surface, leading her to decide that this man had a life anyone might envy, she'd been wrong. He and she had more in common than Laurel would ever have guessed. She preferred to think of him as the bourbon king. But like it or not, Hazel's album touched both their lives. And that made Laurel even more uncomfortable. Reining in, she deliberately dropped back.

"Hey, where'd you go?" He twisted in his saddle.

"We're coming to that thickly wooded area you told me about yesterday. I need to untie my jacket and put it on. I'm feeling chilled. As well, it looks as if the trail narrows quite a bit."

"It does for a half mile or so. Then it breaks out into a natural clearing. That's where the stream forks. We'll rest our horses there and let them drink their fill. From that point, on the grade steepens and the going gets tougher. I hope heights and switchbacks don't spook you. Over the years, the creek wore grooves in the limestone, but it follows the ridge switchbacks."

"I'll keep up, don't worry. So far this is nothing compared to finding some of the weavers' homes I've gone to visit."

"Right. I forgot you travel the hill country in search of…what exactly?"

"Weaving patterns handed down from generation to generation. My grandmother left a scrapbook full of them. Her mother started it."

"If they're handed down, you must be duplicating the same ones over and over."

"A nonweaver might think so. Good weavers are always trying unique variations on tried-and-true patterns. Hill-country women still make cloth for what they wear and use in the house. Well, except for men's overalls, which they buy through a catalog or at a company mining store. I'm awed by their skill, to say nothing of their grit. Most of the homes have electricity now. Some folks own a car and a TV. But basically they still wash dishes in a sink that empties straight onto rocks. They sew on treadle machines. It's fascinating. I may be one of the last to record their designs."

"Oh? Why is that?"

"The kids flock to the city to be educated. Their parents hate to see them go, but want them to have easier lives. And the mining is almost gone. The truth is, once they leave, the kids almost never return home."

"In addition to the loss of mines, the tobacco industry has taken such a huge hit, those jobs are gone, too. One day, estates like Windridge will be fighting urban skylines, too. Unless we expand."

"Hard to imagine urban sprawl out here where the pine needles are so thick our horses' hooves don't make a sound. Oh, God, will you look at that!"

Alan whirled around to see where Laurel was pointing. They'd reached the edge of the clearing he'd mentioned. In the distance, sun filtered through wisps of white cloud. There was a smattering of deciduous trees, which in a month would shade the forked stream. Sunlight glinting off the water seemed to merge earth and sky and stream. A pair of hawks floated on early spring updrafts, putting the finishing touch to the picture. "That would make a perfect photograph," he said. "I have a camera, back in the Jeep."

"I should've brought one. I never remember until times like this." Laurel nudged the mare with her heels. She whistled up Dog, who'd raced after a burrowing animal of some kind. A small rabbit, probably. Rising to stand taller in her stirrups, Laurel exclaimed, "Have you ever seen a more gorgeous place in your life? If I'd been Granddad, this is where I would've built my home. Right in this clearing."

Alan's heart sank. He hadn't counted on the view making her even less likely to sell him the land. If she saw this as a prospective home site, hell, his chances of talking her out of twenty acres had just gone down. Hardy and the board wouldn't thank him for meddling in something they wanted their lawyers to handle.

"Where your cottage sits is more protected from the elements," he ventured, attempting damage control. "Like I told you, during a harsh winter you'd be snowed in for months up this high. Hard rains mean flooding even below."

"Says you. Show me water marks proving that."

Alan leaped off his horse. "Let's take the horses down to drink. Then we'll cross to the other side and I'll show you."

Laurel trailed him through the underbrush. She let Cinnabar drink, then passed Alan her reins. Scrambling up the side hill, she slipped several steps backward before reaching her goal, an outcrop of stone extending out over the creek by several feet.

"Watch out," Alan called. "Hey, you're making me nervous. What are you doing? Limestone can be brittle. I don't want to be packing your broken body out of here."

"I'm trying to see my cottage. I thought I'd be able to." Clearly disappointed, she came off the boulder in short hops.

"When we get to the top it'll be visible through binoculars. I did remember to bring those. I want you to see for yourself where the last bad rain took a swipe through the trees. You'll see how close the creek came to lapping at your door."

"It can't be too huge a danger. My grandparents never lost their house."

"By the grace of God. Each year the channel erodes more of the soft earth that protects tree roots. I think Ted and my grandfather used to haul chainsaws up here after every major storm to do some selective thinning."

"Ted died nine years ago. If it's been that long since anyone thinned, the problem can't be that colossal."

"How do you know Hazel didn't hire someone to continue on where Ted left off?"

"Did she?"

Alan blew out an exasperated breath. "I don't know. A lot of neighbors would've come if she'd asked for help."

"You said she cut herself off from everyone in Ridge City."

"There were her craft friends from Berea. Their husbands or sons may have helped her in exchange for the wood. A lot of folks in smaller communities put in wood-burning stoves to keep from using so much coal."

"Hazel heated with oil. Which reminds me, I need to have someone check the level in the tank. I'd hate to run out of fuel in the dead of winter."

Leaning over, Alan snapped off a yellow wildflower and twirled it between his fingers. "You're planning to stay, then? People in town were laying odds that you'd keep this place as a vacation property, but spend most of your time back at your home in Vermont."

"I have no home in Vermont."

"You didn't get the house in your divorce settlement?"

Her head shot up. "Oh, I forgot you checked my background. I guess you missed finding out that we lived in a cubbyhole apartment. What I inherited from my marriage was a pile of unpaid debts. Thanks to Hazel leaving me her house and land, if I live frugally I might be able to pay off my ex-husband's creditors in five years."

Alan didn't have to think twice about pouncing on that tidbit. Being the accountant he was, he barely let her finish. "What I'm willing to pay—from this fork in the creek up over the virtually worthless rocky top of that hill—would go a long way toward clearing those debts, Laurel."

If ever she wavered, it was then, as they stood toe to toe, with the sky above and the music of the gurgling waterfall in the background.

"Name your price," he said, recognizing a chink, however small, in her armor.

"I've got no idea what raw land here is worth."

"There are two Realtors in Ridge City. Either would give you an honest appraisal."

"I don't know, Alan. I'm feeling hustled, and I don't like it."

He tucked the wildflower behind her ear and slowly pulled back. "The gold in that flower brings out the hazel in your eyes. Back on the bridge, the reflection from the water made them almost turquoise."

Laurel stepped away and yanked the stem from her wind-tangled hair. She didn't know how to act, what to do, what to say.

Seeing her discomfort, Alan widened the space between them. It allowed them both more breathing room. He rammed his hands into his rear pockets, and smiled briefly. "You'll probably think this is another line of bull, but I wasn't going to bring up one thing today about you selling. I wanted you to see how ill-suited this land is for development. I hoped you'd draw your own conclusions as to its future worth."

Laurel turned her back on him, twirling the flower much

as he'd done. "Yet isn't development exactly what you have in mind?"

"No. Come on. Dog's restless and so are the horses. Let's ride on. From the top you'll be able to visualize what my manager and architect have planned."

"All right." Unwilling to throw the silly flower away, Laurel wound it around the bridle up near Cinnabar's ear. The mare twitched her ears a few times, but didn't dislodge it. Once Laurel had stepped up on a rock to remount, and settled in the saddle again, the mare clearly decided the flower wasn't a fly.

Alan had been right, the steady climb, even with occasional switchbacks, was grueling. Her mare moved in fits and starts. She'd have balked completely had Coal Fire not led. Dog panted, pausing often to poke his nose under low-growing shrubs.

"What's he hunting, do you think?" Laurel yelled to Alan as they crowded close to the wall of one overhang.

"Ground squirrels. I've seen their burrows here and there."

"I'm too busy trying to stay in the saddle to watch the ground."

"Ah, greenhorn. That's exactly what you need to watch for if you're out riding these ridges. Your horse can step in a chuck hole and break a leg in seconds. I'll bet you don't carry a rifle to put him down if that happened."

"I couldn't! I couldn't kill any living thing. I wish you'd stop imparting such depressing information. Besides the obvious sheer beauty, tell me something else that's good about Kentucky."

"Well, our preacher once described heaven as a Kentucky kind of place. If you haven't already figured that out, though, I reckon you will after you've lived here awhile. Few states can hold a candle to ours."

"Funny, that's what the tour books for Vermont say, too."

"That's good. I'd hate for everyone up north to rush down here to live."

Laurel cleared her throat. "Is that a polite way of saying *Yankee, go home*?"

"You have roots here. And kin buried in Kentucky soil. Before we learned you were related to Hazel, I told Grandmother it was curious a stranger would choose Ridge City."

"I should probably take offense. But I suppose I can see why you might be suspicious of me."

"Not suspicious of you, but of why someone like you would move to an out-of-the-way town."

She laughed and the sound rained over him. "Distrust was written in every twitch of your jaw that first day we met. Maybe even the second and third times."

Alan, who'd reached the top of Bell Hill, reined his horse to the right, giving Laurel room to join him at the crest. He rested a forearm on the saddle horn and propped his elbow on his thigh, smiling at her. "I have to say, Laurel, I didn't notice you rolling out the welcome mat for me at first." Holding her gaze, he casually reached in the knapsack lying across Coal Fire's rump and pulled out a pair of field glasses, which he offered her.

Even though she'd ducked her head, Laurel failed to hide a guilty flush as she dismounted and tied Cinnabar to a branch. She marched up to Alan and took the glasses. "Just so you know, my welcome mat still isn't out." Spinning on a boot heel, she went to the rim and adjusted the glasses.

He sat still, watching her and her dog for a long moment as he digested her words. Weighing his choices, he decided silence might be the better part of valor. He, too, swung down, but stayed where he was, leaning against a boulder.

"If you angle the glasses twenty degrees left of where you're looking, you'll see the roof of our distillery. Adjacent to that is the warehouse. About a mile farther downhill, you can probably see the lawn around the house. Right under your feet, bubbling out from the limestone you're standing on, is the mouth of the spring. We'd like to build a canal, and channel the left tributary into it. Instead of letting the arms reconnect at the fork, we'd funnel our branch into a new mash barn we plan to add onto the rear of the existing facility." He thought it best to be straightforward, despite her avowed disapproval of anything to do with liquor.

"What makes you think there's enough water to support your…needs and yet not cause my creek to dry up?" Laurel perused the entire area below, identifying damage created by the flood he'd mentioned. Lowering the glasses, she made her way back to him and sat on a flat rock balanced on two smaller ones.

"You're sitting on our lunch table. And I'm starved. Shall we see what Birdie concocted before I bore you with engineering details?"

Laurel slid off the rock. She swiped a hand across it, then across the back of her pants. Removing her jacket, she spread it out as a tablecloth. "Didn't you say you'd asked for peanut butter-and-jelly sandwiches? That looks like a whole meal."

"I asked Birdie to fix something simple. But she never does anything halfway." He set out a container of cold chicken before handing Laurel the knapsack.

He'd piqued her interest. She dug inside like a kid searching for candy, and pulled out a bottle of red wine and two glasses. Wrinkling her nose, she hastily set them on the table rock. "Did you request wine?"

"What? No. I specifically told her sodas or bottled water. So, you don't drink wine, either?"

"No." The bag's next layer produced a container of mixed fruit, another of a green salad sprinkled with olives, cherry tomatoes and blue cheese. Birdie had packed dressing separately. "This all looks delicious, but—" Laurel glanced distastefully at the wine.

"There's no water? Give me a glass, and I'll fill it at the spring. It's ice cold and drinkable, I promise."

"Are you planning to drink all that wine yourself?" she asked nervously.

"Not all of it. I don't drink to excess, Laurel." Then he hesitated. "I won't have any if it bothers you. I think, though, I deserve an explanation," he finished quietly. "I don't know anyone with quite your aversion to alcohol." But he wondered if she was a recovering alcoholic—which would explain a lot.

Laurel had picked up a goblet and stared vacantly into it. Deep frown lines creased her brow, and her fingers shook slightly.

"If we're going to be friends—" he began.

She interrupted him. "We're not." She set the goblet back on the rock. "I'm a loner. Always have been, and I prefer it that way." Laurel clasped her hands tightly over her elbows and turned to face the valley again. Above them, the wind whistled through a cell tower that seemed at odds with its surroundings.

Alan walked up behind her and gently squeezed her shoulders before brushing his fingers to her elbows and back. "Neighbors, then. You can't deny we're neighbors."

She shivered from the friction of his flesh against hers. It had been so long since anyone had touched her with such care. The seductive movement of his palms set off alarms in Laurel's head. Her voice caught in her throat. Whirling, she found they were standing much too close; their knees collided, and he kept her from stumbling.

Suddenly she blurted, "I was married for seven years to an alcoholic. I…tried so hard to make the marriage work. I'm sorry if I don't respond the way you're used to women responding, Alan. I've heard all the pretty speeches. All the charming, endearing lies. I'm immune. Completely." She took a step back, then ran to Cinnabar, where she began tightening the mare's cinch.

Alan supposed he should've been prepared. Should've added it all up, considering what she'd said earlier about being left with debt. *Seven years. Her life must have been hell.* "We've got a hard ride ahead of us. I'm still hungry. Aren't you?" Not looking at her, he shoved the wine bottle back in the knapsack. Grabbing both glasses, he dropped flat on his stomach and leaned over the ledge to fill them with water. He heard Laurel slowly loosen Cinnabar's cinch. Under other circumstances, he might have smiled. But, that remark she'd made about other women, as if he made a habit of seducing them—annoyed him.

Scrambling up, he faced her, ready to set her straight. The vulnerable expression on her pale face changed his mind. Laurel Ashline affected him as no woman had for so long he'd nearly forgotten the exciting escalation of a heartbeat. "Tell me how you got started weaving," he said, handing her a frosty glass.

Laurel took it and drank deeply. When she set the glass aside, she picked up a plate. "If we're going to make small talk, I don't think either of our jobs is a good topic."

"What, then?" Alan said, settling on the ground with his back resting against a boulder.

"Louemma. You have a dear, sweet daughter. I can see she badly wants to join her friends. If I'm to have any hope of helping her achieve that goal, I need to know exactly what the doctors say is holding her back." Laurel filled both plates.

Alan picked at his salad, releasing a shaky sigh. She might as well have asked him to turn his soul inside out. "I begin and end every day praying that she'll miraculously wake up one morning and be her old self. I have stacks of files from dozens of doctors. Between now and her next lesson, I'll run off copies and drop them by your house."

"So many doctors? I had no idea. Alan, if you're expecting me to pull off a miracle, you have the wrong woman. I barely have my own life back on track."

"Vestal's the one who called you the miracle worker. I'm going along with it, albeit reluctantly, because it's the most interest Louemma's shown in anything since the accident."

"Well, that's brutally honest," Laurel mumbled, biting into her chicken. "But it takes us back to my job. Like I said, it's dangerous for either of us to talk about our work. So I suggest we eat fast and call it a day. Unless you can give me more specific details about Louemma…"

As always, when Alan felt put on the spot with regard to his daughter's accident, he clammed up. It was just simpler all the way around.

CHAPTER EIGHT

OVER THE DAYS AND NIGHTS following her ride with Alan up Bell Hill, Laurel replayed many of their conversations in her head. They'd settled nothing, she realized, including her question concerning the amount of water supplied by the spring. Alan had jumped in to say something about not boring her with engineering details, and then never returned to the issue. He was a master at dodging questions he didn't want to answer. But…so was she.

Or maybe Alan had changed his mind. She hadn't heard from him. She didn't dare believe he'd lost interest in diverting the water. Hazel's lawyer had pointed out that the creek was what made Laurel's inheritance worth a lot in monetary terms.

At the time, money hadn't interested her nearly so much as having a place to disappear. Now, she knew she should think more long-term. Before, she'd rarely considered anything beyond a day at a time; living with Dennis had caused that. Even after her move, he'd tracked her down. Often drunk, he phoned at all hours, day or night. For two weeks, though, he'd been blessedly silent. Either the phone company had cut off his service or he'd been evicted or both. She could only hope he'd given up. Now there was Alan… He'd arrived on the scene to complicate things further.

Laurel rubbed under Dog's collar. "You're misnamed," she murmured. "You're woman's best friend," she murmured, "not man's." He raised his head from the rug she'd spread at the foot of her jack loom, and licked her left hand.

Pushing back her chair, Laurel decided it was time to phone Alan. If he had reports on the creek and its water flow, he might as well bring them along with Louemma's medical file. Unless he didn't plan to let his daughter continue with her lessons. Hard to tell. Laurel and Alan had hardly spoken on the return ride. He'd unsaddled Coal Fire and said goodbye. But…why put this off?

Going to a wall phone she'd had installed in the loom cottage, she punched in his home number, and was startled to hear a woman's soft Southern drawl. Not his grandmother, Laurel knew her voice. "Have I reached the Ridge residence?"

"Yes. Who's calling, please?"

"Uh, Laurel Ashline. I'd like to speak to Alan. If he's busy he can call me at his convenience." Laurel thought the woman covered the mouthpiece. She heard mumbles in the background. Glancing at her watch, she saw it was just past 8:00 a.m. Early. But he'd phoned her earlier that first day. Had she interrupted him and a woman friend? Laurel debated hanging up. Then his deep voice crossed the line.

"Laurel? Is it really you? What's the matter? I hope you're not calling to cancel Louemma's lesson tomorrow."

"No. Is the lesson tomorrow? Goodness, I'm afraid I've lost track of time. I've been putting in long hours on a project—a tablecloth and thirty matching napkins for a woman who's giving a political dinner party this weekend." She stopped, realizing she was babbling. "Uh…why I'm calling. You said you'd let me read Louemma's medical record. If it's not too much trouble, I'd also like to see the spring's hydrology study."

Alan was in the middle of his quarterly conference with Louemma's tutor. Rose Robinson had Louemma's school-work spread out on his desk and had temporarily set the phone on the floor by her feet.

He'd assumed Hardy had ordered the study Laurel was asking about; he'd have to check. But in his shock over the fact
that she'd actually called him, Alan was thrown off-kilter. "If
you're home," he said, "may I call you back, in say, half an
hour? Better yet, I'll gather together what you need and run
it over. That might take me more like—" He turned to the
tutor. "Can I see you later, Rose?"

At the other end Laurel heard the same soft voice assure
Alan they could resume anytime he wanted. "Wait, don't cut
short your, uh, visit for me," she said. "Just bring the information tomorrow."

"But I thought you needed to go over it before the lesson?"
Alan clearly didn't understand Laurel's sudden backpedaling.
Why take time out of her busy schedule to phone, he wondered, if it was okay to look at the records later? He stretched
the phone cord to its limit. "I've been inundated with work,
too. I'm glad you called. Otherwise I'd have forgotten you
needed those records. If you do have a few minutes, I'll come
by shortly. Louemma's tutor just said it's no problem resched-
uling our conference."

"That was Louemma's tutor? She's the one who answered
your phone?" Now Laurel sounded flustered. Furthermore,
she felt like a fool. What would Alan think now? He'd probably decide she cared who he was seeing romantically.

Alan was baffled by Laurel's erratic comments. "So, you
do have a few minutes, or not? Is everything okay over there?"

"Um, I'm at the loom cottage. When Dog announces your
arrival, I'll come down and meet you in the clearing so you
won't even have to leave the Jeep."

"That's not necessary," Alan objected. The buzzing in his ear
told him she'd hung up. Rose Robinson was eyeing him speculatively. "Sorry," he muttered. "That was Laurel Ashline."

"I answered the phone, remember?" She laughed. Rose had
been Alan's third-grade teacher; after teaching for thirty years,

she'd retired. A member of the same garden club as Vestal, Rose had volunteered to help her friend and her former student by tutoring Louemma when it became apparent she was having difficulty in the classroom.

"Vestal said Ms. Ashline's an occupational therapist."

Alan watched Rose stack his daughter's test scores. "She's not. But Laurel had success helping Donald Baird regain the use of his left arm after his stroke. She's a master weaver, but she's not medically certified. So I'm not expecting a major breakthrough for Louemma," he said philosophically.

"Don't be such a cynic, Alan. I keep telling you faith can move mountains."

He laughed. "Well, that's appropriate, too. I need Laurel to move a mountain. More or less." He raked a hand through shaggy hair that probably needed another cut. "She's standing in the way of our expansion. I'm sure Vestal told you we'd like to dramatically increase our foreign trade."

"Yes, and I've also heard her muttering over how Hazel Bell pulled a fast one. She and I were once friends, too. Until I suggested Hazel clamp down on Lucy's wild ways. Young as your father was, even he'd washed his hands of Lucy. Oh, that must've been six months before she left town. Of course, Carolee could never abide Lucy Bell."

"Why? I don't know much about any of them. Were they classmates?"

"Yes. And Carolee hated that Lucy and your dad hung out so much. Pure jealousy. Mark and Lucy were raised practically like siblings. But not even Mark could influence Lucy once she met that laborer she eventually ran off with. He was at least ten years older and lived in his car. But Lucy Bell was as stubborn as she was wild."

"I've heard that. I guess I never realized Dad had been such good friends with Ted and Hazel's daughter."

"Before your time. It was great gossip around town. Everyone assumed Ted would have Mark go after Lucy and bring her back. Some believe that was the catalyst for his marriage to Carolee. Mercy, is that news to you?"

"Yes and no. Not that anyone said stuff like that within earshot. But I know my parents argued constantly. They were often the talk of the town," he added wryly. "Mom needled Dad over women, although I can't recall her naming names. It's interesting what you said about Lucy Bell being stubborn. It's a trait her daughter inherited."

"But not the wildness, I hope."

Alan thought over what he did know about Laurel. Her movements were graceful and calm. Her skin was as velvety as her voice. Not that he should be remembering how her skin had felt under his hands. "No, not the wildness," he murmured, shaking his head to dislodge the vivid picture. "Well!" He blew out a breath. "In the time we've spent talking about the past, we could've completed our conference, Rose. But you heard me tell Laurel I'd bring her those reports."

"No problem. I left Louemma listening to a talking book." Rose heaved her matronly body out of his chair collected her papers. The door had barely closed on her when Alan began leafing through the file Hardy Duff had left. He didn't find a water assessment, and picked up the phone. "Hardy, Alan here. I'm looking for a copy of the architect's civil engineering report. Dave requested an analysis on the total cubic feet of water produced by the spring, didn't he? Fact is, I don't see any water volume impact studies in his folder."

"Dave Bentley said it'd be a wasted expense. Hell, Alan, we all know that stream floods twice a year, in spring and fall."

Alan shut the folder. "Floods, yes. From rain runoff. Before we go diverting half the creek, I want to see the predicted long-term effects. Tell Dave it's my money, and that I want an expert's opinion on how much water they estimate the spring will produce over the next hundred years."

"What? That's nuts! Oh, I get it. Is that Ashline woman stonewalling?"

"I'm not voting to put money into an expensive new building if our operation is going to deplete the deep water table. And Laurel Ashline isn't stonewalling. Well, not exactly. How can you expect her to agree to give us access if we can't prove her creek won't dry up?"

"It's *your* creek, Alan. What's this *her creek* crap?"

"Just call Dave. I'm trying to save us time and money and avoid going to court. Hazel Bell didn't do anything illegal according to Kentucky squatter's rights statutes."

"Oh, all right," Hardy grumbled. "Dave's gonna ask why you can't go straight to Judge Hollowell with your original land grant. He'll have that squatter petition reversed."

"This isn't Dave's business. It's mine." Alan slammed down the telephone in irritation. He knew Duff and the board didn't see things the way he did. Too damn bad.

Alan found Louemma's medical records. Not bothering to make copies, he informed Birdie and Vestal where he was going and tore out of the house. If he drove fast enough, maybe the wind rushing in through the open windows would drown out the little voice that sounded a lot like Hardy's. A voice asking why Alan wanted the grief he'd invited by admitting he'd begun to harbor an attraction for Laurel Ashline.

DOG TROTTED TO THE LOOM cottage door, pricked up his ears and began a deep-throated barking. Shushing him, Laurel opened it a crack and listened. "What is it boy? All I hear is wind in the trees." But the dog wouldn't let up and Laurel accepted that Dog's sensory perceptions were far superior to hers. Soon she was able to distinguish the rumble of an engine down the road. Thanks to her early detection system, she crossed the bridge and met Alan's Jeep as he parked next to her pickup.

He climbed out, pausing only to pat Dog. "You shouldn't have come out here to wait, Laurel. Now I feel doubly bad for tying up your valuable time."

She could've told him that because of Dog, her wait had been short. But Alan had already moved on with an explanation for his delay. "I couldn't find the hydrology study in the folder Hardy brought me the other night. Turns out our architect never ordered one. I've remedied that. I should have results within two weeks."

"I'm in no rush. The money sounds tempting, but…" She gave a quick shrug. "I really don't know how you convinced me to consider selling, anyway."

Alan had retrieved Louemma's medical folder from the Jeep. "What does that mean? You're backing off because we didn't order one study?"

"It could be an omen."

"Maybe you spend too much time hobnobbing with superstitious mountain folk. Promise you'll keep an open mind until I can get an honest answer to your question, Laurel."

"All I said was that I didn't know how you'd gotten me to consider your offer. Yes, I'll reserve judgment until I see the tests. Is that folder you're mangling the findings on Louemmm's medical exams?"

Realizing he'd rolled up the thick folder, Alan straightened it out again. "Originals. I decided not to take the time to make photocopies. If you don't mind, I'll wait while you look them over. That way, maybe I can clarify anything you don't understand."

"Oh. Then come inside while I read them. I'll fix us a glass of lemonade." The moment the offer left her lips, Laurel wanted to snatch it back. Since she'd moved here, the cottage had been her sanctuary. No one except she and Dog had darkened its door. But…at some point she had to start expanding her social circle. If she didn't, she might as well say goodbye to any hope of living a normal life, ever.

"Lemonade would sure hit the spot." Alan handed her the file and matched his stride to hers.

The first thing he noticed after Laurel had unlocked the cottage and stood aside so he could pass was that she made no apology for the condition of her house. It struck him as odd, because Emily and Charity Madison, too, always made some comment, even if their homes were scrubbed and polished to perfection.

Laurel excused herself to get the lemonade, leaving him to his own devices. Which suited Alan just fine, as it gave him a chance to observe her tastes without having to hide his curiosity. The room gleamed. She was uncommonly neat. Alan saw evidence of her talent in every direction he looked. Whether it was in a couch coverlet, a chair cushion or wall hangings, her eye for color had turned what was once a drab interior into a place of warmth. By contrast, he'd have to call his home formal. He chose an overstuffed chair and then fought an urge to kick off his boots as he sank down.

Laurel returned with a tray holding a pitcher of iced lemonade and a pair of unmatched glasses, also without apology. "I see you made yourself at home." She set the tray on the low coffee table. As she picked up the pitcher to pour, her nervousness became patently obvious in the rattle of glass against glass, a result of her shaking hands.

"You've done a fine job sprucing up this old place, inside and out." Alan let the remark fall casually, wanting to dispel some of her unnecessary misgivings.

"You're my first guest," she blurted.

"I'm honored, then." Leaning toward her, he took a glass out of her hand. He didn't want her to spill lemonade all over a rag rug woven in autumn shades. "I'm guessing you made the rug and the other weavings. They're great," he rushed to add. Standing, he walked over to examine a wall weaving, a mountain scene. "I know every step that goes into producing a bottle of good bourbon," he said. "The right charred white-oak barrels, the depth of an earth floor. In winter I know exactly when to pump steam through a warehouse. It's a balancing act. I imagine your craft's the same."

"I hardly think the two comp—" Laurel broke off, swallowing the hostility that automatically flared. She picked up her glass, feeling Alan's eyes on her suddenly stiff shoulders.

"Alcoholism is a disease, Laurel. Healthy men and women can enjoy the smooth, mellow taste of my bourbon without ill effects. I accept that you have reason not to drink, but I won't be held accountable for one man's weakness. Or even one man multiplied by hundreds."

Alan set his unfinished drink on the tray. He lifted the files he'd left on an end table between the couch where Laurel sat and the overstuffed chair. "You probably feel sorry for Louemma, being born into a home you can't bring yourself to set foot in."

Laurel gripped her glass tightly in both hands and yet the lemonade still sloshed over the edge as she jumped up. "Now who's being unfair? Anyone with eyes can see you're a devoted father. A good man. I…can't help how I feel about what you do for a living. But I'd *never* project that onto your daughter."

"How about my grandmother? She and Birdie are bugging me to invite you for a meal. I've run out of excuses. What do you want me to tell them?"

"I don't know. That I'm too busy. I am, thanks to Vestal. She recommended that Charity Madison invite me to give her Camp Fire troop a demonstration, and I'm getting invitations from women's groups, too. But with the girls…I felt compelled to offer them classes. And one class has become two. Unless you're now saying you've decided to withdraw Louemma."

That had indeed run through Alan's mind. But if he walked

out and severed this tie with Laurel, he'd not only disappoint Louemma, Windridge could say goodbye to any kind of a compromise regarding the creek. Alan had to decide whether he had the stomach for letting Hardy and the board take Laurel to court.

And he discovered he didn't. If it lay within his power to settle things amicably, he would. Not only was that his natural inclination, he didn't want to be yet another man causing Laurel pain. He placed the file next to the tray on the coffee table.

"I don't think you really need to wait while I read Louemma's file, Alan."

He bounced his hands on his thighs. "Okay. Sure…I'll collect it when we come for her lesson tomorrow. If you have any questions, you know my number." He skirted the couch.

Laurel's phone rang just then, interrupting Alan's walk to the door. He could have let himself out, but he'd left his cell phone in the Jeep, and it crossed his mind that the caller might be family trying to reach him. Vestal and Birdie knew where he was.

Before Laurel answered the ringing phone, she sensed who it was. Damn, Dennis had surfaced again, just when she'd begun to relax her guard. She shut her eyes and clamped a steadying hand against her stomach.

Even from where he stood, Alan could hear a loud stream of vitriolic language pouring from the receiver Laurel gripped in a white-knuckled hand. He was seconds from ripping the phone away and taking on whatever madman had called her. But Laurel seemed entirely in control. She spoke in a calm and level tone, with the barest hint of taut nerves. "Dennis, I've told you repeatedly that I won't talk to you when you're in this condition. You need help, and you know where to get it. Stop calling me. Our lives are no longer connected. I'm hanging up now. Don't call again, because I won't answer."

Alan would've ripped the phone out of the wall, or failing

that, would've banged the receiver into the cradle, but Laurel set it down carefully. He saw that her control was quickly disappearing, however. She clasped her hands together so tightly her fingers turned red and then white. Her lips were pinched and her eyes wide open with shock.

"Does he do that often?" Alan inquired in a soft voice. "Can't you get a block put on your phone? Or else have it unlisted?"

She turned sightless eyes in the direction of the voice penetrating the old fears that held her in their grip. Blinking several times, she slowly felt herself emerge. "Oh, Alan. I thought you'd gone." With an effort, Laurel separated her hands and raised a badly shaking one to smooth back her hair.

He crossed to her side and gathered both of her hands, chafing them gently. "I asked why your phone isn't unlisted, Laurel."

"I need it for business. Anyway, Dennis is clever and devious. I actually did have it unlisted when I first moved here. Somehow, he got hold of the number. The phone company apologized and gave me another, which Dennis also found."

"At the very least, get caller ID."

She realized suddenly why warmth and feeling were returning to her body, and she disengaged their hands. "My Women's Legal Aid divorce lawyer said some alcoholics feed off an ex-partner's attempt to thwart them. A counselor at a women's survival group recommends repeating the same firm message I just gave Dennis, each and every time he calls while drunk."

"So, then eventually the calls stop?"

"I certainly hope so. But really, Alan, this is my problem. You have quite enough worries of your own, what with Louemma's condition and all."

"I know, but I have a support team of doctors and others to call on when I need them. Like Vestal and Birdie and Rose…"

"Louemma seems so isolated. Don't forget, I've witnessed

how her friends acted toward her." She paused. "The gossips in town say you're determined to weather your storms alone."

"Who said that?" But as the words left his lips, Alan experienced a wash of guilt. He'd cut off everyone he and Emily used to see regularly—so he wouldn't have to deal with their sympathy, or with their ill-concealed speculation as to what had prompted Emily's unscheduled trip. He paced in circles around the chair.

"Don't let me keep you, Alan," Laurel said. "I've already taken too much time from a project I need to complete before the girls' lesson tomorrow. As well, I want to set aside a couple of hours to study Louemma's records." She grabbed up the thick folder, glad it gave her something to do with her hands.

"I've been thrown out of other places. Notice I didn't say better places, and certainly never as nicely," Alan drawled.

A flush crept up her neck. "I wouldn't exactly call it throwing you out. Before the phone rang you were already headed for home."

"So I was. I only stopped because I'd left my cell phone in the Jeep. With my grandmother's recent illness, and of course with Louemma, I ought to keep the phone on me at all times. I thought maybe the call was for me. Then I heard the garbage spilling out of that jerk's mouth. I wouldn't have left you on a bet."

"What's so sad is that…if and when Dennis sobers up, he won't remember a word. He may not even remember my phone number. He hasn't called except when he's three sheets to the wind."

"Doesn't make a lot of sense, does it? But I have to admit I've never spent any time around an alcoholic."

Laurel seemed surprised by that. "In your business? You mean Ridge City hasn't got any town drunks? That hardly seems plausible."

"I'm not saying there aren't guys around who get buzzed

occasionally. And those who stop at the tavern every night for a beer or two. But I guarantee I'd know if anyone around here had a problem—or a mouth on him—like your ex."

Again Laurel's face reddened. "It's not pleasant. Please, can we forget it happened?"

"I doubt it. Laurel, what if he shows up at your door one day?"

She shivered and wouldn't meet Alan's eyes. Her lawyer had said that Laurel shouldn't be naive. Sometimes men decided to wreak vengeance on ex-wives who, in their alcohol-soaked minds, had wronged them, and they too often succeeded.

"I can tell that thought's entered your mind." Alan walked back to the coffee table and ripped off a corner of Louemma's file folder. Taking out a pen, he scribbled down three numbers. He labeled them *H*, *W* and *C*. "The first is my home, which I know you already have. The second is the distillery, and the third is my cell. If for any reason, day or night, you need help, I want you to phone me."

She shrugged and started to refuse the scrap of paper.

Striding up to her wall phone, he tucked the paper under the edge. "I mean it." He glanced at his watch. "Time for me to stop saying goodbye and actually go. Louemma's last class is almost over. If I hustle I can probably catch her tutor and wind up the conference I postponed."

"By all means. Go. Her tutor sounds…young," Laurel said before she could stop herself. Having made the observation, she quickly added, "Is she a certified teacher or just a college student working toward a teaching degree?"

"Rose? You think Rose Robinson is young enough to be in college? She'll love it. Laurel, she taught me. Rose is my grandmother's age."

Once again, Laurel felt her face explode in heat. It was bad enough to appear curious about a woman who might be more to Alan Ridge than his daughter's tutor. It was even worse to be caught probing so blatantly for information. "It's hardly my concern," she said dismissively.

Alan's foggy brain could come up with only one reason Laurel might be so flushed over their latest exchange. If she'd thought he and Rose—no, that was preposterous. Laurel had all but told him to stay out of her life. Clearly she couldn't wait for him to be gone.

He didn't stick around, although he stopped more than once to cast a backward glance in her direction. Surprisingly, she remained standing in the doorway. Alan didn't wave, and neither did she. All the same, there was a new connection of sorts. As he drove home, Alan discovered he was looking forward to returning the next afternoon.

THE NEXT DAY, Louemma badgered her dad to stop at the supermarket in town before they went to Laurel's. "I want to buy treats or a toy for Dog. He always puts his head on my lap, Daddy. It'd be cool if I had a present for him."

"He may be a little old for toys, honeybee. Anyway, we have no idea what he might like."

"Nana told me you used to have a dog. She said he died and you never got another one. Why? Were you too sad?"

"I was. Boone was a good old dog. A coon hound. Out of the same litter as Pete Madison's Crockett. Pete and I named our dogs after mountain trackers—Daniel Boone and Davy Crockett. Hey, squirt, don't you remember how you and Sarah used to try and dress up old Crockett?" Alan smiled as he cruised through fond memories.

"I don't remember. Why did your dog die and not Mr. Madison's?"

"Boone picked up a tick. His fever shot sky-high before I could get him to a vet. Sometimes sickness spreads so fast there's nothing anyone can do, Louemma."

"Why didn't you get another dog?" she asked again.

"I didn't have time to train a new pup, and...your mother, well, she...was never too wild about dogs."

"We could get one now."

Alan should've seen that sneak attack coming, but he hadn't. "It's not just up to us. Nana has a say. Look, here's the pet aisle. Let's see what they have."

Louemma finally settled on a soft rubber bone that had a bell in one end and a squeaker in the other. It took her so long to decide, Alan thought they might be late for her lesson. On their way to the checkout, Louemma saw a display of African violets. "Stop, Daddy! Ms. Ashline loves flowers. Those ruffled white ones with the pink centers are beautiful. Can we buy them? The other day Brenna showed Jenny and me a vase on the windowsill above Ms. Ashline's loom. Her flowers were wilted. Buy her these, Daddy, 'cause they're in a pot and they won't get all yucky."

"Honey, it's one thing to take Dog a toy. A gift for your teacher—well, she might get the wrong idea."

"How? I don't understand. She likes flowers, and hers died."

Sighing, Alan added the small green pot to their purchase. Some rituals of the type that went on between men and women he'd rather not try explaining to a nine-year-old.

They were only marginally late, for which Alan was glad. He passed Brenna's mom on the gravel road a half mile from Laurel's cottage. He wouldn't have liked that chatty woman to see him carrying a potted plant to a single, and therefore eligible lady. Gossip again. Lord, Alan hated those wagging tongues. In small towns, though, gossip was like the lifeblood.

Seconds after Alan had pushed the wheelchair across the threshold into the loom cottage, the violet pot wedged on one side of his daughter and Dog's toy on the other, he rushed to assure Laurel that both gifts were from Louemma. After all, he remembered the fate of the fruit basket Vestal had sent in his name.

"For me?" Laurel knelt and wrapped her arms around the

child. "You shouldn't have, sweetheart. But they're gorgeous. I have the very spot for violets. Where I can see them whenever I work." Standing on tiptoe, she stretched to place the pot on the ledge above her loom.

"See, Daddy?" Louemma said smugly. "That's where me, Jenny and Brenna saw her dead roses."

Laurel froze, then dropped slowly back on her heels. Had Alan, too, noticed how long she'd kept his vase with the three rosebuds? If so, he said nothing to rub it in.

"Shall we get started?" Laurel said brightly. "Half an hour will go by fast."

"Where's Dog?" The child seemed upset when she didn't see him.

"Oh, I left him at my house after Jenny and Brenna's class. Dog generally eats about this time and I didn't want to interrupt your lesson to go feed him."

"I brought him a toy bone," Louemma said excitedly. " I want to give it to him."

Laurel opened her mouth to suggest waiting until after the lesson. But it was plain that Louemma wouldn't settle down to work without first delivering her other gift. "I'll run and get him."

"Let me." Alan reached for the doorknob at the same moment Laurel did. Their fingers touched, and something like an electrical impulse shot up Laurel's arm. "I'd better go," she rushed to say, yanking back her hand. "He knows you, but he might be unwilling to let you in if I'm not home."

"Ah. Of course." Alan's arm fell limply to his side. As Laurel dashed out, he was left wondering what had happened.

He hardly had time to gather his wits before she returned. Her hair was mussed by the wind and her cheeks pink from the run down and then up the hill. She was *beautiful*. How had he missed that in the beginning?

Louemma immediately called Dog. The big lummox loped

over to her chair, his tongue lolling out one side of his mouth. He zeroed right in on the bone lying across her knees. He nudged it with his nose. The toy rattled and the dog sprang back.

Giggling, she coaxed him forward again. This time he grabbed the bone, but when it squeaked in his teeth he tossed it straight up in the air. It fell with a squeak and a rattle. Acting like a pup, Dog pounced once, then twice, shaking it wildly in spite of the noise.

The trio watching the show shared a delighted peal of laughter. Laurel sobered first. "Well," she exclaimed dryly. "With luck that'll keep him occupied throughout your lesson, Louemma. But you're here to learn weaving. I'll start by sliding your chair under the table. You've watched your friends work a loom. Now I'm going to show you up close how easily the beater bar moves."

Louemma's eyes grew round. It was obvious she wanted to touch the wool.

"What color yarn is your favorite?" Laurel asked.

"Red," the girl whispered. "Or yellow. I like yellow, too."

Edging the wheelchair back, Laurel plunked a huge coil of bright red yarn in Louemma's lap. She added a yellow one of equal size. Taking Louemma's inert hands in hers, Laurel carefully arranged the lifeless fingers around each ball of yarn.

Laurel felt Alan grow tense. "Alan, we'll be at this awhile. Please take a walk or at least find a seat."

Dropping cross-legged to the floor, she smiled serenely, inducing an answering smile from Louemma. "These colors would make such a nice, bright winter scarf. I want you to imagine how soft it'll feel warming your neck."

"Will it be a scarf like skaters wear?"

"Sure," Laurel murmured, almost afraid to think she felt a ripple along the backs of Louemma's hands. A faint tightening of her muscles.

"I wanted to learn to ice-skate on the pond. Mama wouldn't let me."

"Think of your scarf. Imagine how it'll look flying behind you in the wind."

Slowly, ever so slowly as Laurel painted pictures with words, she also withdrew her fingers. Louemma clutched both balls of yarn without assistance.

Directly behind Laurel, Alan leaped up from his chair and drew in a sharp breath. The hiss startled his daughter. Her right hand fell to her side and the red ball skittered across the floor.

Upset over dropping it, she started to cry. The yellow ball joined the red.

Dog bounded across the floor. He sniffed the yarn, then picked it up in his mouth and gently deposited it on the child's lap. He held the ball steady, a low whine urging her to take it. And she made every effort. The strain showed on her thin face. Laurel thought Louemma's wrist might have moved a quarter inch.

"Thank you, Dog," she said calmly. "Louemma needs you to bring her the yellow ball."

"Yes, please," the child said, sniffling through her tears. Laurel took a clean tissue from her pocket and dried her face.

When the shepherd obeyed at once, Louemma broke into a happy laugh. "He did, Daddy! He brought me the yarn."

And ham that he was, Dog expected to be petted in reward. He nuzzled his way under the girl's stiff arm. "I love you," she cried, making her best attempt yet to stroke his soft fur. "I wish you were mine! I drop stuff all the time. If you lived with us, Nana wouldn't have to bend so much. She's getting old, you know."

Pleased, feeling that a tiny breakthrough had come far earlier than she'd expected, Laurel was unprepared for Alan's response.

"How much for the shepherd?" he demanded, digging out his wallet.

"What? You're joking!"

"No. You saw what I saw. It's the dog, not the lessons, that'll help her."

Clambering up, Laurel frowned as she pulled him aside. "If that's what you think, we'll stop the lessons right now. Dog is not for sale."

"You can go to the shelter and find another pet."

"Leave, Alan. I don't care if you own the entire town. You can't barge into my life and think you can buy everything I have. First the creek. Now Dog."

For a moment Laurel thought he'd argue. He didn't. He walked stiffly over to his child, grasped the handles of her chair and wheeled Louemma to the door.

"Bye," the girl called. "I'll be back for another lesson in two days. I love you, Dog. And you, too…Laurel." The door slammed on her words.

Laurel sighed and glanced at the nodding violet, doubting she'd ever see Louemma again. It was some time before the incident faded and she was able to return to her own project. Even then, she worked with a heavier heart.

CHAPTER NINE

WELL AFTER DARK that same day—Laurel had lost track of the exact time—Dog leaped up from her feet under the loom and raced to the door. He barked, but this wasn't one of his I-hear-a-squirrel yips. A couple of weeks ago, when he'd had a similar barking fit, Laurel had discovered a pair of raccoons waddling up the path. "Easy, boy," she called, rolling her shoulders. It was later than she'd realized; she'd worked through supper again. However, she'd forgotten her irritation with Alan Ridge, and in one more good sitting she'd finish this project.

Dog didn't let up. He was definitely acting strange. He snatched up the bone Louemma had given him, and still attempted to bark without dropping the toy. "Come here, you crazy mutt." Laughing, Laurel spun around in her chair. Dog didn't budge, so she got up to check. She'd nearly reached his side when she heard the unmistakable crunch of footsteps on her gravel path. Still, Dog was no longer sounding an alarm. Unless you could call emitting happy little woofs—around the bone he continued to hold—a warning.

She yanked open the door and screamed as a dark, somewhat blurry shape with an upraised arm appeared on her porch. Her mind stopped functioning. Dog—her protector—wagged his tail.

"Laurel." Alan's low, deep voice penetrated her fright.

She flattened her right hand over her galloping heart. "Why on earth are you sneaking up on me at this time of night?"

"It's just past eight. I…should've phoned first, but I was afraid you might hang up on me, considering what a jackass I made of myself this afternoon." Noticing the dog, Alan bent and the two played tug-of-war with the squeaky toy.

"If you've come to up the ante on your offer for my dog, the answer is still no." She resented the way she'd let him frighten her out of her wits.

He straightened, looking repentant. "I seem to spend half my life lately apologizing to you. Of course you don't want to sell him. I was blinded by Louemma's first sign of improvement. At dinner I told Vestal and Birdie what I'd witnessed. They both believe if there's a breakthrough it's due to both of you and Dog."

"Come in," she said finally. "We're letting the mosquitoes in. We need to talk. Better yet, let's go to my house. I haven't eaten, and I've sat at the loom long enough."

"I hate to interrupt your meal, Laurel. May I take you to a restaurant instead? God knows, a substantial meal is the least I owe you."

"It's late, Alan. And you owe me nothing." They walked down the path with Dog trotting between them. Laurel unlocked her well-lit house.

"I stopped here first because so many lights were on."

"If I turn them all on when I feed Dog at five, then when I work late, as I often do, I'm not walking into a dark empty house."

"Makes sense." Alan trailed after her into a small but serviceable kitchen.

"I'm going to make tea. Would you like a cup? Or I have soda."

"Tea's fine. Or nothing. What did you want to talk about?"

Laurel set up the teapot, then took out a plate and began to fashion a sandwich of ham and cheese. She sliced tomatoes, periodically staring at Alan as if trying to decide where to begin. "Our backgrounds are so different, Alan. I was ten when a doctor at a welfare clinic diagnosed my mother as having an anxiety disorder. It wasn't the first of her mood swings, but the most severe, to that point, anyway. I think he explained it to me, because I was the only other person there. He prescribed pills and said she'd be fine. Except she alternately used and abused her pills, I learned later. She got and quit jobs, then didn't fill her prescriptions. To make a long story short, my mother suffered chronic and recurring episodes in one form or another until she died suddenly of a brain aneurysm. I was fifteen—the age she was when she had me."

As Alan rose, he evaluated what life must have been like for her. He couldn't resist wrapping her in a warm embrace. When she stiffened, he rubbed her to relax her. "Did you end up in a foster home?"

She gravitated to his warmth. "No, I didn't tell my counselor Mom was dead. I struggled to stay in school, the only place I enjoyed. I managed."

"Why didn't Hazel take you?"

"A year passed before I found Mom's parents' names in a keepsake box. Since she'd never said anything good about them, I made excuses not to contact them, either." The kettle whistled and Laurel slipped out of Alan's embrace. She prepared the tea and poured them each a cup. She half expected Alan to interrupt again. He didn't. He murmured sympathetically and continued to observe her out of dark, turbulent eyes.

She took a seat at the table in her breakfast nook, which forced him to wedge himself in, too. Alan sipped his tea and Laurel picked at half of her sandwich until the silence grew excruciating. "After graduation—I don't know—I guess seeing all the other kids' families at the ceremony made me want…someone. I wrote to my grandparents. Hazel wrote back, and we began a weekly correspondence.

"The main thing she did through her letters was spark my

interest in weaving. I visited an old school counselor, and she helped me get into an apprentice program in Vermont."

"And that's where you met and married the bozo I heard on the phone."

"Right. Alan, I'm not telling you this story to make you feel sorry for me, but to explain why I hate scenes. And confrontation. I've had enough to last a lifetime. I had to accept erratic behavior from my mother. I accepted it from Dennis. But this seesawing we've been doing over Louemma's lessons isn't something I have to put up with. It's got to stop. Otherwise, I won't be able to continue teaching her, no matter how much you or anyone pleads."

"Okay! Believe it or not, I understand." Alan closed his eyes and pinched his nose between finger and thumb. He opened his eyes slowly. The truth is, I dislike arguments and face-offs as well. My parents couldn't be in the same room for more than ten minutes without Mom blowing up at Dad. Retreating or conciliation is how I handle situations I can't control. So there you have it. Both sets of cards are on the table."

"That does explain a lot." Laurel eyed him obliquely. "No more sneaking up on me, either. You have no idea how difficult I find situations that cause even a moment's panic. It doesn't matter that doctors have told me that my mother's disorder usually isn't inherited. The worry is always hanging over me."

"Listen to the doctors," he said. "You know, you have a lot of guts, Laurel. It sounds to me as if you were literally the adult in the house from the age of ten. And maybe your mother was always ill. I'm told she caused quite a stir in Ridge City."

"Alan, you said your parents argued a lot. Did they ever fight over anything to do with my mother?"

"This is déjà vu. Rose Robinson, Louemma's tutor, and I had that very discussion yesterday." He shifted uncomfortably on the narrow bench seat. It was one thing to reveal his own shortcomings, quite another to air his parents'.

Laurel noted his hesitancy. "Remember that album of Hazel's I found?" She slipped out of the breakfast nook. "I'll show you." Rushing off to the bedroom, she came back with the leather-bound volume. Setting it in front of Alan, she thumbed to the page where Vestal—and pages later, Hazel—showed off their pregnancies. "Take a look at the pictures from here on. See what you think."

He did, seeing Lucy Bell for the first time. "Outside of being blond, you don't look much like your mom," he said as he examined a teenaged Lucy. "You're much prettier."

Laurel blushed and glanced away. "Lucy and Mark Ridge spent a lot of time together."

"Mmm. According to Rose, they were raised like brother and sister. Until, as she put it, 'Lucy went wild.'"

"Became rebellious, you mean?"

"I suppose that was the implication. There was apparently a furor over her dating an older man, a guy who worked at the distillery. Rose said Lucy was stubborn. She indicated that my dad even quit being her friend some months before she ran off."

"How many months?"

He frowned. "Pardon?"

"When did their relationship dissolve?"

"I wasn't there. Five or six months, I guess. Evidently Ted and Hazel expected Mark Ridge to track Lucy down and bring her back. He didn't. He and my mom got married right around then." On their horseback ride, he'd already told Laurel his mother had left school and his father went on to college. "Vestal remembered that Ashline was the name of the man Lucy Bell left town with."

"Then it would seem I'm probably an Ashline and not a Ridge."

"Wh…at?" Alan let the album flop closed. "But that would make us—you and me—" He broke off with a dumbfounded shake of his head. "Why would you even *think* anything so preposterous?"

Laurel sighed and clasped her arms around the book. "Maybe hope on my part that one parent, at least, wasn't a disaster." She sighed. "Lucy went by the name Ashline. I know she would've said if he wasn't my real dad."

Alan relaxed again. He'd worried for a minute that Hazel had made up a tale to establish a different kind of validity for filing squatter's rights. But Alan thought Laurel would say as much, since they were shaking out the skeletons in their respective closets. "You turned out okay," he said offhandedly.

"Well, thank you."

"A little too skinny, maybe," he teased when it became clear his remark had embarrassed her. "Is it any wonder, if this is your usual supper?"

"Haven't you heard that women can never be too thin or too rich?" She wrinkled her nose at him. "Weavers are never rich, so I figure one out of two is the best I can ever do."

"Kidding aside. Like I said, if you want the real facts on your family, you need to come talk to my grandmother." He held up his hands, palms out. "I know what you're going to say about our shady occupation. But the house is set totally apart from the distillery. We don't force our product on any guest, I promise."

Laurel wavered. She couldn't say he wasn't making his invitation more tempting every time he issued it. She'd driven past the Ridge estate a few times. She wouldn't be female if she didn't wonder how someone whose ancestors had founded an entire town lived. She herself had existed pretty much hand to mouth, even after her marriage.

"Is that indecision I see in your eyes? Trust me, Laurel. You don't want to play poker. Your expression gives you away."

Looking disgusted, she pulled the meat and cheese out of her sandwich and fed the slices to Dog. Closing the bread back over the lettuce and tomato, she bit into what was left.

"Come on," he wheedled, in much the same fashion he employed to get Louemma to eat more at mealtimes. "We'll feed you a hot meal. Grandmother would come here, but she's still stove up from that spill she took in the garden."

"I don't know."

He leaned back and tucked his thumbs under his belt. "So what do you say? Have I convinced you?"

"Can't you just be happy I've decided to continue Louemma's lessons? And that reminds me—you've got to quit hovering at her lessons. I'll provide regular updates on her progress."

"I thought we'd agreed I could sit through today's lesson."

"Yes, but you didn't sit. You interfered. Unintentionally, but you broke Louemma's concentration. Success is all about focus, Alan."

"Well, I sure pray it works. All right, Laurel. You have my solemn word." Alan rose and extended a hand.

Laurel slid her hand into his, again suffering a jolt like the one that had occurred before the start of the lesson, when their fingers had accidentally brushed. Drawing back, she crossed her arms in an effort to act casual as they walked toward the door. Dog, who'd been snoozing in the corner, bounded over to say goodbye.

Alan rubbed the animal's sides. "Too bad I can't clone you, boy."

"You could get Louemma her own dog. The shelter has plenty to choose from. I'd recommend an older one. Or a cat. One content to sit on her lap. It might encourage her to begin flexing her fingers more."

"I'll consider it. Thanks for your understanding, Laurel. And…" He hesitated. "I wish your childhood had been nicer."

"Thanks. But you know, it wasn't all bad. When Mom worked, we spent weekends in the park. She splurged on movies and ice cream."

They lingered on the porch a moment, chatting about how big and bright the moon happened to be right then.

Laurel looked especially pretty bathed in moonlight. Alan had to make a conscious effort to not blurt out that comment. He hadn't supposed he'd ever want to venture into the relationship market again. Particularly since his marriage had been less than he'd hoped for. He wasn't even sure how it'd broken down so completely, or exactly.

"Well, I won't keep you any longer," Laurel murmured, beginning to rub her arms to keep warm.

Alan jerked himself out of the daze he'd fallen into, and realized he must have been standing there gaping at her for some time. As well as contemplating the demise of his marriage, he'd entertained a couple of lust-filled thoughts about Laurel. She had the kind of body he admired. And since he was slowly emerging from a self-imposed isolation, there was no denying there were *some* things a normal male missed, no matter how much he tried not to. "So long," he said, probably sounding a whole lot gruffer than he wanted to.

He left quickly then. Before he did something foolish that would ruin everything. Like kiss Laurel. Or— He shook his head. He could chalk this feeling up to moon madness.

On the drive home, though, he spent a lot of time analyzing why Laurel was the woman to lure him out of his shell. Emily had had beauty-queen perfection. Everyone said so. And she'd spent hours in salons and spas to ensure she didn't lose that beauty.

Laurel had probably never been inside a spa. She wasn't a classic beauty. Until she smiled. Then her face lit up from the inside. Louemma and Dog were on the receiving end of most of her smiles; now he'd figured that out, Alan knew he'd have to concoct ways to share in the wealth.

THE TWO DAYS between Louemma's classes crawled by for Alan, in spite of the fact that he had plenty to do at the distillery and in the office. Louemma cleaned her plate at breakfast, unheard of in the past.

"Nana, you'd really like Laurel and Dog. I know it. Daddy likes them, don't you?"

Since Laurel was frequently on Alan's mind, the question jarred him.

Vestal glanced up from pouring orange juice. "Alan, why haven't you brought Laurel around yet? Yesterday Millie Honeycutt stopped by to see if we wanted to donate the usual four bottles of our special reserve to the Hill'n Holler Art Festival this fall. She said she's been trying to contact her."

Ignoring the references to Laurel, Alan said, "Have Hardy set aside what you need. Did you put the festival dates on my calendar? He'll need them on his, as well."

"It's in late September. Hardy came over last night, so we did coordinate dates. Were you aware that the plans to have the new mash bins operational so we can set our first open house to coincide with the festival's fall flower tour?"

Alan held a forkful of scrambled egg halfway to his mouth. "Who decided that? Even if we had all the permits, which we don't, that'd be pushing it."

"Hardy doesn't think so. He's all pumped up. All the Kentucky distilleries are linking up in a single brochure to promote a tasting tour like wineries do."

"It's not that I don't think it's a good idea. My question is, why are we just hearing about the plans now? Shouldn't it be a board decision?"

"Hardy more or less said you'd been too distracted, Alan. First in running Louemma all over the state to various doctors. And now with Ms. Ashline. Oh, by the way, I promised Millie you'd ask Laurel about donating one of her chenille shawls to the auction. I haven't seen them because I've been housebound, but Millie bought one at the Craft Corner and she was full of raves."

Shoving back from the table, Alan stood. "If you need me this morning, I'll be at the distillery. Between us, Grandmother, we own the controlling shares in Windridge. Hardy shouldn't make arbitrary decisions of any sort without talking to us."

Vestal seemed surprised. "Isn't that why we promoted him after you got too busy and I decided to retire?"

"Have I neglected the business?"

She nodded, then looked sheepish. "I'm not blaming you, but in this past year you've let a lot of things go. Our night watchman sees you wandering the warehouse in the wee hours. And our official taster called the other day to see if you were on a six-month leave. It all adds up."

"Come on! I leave notes after I've checked the barrels. Joe's just pulling your chain, Vestal."

She gave a halfhearted shrug. Alan stalked out, only taking time to drop a kiss on Louemma's nose. "I'll be home to drive you to your lesson with Laurel, honeybee."

It was a promise he barely kept. He wheeled in at 4:39 and took the porch steps two at a time. "Ah good, I see Birdie has you ready to go, Louemma. Sorry I'm running so slow. What's that?" Alan pointed to a sack sitting on Louemma's lap.

"Nana helped Birdie make spice cake today. She fixed an extra one for Ms. Ashline. Daddy, may I call her Laurel?"

"Ask her. Nana must be feeling better if she's up to puttering around in the kitchen."

"Birdie complained all morning to Miss Robinson." Louemma mimicked the older woman's gruff manner. "She said when *that woman* takes a notion to prepare for comp'ny, she's like a whirling dervish. What's a dervish, Daddy? It's not in my talking dictionary."

"It's a term that describes someone working in a frenzy. Like a whirlwind. People can't be whirlwinds, but it makes a good description. You know Birdie likes order. She's big on removing clutter. And Nana Vestal is big on collecting…everything. Uh, out of curiosity, what company are we preparing for?" he asked, stowing Louemma in the Jeep.

"Laurel. Birdie says there's a special note with the spice cake. 'Cause Nana thinks you're stalling instead of inviting Laurel over. Daddy, what does stalling mean?"

"Something I'm not doing. I explained numerous times that I did invite Laurel, but she's too busy to come. Why can't Vestal take me at my word?"

The nine-year-old wisely watched the passing scenery, saying nothing.

When they arrived at Laurel's, she had all the doors and windows at the loom cottage standing wide open.

"Hi," she greeted them gaily. "Isn't this a glorious day? We can hear the birds singing and the bees buzzing while we work."

Dog loped up out of the woods. He shook off twigs caught in his coat, and ran inside immediately to grab his toy bone. Heading straight for Louemma, he deposited the toy in her lap, on top of the sack. Dog pawed her knee gently, then snuffled the bag that held the cake. The girl giggled. "Dog remembers me. He remembers who brought him the bone."

"He wants to play, but today you're going to work, young lady. Tell your father goodbye. He has other things to do." Laurel's gaze lit pointedly on Alan.

He rescued the spice cake before Dog took it in his head to have a snack. Handing the bag to Laurel with a flourish, he said dryly, "The other women in my life send you gifts. I swear it's not my doing, but you need to prepare yourself for the fact that they're plying you with goodies because they feel

I've fallen down on my job as the Ridge family host. Vestal's decided to issue you a dinner invitation by courier."

For a second Laurel resembled a guppy hunting food. But she recovered and passed Alan the sack. "Whatever they've chosen as bait smells delicious. If you're availing yourself of my patio, do you mind dropping this off in the kitchen?"

"You're not even going to read the note so I can bring home an answer?"

"Later. Now, vamoose."

"What's vamoose?" Louemma asked, her eyes moving between the adults.

"It means I'm leaving right *now,*" Alan drawled. "Ladies, have fun. Mm-mmm, this does smell good. It may not make it to your kitchen."

"It had better," Laurel warned, hollering out the door after him.

"Daddy's teasing," Louemma said solemnly. "I think he likes you, Laurel. Oh, I'm supposed to ask if I can call you that, 'cause it's disrespectful otherwise."

Laurel's brain had stuck on Louemma's pronouncement that Alan liked her. "Er…up north, kids often call adults by their first names. You may call me Laurel, if you like. I already gave Jenny and Brenna permission."

"I'll tell Daddy you said okay. 'Cause Nana Vestal is a stick—uh, stickler for manners," she said in a rush.

Laurel noticed with interest that the whole time the girl nattered on, her fingers were kneading Dog's fur. "Louemma, I've really been looking forward to our lesson. Yesterday I had a brainstorm. I prepared a special loom for you." Wheeling her across the room, she then connected a lap loom to the arms of the chair. Skeins of yarn sat in a basket that hung over her legs. The handle on a much longer shuttle bumped Louemma's limp right hand.

"This chain operates the beater bar," Laurel explained. "I've seen you petting Dog, so I know your fingers work. What you have to remember is that weaving should be fun. Do what you can, when you can. No pressure. No rush."

Laurel guided the girl through several rows until she got the hang of how the converted loom worked.

"Look," Louemma exclaimed. "I have four rows, and they look 'xactly like the ones Jenny and Brenna made."

Her smile was reward enough for Laurel. "That's right, hon. You're making cloth. It's the same process over and over. Now, you try a row on your own. I have some work to do. I'll be pulling spools off the spinning mule and loading them on the skein winder. Right there." She pointed to an apparatus some ten feet away.

Laurel didn't know if Louemma would even try it by herself. For approximately fifteen minutes, she didn't, and Laurel worried that her experiment had failed. But darn it, she'd pored over Louemma's medical records. Each and every doctor Alan had taken her to said there was no physical nerve damage. None. Her block was mental. And it would stay in place until something induced her to want to break out. Which they all hoped would be weaving. But maybe it wouldn't happen. Or maybe…yes. Laurel darted another glance. Unless her eyes were playing tricks, Louemma's fingers had begun to move on the shuttle. Yes! Laurel wanted to fling her arms in the air and dance a heel-clicking frolic around the room. Instead, she pretended not to notice and continued to empty the spinning mule.

After a while, a knock startled her and her pupil. Alan stood framed in the open door. Twilight shadows had replaced the warm May sun. "Hey, this half hour lesson should've ended forty minutes ago."

"Daddy, Daddy, come see," Louemma cried. The shuttle slipped from her hand and struck the metal footrest of her chair. Dog flattened his belly against the floor, crawled under the loom and retrieved the shuttle as Laurel had watched him do dozens of times throughout the lesson.

Alan crossed to his daughter's side. His eyes widened. "Laurel wove these rows, right?"

Dumping a lapful of spools into a bushel basket, she slid off her stool and walked over to inspect the project. "Wow, Louemma. Great job! I helped weave the first few rows," she said, hugging her student. "She's done four on her own."

Louemma's eyes were shining. "I did. I did it by myself. Well," she admitted, "Dog helped. I dropped the shuttle a million times maybe. He picked it up and gave it back to me each time, didn't you, boy?"

Laurel was surprised to see tears glinting in Alan's eyes. Or perhaps it wasn't so surprising, given his great love for his child. The sight touched her more than she was prepared for, however.

Alan found it hard to control the range of emotions he felt just then. Louemma's bright smile felled him. Closing his eyes, he sank to his knees and enfolded her and the dog in a hug that had both recipients struggling for release. "I can't help it," he mumbled time and again as Louemma said he was squishing her. "Damn, but this calls for a celebration." Scrambling up, he checked his watch, and ignored the fact that Louemma scolded him for swearing.

Laurel tried to discreetly wipe away her own joyous tears. But when she noticed the moisture gathering in Louemma's eyes, she gave up, knelt opposite where Alan stood, and cried with the little girl. "It's a start," she murmured. "Sweetie, your back and arms will ache tonight. You used muscles you haven't used in quite a while. Alan," she instructed, gazing into his still-stunned face, "do you understand what I'm saying? She may be wakeful. May need her muscles rubbed."

He reached for Laurel's hands, rose with her and danced her around the room. "Come home with us. We'll have Birdie prepare a proper feast. And you can take a gander in our medicine cabinet to see what lotions and potions will work on Louemma's muscles."

"It's Birdie's night off," Louemma reminded her dad. "And Mrs. Honeycutt's taking Nana to the Hill'n Holler planning meeting tonight. It's a potluck at the Methodist church. You were supposed to ask Laurel if she'd donate a scarf, remember? Nana knew you'd forget."

"What's this about a donation?"

"A local festival. Something town patrons came up with to get in on the tourist trade that descends on our area during the fall foliage tour. It's not until late September. We've got the rest of spring and summer to go before they need your donation. I just assumed I had plenty of time to work up to asking you."

"I'll be glad to donate a scarf. See how easy that was, Alan?"

"Okay, but that still doesn't solve our celebration problem. Come home with us anyway. I'll cook. Birdie will have left something for us to pop in the oven."

"Alan, I know you're bound and determined to get me to visit Windridge. I will. I'm...just not ready yet. But if you two are really on your own tonight, why not let me feed you? We'll share that great-smelling cake. Unless you gobbled it up as you threatened."

Alan seemed unsure now that the offer had been made. "How does eating here sound to you, Louemma?" He hesitated because she hated to eat in front of strangers. Lunchtime at school had been one of the deciding reasons for home-schooling her.

"Does Dog get to be at your table, Laurel? Oh, Daddy, she said I could call her that."

"He doesn't as a rule, Louemma. I suppose I could make an exception tonight in honor of your accomplishment."

"Okay. Can we have chicken'n dumplings? Birdie fixes that when it's my birthday."

"Louemma," Alan cautioned. "When someone's nice

enough to invite you to dinner, you don't put in a request. Laurel's not running a restaurant."

"Well…I may just be able to manage chicken and dumplings. I roasted a chicken the day before yesterday. It won't take any time at all to prepare everything else. Although I'm sure Birdie probably makes fluffier biscuits. I never quite got the hang of making light biscuit dough."

"I wouldn't have guessed you cooked at all," Alan said as he helped her close the windows and lock up.

"How did you suppose I ate?"

"That didn't come out right," he said. "I just meant you're busier than any woman I know." Their eyes connected briefly over Louemma's head, his brimming with admiration, hers unreadable.

She led the way down the path, but turned to walk backward to check the others' progress.

More relaxed than he'd felt in longer than he could remember, Alan playfully grabbed Laurel and held her so she wouldn't trip and fall. The path was engulfed in shadows, making the light unpredictable. He discovered enough to worry about her. Now, if he could figure out a way to steal a kiss…

Laurel chatted easily with Louemma once they went inside, less so with Alan.

He sat back at first, apparently content to listen. But on more than one occasion he chimed in, and the conversation grew increasingly amicable—and interesting. Laurel was impressed that he was so well versed on a such wide range of subjects. Plus, he seemed genuinely interested in what she said. Dennis, even when he was sober, usually wanted absolute silence during meals so he could watch sports.

Only after Louemma yawned loudly, and Laurel and Alan turned to see her nodding off, were they ready to end the evening.

Laurel sprang out of her chair and began gathering up leftovers. "Would you look at the time? Nearly nine. I can't think what's gotten into me. I haven't offered to cut your grandmother's cake, nor made a move to fix you coffee."

Alan studied Louemma with an appraising eye. "Save the cake for our next visit. Freeze it. Or go ahead and eat it. We'll ask Vestal and Birdie to make another, won't we, Louemma?" He'd already risen out of deference to his hostess.

His ingrained manners were also something Laurel needed to get used to. The more time she spent around Alan Ridge, the more she realized had been missing in her marriage. Now she wondered how she'd let herself be so blind as to fall in love with Dennis Shaw.

"I should offer to help wash dishes," Alan said, casting a worried glance between Laurel and Louemma.

"Don't be silly. Louemma's had a tiring afternoon. I hope you and your grandmother appreciate how much effort it took her to make the progress she has."

"I do, and she will. Vestal always had the faith I lacked. How can I ever thank you, Laurel?"

"It's a tiny beginning, Alan." She picked up an empty plate and the soup tureen, and from motions she made with her head, he got the message that she wanted a word with him alone.

"I'll be right back," he told Louemma. He stacked the remaining bowls and hurried after Laurel.

"You have something to say that Louemma shouldn't hear?"

"Yes. I want to prepare you for the possibility that her next lesson could be a setback. At the hospital, patients don't all keep making strides forward. Sometimes it's one step forward and three steps back."

"I hadn't thought of that." As Laurel gestured with her hands, Alan found it easy to capture them and kiss her knuckles.

She snatched them back. "Why did you do that?"

"I felt like it. Your hands wrought magic with my daughter. A kiss expresses something words can't convey. I saw the engineering you did on the loom. You gave Louemma a positive experience today." He ran his palms lightly up and down her arms. "I'm truly and profoundly grateful, Laurel."

A shivery joy seemed to spring from his fingertips and settle warmly in Laurel's abdomen, stirring desire—something she'd assumed was long dead. Because it felt so natural, she edged closer to Alan and placed her hands flat against his chest. "You're more than welcome. Louemma's a wonderful child. Keep fighting, Alan."

He couldn't deny the tug on his senses, which urged his head closer to Laurel's inviting lips. It was more than gratitude he felt. And he was a millimeter away from an honest-to-God kiss when Louemma's plaintive call made them spring apart.

"I have to go," he said reluctantly. "Please, though—tomorrow night, join us for dinner. Six o'clock?"

"Yes," Laurel murmured.

It wasn't until her guests had gone that she wondered how Alan had persuaded her to agree. Still, she couldn't be too upset. Not when they'd shared something so precious with Louemma. Not when Alan had almost kissed her. She'd *wanted* his kiss, and that shocked her most of all. She felt an urge to see him in his own surroundings. An urge to discover whether these feelings were only a spell cast by a big Kentucky moon.

CHAPTER TEN

LAUREL MADE IT A HABIT to be on time. Dennis's drinking had caused them to be late a lot, or to cancel at the last minute. Tonight, ten minutes before the appointed dinner hour at Windridge Estates, she sat at the end of their winding lane, pondering whether to stay, or leave and make up an excuse. She'd gotten good at fashioning excuses while she was married. Now her sweaty palms felt slippery on the steering wheel. Was she dressed okay? Would the woman she'd met at the hospital see at a glance that Lucy Bell's daughter didn't fit in here?

The stone structure on the hill must have come straight from Laurel's childhood fantasies. White pillars supported a full balcony. Three cupolas added old-world charm. Growing up, she'd whiled away hours imagining her adult self as a wife and mother in a fairy-tale house like the one her mom had described in maudlin moments. It resembled exactly the home Laurel faced, telling her that her mother had probably longed for Kentucky.

Laurel sat there so long remembering that when she glanced up, she saw Alan Ridge charging downhill on foot. He wasn't wearing a suit as she'd expected. In fact, he looked the same as he did on days he brought Louemma for lessons. Now Laurel worried she might be overdressed.

Chest heaving, he jogged up to her pickup and knocked on the window. "Did you run out of gas?" he asked as she cranked down the window.

"I ran out of nerve."

"That's what I was afraid of. Move over. I'll drive from here."

"No, I will." She latched on to the door he'd opened, and tugged it shut. "I need to stop being—well, I'm okay now, Alan."

"Cold feet gone?"

"Let's say they're warmer."

"Good. I'm still hitching a ride. I hate to admit it, but I'm getting too old to do hundred-yard sprints."

She raised her eyebrows. "My mama lectured me about never picking up strange men."

He stepped up on her running board. "Drive. If I walk around to the passenger side it'd be just like you to leave me here."

"I wouldn't. Only…how will this look to—to your grandmother?"

"She's used to me, Laurel. Take off, before I lose my grip."

She did, creeping up the hill. What if his grandmother watched this sideshow from one of those massive, mullioned windows? What would she think?

Apparently Vestal Ridge had better things to do. The couple entered a house that might well have been empty.

"We're here!" Alan's booming voice ricocheted around the vast marble entry.

Laurel gaped up at a glittering chandelier that cast a prism of rainbows on gilt-edge mirrors flanking a polished, antique pedestal table. She tripped on the threshold and almost fell flat.

Alan caught her elbow in time. "Don't let the foyer intimidate you," he murmured with a grin. "The Ridge who built this house greeted business clients here before he hustled them on up to the distillery. This, and the old office up there, are the estate's grandest rooms."

Louemma peeked around a corner. "Where's Dog?"

"Oh, hi, honey. He's at home."

The girl disappeared, but Laurel wished she'd stayed. She was guilty of gawking as Alan ushered her down the hall. She admired what she saw of polished cherry floors and wainscoting in what probably was the living room. They crossed into an impressive dining room with high ceilings, filled with French provincial antiques of the type Laurel coveted.

Suddenly, the woman she'd met at the hospital appeared, pushing through an adjacent French door. Perfectly set white hair softened the lines of her face. "Forever more, Alan, dinner's ready. Why were you lollygagging? And where's Louemma?"

"I'll fetch her," Alan said.

He left, and Laurel wanted to snatch him back, but Vestal was extending an age-spotted hand, its slenderness set off by a sparkling dinner ring. "Welcome to Windridge. Honestly, men have so little common sense at times. Oh, what a pretty suit. Red becomes you, my dear. Your grandmother was partial to red, too. Come to think of it, you remind me of her as a girl." Her voice cracked.

Laurel saw a vulnerability in the faded eyes she hadn't expected. Before she had time to think about it much, Alan returned, Louemma at his side. Laurel realized she'd never seen Louemma take more than a step on her own.

"I wanted you to bring Dog," she said, eyebrows lowered, lips pouting.

Laurel smiled. "Honey, he's home doing his duty as a guard dog. You'll see him Monday at your lesson."

"But I want to see him *now*. He'll be lonesome. You and Daddy go get him." The child kicked a foot against the table leg.

Not knowing what to say, Laurel deferred to Alan. He spoke rationally to Louemma, reinforcing Laurel's words, but was interrupted by a woman wearing a ruffled apron backing into the room through a swinging door. She set a steaming roast on the table, along with a dish of creamed peas. "What's all this fuss, missy-lou? Birdie can't have you feeding her crown roast to no dog."

Alan introduced Laurel to the short, plump woman of indeterminate age.

Before Birdie bustled out again, Laurel felt thoroughly vetted. No one seemed bothered by the fact that the housekeeper shook salt over her shoulder and set the shaker back on the table. Or that she engineered the seating to suit herself, which included moving a pedestal holding a vase of flowers from the corner between Alan's and Laurel's chairs to the other side of the room. Already shaken by Louemma's sulking, Laurel was glad when Alan carved slices of meat and laid one on her plate.

Vestal passed her the peas, followed by a bowl of red potatoes. "Thank you," Laurel murmured. "I trust Alan's told you how excited we all were yesterday to see Louemma weave several rows without my help."

Alan dished up peas for his daughter and mashed her potatoes. "A fork handle is shaped like the shuttle Laurel fashioned for you, honeybee. Show Nana how you can close your fingers around something solid."

The girl flatly refused. She tightened her lips against a spoonful of peas Alan lifted to her mouth. She balked at everything and began crying for Dog.

The more Alan tried, the louder and more uncooperative Louemma became. Finally, he slid back his chair. "Please excuse us. I think Louemma will be happier in a time-out."

Laurel felt bad for both Alan and Louemma. She hoped her visit wasn't the cause.

The whole time Alan was gone, Vestal fussed and fretted about the medical profession's failure to cure Louemma. The old woman seemed frailer than Laurel had judged her to be at the hospital.

Even after Alan returned and took his seat as if this there wasn't a problem, Laurel thought the meal was a disaster.

At one point he leaned over and whispered, "Relax. Kids

are quick to explode and as quick to make up. Louemma will ask for something when she gets hungry."

Laurel smiled feebly.

Vestal, who hadn't eaten much, placed her silverware on her plate and turned to Laurel. "I suppose Alan told you I didn't know Hazel exhibited her crafts over in Berea. Not until her funeral. As girls, she and I were inseparable. And during our early married years. Then we…took different paths. I regret that. I hope you'll consider our home yours while you're visiting Kentucky."

"Oh, that's kind of you, Mrs. Ridge, but…I'm not visiting."

"Please, call me Vestal." She fixed her attention on a napkin she'd begun to pleat and fold. "I'll never understand why Hazel felt the need to go behind our backs and file for that land. My door was always open to her."

"File for what land?" Laurel asked politely.

"Grandmother." Alan reached across the table and stilled Vestal's nervous fingers. "I promised Laurel a stress-free evening. Why don't you tell her about some of the great times you and Hazel did share? Laurel never met her grandmother, remember?"

Laurel sent a questioning glance between the two, sensing an undercurrent of tension. A moment passed in silence.

Alan probably didn't want her to hear anything negative about Hazel, as she had so few memories as it was. Undoubtedly the women's falling out made it hard for Vestal to talk about their happier days. Laurel watched her tug her thin hand from under Alan's. Her eyes cleared and she launched into stories Laurel had difficulty concentrating on.

Nevertheless, she forced a smile, and picked at the food remaining on her plate. As the evening wound down, so did Vestal. In a last-ditch attempt to salvage the night, the old woman turned to Alan. "It's a shame Birdie's meal went begging. So Laurel's trip isn't a total waste of her time, Alan, take her on a tour of the distillery. People are always hounding us for private tours," she said to Laurel, then rose with visible stiffness, adding, "I'll go check on Louemma." Unhooking a cane from the back of her chair, she patted Laurel's shoulder in passing. "We must get together soon, my dear."

Alan had risen from his chair, but as he prepared to sit again, he noticed Laurel folding her napkin. He tossed his haphazardly onto his plate. "I guarantee you'll find a tour of the distillery more stimulating than tonight's meal," he said, trying to break the tension.

Laurel jumped up. "No, thank you. I can't. You know that, Alan. Please tell Birdie my poor appetite had nothing to do with her cooking."

"At least stay for coffee."

"It's better if I leave. Maybe Louemma will come out and eat." Without further ado, Laurel all but ran from the house.

Not sure how the evening had fallen apart so fast, Alan heard her engine start. Hurrying to the front door, he threw it open in time to see the pickup disappear into a low fog that had rolled in. Swearing, he dawdled on the porch until he heard Birdie demanding to know where everyone had gone. Sighing, he went back to explain.

Emily had been prone to outbursts. Even as a grown woman she'd thrown tantrums at the least provocation. He could still effect a change in Louemma through consistent discipline. But did he want *another* volatile woman in his life?

The answer came from somewhere deep inside. No, but Laurel hadn't thrown a tantrum. The evening had been uncomfortable for her, and she had reasons for not touring the distillery. And therein lay the real problem. Bourbon was his livelihood.

LOUEMMA'S FIRST LESSON following the unsuccessful dinner began with both the girl and Laurel keyed up. However,

Louemma apologized, and her pleasure at being with Dog softened Laurel. And the girl added three more rows by the end of her half-hour class, which set things back on an even keel.

"Will you ask Daddy if I can stay longer?" she begged Laurel, who hesitated.

"Honey, I don't want you to overdo it. Let's put the project aside for now. We'll go down to the house and ask your dad about lengthening your time next Wednesday."

"Okay. Can we eat here again? Dog wants me to stay."

Laughing, Laurel agreed, provided Alan approved that, too.

"Louemma Ridge," he gasped. "I can't believe you invited yourself to dinner! There's no excuse tonight. I happen to know Birdie and Nana are both home, waiting for us."

"Call them. They won't care," the girl said unrepentantly. "Laurel said it's okay."

She nodded because, in truth, the prospect of having company this evening appealed to her. Dennis had called twice the night before. His slurred commentary had left her feeling out of sorts. If it weren't for the fact that his calls were so erratic and many of her clients phoned her in the evenings, she'd ask the phone company to rewire the cottage with phones she could unplug. Still, she'd been told there'd be a hefty charge for rewiring. She'd placed it way down on her list.

"If you're sure we're not being pests," Alan said, "I'll call Vestal."

Laurel directed him to the phone that sat on her kitchen counter. Then she left him to go rummage in the fridge. "Louemma, do you like ham and cheese omelettes?" she called.

"And biscuits?" the girl yelled back from the living room. "I liked your biscuits. So did Daddy. He thinks you're a good cook."

Laurel felt a curl of warmth in her stomach. "Okay, biscuits and an omelette."

Alan hung up, smiling contentedly as he listened to their banter. The phone rang almost immediately. Without thinking, he lifted it and said, "Hello." Then he jerked the phone away from his ear as a man swore nastily. Alan recognized the voice.

So did Laurel. She straightened and the block of cheese slipped from her hand.

Taking a deep breath, she reached out to take the phone.

Alan gave a firm shake of his head. "This is Alan Ridge. I'm a friend of Laurel's. No, I won't put her on the line. Not until you can speak civilly. Same to you, bud." Grimacing, Alan dropped the receiver back in the cradle. He leaned down and picked up the plastic-wrapped block of cheese.

"Was he horrid?" she asked, placing the cheese on a wooden cutting board and peeling off the wrap.

"I have a friend, an old college roommate, who works in management at the phone company. Let me ask if there's something you can do short of unplugging your phone."

"I can't even do that. I gather it wasn't cost-effective for phone companies to change backwoods phones when they switched to plug-in ones in the cities. Now, they rewire in the country only if you need other work done. But I've ordered caller ID. The calls have increased, and after you suggested it before, I put in a request. It's a matter of the work order catching up to whoever installs out here."

"That's a relief. I hope it's soon and that it helps. Where are your plates? I'll set the table."

Alan expected her drunken ex to phone again. So did Laurel. Throughout the meal, she watched the phone as one might watch a snake. She could have turned off the ringer, but she was expecting a call from a client and was afraid to miss it.

While they ate, Alan introduced as many lighthearted subjects as he could think of to distract her. When they'd finished, he was strangely reluctant to say goodbye. But Louemma needed to get home. She was the one who caught him—and Laurel—off guard.

"I wish I had a weaving lesson every day, Daddy. I'm teaching Dog to do tricks. If I was here more, he'd remember them better."

"Every day isn't possible in my schedule. We could add a Friday class, though," Laurel said, surprising herself as well as Alan.

"Fine with me." He was quick to agree.

"Okay. Same time? If you like, we can have dinner, too—until you guys get sick of my cooking. Eating alone gets…well, old," she admitted, giving away another of her closely guarded secrets.

Delighted, Alan elaborated on her suggestion. "If Louemma continues to improve, we could go out once in a while." He noticed that neither Laurel nor Louemma jumped at his offer. Which was all right. Louemma was still uncomfortable about restaurants and, oddly enough, she ate more here than at home.

The three of them and Dog lingered a moment on the porch. Suddenly Laurel said, "I almost forgot my other news. My mare's going to have a baby. The man who sold her to me in February said it was possible she'd gotten with his stallion accidentally. He asked if it'd be a problem for me. Of course I was excited. Anyway, she's exhibiting the signs he told me to watch for. The vet came yesterday to do an ultrasound and he confirmed it. Do you want to see her before you take off? I think she may be getting pudgy even though the vet laughed at me. He said horses don't show that early."

Alan followed Laurel down the steps. They were turning toward the corral when all at once Louemma burst into tears. Real tears, not phony ones.

"Ohmigod," Laurel whispered. "I forgot she's scared of horses. Louemma, sweetie," she crooned, returning to kneel and gather the distraught girl in her arms. "You don't have to visit Cinnabar. Shh. Alan?" she implored.

He scooped the girl off the steps. Then, for whatever reason, he leaned over and brushed a light kiss on Laurel's trembling lips. "Don't fret. She'll recover. These reactions are something I've never fully explored with Marv Fulton, our family doctor. I'll phone him. So, we'll see you same time, same station on Friday? Or maybe I'll see you sooner," he called softly over his shoulder.

She traced her tongue over her lips and watched them drive off. A lot had changed in their relationship in a relatively short time, but she almost wasn't sure that she hadn't imagined the kiss. Yet he tasted of the mint he'd swiped from her candy bowl after dinner.

A few hours later, it didn't altogether surprise her when a knock sounded at the door to her loom cottage. She opened straight away, knowing it was Alan. "Is Louemma all right?" she asked promptly.

"Yes, but she took a long time to settle. I have to admit that neither Vestal nor I can shed any light on Louemma's dread of horses. Her actions make even less sense when you consider how devoted she is to Dog." Alan rubbed the dark muzzle as he greeted the animal. "I didn't come back to talk about Louemma," he said, straightening. Bumping the door closed, he picked up both of Laurel's hands.

"Dennis hasn't phoned again if you're worried about that," Laurel said, not letting herself think about the prickles of awareness skittering along her nerves.

"You know why I've come again. You feel it, too," Alan said in a voice that wasn't completely steady. "I can't explain our mutual attraction, but we both know it's there."

She nodded and bit down hard on her bottom lip.

"Listen…" Alan took her gingerly in his arms. He cupped a hand around the back of her soft hair and pressed her cheek to his chest, aware that she'd feel his rapid heartbeat. "I'm not very adept at this." He chuckled a little. "A man probably shouldn't admit to falling down in that area, huh?"

"I don't mind. I'm not ready to…leap into another relationship." She leaned back. "Oh—you never said anything about wanting a relationship. I just meant—"

"Hush." He kissed her, taking his time to simply savor her lips. When at last they drew apart, Alan gently combed his fingers through Laurel's silky hair. "I want, all right! I know you can tell." Again, he laughed. "I guess I'm trying to say I'm not falling down that much. I *want* the whole nine yards, including bed. Bank on it, Laurel. But…I'm okay with taking our time. We need to let things build naturally."

Her breath trickled out. "I'd like that, Alan." She ran exploratory fingers up and down the soft cotton of his shirtfront, pausing to brush a well-manicured nail across button after button.

Tightening his arms, Alan lifted her feet off the floor. "Much more of that, and I can honestly say the natural progression's gonna be drastically cut."

They traded soft kisses then, without words. It wasn't until Alan realized he'd backed Laurel flat against the door and they both needed breathing room that he eased his body away from hers. "Old as this building is, I'd say we're lucky we didn't plunge straight through the door," he joked.

"Umm." She licked tingling lips. "I'd say we're on the same road—and moving faster."

"Yeah. But I really didn't come with *that* in mind tonight—and I haven't even thought about protection for years."

"Protection?" Laurel's eyes widened appreciably. "Whatever must you think of me, Alan? Uh…it never entered my mind."

"Probably since we agreed to take it easy. I'm sure you would've thought of it if we'd gone further." He stood, massaging the back of his neck. "I'll take care of it. It's a good thing we didn't wait until we'd reached the eleventh hour."

She began righting her clothes. She couldn't believe the mess she was. How far she'd let things go—considering. Or maybe that was exactly the reason she'd lost control. In the past she'd always hated the smell of liquor on Dennis's breath. During the last three years of their marriage, she'd dodged his kisses and anything more intimate. "You probably wonder if I'm promiscuous," she ventured without turning.

"I wonder nothing of the sort." Alan wanted to touch her, but every line of her taut body told him not to. "Why would I think anything like that, Laurel?"

"Are you kidding? You're well-versed in my mother's history in this town."

"You aren't your mother. It sounds as if she was unhappy as well as ill. If your dad hadn't walked out, maybe she'd have been a different person. But then…maybe she wouldn't have had you. From my perspective, that would be a damn shame."

"Thanks. Living with her was hard. But she was all I had."

He'd walked over to inspect the loom Laurel had been working. "I obviously interrupted your evening work. This loom looks a thousand times more complicated than the ones you use to teach the kids. Do you mind letting me watch you weave?"

"I don't mind. Starting—or tying up—gets complicated. It's important to read each step of a pattern correctly. I keep the steps taped to the loom until a project is complete. Then it's simple to check that the colors are introduced at the proper places." She sat.

Dog, who'd paced constantly as they were kissing, flopped down near her foot pedals.

Alan dragged a chair to the other side so he wouldn't block her light.

Doing something routine with her still-shaky hands and legs allowed Laurel to relax. Work was soothing. Kissing

Alan Ridge wasn't. She began to toss both shuttles expertly through the warp threads, rattling the reeds—the metal rods that fit into the beater bar—once she'd developed a rhythm. After running eight or so lines, she lifted her head and smiled at Alan. He looked so serious.

"Say what you want, it seems damn difficult to me. I suspect if making cloth back in the pioneer days depended on men, nudist colonies would've come into fashion centuries ago."

"I'm sure the cold Kentucky winters had something to do with keeping the art alive here."

"Yes, but why carry on today? Not out of necessity."

"Not usually. Remember how you said bourbon making got passed down in your family? Hand weaving's like that. In fact, weavers refer to the process as 'passing it on.' The baton, the torch, whatever. If each weaver trains three others, the craft will never die."

"You like that idea, I can tell." Alan crossed his arms over his wide chest and stretched out his long legs, settling in to observe. "I'm sure you don't want to hear it, Laurel, but there's an art to making fine bourbon, too. At Windridge we don't bottle every batch. Not by a long shot. It's costly to toss out mistakes. But its our pride and our name out there on every bottle."

"I must be mellowing in my old age. I do understand what you're saying, Alan."

"Good. Great, in fact. If we're going to—you know—let what's between us go galloping forward—" He broke off.

"*If* we proceed, I think what you're trying to say is that I have to stop blaming you for Dennis Shaw's condition."

"Exactly. Can you do that?" Alan asked, sounding apprehensive.

"Why would you trust my judgment? Dennis's problem didn't become evident until after we'd met and married. At any rate, I failed to see any sign of it."

"Well, they say love is blind."

"Love. I can hardly remember back to when I loved Dennis."

Alan realized it was the same for him. In high school, he'd thought his feelings for Emily amounted to love. So long ago, and so much water under the bridge since then. But he couldn't speak of that to Laurel, or anyone. Maybe because his feelings were all wrapped up with a sense of failure. Lord knew he had flaws. He'd never expected Emily to be perfect. But still.

He roused himself suddenly. "I didn't tell anyone at home where I was going. Guess I'd better scoot back. If I'm needed, they'll think I've gone to the distillery."

"Oh. Don't let me detain you. I'm, uh, glad you came back." Laurel stopped weaving and blushed hotly.

He stood, and drew her up, too. Looping an arm around her shoulders, he ambled to the door. "There's one thing we shouldn't do. Be embarrassed to speak honestly."

"Oh, I couldn't agree more, Alan. Hardly anything is more important in any relationship than openness."

Alan thought for a minute that she was going to lock up and walk him to his Jeep. She didn't, and he was almost glad. He needed time to—what? Digest their exchange? *Maybe.* As of tonight, if they were keeping score, Laurel was several steps above him on the honesty scale. He'd catch up, he just needed time to get more comfortable talking about his marriage to Emily.

Plus, he and Laurel needed to come to terms about the issue of the creek.

Although…maybe that didn't count. Once Dave Bentley provided a copy of the hydrology report, Laurel would agree to his plan, Alan was sure of it. And once she agreed, Hardy would get off his back. Windridge's expansion would go forward. Laurel would have her cottages. Everything promised to work out.

Driving home with his windows down, admiring the starry night, Alan couldn't help feeling pleased about Laurel's softening on their other problem—her adamant stance about his profession. That might have been a bigger sticking point than any of the others. No matter how he looked at it, Alan *was* Windridge. He'd hoped one day to pass the land and his stock in the distillery to his children—and it had never been his choice to let Louemma be an only child the way he'd been.

As he entered his lane, he felt as though his burdens had been lifted.

THAT NIGHT, Laurel couldn't sleep. Sparks had shot into flames between her and Alan, so quickly she hadn't had time to think. But in the midst of her worrying, she admitted the heat had simmered beneath the surface almost since their first meeting.

Still, she had to examine the facts. She wasn't very good at picking a man.

But they were talking Alan Ridge. Pillar of the community. Father extraordinaire. Entrepreneur. Breadwinner. All arenas in which Dennis had failed.

Despite all that, Laurel remained nervous over the prospect of taking the next step. So nervous, she saddled Coal Fire at dawn. She and Dog set out to visit another mountain weaver.

Laurel spent a glorious day. The mountains were dappled with sunlight, and at the threshold of summer, the wilderness was fresh and beautiful. There was so much more to Kentucky than its famous bluegrass. She had her first look at the peeling bark on the mountain laurel, for which she was named.

Essie Johnson, who at ninety-one still lived alone, bolstered Laurel's sense of self. On the old woman's rough-hewn cabin walls hung some of the purest weavings Laurel had ever seen. Hours later, when she untied Coal Fire and left, she was clutching Essie's patterns for variations of the Whig Rose and Chariot Wheel. Essie swore they'd come to her through a family member who'd served in the household of Thomas Jefferson. Laurel thought it could be true. In Hazel's pattern scrapbook were notations indicating Jefferson himself had named the Whig Rose design.

Also stowed in her saddlebags was a salve brewed from chittam bark. Essie claimed it cured any number of infections. Oh, and two loaves of fresh persimmon bread. The smell tantalized Laurel as she rode, Dog at her side.

It was a refreshed, exuberant woman who cantered in after dark, only to find a near-apoplectic Alan Ridge racing around the perimeter of her house. His brown hair stood up in spikes. He waved a wilting bouquet of daisies like one might a Fourth of July flag.

"Oh, Alan, are those daisies for me?" Laurel asked, sliding from her saddle.

"Where in hell have you been? It's nine o'clock!" In his agitation, he roughly bumped Dog aside. And for the first time in ages, the shepherd growled.

Laurel took a step back. She clutched Coal Fire's bridle. A wave of fright sent goose bumps up her spine. But then the porch light revealed the anguish and worry in Alan's brown eyes. Worry for her safety, she realized.

Stepping forward, she rose on tiptoes, grabbed Alan's collar and kissed him.

He lost his footing and his arms flailed, but she managed to telegraph her pleasure at finding him on her doorstep. Alan couldn't check his backward momentum, and Laurel followed. His boot heel struck the bottom step. He went down on his back, with Laurel on top of him.

His arms circled her for support and neither of them noticed how the daisies rained down over them.

Relief at seeing her safe and sound gave way to other feelings. Alan was ready and willing to make love to her right there in the moonlight on the worn boards of her porch.

She had other ideas. She somehow managed to tie her horse and unlock the front door still clutching his shirt. She began unfastening buttons, the ripping some off.

It'd been so long…the shudders coursing through her took over.

Alan, his nerves already stretched to the limit from worry, needed no other invitation. Though he probably lacked finesse, he was able to find Laurel's couch in the dark. And he got them both naked in less time than it took to shut the dog out. Alan didn't want a cold nose interrupting what he'd come prepared to do—make love to Laurel Ashline until neither he nor she could stand.

He wished he'd thought to switch on a lamp so he could see every beautiful inch of her. He had to settle for communicating his urgency with his lips and hot, skimming hands.

Both athletic and agile, Laurel matched his hunger. She refused to pay heed to her saddle-weary body tonight. "This is a perfect end to a wonderful day," she murmured as he turned her on her back and took a second to sheath himself.

"I can't think beyond now. Don't talk. If you do, I'm going to explode."

Her heart raced. She didn't need words. But she couldn't help worrying that the coupling would be awkward, or that she'd forgotten how. *Silly girl!* The phrase pounded in her head, along with the rising heat in her blood as Alan entered her smoothly and slickly. All words, all thought—everything flew straight out of her head.

If it'd ever been Alan's intent to start out slow and easy, that went by the wayside as soon as Laurel's welcoming warmth closed around him. She made love with the same expertise she'd used to operate her looms. As heat, light and joy all coalesced in a climax that Alan was sure rocked the very foundations of the cottage, he knew he'd never again watch Laurel weave without remembering this night. Without remembering it and wanting to repeat it.

They lay entwined in the darkness, both content to let their heated bodies cool naturally. Alan couldn't get enough of touching her soft skin. She seemed to want the connection, too, as her fingers made forays up and down his right side. Every so often she murmured, "I ought to get up," but then she'd brush her lips across his chest.

"I should move, too," he finally said halfheartedly. "I'm probably squashing you."

She stroked his nipple with her fingertips, and smiled against his bare skin when she felt him stirring again. "I notice your body says something entirely different, and I'm oh, so tempted," she murmured, moving a bit to ease out from under him. "Do you realize I left Coal Fire tied out front? He's fully saddled. And Dog's trying to scratch down the door. I think he's starved."

Alan swung his legs around, sat up and reached for his jeans. "Oh, damn. Maybe he *won't* be hungry. I set down a picnic basket when you rode in, and I can't remember where. But maybe he doesn't like cold lasagna. Louemma ate, then fell asleep watching *102 Dalmatians*. I swiped the leftovers and—well, you know the rest."

Laurel rose to her knees and snagged her panties off the lampshade. She scooped her bra off the picture frame that hung behind the couch. "Daisies and a meal. I'm so sorry, Alan, I didn't mean to spoil your—"

"Seduction?" he asked in a low growl, pausing to kiss her belly button as she wriggled into white cotton panties. "I'd say that part happened just right. All the rest was window dressing."

"I didn't expect you." She braced a hand against his shoulder, holding his lips at bay so that she could button her blouse.

"It was obvious you didn't expect me. Here, let me help. You buttoned that all wrong."

Laurel let her hands fall to her sides. She stood before him in her half-buttoned blouse and her panties, and wondered if he had any idea how far she'd come in leaving herself open to his scrutiny. Before their divorce, things between her and Dennis had deteriorated to the point that she was locking him out of the bedroom. Half the time she slept fully clothed, so that if he broke through the door she could escape out the window and shinny down the tree that shaded their second-story apartment.

"You look pensive." Alan retrieved his shirt and handed Laurel her jeans. "I didn't mean to come off sounding like a jealous jerk."

"I know. I could tell you were worried sick or we wouldn't be here right now. I just…haven't had to account to anyone for my whereabouts in a long time."

"And you don't now." He sat and dragged on his boots. "Would you like to see if there's anything left of that picnic? I'll go put Coal Fire up."

"You don't have to."

"I want to." He stilled her protest, framing her face with his hands.

Laurel circled his wrist with trembling fingers and felt the kick of his pulse under her thumb. "I rode out at dawn to go visit a mountain weaver. I did that partly because last night I began to think I might be making another huge mistake."

Alan's hands slipped to her shoulders. Unconsciously, he traced her collarbone with his thumbs as he gazed into her eyes. "So, was tonight an experiment? A test? I guess I'm asking…is this goodbye?"

Her face flushed with the passion that had ignited earlier. "It can be hello, if…you think everything, uh, went okay." Although it was the last thing she wanted, her insecurity hung between them.

Whooping, Alan caught her in his arms. "Don't ever scare

me like that again. It went, okay? No, it was wonderful. Damn wonderful."

She slapped at his shoulders and asked to be set down. He did so, but only after a last kiss.

They separated reluctantly. Laurel searched her vocabulary for a more descriptive word than *wonderful*. Happy. Ecstatic. Content. What she really felt was that, at long last, the chaos of her life had faded. She felt as if nothing could go wrong again. And did she dare hope there might be another word linked to Alan Ridge—such as *love*?

CHAPTER ELEVEN

MAY SLID INTO JUNE without fanfare, then June became a sultry July. Louemma progressed slowly but steadily. Every lesson ended with her gaining fractionally greater use of her arms. She was walking a lot more and was less dependent on her wheelchair. Alan continued to hope for a full recovery.

In between lesson days, if he managed to break away from his duties at Windridge, he slipped back to Laurel's. They didn't always end up in bed, just enough times to keep them both content....

Sometimes they took moonlit walks in the woods, holding hands or whispering silly things with their heads together. On the days Alan couldn't get away, Laurel spent her empty hours photographing colorful mushrooms native to the area. She framed a trio of her more exotic-looking prints and hung them in her kitchen. A craft store in town sold the others on consignment.

"There's just no accounting for the junk tourists will buy," Alan teased her one night, being sure to punctuate his words with not-so-teasing kisses.

While they laughed and joked, both were aware that they'd never discussed a future together. They'd made such a habit of sidestepping any mention of Windridge or the creek that Laurel was shocked one Sunday afternoon when Alan rolled over in bed, propped himself on his elbow, and blurted, "It's been more than a month since I gave you Dave

Bentley's report on Bell Hill's water table, Laurel. What have you decided?"

"A month? So long?" She covered her breasts with the sheet and slid up to lean against the natural pine headboard of a new king-size bed she'd bought once it became clear she and Alan would be sharing it often.

"Hardy left the report on my desk weeks ago and I brought it to you almost immediately. I should think you've had ample time to study it."

She shrugged. "I suppose. Why the rush?"

He studied her from dark, fathomless eyes for quite some time before he rubbed his nose and finally offered a crooked grin. "Uh, the object behind requesting the study was so you could make an informed decision—and ultimately allow us to tap into the spring. I need a verdict soon if we're going to meet our targeted expansion date."

Laurel drew up her knees and wrapped her arms around them. "I think the person who wrote that report has a master's degree in double-speak."

"That's typical of engineers. It read fairly straight forwardly to me. The perk tests and water table tallies indicate the headwaters come from an infinite source."

"Does it? Or are they guessing? The pages are filled with words like 'in our estimation' or 'so far as this surveyor is able to ascertain' and 'based on the most sophisticated equipment available today, we think…blah, blah.' One engineer is guessing the underground spring will continue at its current rate ad infinitum. He can't *guarantee* it will."

Alan stole a portion of the bedsheet and faced her. They both sat cross-legged. A muscle in his jaw flexed as he tapped his fingertips together. "I guess something like that's impossible to guarantee, Laurel. The firm doing the study has to cover their butts. They can't afford to be sued down the line should something unforeseen, like a ten-year drought, dry up the spring. But theirs is the most educated assessment available. They're a reputable group."

"I'm sure." She breathed out a sigh.

"You can call the state and see if anyone's ever logged a complaint against them. Would that go further toward relieving your mind?"

"I don't know. Frankly, I'd hoped you'd dropped the idea of proceeding with that scheme."

"It's not a scheme, Laurel. Why would you call it that? My company's plans have been hanging fire, waiting for your okay. Hardy Duff has a construction crew on a retainer that's about to run out."

She picked at her fingernail polish. "I see. I didn't know that. So, how much longer do I have before I absolutely must decide?"

"Hardy phones every night, and a few members of our board have been on his case. Your indecision's causing a domino effect. It's the board's job to keep company growth on track, and they get edgy about retainer fees and building loans left in limbo. In essence, we're paying Dave's crew to do nothing."

"That doesn't tell me how long I have."

"A week. Maybe I can buy ten days. The sooner, the better. That's assuming you're going to say yes. You are, aren't you, Laurel?"

"Don't pressure me, Alan. You know I don't respond well to pressure tactics."

"Okay. Jeez!" He held up his hands. Then he wrung out another smile and reached for her, but she deftly avoided him. She yanked away the sheet as she jumped off the bed.

Feeling exposed, he grabbed his pants. He'd started for the bathroom to shower, as was his habit, when the phone beside the bed rang.

Since Laurel was closer to the nightstand where it sat, she checked the caller ID readout. A look of dismay crossed her face.

"What is it? Who?" Alan asked, hesitating even though he stood naked, half in, half out of the bathroom.

"Dennis, I think. At least it's a Vermont area code. I don't recognize the number as one he's used in the past. To be truthful, it's been weeks since he called."

"I know. I'd hoped we'd seen the end of him," Alan said, raising his voice to be heard over the third insistent ring. "Don't answer. He'll assume you're not home."

As if to show Alan she didn't like him making decisions for her, Laurel jerked up the receiver in the middle of the fifth ring. "Hello. Ah, yes, Dennis. I did suspect it was you. Yes, I have an ID service, but this time I only got a number. I didn't recognize it. What? I didn't answer earlier because I was busy." Color streaked her cheeks as she wound the cord around a finger and cast guilty glances at Alan. "Actually," she said with a toss of her head, "I have a visitor. Why are you calling?"

Alan had noted it was customary for Laurel to pace in circles whenever she spoke with her ex. Today she fell back on the bed. Before she'd interrupted his tirade with her canned speech, but today she appeared to listen raptly.

Unsure as to whether to stay or go and shower, yet feeling foolish for waiting there naked, Alan stalked into the bathroom. He turned the faucet on full bore and as cold as the water would go. Which was quite chilly, considering that Laurel's water came from a deep well. But even the sharp, icy sting against his skin didn't keep him from wondering about what was being said in the next room.

He soon found out. He walked out carrying his socks and boots, to find Laurel fully dressed.

"You will not believe what I have to tell you," she said. "The reason Dennis has been so silent is he's checked himself into a rehab facility. Some private program. Apparently a former boss pulled strings to get him placed. They admitted Dennis under a grant-funded program. I'm not quite sure how it works. He just said he had to remain sober for six weeks before they let him make phone calls to friends or family."

"Has he ever been sober for six weeks before?"

"Yes. He got sober when it was required by various companies as a condition of employment. Never because he *wanted* to stop drinking. Maybe this time will be different. He sounded almost upbeat today."

"Right…and babies just show up under cabbage leaves."

"That's not nice, Alan. He gave me some impressive success rates for this particular program."

"Hmm. Why the big change now? What's his sudden catalyst?"

Laurel's words came out in a flood. "Me. I'm his catalyst. He said it's because he hit bottom and suddenly realized he'd lost me because of his constant drinking. He said he's doing this to win me back." A red flush slowly crept up her face.

Alan's boot hit the floor. *"What?"* Dog, who'd been snoozing in the corner, bounded up and started barking.

Laurel calmed the dog with a soft command.

"You told Dennis to hop a westbound freight, I hope."

She laced her fingers and rubbed her palms together nervously. "What purpose would it serve to squash the one hope that might keep him in the program?"

Alan said nothing for a minute. He finished tugging on his boots. As he got to his feet, he saw that Laurel hadn't moved. Rounding the bed, he pulled her up against him. "Don't you see? Dennis is still making his success or failure dependent on someone other than himself. On *you,* Laurel. Surely you're not entertaining any wild notion of letting him back into your life."

She tensed briefly, then snuggled against Alan's solid body, pressing her cheek to his chest. "No. Of course it'd never work."

Alan thought he heard both hesitation and doubt in her statement. And she'd considered her answer far longer than he would've liked—longer than he would've thought possible, given their growing relationship. A heaviness invaded his chest when Laurel changed their earlier plans of going somewhere for brunch. She left his arms, saying, "I forgot to mention that I got a commission for a new piece yesterday. A woman from Louisville. She and her husband own one of the big Thoroughbred horse farms. Anyway, she saw my work and ordered a monogrammed tablecloth and forty matching napkins. It's a coup, not only in terms of money, but referrals as well."

"But—"

"I have no choice, Alan. If I work all afternoon and evening uninterrupted, I can have the larger piece warped. I've goofed off. Now I have to find time to finish the job."

He felt her pulling in. Pulling back. Alan thought he probably ought to insist they take a minute to discuss where this left them. Where it left their relationship. But he wasn't good at that—wasn't good at spilling his guts, or hanging on to someone he cared for. He'd let his mother leave the company, and him, without a word. He'd let Emily close him out. Now it was happening again. Or…maybe it really *was* about Laurel's new project, and he was making too much of it. But Louemma… She and Laurel had made plans.

"You promised Louemma she could sleep over after tomorrow's lesson," he reminded her. "Do I need to let her down gently? She was so excited, she actually went to Brenna's birthday party this afternoon. I was going to pick her up after our brunch."

Laurel had led the way down the hall to the front door. She stopped with her hand on the knob. "Darn, Alan. That completely slipped my mind. She and I were planning a girls' night. We'll do some cooking, stay up late and watch a movie or two. I'm so glad you mentioned it. No, I'd never disappoint her. Will you pick her up Tuesday morning or shall I deliver her to Windridge?"

"I'll pick her up. Rose arrives at eight-thirty to give us the results of the exams Louemma took in June. Shall we say eight? Unless, of course, Louemma can't sleep and you need me to come get her during the night."

"I hadn't thought of that. I never did sleepovers as a kid," she said wistfully. "I hope it goes well."

"So do I," he said gruffly, unable to keep himself from kissing away her sad expression.

"Mmm," she murmured once he finally released her. "What was that for?"

He almost said *because I love you,* but checked himself. It didn't seem the right time. "Do I need a reason to kiss you?"

"I guess not." She smiled a genuine smile—her first of the morning. It went a long way toward loosening the knot in Alan's stomach.

"Well, since kissing you has a habit of getting out of hand, and since you have to work, I'd better scoot while the scootin's good."

"Right. Duty calls. Frankly, your family's probably feeling neglected. You should take Vestal to pick up Louemma from her birthday party, then go on an outing. The Shaker Village has special presentations all weekend. Hot as it's been, I should think a trip downriver on the *Dixie Belle* paddle wheeler would be nice."

"I wanted you to come with us when I took Louemma on the boat. Anyway, I've ignored spreadsheets and billing. I'll put my afternoon to good use."

"See you tomorrow, then, when you drop off Louemma for her lesson. Oh, if someone could jot down a typical evening's schedule for her, it would help me."

"Sure. I'll stick it in her bag, along with her favorite teddy bear. She likes him on her bed at night. It nearly kills me that she can't hug him like she once did."

"She is improving, Alan." Laurel squeezed his arm. "I'm

afraid I agree with the doctors who said it's a subconscious affliction. There are times I see her almost reaching out. She wants to, but just as fast, the spark disappears."

"She loves Dog, and she looks forward to coming here. If anything happened to take that away…" He blinked rapidly and stared into the distance.

"What could, Alan? Goodness, I'm only asking for a little time to myself." She hooked her arm through his and moved with him toward the footbridge.

He waved as he drove off. It felt as if she was asking for more than a breather. But he might be reacting to her ex's call. The man had been silent for months, then wham. Yes, that was probably all it was, Alan decided, feeling slightly foolish once he reached home.

He phoned Laurel that night before he went to bed, which had become their habit. They didn't talk long, but she sounded like her old self, and he fell asleep happy.

In the morning, a lost shipment to one of Windridge's best clients caused Alan so many headaches he had to sweep everything else from his mind. Everything except Louemma. She practically bounced off the walls in her excitement about the sleepover with Laurel. All afternoon, she drove Alan crazy, wanting him to pack half the treasures in her room.

"Land's sake, child," Vestal said at three, sounding exasperated. "Alan, didn't you make it clear she's only staying one night, not two weeks?"

"Laurel said for me to bring puzzles and games and my favorite video."

"Maybe one puzzle and one game," Alan suggested.

"But what if Laurel doesn't like what I pick? I want her to invite me again."

"Honeybee," he said, unable to resist her plaintive cry, "take whatever you want. I'm sure Laurel can find someplace to store the stuff you want to leave. I have no doubt she'll invite you more than just this once."

"I hope so." At last Louemma had pared down her luggage to one small suitcase and one bag of toys. By then, Alan knew that if they didn't leave immediately they'd be late for her lesson.

"I'm warning you," he murmured to Laurel some time later, when he was preparing to leave after depositing Louemma's things in the cottage, "She's going to try to pin you down to a time to do this again. She might be thinking once a month. She even brought a calendar for you to mark the nights she can stay. You'll have to be firm and limit her, or she'll be over here every night."

Laurel smiled. "Maybe I wouldn't mind. I always wanted a little sister."

"Not a daughter?" Alan asked, realizing he didn't know if Laurel wanted children or not. That sort of information fell in the realm of intimate details they'd shied away from sharing. Now he wished they hadn't been so…careful.

"I'd love a child. Children," she corrected. "But I decided a few years into my marriage that I couldn't, not with Dennis. Keeping food on our table became enough of a struggle. Imagine the nightmare if we'd had babies. And you, Alan, produce and sell a product responsible for putting millions of women in that position."

"Stop it, Laurel. This argument hasn't come up in months. Why now?"

"I've been rereading the engineering study. I'm having trouble saying yes to something I know will put more whiskey out in the world."

Alan took her by the elbow. "If you're going to yell, let's step outside, out of Louemma's hearing."

Looking guilty, Laurel glanced over her shoulder to where the girl worked at her loom, all the while chatting nonstop to

Dog. He had his chin planted firmly on her thigh, his eyes shut in doggy ecstacy.

"I don't want to pick a fight with you, Alan. It's my frustration over not being able to tell you yes that you're hearing."

"Slow down. You're stuck in one rut. For every alcoholic, there are many more responsible, perfectly rational social drinkers. I told Hardy this morning that you hadn't made up your mind, and that I wouldn't push you. He's unhappy, but I want you to reach a conclusion on your own."

"Thank you. I know it means dollars and cents to you. That's eating at me, too. I will decide soon, Alan. By the end of the week. You have my word."

"Hey, that's good enough for me." He tugged her partially out of the loom cottage, so he could steal a kiss. So far they hadn't kissed in front of Louemma. Alan assumed it was because they were both hesitant. Now he wondered if it was only *his* problem. When the kiss ended, he asked abruptly, "Is there a reason we're hiding our—you know—relationship?"

"From your family? The town? Who, exactly, would we be hiding from?"

"Everyone. You find reasons to refuse to go to a restaurant with me or elsewhere in town. Is it because you don't want people to think we're a couple?"

"Not at all. I, uh, we agreed to let any relationship develop naturally. I'm a private person. I got the idea you were, too. Is something wrong?"

"Not if that's the only reason. Oh, I hear Louemma calling you. She probably broke a thread." Alan dropped another fast kiss on Laurel's mouth. "I'm crossing my fingers that tonight goes well. Call if you need me for anything." He backed down the steps.

As she turned aside, Laurel had no intention of calling him. Did he think her incapable of entertaining one small girl for one night? She loved Louemma. It was certainly no hardship. The child was smart. She learned quickly, and she had Alan's laugh.

Laurel very much feared she was falling in love with Alan Ridge. She'd thought she'd gotten past his occupation. In fact, she'd been making headway—until Dennis called from rehab, reminding her of all the problems whiskey caused. He'd called again last night, and once this morning. To clear the air between them, he said. To explain about his childhood. In all the years they'd been married, he'd never referred to his childhood. As Laurel suspected, Dennis came from a broken home. If only she'd known he was a product of two alcoholic parents...

She'd asked him not to call tonight because one of her students was spending the night. That was when she'd seen the first sign of the old Dennis. His jealousy was palpable, even over the phone. Laurel had no doubt that he'd call to make sure she was entertaining a child and not another man.

Well, if he phoned and Louemma figured it out and told Alan, there was little Laurel could do. Alan had his own jealous streak. Why couldn't he see that after investing seven years trying to save Dennis from himself, she couldn't turn her back on him when he finally seemed to be making an honest effort to put his life together?

Dennis hadn't phoned by the time she and Louemma had finished their evening meal. "Hey, want to help me bake chocolate chip cookies? I bought all the ingredients yesterday."

The girl's eyes lit with interest, then she banked the flame. "I can watch. I can't stir or dump stuff in the bowl. I watch Birdie make cookies. She says I'm a big help 'cause I keep her company when Nana takes a nap."

"That's good. That's important so Birdie doesn't feel lonely. I know a lot about loneliness. It's not enjoyable."

"Yeah, but you have Dog." The girl smiled down at the animal, who'd stayed close to her side.

"And I have Cinnabar and Coal Fire. By Christmas, I'll add a colt or a filly, as soon as Cinnabar has her baby. Before I start the cookies, I need to go feed the horses and give Cinnabar her vitamins. Want to come?" she asked casually, setting aside a bowl she'd gotten out.

"No! No, please no. Can I stay here with Dog?"

Not wanting to upset the child, Laurel paused to give her a reassuring hug. "That's fine, sweetie. I won't be long."

She rushed through her chores. Laurel didn't know how Alan would feel about her leaving a nine-year-old alone for the fifteen or so minutes it took to feed her stock. That was something else they hadn't discussed. At that age, Laurel had cooked, cleaned house and even shopped for groceries. But fifteen minutes alone might seem an eternity to Louemma Ridge, who had a real childhood.

Calling out to the girl as she opened the door, Laurel skidded to a halt at the sight of a man, a stranger, standing in her living room calmly chatting with Louemma.

"Who are you?" She glanced around for a weapon. "What are you doing walking uninvited into my home?" Her heart hammering in fright, Laurel found her first thought was to place her body between the man and Louemma.

"Louemma invited me in." The man, who was probably about sixty, looked Laurel up and down before he extended a hand.

"I'm Dale Patton, principal attorney for Windridge Distillery. I assume you're Laurel Ashline."

She inclined her head, not making sense of the man's words. How had he gotten here? And how had she missed hearing the approach of an automobile? "I'm afraid I don't understand why you're here. Is there some legal form Alan needs in order for Louemma to spend the night?" She touched the girl, who was suddenly clinging to her leg. "If so, I should sign a stack. Louemma and I have already made three future dates."

"I'm here regarding the creek. This land. The forty acres you think you inherited from Hazel Bell."

Laurel frowned. "I did inherit. I'm Ted and Hazel's granddaughter. Their only relative, I've been told."

"I'm not disputing your relationship. I have here a copy of a land grant that supercedes the deed of title Hazel received from the circuit court when she petitioned for squatter's rights."

Taking the faded parchment paper, Laurel stared dazedly at a document she had difficulty making heads or tails of because it had been written in flowery script with a wide-tipped pen or quill. "Who? Uh—who does own the land?"

"Alan Ridge. Well, and Vestal."

"Alan?" She gaped.

"How…uh, long has he known? Or does he?"

"It'd be hard for him not to, little lady. He's the one who found the document in his grandfather's office up at the distillery about six months ago."

"Six months ago?" Laurel swallowed her disbelief. "Mr. Patton, just tell me what this is about. I want to know precisely what your visit means."

"I've been out of the country on vacation, or this would've been cleared up before now. Our state superior court recognizes the validity of original land grants. This document tells you I've filed to rescind the decree issued to Mrs. Bell by the circuit court. And this one…" he paused "…is your thirty-day eviction notice. I hate being the bearer of bad tidings. And I can see you've settled in here." He cleared his throat. "To say nothing of the fact that my wife thinks you're a fine addition to Ridge City. She's already bought two of your shawls." The man flushed.

Fireworks exploded inside Laurel's head. The light, the sound, the rending pain blinded her. The papers fluttered as her hand shook; she made an effort to keep them still—made an effort to understand what the lawyer said. Very little beyond the remark about eviction had penetrated. She was being thrown out of her home. Something that had happened too many times during her childhood. *And Alan—Alan had known for six months.*

"Well, I need to be going. My wife's keeping my supper warm. She's none too pleased that Hardy insisted I handle this ASAP. 'Course, they've got a construction crew on an expensive retainer."

"Wait. Alan didn't have you bring me these papers?"

"No, and yes. Hardy's the GM at Windridge. Alan is president and Vestal is board chairman. It's all in the judge's report that I'm giving you."

"I see." Laurel didn't, though. "And you represent the family or the distillery?"

"Ultimately it's one and the same, little lady. Since Jason died, I deal more with Hardy on legal issues than I do with the family. But fundamentally it's all the same."

"So if I wanted to fight this in court I'd be fighting…who?"

"Windridge and the Ridge family. Take my advice, that's a fool's game. You'd be shelling out money for nothing. That's free advice, and lawyers rarely give anything away for free, Ms. Ashline." He had the audacity to wink.

"The lawyer who handled my grandmother's affairs said she had clear title to this property. All duly recorded with the county assessor. She paid property taxes. I did, too, plus an inheritance tax. I think, Mr. Patton, that you need to inform your clients they'll be hearing from my counsel very soon."

Dale Patton revealed nothing of his personal feelings as he snapped his briefcase closed and walked out. Laurel imagined him rubbing his hands together, adding up future fees in his head for all this "little lady," as he'd called her, would cost his clients in billable hours.

"Are you mad at my daddy?" Louemma ventured timidly as she watched Laurel take out her irritation on the cookie dough.

Laurel's head shot up. "Here I thought I was doing a fair job of hiding my anger. I should know you can't fool a kid. Honey, I don't want you worrying about any of this. The big bonus attached to being your age is that you don't have to fight any battles. You get to leave all of that up to the adults in your life."

"You *are* mad at Daddy." She sighed. "He made Mama mad, too. But I thought you were different, Laurel. I thought you made my Daddy happy."

Dog, as if sensing his little friend's distress, whined repeatedly, sounding almost human. Clearly, Louemma was upset. Laurel felt rotten, because if anyone knew how badly thoughtless adults could hurt a kid, she did.

"I won't lie and say your dad didn't disappoint me. He did. But I'm not mad. And I cross-my-heart swear that our differences won't change my friendship with you. Will you trust me on that?" she begged, setting the dough aside as she bent to the child's eye level.

"Those days marked on my calendar? I still get to sleep over?"

Laurel nodded vigorously. "I promise I'll do everything in my power to make sure we have those times together. And we'll continue your lessons." She didn't add that the lessons might not be in the loom cottage. Merely thinking about having to move her grandmother's old looms, spinning wheels and spinning mules threatened to bring on the tears that hovered very near the surface.

Yet she hadn't lied to Louemma. It wasn't anger she felt toward Alan. There was only pain. Her heart felt shredded by the betrayal. She'd trusted him, body and soul. They'd been as intimate as it was possible for a man and a woman to be.

And he'd done *this* in return. Through his henchmen. She honestly didn't know how she'd even make it through the night.

But she'd do it the same way she'd managed to survive

every other heart-bruising episode in her life. She would weather this setback, too. But not until it was almost time for her alarm to sound a new day did she actually believe she'd mustered enough strength to face Alan when he came to collect Louemma.

He might consider himself better than Dennis, but Laurel put them on the same level. Alan didn't even have an illness to excuse his underhanded tricks. He'd slept with her, then pretended to let her think she had a choice over allowing him access to the headwaters of the creek. All the while, he'd possessed a document virtually guaranteeing he'd win.

Dog alerted them to Alan's arrival just as Laurel finished feeding Louemma a breakfast of toast, eggs and melon.

Wiping her sweaty palms on her jeans, Laurel opened the door. She soon discovered she wasn't at all prepared to face a freshly shaved, bright-eyed, whistling traitor. Her fingers curled into her thighs the moment Alan stopped whistling and leaned in the door to kiss her full on the lips.

"D-don't," she stuttered, so totally wrung out of all emotion she couldn't say any of the things banging away inside her brain. She felt like a wretched mess of tears, mourning the loss of yet another dream.

"Laurel?" Alan reared back as soon as it dawned on him that she wasn't returning his kisses. "Uh-oh." He stepped inside, closed the door softly. "Louemma's been a trial for you."

She knew red must be streaking up her neck, even spilling into her cheeks. "Louemma and I got on famously. But you, Alan Ridge, have some nerve. Too bad you're a snake in the grass instead of being more like your precious daughter." She shoved the suitcase and bag of toys into his stomach. "Here are her things."

"Oof!" Alan grabbed twice to keep from dropping everything.

"Louemma," she called. "Your father's here to pick you up."

"What the hell's eating you?" he muttered. "You get up on the wrong side of the bed?"

"My sleeping—or waking—habits are no longer your concern," she retorted, frantically checking over her shoulder, anxious for Louemma to get in here. Girl and dog slowly made their way toward the kitchen door. Relief flooded Laurel.

"Great. You toss out a comment like that just as my big-eared daughter shows up," he said, frowning. "I have to dash home, too. Vestal left me a memo about a board meeting I didn't have on my calendar. It starts at nine, apparently."

"Surprise, surprise," Laurel said sarcastically.

He gave her a puzzled look. It is. God, but I'm having a hard time reading you this morning."

"You know what, Alan? You've never read me correctly."

Louemma had finally reached the door, even though it was obvious she'd rather not leave Laurel's.

"Hi, honeybee." Alan bent awkwardly around the stuff he held, and kissed the tip of her nose. "Hey, did you grow two inches overnight? No?" He waggled an eyebrow, and Louemma giggled. "Okay, I've got it. Laurel fixed your hair. That's why you look all grown-up to me."

"Oh, Daddy!" She preened a bit. "I like having it off my neck. Do you think Nana or Birdie will be able to fix it this way tomorrow?"

"I have no idea. If not, maybe Laurel will swing by the house to show them how."

"No. No, I have an appointment in Lexington tomorrow." She'd phoned Avery Heeter, Hazel's lawyer, on the dot of eight. He'd agreed to see her, despite the short notice.

"You do? What time are you getting home? I made us dinner reservations at the Shrimp Boat. I intended to surprise you. But…well, shoot. Surely you'll be back for a nine o'clock reservation."

She tried to keep her jaw from dropping. For the first

time, pure anger swept through Laurel. Marching past him, she yanked open the door. "Forget it. You may think you'll have cause to celebrate, but I wouldn't yet if I were you. Now, please just leave so there's no need to play this cozy scene out further in front of Louemma."

Because Alan's arms were filled with unwieldy luggage, and as Laurel was obviously ready to explode, he walked his daughter out the door.

When he turned back to mouth something to Laurel, she answered in a low, furious voice, "Don't come here again. I'll meet Louemma at the bridge when she comes for her lessons. As long as I have a bridge to cross, that is."

Then she slammed the door in his face.

He was about to drop everything and get to the bottom of this, but Louemma started to sob. "I knew Laurel was mad at you. She said she's not, but she is. You've gotta fix it, Daddy. I love Laurel. And…Dog."

"So do I," he muttered. "Why is she upset?"

"I don't know. You should ask Mr. Patton."

"Dale? What's he done?" The load Alan carried was cumbersome, and Louemma wasn't moving too well, even though she'd been walking more.

He was torn, thinking he ought to go back and ask what his lawyer had to do with anything. But he had that damn board meeting. And he was supposed to see Rose about Louemma's results. He'd have to talk to Laurel later in the day.

CHAPTER TWELVE

ALAN ESCORTED VESTAL into the boardroom at their bank, which was where Windridge meetings were held. He'd left Birdie with Louemma, who in spite of claiming she'd had a good time, had been moping since they'd left Laurel's. As a result, he and his grandmother arrived late. The others were seated and had already had their coffee. Everyone glanced up, and talk stopped.

Taking his seat at the head of the table, after pulling a chair out at the opposite end for Vestal, Alan opened his board notebook. "This may be the shortest meeting on record, folks. I never received an agenda."

"There's only one item," Hardy announced. Wasting no time, he deferred to Dale Patton. And at that moment, when Alan saw a look pass between his general manager and the company lawyer, a sick feeling hit him.

"Does this by any chance have to do with Laurel Ashline?"

Patton got up and passed around copies of a set of documents, the top one being a replica of the original land grant. "What's all this?" Alan asked.

"A copy of what Hardy had me deliver to Ms. Ashline last evening. Your option to hold Mountain Builders on retainer is about to expire, Alan. It's plain you haven't convinced Hazel Bell's granddaughter to let you dig the canal. Hardy sent me the land grant you found up at the distillery in March. I ran it by a judge. He gave us good advice. The documents in this packet are simple and straightforward."

Alan skimmed the pages. His head shot up. "You call a thirty-day eviction notice *simple*? Dammit, Hardy, if I had a résumé on file of just one man with even half your experience in bourbon-making, I'd fire you and hire him on the spot. I said I'd handle the creek problem."

Hardy slammed a ham-size fist down on the slate table. "If you weren't Jason's grandson, I'd have walked the minute I could see that little tart of Lucy Bell's was leading you around by the balls."

"That's uncalled for, and you're out of line," Alan roared.

Dale Patton, first deacon of the United Methodist Church and a devout conservative, cleared his throat. "Now, gentlemen, take a minute and let tempers cool. Remember, please, we have a lady present."

"Sorry, Vestal," Hardy muttered.

But Vestal, who'd run the company for a number of years after Jason's death, seemed nonplussed. "You've *all* bungled the job," she said. "Why didn't either of you come to me so I could meet with Laurel and settle this woman to woman?"

"You haven't been well," Alan said. "Frankly, I saw no reason to tell Laurel what Hazel did. Laurel walked into this unaware of past dynamics. So, which one of you has been appointed to break the really bad news? There's more to this, right?"

Vestal shifted so she could eye Hardy and Dale. "There's worse? Like Dale said, these forms spell out that the forty acres is ours. I see no reason we can't just offer to lease Laurel the cottages, Alan."

"None of you gets it. This is the first time in her life she's had anything to call her own. Just so you all know how strongly I feel about this, I offered to buy back her upper twenty acres. Not with company funds, but with a personal check."

"That's damn stupid," Hardy snapped. "Why buy land that's already ours?"

The banker on their board kept clicking his ballpoint pen. Dale removed his glasses and cleaned them vigorously with a pristine handkerchief. "Ms. Ashline's not going to leave meekly," he said. "Doing it Alan's way might have helped you avoid unnecessary legal wranglings. Now I suspect she'll tie you up in court. Or try to."

Alan drummed his fingers on the table. "Is that why Laurel's making an unplanned trip to Lexington tomorrow? Grandmother, isn't that where Hazel's attorney practices law?"

"Avery Heeter," Dale interjected. "He specializes in real estate litigation. I took the liberty of checking him out after I discovered he's the one who filed the squatter's rights petition for Hazel. My colleagues say Avery's like a fighting rooster. He goes beyond the call of duty to help widows and orphans."

Hardy slumped in his chair. "That explains why Heeter took Hazel's case," he growled. "Although the Ashline woman's not a widow. Isn't she divorced?"

"But an orphan," Vestal added before Alan could. "Lucy Bell died when Laurel was still in high school. She's come a long way on her own, considering."

"In my opinion, she deserves better than she's getting from us," Alan said.

No one argued, possibly because he looked ready to chew nails and spit tacks. That morning's encounter played over and over in his head. Laurel's attack made total sense. She assumed he'd double-crossed her. No wonder she thought he was out of his mind for inviting her to dinner tomorrow night.

He groaned, remembering when that idea had taken root—when he'd passed Olson Jewelers and had seen an eighteen-carat gold pin in the window—a replica of Laurel's old spinning wheel. Alan doubted anyone had ever given her a just-because gift. And dammit, now he'd probably never get to see the pure joy in her eyes. He loved watching her eyes change color with her moods. During lovemaking they turned a deep, smoky brown.

Jumping up, he banged his notebook closed, not giving a damn that everyone gaped at him. "As president and majority stockholder, I rarely if ever pull rank. As far as I'm concerned, this meeting's adjourned. I'm giving you all one edict—fix this screwup with Laurel Ashline. Some of the finest minds in town are at this table. Collectively, I'm sure you can figure out how to access the water we need to expand Windridge without throwing a defenseless woman out on the street."

"You didn't," Hardy said under his breath once Alan had started for the door.

Vestal left her chair, and the remaining men, as dictated by good manners, also rose. "Hardy, we'll never know if Alan would've succeeded, because you took matters into your own hands."

"I expected you to stand by us, Vestal. You were mad as hell at Hazel, if I recall, when that squatter's deed came to light after her funeral."

"That was personal. And this is family. The reason Windridge has never completely left Ridge hands is because our stock votes as a block. Always has. Always will. Where I stand, gentlemen, is squarely behind my grandson." She left some sagging jaws behind when she swept regally from the room.

"Thanks for backing me," Alan said, gazing lovingly into her eyes. "You were free to do whatever you liked. Hardy just made me so damn mad." Taking Vestal's arm, Alan cautioned her to watch the step as they entered the parking garage.

"What I'm doing is kicking myself for being asleep at the switch," she muttered.

"How so?" He unlocked the heavy door to Vestal's luxury car and helped her in.

"I'd like to think that even a year ago, I'd have been sharp enough to see something this obvious—that you'd fallen in love with our new neighbor. As late as this meeting, I'm afraid I was still on the page in the script where I practically had to beat you over the head to get you to take Louemma to one of Laurel's weaving demonstrations."

Alan had already slid beneath the steering wheel before his grandmother's observations slammed him in the gut. It was a good thing he was sitting, although he did fumble the keys and drop them on the mat. "Who said anything about love? I, ah, recall saying I didn't want her thrown out on the street."

His grandmother smiled like a cat with her nose and both paws in thick cream. "It's plain as plain can be. Don't argue with your elders. Women sense these things. *Those* powers of mine still operate just fine." Vestal folded her hands primly across the Gucci bag that had been Jason's last birthday gift to her. She carried it everywhere, despite being a stickler for every other fashion rule.

"We'll have to scrape Birdie off the ceiling," she said dryly. "Or maybe you haven't noticed she's been planting old Kentucky good-luck charms in every corner of the house, hoping for this outcome since the day you had her pack the two of you a picnic lunch. She throws salt over her shoulder for luck. She moved the pedestal table from between your chair and Laurel's to ensure you won't quarrel."

"Ha! You can tell Birdie *that* one didn't work."

"The most I ever hoped for, Alan, was that you'd one day escape the shell you disappeared into after losing Emily."

"I haven't been in a shell."

"Huh!" she snorted. "Are we going to sit here all day trading words that insult my intelligence? Pick up your keys and take me to breakfast at the Garden Room. And on the way, tell me how Louemma's going to react to having a new mother."

Alan stabbed the keys in the ignition and rolled his eyes.

"You're getting way ahead of the game. After Dale's impromptu visit, Laurel's no longer speaking to me. Honestly, to think I was completely clueless as to why she was so angry."

"Surely she'll listen. The woman doesn't exist who can resist a Ridge man once he turns on the charm."

"Laurel may be the first," Alan said, his tone glum.

"Pshaw! And while you may think you've evaded my question about Louemma's feelings for Laurel, you can be sure I'll ask it again and again until I get an answer."

"I *can't* answer that. And you're forgetting I haven't said I love her."

"Is it because you live under some misguided notion that you need to remain true to Emily forever? Because that's utter nonsense, Alan."

"I'm more worried about the fact that I've begun to question if I ever really loved Emily. I'm afraid that in high school I lusted after her, and then got washed along on a small-town tide where everyone assumes high-school sweethearts get married."

"I don't like to speak ill of the dead, but Jason always said Emily was a piece of work. I interfered in my son's life. Once. I swore I'd never mess in yours, Alan."

"I'm aware you and my mother had differences. But I thought you liked Emily." Alan pulled up at the curb and parked near Vestal's favorite restaurant. They put their conversation on hold while he got out and guided her inside to await a table. Even then, she didn't take up where they'd left off.

After they'd been seated and she'd said again how much she loved this restaurant, Alan figured she'd chosen to let his remark pass altogether. It wasn't until the waiter had taken their order that Vestal sipped her lemon water and said, "Perhaps everyone but you and Louemma knew Emily was a chameleon. She was adept at being exactly what any given person wanted her to be. In reality, she was all of them—and none."

Alan poured cream in a cup of coffee the waiter placed near his right hand. "In hindsight I realize that's true. I began to see a different Emily after Louemma was born. I haven't always been in a shell, Grandmother. I'm also aware that our friends gossiped after she died. Were the rumors of her infidelity true, do you think?"

"I don't know. And what good can come of knowing now? I'm proud of you for ignoring hearsay the way you have for Louemma's sake. Which didn't stop me from aching for the way you'd shut yourself off. I hope Laurel Ashline is worthy of your love."

At the very mention of her name. Alan felt his face soften. Vestal stretched out a blue-veined hand and patted his arm. "I can see she is, and I'm glad. Lucy was such a trial for Hazel and Ted. Close as Hazel and I once were, I'm guilty of forsaking my friend in her time of need. Few people— not even Jason or Ted—knew about the huge fight she and I had over Lucy. Well, over Mark's friendship with her. When Lucy left with that man, I was secretly glad. Only…" Vestal straightened her silverware. "Hazel came to the house wanting Mark to track Lucy down and bring her back. I flatly refused to let him go. Hazel severed our friendship. We never spoke again. Ted used to sit in our kitchen lamenting the change in his wife. My fault, and I never told a soul until now."

"Why did you stop my dad from going?" In the back of Alan's mind hung Laurel's question about whether or not his dad might also have been *her* father. Wouldn't that be the irony of all time?

"Mark had a soft heart. Softer than yours, Alan. He was forever getting Lucy out of trouble. Mark told no one else that Lucy was pregnant by that workman, but he confided in me. I was afraid that if Mark went after Lucy he'd feel obligated to provide her baby with a name. It would've been a disaster. A more restless girl was never born. She'd have done anything to get out of Ridge City. Did, and then she ran off. I know she would have talked Mark into leaving, too, which would've killed Jason. No one but me knew his heart was failing. I also knew Mark had been seeing Carolee—and that Carolee was expecting. I used that fact to keep Mark home. If I hadn't, Carolee might not have gone through with the pregnancy. That's what she threatened, anyway."

Alan roused from a stupor. "Wow. Then I wouldn't be here. Laurel has an album of Hazel's. There are all these pictures of Dad and Lucy together. Since I've developed, uh, feelings for Laurel, I have to be sure, Grandmother, that there's no chance the two of them might have been…lovers."

She arched a regal eyebrow. "Funny, I asked Mark that very question. As well as soft-hearted, he was unfailingly honest. I embarrassed him to death by asking. Young men just didn't discuss their sex lives with their mothers back then."

"Nor do they now," Alan retorted.

"Be that as it may, his denial came without hesitation. I startled him so badly, he admitted he'd been intimate with Carolee, but no one else."

Alan found a weak smile. "I'll bet that got him an hour's lecture."

"It did. Of course, he married your mother, but he was never happy. I used to tell myself, that all things happen for a reason. Now, I don't know. Did I ruin a lot of lives by trying to add years to Jason's?"

"Grandmother, Lucy could've come home when Ashline walked out. Dad didn't have to stay in a bad marriage. People do what they do."

Relief blew through Alan like a pleasant breeze, now that the niggling question about Laurel's parentage had been answered by someone who knew. Their breakfast arrived and he was able to eat with gusto. Which didn't mean he had no hurdles left to scale with Laurel...

After the meal, Alan drove Vestal home, and they parted ways in the hall. He detoured into his office to put away his notebook. While there, he decided to phone Laurel. No answer. He knew she had an extension in the loom cottage, but she might be in the corral.

He checked on Louemma, then read her a story. The minute it ended, he excused himself to try Laurel again. She still didn't pick up. Only after a third attempt some two hours later did he suspect he might be a victim of the caller ID he'd convinced her to install. Determined to square matters before a bad situation got totally out of control, Alan grabbed his car keys. "Birdie, I'm going to be gone for an hour or so. Can you keep an eye on Louemma?"

"Sure 'nuff. I'm going to make custard cups. I'll see if she wants to help. Your grandmother's resting?"

Nodding, he hurried to the Jeep and drove quickly to Laurel's. A few weeks ago, studying a map of the proposed expansion, he'd found a little-used fire road that brought him less than a quarter of a mile from her clearing. He took the shortcut now.

Her cottage showed no signs of life. In fact, the silence reminded Alan of his first visit, except this time no fruit basket protruded from her garbage can. And he knew enough now to head for the loom cottage.

Dog barked a greeting from inside. Alan knocked once and tried the door, which normally wasn't locked. The handle didn't budge. He rattled the knob and called, "Laurel, it's Alan. Listen, I didn't send Dale Patton. Hardy took matters into his own hands."

He thought he heard Laurel order Dog to be quiet.

"Sweetheart, it makes no sense for me to stand here shouting through the door."

"Then go away! Don't be sweet-talking me, Alan Ridge."

He barely made out her retort. Leaning his forehead against the smooth wood, he placed his mouth against a thin crack. "You don't mean that!"

"Yes, I do. In fact, if you don't leave I'm going to phone the sheriff and say you're harassing me."

"Don't do that." Sighing, Alan backed off the porch. All he needed to complicate matters more than they already were would be for Laurel to have him thrown in jail. "Laurel, please, I know we can resolve this without involving lawyers if you'd just open the damn door."

"You involved a lawyer, Alan. Go…away!"

She had him there. Patton was his attorney. "Okay, I'm leaving. But I'm not giving up. You'll have to see me Monday when I bring Louemma to class."

MONDAY AT NOON, Laurel phoned and asked to speak with Louemma. Birdie said she'd hold the phone for the girl.

"Hi, honey. I'm in Lexington and I won't be back in time for our lesson. I have to cancel. I'm really sorry."

"Did Dog go to Lexington with you?"

Laurel laughed. "He's guarding the house. Would you like me to bring over your loom and project tomorrow so you can work at home?"

"No, I don't want Nana to see the scarf. It's her Christmas present."

"Oh, right. Listen, I have to go. We'll work something out, okay?"

"Okay. Are you still mad at Daddy?"

Laurel mumbled something noncommittal and signed off.

Birdie relayed the conversation to Alan when he dashed in from the distillery to collect Louemma.

"Ms. Laurel sounded really sorry," she said. "Hardy Duff needs to have his ears boxed for causing this stupid tug-of-war over water."

"It's become more than a tug-of-war, Birdie. This afternoon, Windridge got served a subpoena and we'll have to appear in court. Where's Vestal? The summons lists Hardy and me by name, then lumps the other principals together. Dale wants to try and get the case thrown out based on the fact that Vestal and I together own a majority of the voting stock. Hardy's a minority owner."

"Huh, if you ask me, and nobody did, you and your grandmother own a majority of a big headache. Speaking of which, she's lying down now trying to get rid of one. Headache, that is."

"Oh, well, don't disturb her. If Laurel wasn't so stubborn, if she'd meet me halfway, we could save everyone time, money and headache remedies."

Louemma, who'd heard Alan's voice, entered the kitchen in search of him. "Daddy, I forgot to ask Laurel if I can have my lesson tomorrow. Will you ask her?"

"Well, uh…she's not exactly talking to me, honeybee."

"Is that because you and Mr. Patton made her mad the other day?"

"Correction. Mr. Patton's the culprit. Laurel's choosing to include me."

Louemma's eyes filled with tears. "Why's she 'cluding me? I don't even know why everyone's mad."

Because it suddenly felt to Alan as if Laurel had put his daughter in the middle, as Emily so often had, he was overwhelmed by a sense of sadness. "Shoot, honey, let's go to town and see if a couple of big chocolate milkshakes will help us forget Laurel."

"I don't want to forget her. Or Dog." Huge tears poured down her cheeks. She tried to turn and run down the hall. Alan and Birdie were left to watch the awkward sight. Most people relied on upper body strength as well as legs when they ran. Louemma's arms swung limply at her sides. With a sinking heart, Alan thought the flaccidness more pronounced than at any time since her breakthrough.

Vestal emerged from her room. "Mercy, what's all the noise? Is my anniversary clock losing time? I set it to chime so I'd get up to dress for the library association meeting. I thought you and Louemma would be off to her lesson by now."

"Laurel canceled, and Louemma blames me. I just told Birdie that Hardy and I were subpoenaed an hour ago. You weren't specifically named in the suit Avery Heeter filed on Laurel's behalf. Dale wants to petition the court to drop the case because they left you off the list. I can't even believe it's reached this point. If Laurel would let me explain, I think we could come to an amicable agreement."

"Sometimes differences compound so fast they're irreparable."

Alan guessed from Vestal's tone that she must be thinking of her falling-out with Hazel. "This thing became a mess through no fault of mine. If Hardy had let me take care of it, we might already have Mountain Builders clearing a path for our canal. I was this close to convincing Laurel." He held his thumb and forefinger half an inch apart.

Vestal rummaged in the hall closet and came out with a plaid chenille shawl that looked suspiciously like Laurel's work. "Don't frown at me like that, Alan. I know the calendar says it's summer. But the fog's rolling in every night. Marv Fulton cautioned me about taking a chill, and. I've noticed a damp mist some mornings. I wonder if our rains will come earlier than normal."

"I—it's—I've never seen you wear that shawl before. Laurel does similar things."

"She wove this one. Is there any reason I shouldn't support her work?"

"None whatsoever. Her weaving work is all the more reason we shouldn't kick her out of the cottage."

Birdie announced that she thought Vestal's ride had pulled in. To Alan, the housekeeper said, "This business with the shawl? It's more a matter of Miss Vestal wanting to keep up with the Joneses. The day she asked me to take her shopping for it, she admitted she didn't like being the only member of the garden club not to have one. Isn't that what you said?"

Vestal sighed impatiently.

"I said it would look bad if people in town heard about this hullabaloo over the creek. They'd say I'm shunning Laurel's work, and I'm not. Our battle in the courts should've been with Hazel, not her granddaughter. She's innocent."

"Agreed," Alan declared. So, if we all think alike, why are we going to court?"

"I don't know, dear. Can't Dale Patton fix things?"

"Dale says since Heeter filed first, we have no choice but to show up on the appointed day. It's like this whole damn debacle has a momentum of its own."

A horn honked, and Vestal reached for the doorknob. "I mustn't keep Mary Lynch waiting. Think about this, Alan. If you do go to court, Laurel will have to listen to your side, won't she?"

Crossing to her, Alan leaned over and kissed her rose-scented cheek. "You're brilliant. Now, if only I can win Louemma around so easily. I figure a kid's seriously mad if she refuses to be bought off with chocolate milkshakes."

After Vestal left, Birdie marched back into the kitchen, "Louemma don't need chocolate," she flung at him. "What that girl needs is folks in her life who ain't all the time fightin' and carryin' on."

Her words stung. Alan wasn't used to Birdie being quite so outspoken. He didn't want to fight with Laurel. Granted, they'd started off badly, but for more than three months they'd gotten along idyllically. If he had his way, they would again. He already missed her. Missed everything they'd shared. Not just the sex, though that was fantastic. There had to be a way to regain what they'd lost.

Alan tried reaching Laurel many times as July gave way to August's humid thunderstorms, but the next time he saw her was in court ten days after their breakup. Alan and Vestal had ridden to the courthouse together. As his grandmother wasn't listed by name in the suit, she chose to sit in the back.

He left her and made his way forward to where Laurel stood talking with a short, bulky man who had receding hair and a handlebar mustache. Alan's first reaction was that he yearned to see her far more than he'd dared acknowledge, even to himself.

Always slender, she seemed thinner. *Probably lost weight worrying over this,* he thought, rubbing at a sudden pain in his chest.

Laurel glanced up, straight at him, and her expression didn't change. The fact that she didn't react in any way to his smile didn't bode well for what Alan planned as his last-ditch effort to prove his good faith. He shot the cuffs of his snowy dress shirt and checked to make sure he'd shaved. He nervously straightened the knot in his tie. He'd had a hell of a time tying it earlier.

"It's now or never," he muttered under his breath.

He bypassed the table where Hardy Duff sat with Dale Patton, the company lawyer; they clearly expected Alan to sit with their team. Alan strode up to Laurel instead.

"You haven't returned any of my calls," he said, flatly ignoring the man standing beside her. "Could I have just one minute? This court fight isn't what I want. I'm sure it's not what you want, either."

He'd never know whether or not his plea would have breached her resistance. Just then, a court clerk stood and ordered everyone to find a seat. "Prepare to rise for the entry of Judge Wesley Parnell," the woman said.

"That means you, young man," Laurel's lawyer told Alan.

Heeter effectively brushed him aside. He and his client sat, leaving Alan no choice but to join his group—or risk a contempt charge.

Dale, normally easygoing, gripped Alan's arm and yanked him down so he could whisper in his ear. "What are you trying to do to our case? We've got a small edge in drawing Parnell. But any judge can rule the other way if he sees the opposition cavorting with the plaintiff."

"We weren't cavorting. And maybe if I'd had an opportunity for a few words with the plaintiff, we'd be able to call this travesty off. How in hell did we end up here in front of Parnell? At the board meeting, I specifically told you and Hardy to fix things with Laurel."

"I tried, Alan. I phoned. Then I wrote, asking her to sit down with Hardy, me and you. Sent it by courier, so I know she got it. We didn't request this adjudication hearing, Alan. We're here at her behest."

The judge entered, forcing them to stand. He was a big man with a ruddy complexion. Alan knew Wes to be an avid outdoorsman. Having never seen him wearing anything but chinos, boots and a lumberjack plaid shirt, he had difficulty adjusting to the sight of him in a flowing black robe. There was no denying, however, that Wes's taking the bench precluded further conversation.

Judge Parnell acknowledged Dale Patton with a thin smile and a brief inclination of his head. The look he bestowed on Laurel's lawyer could only be described as chilly. Alan immediately found himself feeling sorry for the out-of-towner.

Something Alan probably should have told Laurel was that men like Dale and Wes Parnell hadn't taken kindly to the upstart from Lexington pulling a fast one when he represented Hazel Bell.

It'd been no accident that Heeter had avoided filing the squatter's rights papers with the Ridge City court and had instead gone directly to the county seat. The recording and the deed were finalized before Vestal ever received a copy of the claim. At the time, she'd been grieving over her husband's death; as well, the prospect of helping Carolee run the business had overwhelmed his grandmother. It really wasn't until Hardy had begun to explore expanding their current facility that any of them worried about the ramifications of Hazel's action.

Parnell perched half glasses on his bulbous red nose. Wesley wasn't a pretty man in any sense of the word. Alan thought the attire and being perched above everyone in the room made him look like a giant troll.

Alan glanced over at Laurel and discovered her gnawing on her upper lip. She'd pulled her hair back in a tight little knot, reminiscent of the first day he'd seen her. Tendrils still escaped, and in the stuffy courtroom, two or three strands stuck to her pale neck. Alan remembered toying with those curls after they'd made love. Blood surged to his groin. He was forced to shift in his seat and turn aside.

The judge had finished perusing the items in the folder handed to him. "It's plain this case is a waste of the court's time, and mine. I don't understand why Vestal left ownership of the forty acres in doubt as long as she did." He folded his hands atop the file and glared at Laurel over his narrow glasses.

"Your honor." Avery Heeter hauled himself to his feet. "My client's grandmother and grandfather resided on that property far longer than required by Kentucky law to make the claim. They did more than the required improvements. Mrs. Bell meticulously paid taxes, as has my client since her inheritance. We contend all of that gives her the legal right to the land in question."

"Last time I checked, I made the decisions in this court, Avery. On the basis of the original land grant—which not even a Lexington lawyer can refute—it seems obvious to me that the acreage still belongs to the lawful descendants of one Luther Ridge. That's Vestal and Alan. Unless you can prove there was ever a time a Ridge sold off any part of the parcel outlined in the grant, I'm ruling in their favor. Your client has thirty days to vacate the premises or is subject to forceful eviction." Wesley slammed down his gavel.

Heeter started to sputter in protest. It was Laurel who jumped up. "I see what's happened here. You, sir, are biased in favor of Alan Ridge. Not because his claim to the land is more lawful, but because *you* obviously like sampling Windridge's wares."

Parnell slammed his gavel five times. His red face and prominent nose grew even redder. "I find you in contempt of court, young woman, and fine you one hundred dollars. Open your mouth again and your fine jumps in increments of a thousand dollars." Rising behind the podium like an apparition, Wes Parnell began shuffling together the papers that had scattered when he'd whacked his gavel.

"Judge, wait a minute." Everyone gaped as Alan sprang from his chair. The court stenographer's fingers flew across her keys. Dale yanked on Alan's suit coat.

"Alan, sit," he hissed.

The judge adjusted his glasses and scowled at Alan's intrusion. However, he had to be aware that this was an election year and he was looking at a patron he knew held a powerful position in their community. "There's more you want?" Wes asked.

"Less. I want less," Alan stated loudly and firmly, turning to locate his grandmother. "We only want the property that gives us access to the headwaters of the spring. In all, we calculated it's roughly seventeen acres, plus an easement allowing our workmen a right of way up the hill. Call it twenty acres for a good round number."

"This is highly irregular." Judge Parnell sank heavily back

into his chair. "I ruled on forty acres, but now you say you only want twenty? What about the other twenty acres in the original parcel?"

"I want the land with the two cottages and outbuildings constructed by Ted Bell either left as is under Hazel's grant, or deeded directly to Laurel Ashline." Alan turned with a smile meant to include Laurel. But if he expected to see her face wreathed in joy, he was disappointed. She stared at him with burning eyes.

Parnell extracted a pen from underneath his robe. He scribbled on the papers in front of him with a theatrical flourish. "Am I to assume this request of Alan's meets the approval of all remaining board members?"

Hardy Duff wore a thunderous expression. The bank president clearly didn't follow what was going on. Finally, Dale Patton half rose and said, "Aye."

"My grandmother is here if you'd like to poll her. But I think our legal counsel will tell you the remaining Ridge family still controls decisions of this nature. Only a few days ago, the board had this discussion and it was duly noted that she and I vote in a block."

"That's true," Dale said, rising again. "If Vestal agrees with this request of Alan's and if it pleases the court, then it's a done deal."

"Nothing about this case pleases the court," the judge said stiffly. "Vestal, what say you on the matter?"

Those few gathered in the room all followed Parnell's gaze. "I say those forty acres have been in limbo for long enough. Just let it be done so Hazel, Ted and Jason can rest in peace."

"So be it." Parnell signed his name, then smacked his gavel a final time before requesting that his secretary record, copy and distribute his ruling.

Alan barely listened as Hardy ranted on about how he had rocks where his brains belonged. All Alan cared about right now was patching things up with Laurel. But he saw that she and Heeter were making their way to a side door. He left Hardy talking to thin air and cut Laurel off a heartbeat before she cleared the door. "Hey, what's your hurry?" Alan caught her by the elbow. She was pale and didn't look happy.

"I can't talk to you now, Alan. I need time to cool down."

"Why are you still mad? I just solved our problems. Gave you a home and twenty acres of prime *Kaintucky* property," he drawled.

Pain lay buried deep in Laurel's eyes. "Well, thank you. I grew up depending on charity. I hated every minute of it."

"But…charity implies there are strings attached. There are no strings in what we did for you, Laurel."

"No strings? Then don't come 'round expecting to take up our relationship where we left off. Excuse me, please, I'm keeping Avery waiting."

"Wait! Don't you think this is what Hazel wanted? Why she went to the trouble of filing? She wanted you to have the home Lucy never did. We'll never know why she grabbed the land, but that's the only reason that makes sense."

Laurel kept on walking, her head held high. She probably hadn't heard half of what he said.

CHAPTER THIRTEEN

AVERY HEETER HUSTLED to keep up with his client's long strides. "The judge was biased in their favor, Laurel. I'll appeal. We deserve a fair hearing. I'll need to go back to the office and review your options."

Having reached her pickup, she stopped digging in her purse for her keys to wait for her shorter-legged ally. "I thought we…he could've had it all, couldn't he, Avery?"

"Yes," the lawyer said angrily. "I'll need to research. I'm sure there are millions of loopholes in those old land grants. Meanwhile, you haven't been deprived of a place to live, thanks to Alan Ridge's magnanimous posturing."

"Oh, but Alan's not like that. I know him. It's the way they went about it, Avery. I feel—I don't know, like maybe I ought to leave this town, anyway."

"And go where? Your grandmother wanted you to carry on her work here. She came to me when she'd heard of the squatter's provision in our statutes. Hazel was a lonely, bitter woman. You truly were the only bright spot in her life."

Laurel hugged both arms around her purse as she considered her lawyer's words. "I love this part of the country. Maybe Grandmother's friends in Berea know of an inexpensive place I can rent. There's a fine weaving gallery there. I'd have to promise not to duplicate their patterns but we could coexist."

"No need to make a hasty decision. I've always found it

best to sleep on a difficult situation. Things usually look better the next morning."

"That's good advice. I need to think this through. I shouldn't be complaining. Instead, I ought to thank you for all your support." Laurel extended her hand, and Avery Heeter shifted his briefcase so he could shake it.

When the van beside them pulled away, they were rocked by a blast of wind. Avery stepped back and glanced uneasily at the sky. Dark clouds had begun to scuttle overhead. "I'd better move along. Seems to be a storm brewing. I hope I can beat the rain to Lexington."

Laurel hadn't noticed the ugly dark clouds that were moving fast across an otherwise unremarkable navy sky. "I didn't expect thunderstorms until mid-September."

"Depends."

"On what?" Laurel asked, still studying the swirling black clouds.

"Oh, I'm no weather authority." Heeter laughed. "Early storms are rarely anything to worry about. And you're right, the fall Gulf hurricane season brings our worst downpours. This is likely a teaser. It's been so hot—we should be glad if we do get some rain to cool us off."

She smiled brightly. "Take care on the drive home, Avery. I do so appreciate your coming all this way to represent me."

They waved and climbed into their respective vehicles.

Driving back to her cottage, Laurel felt that the weather matched her mood. The darkest of the black clouds broke open before she reached the clearing. Her favorite parking spot had already turned muddy underfoot by the time she shut off her engine and crawled out.

Dog bounded off the porch and ran to greet her. His wet paws made a mess of the light blue suit she'd bought to wear for the trial, at Avery's suggestion. "Got my skirt all yucky," she told Dog, brushing at the worst spot.

She kept a hand on the big dog's head as they crossed the bridge. Laurel couldn't help noticing that her normally placid creek was now churning up mud from the bottom of the streambed.

Fat raindrops soaked her hair and all the way through her suit coat. Rather than linger on the bridge to watch the fascinating turbulence of the water, she dashed on across the yard and took refuge on her covered porch.

She sniffed, and thought the air smelled fresh and clean. "Instead of going straight to work, Dog, let's play hooky." It crossed Laurel's mind that this might be her last opportunity to ride to the top of Bell Hill without risking trespass. Or was that already defying the court order?

A good ride always cleared her mind. Saddling Coal Fire some twenty minutes later, she felt as if she'd assumed some semblance of control over her life again.

The rain slackened as the gelding climbed the lower section of the narrow, scarcely traveled path. When she reached the fork where her branch of the creek split from the one Alan had claimed, Laurel couldn't help thinking of their last visit here. She and Alan had laughed and talked a lot that day. It was really the beginning of their deeper relationship. A relationship she hated losing.

Resting at the spot that held so many memories and broken promises, Laurel kept her gaze on the path ahead. Her eyes were wet from tears, not from the rain, which had virtually stopped. Her goal in reaching the top of Bell Hill was to make one last survey of what had been her grandmother's legacy.

She whistled for Dog. He crawled out from the thick underbrush and shook his wet fur, making her laugh. Laurel nudged the big gelding into the switchbacks. Some areas of the trail were still slick from the recent downpour, and muddy. Others had already dried. She slid out of the saddle, leading

Coal Fire the final hundred yards. As a result, she, horse and dog were all winded when they capped the last rise.

The last person on earth Laurel expected to find perched on a rock was the man she'd so recently left in court.

A stiff wind ruffled Alan's dark hair. He, too, had changed out of his business attire, and looked elegantly casual in a pair of khaki Dockers. The sleeves of a brown-and-gold plaid shirt were rolled up over his well-tanned forearms. He had the stem of a green blade of wheat grass tucked between his even white teeth. Laurel was so forcibly reminded of the last time they'd been here that the ache under her ribs took away what was left of her breath.

"Give me a minute, then I'll leave. I know I'm trespassing, but…I wanted—I don't know why I came. Are you here to gloat?"

"No." The single word fell heavily from his lips. Slowly, Alan removed the blade of grass from his mouth. Seeing her out here brought such a mixture of joy and pain to his heart. "I thought I might run into you up here, Laurel." He confessed, "I hoped I would."

"Why? What's there to say, Alan?" she finally murmured in a husky voice.

He slid off the rock in one fluid motion, at the same time tossing aside the blade of grass.

She shrank from his imposing height, and then was angry at herself for allowing him to have such an effect on her scattered, shattered emotions.

"Don't. Please don't ever flinch away from me. And don't think about fleeing. You've ignored my calls and evaded all my attempts to discuss the truth about what led to today's court appearance."

"What's the use? It's over."

Because he had a grip on her now—and because, whenever she was in his arms, Alan lost all rational thought—everything that had contributed to their problems fell away. He slid his hands up her back into her wet hair and anchored her mouth to his with an almost savage desperation. His heart slammed in excitement, especially as he felt Laurel dig her fingers into his shirt and kiss him back with abandon.

The kiss went on for what might have been mere seconds or could have been an eternity. Both of them were panting hard, hearts racing, when they finally broke apart.

Laurel ruined everything by wiping the back of her hand across her mouth.

"How dare you take such liberties."

Unable to catch his breath long enough to speak, Alan simply held out an imploring hand.

Reacting to the anger in his mistress's voice, Dog moved his bulk between them and whined. His black ruff bristled.

"I'm sorry. I had no right." Alan knew if he didn't speak quickly, the moment would be lost, and the chance of Laurel ever letting him close enough to explain, to remedy their situation, would be zero. His first attempt came out garbled. "I didn't…it wasn't…I never wanted… Hardy and Dale acted on their own."

"Don't insult my intelligence just because I'm naive when it comes to choosing romantic partners."

"You're not. I mean, you *are* smart, and you're not naive. What I'm trying to get through to you is the God's honest truth, Laurel. I told you the retainer clause with our contractor was running out. Hardy was afraid it would, that I'd be willing to let it go so you'd have more time to make up your mind." He tucked one hand in his pocket and with the other massaged his neck. "I'd give you the moon over Kentucky if I could, Laurel. But it involeved more than just me."

She walked to the center of the bald hill. Holding her arms tight to her sides, she stared out over the rain-washed landscape spread out below. As she chewed at the inside of her mouth, a gorgeous rainbow arched over Alan's distillery. Then, below the first swath of color appeared a second, and both shimmered in the thready sun, casting shades of red, orange, yellow and green over the rooftops and trees.

"Oh, my!" Her lips began to tremble. Laurel had only ever seen one double rainbow in her life, and she took it as a sign that better things were in store.

Alan heard her exclamation while he tried to decide whether to give up trying, and just go. Wanting to see what caused her reaction, clambered up the hill to stand behind her.

"Twin rainbows," she said tremulously, pointing.

"Ah, it's still raining between here and my place and the sun's come out behind us. Sunlight diffused through raindrops is how rainbows are formed."

"But there's a second. Isn't that rare?"

"A reflection of the first. Not nearly as bright. Secondary rainbows never are. Notice how the colors are reversed."

"Oh, no, we're losing the lower one. It's fading." Laurel's disappointment was palpable.

"The clouds are moving in again." Alan squinted up at the sky behind them. "Appreciate it quickly. Once the clouds come between us and the sun, your rainbow is history."

She removed her gaze from the spectacular sight long enough to study him with a frown. "You're an expert on rainbows because?"

He slipped his hands in his belt in a familiar stance. "Comes from home-schooling Louemma," he said with a laugh and a rueful shake of his head. "I'm sure when I studied elementary science I didn't learn half of what Rose comes up with for her. You should've seen us a few months ago. Whenever my grandmother or I walked into Louemma's bedroom, we had to duck. She was studying the planets, so I spent a few nights creating papier-mâché globes to hang from her ceiling. The rings of Saturn were a special challenge.

Louemma gave me directions." He paused. "The other kids probably had the fun of making their own." His pleasure decreased noticeably.

Dark shadows of grief for his daughter's affliction crowded out the light that entered his eyes when he spoke of the normal activities other parents took for granted.

If anything melted Laurel's heart, it was seeing Alan's obvious love for his child exposed in such a raw fashion. "Louemma *is* progressing, Alan," she said, touching his wrist. "If I stay on at the cottage, I want you to know I'll continue to work with her twice a week. More if you see it's helping."

His face registered surprise. "What do you mean, *if* you stay on? The buildings and all the land around them are yours, Laurel. The court recorder will be sending you a clear title deed."

She hopped down from the flat rock where they'd been facing each other. Gathering Coal Fire's reins, she untied him from a shrub. She could feel Alan's unhappy gaze following her to a log she used to make mounting easier. It wasn't until she'd settled in the saddle that she spoke again. "When I finally found the strength to break away from Dennis, I made a promise to myself, Alan. I said I'd never be beholden to another man. Maybe you didn't mean for any of this to happen, and I should say thanks for your generosity, but…it feels like just another form of betrayal."

"Dammit," he said, legs wide. "I would've bought the upper acreage from you. Or leased a path up the hill for the canal. And if Windridge had remained solely in Ridge hands—had my mother not incorporated to improve our cash flow—it would've been strictly up to Grandmother and me. Hell, for all I know, my grandfather may have given Ted and Hazel the impression they could pass this on to their heirs."

"Your grandmother isn't of that opinion, is she? She believes my grandmother filed out of vengeance. And your manager, Hardy, and your attorney think that, too. I saw it in their eyes.

They think I'm a chip off my mother's block—that I seduced you into taking my side." Her laugh was short and cynical.

"Do I look like I give a damn what any of them think?" Alan could see at a glance that this was the wrong approach. Laurel stiffened measurably. "I take that back. If I haven't already, I'll set them straight. But that's the main drawback of living in a small town, Laurel. Other people stick their noses in your business. From experience, I know you can't stop folks from gossiping. The only way I know to get past caring about rumors is to ignore them."

"Easy for you to say. Your name is respected."

"Bull!" Alan leaped down off the boulder. If she only knew the rumors that had spread after Emily's death. And he didn't even want to find out if there was truth to some of them. Damn, if it wasn't still so difficult to deal with, he'd lay it all out now. He'd tell her his best friends thought Emily had been leaving him for the latest in a string of lovers.

Alan landed hard, too close to the gelding. The horse spooked and reared up. Dog sprang forward, knocking against Alan's knees. It all happened in a split second—a second Laurel used to wheel the black around and bolt back down the trail.

By the time Alan regained his balance, she'd disappeared. Dog ran back and forth, whining. "Go," Alan grumbled, waving the animal off. "Go after her. Slow her down so she doesn't break her neck."

The shepherd licked Alan's hand. Then he tore off down the pine-needle-covered path.

Alan, who'd come up by a different route, now faced the arduous task of picking his way downhill, back to the distillery. He wished he'd remembered to tell Laurel about the construction crew that would be starting the canal project on Monday. Hardy hadn't wasted any time. He'd been on the phone immediately after the judge had signed his decree. Windridge's manager was determined the corporation wasn't going to lose out on getting the crew they'd paid to retain. If it was only about money, Alan would agree. But he'd hurt Laurel, and nothing was worth that to Alan.

The sun popped out from behind the clouds again. Warm rays beat down on his back as he trudged downhill. He could hardly believe that he and Laurel were fighting over this spongy earth underfoot and the still-wet branches slapping his arms. On the other hand, wars had been fought over turf from time immemorial.

Dammit, he didn't want to be at war with Laurel. He'd grown comfortable with her. Watching her weave gave him a sense of comfort, of…belonging. A feeling he'd always lacked in his life, despite his family's long history in this area. To him, home had more to do with a sense of sanctuary and safety, a calm center. He'd never found that with his wife; Emily had always been a bundle of frenetic energy.

Until he'd met Laurel, Alan couldn't quite put his finger on why Emily felt a need for other distractions when she had a home, a daughter, a husband and friends in Ridge City. He'd supposed that over time they'd merely drifted apart. Heaven knew Emily had accused him often enough of losing interest. He didn't consider himself inattentive, but somehow he'd never been able to keep up with her.

After spending long, lazy hours sometimes doing nothing with Laurel, he was able to see how Emily had drained energy from everyone around her. She'd moved through life at warp speed, and she'd expected the world to keep pace.

Walking out here alone, Alan had time to ponder a few things. Did some people have a premonition they might die young? Had Emily? With each passing year, especially once they'd had Louemma, Alan became more of a homebody while Emily needed…more.

It was a difference that caused problems over Louemma. Alan had wanted his daughter home, trailing after him, asking endless questions. Emily insisted she take classes, riding lessons, tap and ballet. Swimming lessons. Baton. As well, it seemed they were always shelling out big bucks for her to join one or another organized group. Camp Fire Girls, junior charm school, soccer. Alan much preferred to take Louemma to the library to poke through the kids' section. Emily demanded all their daughter's free time—as if Alan and she were competing for Louemma's love.

Maybe that was why he'd balked when his grandmother had wanted him to take Louemma to Laurel's demonstration at Charity Madison's.

If he explained to Laurel the affect she'd had on his life, if he laid out a before-and-after-Laurel scenario, she might have been willing to let him back into her life. He refused to think *into her bed*; Laurel had always meant more to him than someone to fill sexual desires.

Vestal met him at the door. "Where have you been? I've called all over. Louemma said you said you were going to see Laurel. Her answering machine's taking her calls."

"I didn't go to her house. I suspected she'd want to make one last trek up Bell Hill—or what she'd see as one last trek. Seems I was right. What do you need? Lord, Louemma's okay, isn't she? I turned off my cell phone while we were in the courtroom. I forgot to turn it on again." Taking it from his belt, Alan rectified the situation then and there.

"Hardy's been calling here every ten minutes. Dave Bentley delivered the final blueprint for the expansion and renovation. They want to start at six, Monday morning. Hardy needs you to come to the distillery and sign off on the plans."

"Huh, why wasn't he this conscientious when it came to dealing with Laurel?" Alan heaved a sigh. "That's not entirely fair. I was dragging my heels—unwilling to push her. If he phones again, tell him I'm on my way."

"Seeing how upset she was after Wes Parnell ruled in our favor, well, I got to thinking."

Alan grinned. "Uh-oh. That's dangerous."

Vestal wasn't too frail to cuff his shoulder. "At lunch, I started to wonder why we need our new mash tanks connected to the creek water. Birdie reminded me how Jason used to complain that no matter where he dug on the property, he had to drill through limestone. Why couldn't we attach the new tanks to the existing warehouse, build a new pump house and sink another well?"

"I asked that very question in a board meeting, remember?" At her blank look, Alan chuckled. "You said our meetings are so boring they put you to sleep. That must've been one that did."

"I won't deny it. So tell me, why won't my idea fly?"

"First, preliminary studies proved a canal is cheaper. Second, there's something in the county codes about not placing new buildings in direct proximity to historic dwellings. Dale Patton said our house and the distillery meet the criteria."

"Oh. I might have known it'd boil down to something politicians did to make our lives miserable."

"There's the phone. It's probably Hardy again. Tell him I'm coming."

"Birdie will get it. I wasn't finished talking to you. Louemma is really moping again. She's been in tears most of the afternoon. I'm afraid she overheard me catching Birdie up to date on the hearing. Louemma has it in her head that Laurel's going to leave Ridge City."

Alan glanced out the foyer, down the hall, and seeing it clear, lowered his voice. "That's not altogether impossible. Laurel feels quite uncomfortable over how this whole deal was handled. And I can't say I blame her. You can tell Louemma, or I will, that I'll do everything in my power to convince Laurel to stay. But it'll take time. I'm obviously going to have to win back her trust."

"I have every confidence in you, Alan."

Birdie eased her head around the corner. "Mr. Alan, I didn't hear you come in. I just finished telling that pushy Hardy Duff to stop calling here. I said you'd go see him the minute you got in. So you'd better scat."

"I'm gone." Alan jerked open the door.

THE NEXT TIME Alan saw Laurel, he was walking Louemma to the loom cottage for her lesson. As usual, Dog raced up to his friend, cavorting like a pup. Yet he was always careful around her, as though he recognized the child's fragility.

Laurel smiled, watching those two resume a routine that had been interrupted. "Dog's missed her," she remarked to Alan. "So have I. Would you consider letting her stay for dinner?"

"Used to be we both stayed," he said casually.

"I know, but this invitation is strictly for Louemma."

Alan considered for a moment, rocking back on his heels. He looked downcast, but said, "Sure, it'll be good for her. Grandmother says Louemma's been moping all week."

"I meant to ask you something. At our last class, Louemma said her tutor took vacation during July, August and part of September. I thought she and I could plan another sleepover Labor Day weekend. Would it be okay? I'll rent some kid-appropriate DVDs. I also bought an ice-cream maker I'm dying to try."

"Ask her," he said slowly, not admitting he felt left out. "If she's in favor of it, then I guess it's okay. This is our busy time at work, so we rarely get to town for the Labor Day parade. I don't know how she'd do being jostled along a parade route, anyhow."

"Really? You'll let me stay here again?" the girl squealed. "Does that mean you *aren't* moving, Laurel?"

She shot Alan a veiled glance.

"Don't look at me," he said. "I'm not the one who's been

talking out of turn. Louemma eavesdropped on Vestal and Birdie."

"I said I was sorry, Daddy. But nobody ever tells me anything. I don't want you to go away, Laurel. Neither does Daddy. Isn't that right?"

"Laurel knows what I want, honeybee."

Laurel dragged Alan out the door. "I don't think it's a good idea to involve Louemma in arguments that are just between us," she hissed.

"That's the heck of it, Laurel. I'm not arguing. I want us to forget the past and start over. Is that so hard?"

"It might be easier if bulldozers weren't ripping off the top of Bell Hill. That's another thing, Alan. On top of everything else, I think those reports you lent me lied about the damage being wreaked on the ecosystem. Judging by the racket, anyway."

"What do you mean?"

"Haven't you been up to see what they've done?"

"No, I've been busy. I know Bentley promised low impact on the pines and hardwoods. The plans call for minimal slash and burn to carve out a narrow track for the canal. Right now, they're cutting trees for a path to move in some equipment. That probably accounts for the noise."

She gave him a skeptical glance. "I haven't actually ridden all the way to the top yet. I plan to this weekend."

"Do. Call on my cell—let me know what you find, I'd go with you, but Monday is Louemma's follow-up appointment with the neuropsychologist at the children's hospital in Charleston. We'll fly to South Carolina Saturday and get back sometime on Monday afternoon."

"I hope the doctor is pleasantly surprised by Louemma's progress."

"You could go with us. Dr. Duval would probably like to ask you questions."

"If he has questions, he's free to phone, fax or e-mail me. Do you still have one of my business cards?"

"She, and I'll give it to her. I knew this information age we live in was no damn good."

"It's very good. Dennis's counselor said he should e-mail me rather than phone so often, so I purchased a used computer. Not only are his communiquées getting further apart, but the last one indicated he's discovering through therapy that he was much too dependent on me. He stopped just short of saying we'd have to break off totally if he hopes to fully recover. In my reply, I tried to reinforce that idea." She gave a self-satisfied smile.

Alan cocked his head to one side. "If you think I'll discourage as easily as that, forget it. I liked what we had together. I miss you, and I'm not giving up on us."

"I'm still not comfortable accepting the cottages from you, Alan. But I will—and thank you. Don't misunderstand me, though. We can't turn back the clock…."

Laurel missed him, too. A lot more than she'd expected. She didn't say so because…she couldn't. Deep down, though, she knew the truth.

They settled on a time for him to collect Louemma, and then he left. Once, Laurel would have stood in the open door, watching him walk to his Jeep; now she returned immediately to her seat in front of the big loom.

Louemma had a fabulous day. From the moment Laurel introduced the prospect of another sleepover, the girl reverted to her former cheery self.

At home, later, Vestal noticed immediately. But as Windridge truly had entered its busiest season, a time when a deluge of new orders came in and had to be entered into the system, Alan was putting in long hours. As a result, Vestal and Birdie began shuttling Louemma back and forth to Laurel's. At Laurel's suggestion, the two lessons had become three.

It wasn't until a full week had passed that Alan realized Vestal had authorized letting Louemma eat practically every evening meal at Laurel's.

Wednesday, midway through a wetter-than-normal week, Alan rolled in well after dark. He wasn't surprised to see that Vestal had already retired. He slipped in to check on Louemma, but she wasn't in her bed. Alan could only surmise that she'd stayed at Laurel's after today's lesson.

This was beginning to resemble the year prior to Louemma's accident. Emily had had no compunction about tossing their daughter and a couple of suitcases in her car and heading off to spend several days with her horsey friends near Louisville. At first she wrote him notes; later, she didn't bother. He saw that Vestal hadn't left him a note tonight. And come to think of it, Laurel hadn't left a message letting him know what she'd found at the construction site. That must mean everything met with her approval, but damn, he would've liked to hear her voice.

Tired, hungry and out of sorts, Alan rummaged in the fridge, hunting for something to quell the acid running in his stomach.

He heard a car pull in next to the house and thought he'd been mistaken about his grandmother's whereabouts. Maybe she, Birdie and Louemma had gone to a movie in town, as they did on rare occasions.

Birdie entered the house through the kitchen. "Lordy, Mr. Alan, you near scared me to death. What are you doing lurking about at this hour? Are you the one who made muddy tracks all over my clean floor?"

"I just got in, Birdie. Sorry about the tracks." Alan shucked off his boots. "I probably tracked all down the hall and into Louemma's room, too," he added. "Let me toss a sandwich together and wolf it down. Then I'll clean up."

"You will not. A man comes home looking like he's been

rode hard and put up wet, he don't need to be scrubbing floors. In fact, why don't you go clean up? I'll fix you some buckwheat pancakes, and a couple of eggs and warm a slice of ham from last night's dinner. Another dinner you missed," she said pointedly.

"Birdie, you know what I said when you agreed to live in after Emily died. Your priorities are looking after Louemma and Vestal. If I'm home to eat, okay. Otherwise I'll fend for myself."

The housekeeper crossed her plump arms. "I said then that isn't any way to live. I stand by my words. Jus' you go take your muddy self off to shower." Spinning, she dragged out the old griddle she used for pancakes. "I thought you only did the accounting for Windridge. How come you look like a steve-dore lately?"

"It's time to pay the second installment on our building job. Between rainstorms I went out to find Bentley's foreman and have him sign off on their progress to date. Luckily, I met him partway up the hill from the warehouse. It's a mess out there."

"I guess. Miss Laurel, she thinks they're scraping away too much vegetation. When Miss Vestal and I delivered Louemma today, Miss Laurel showed us some of the debris she's pulled from the creek. Talk about mud. Whoee! Miss Vestal said that creek used to be so clear and cold you could drink from it. Today, there was nothing but mud pies."

Alan's expression soured. "If Laurel has a problem, tell her to call me."

"I don't blame her none, Alan. Inside her loom cottage, the dozers sound like they're comin' through her back wall."

"Jeez, they're two miles away." He paused as he pulled off his boots. "Do you know why Louemma's spending the night at Laurel's?"

"You want the truth?"

"I wouldn't have asked otherwise," Alan said, wearily straightening from having set his boots on the back porch.

"Part of the truth might not set well."

"Is this a ploy to get me to cave in to Louemma's request for a dog? I heard nothing except that during our whole trip to Charleston. Birdie, she's not able to take care of a pet. I don't think it's fair to slough it off on you or Vestal. And I'm too busy right now to even think of training a pup. Besides, after her exam, Dr. Duval suggested the promise of a dog at a later date might be incentive for Louemma to progress faster. While she agrees there's some improvement, the doctor maintains the latest tests show absolutely no nerve damage."

"I wasn't going to mention the dog. Although, now that you've brought up how little you've been home... That's what I intended to say. Louemma likes it at Miss Laurel's because she's *there*. And she's young. They do fun stuff, not just weaving. They talk about books, clothes, hairstyles. Things little girls do with their mothers."

"Laurel isn't Louemma's mother, nor is she ever likely to be," Alan stated. "Louemma was so full of talk about Laurel, Dr. Duval cautioned me about letting her get too attached. If there's a possibility it might end in disappointment, she told me, we should be very careful. She did say the weaving appears to be helping. So lessons are fine. But I think all other activities should stop. In fact, whoever picks up Louemma in the morning needs to tell Laurel that."

"Uh-uh. Not me. I'm not gonna break Louemma's heart."

"Birdie, I don't want to, either. That's why this can't go on. We're setting Louemma up for heartbreak." He sighed. "I'll go fetch her myself and I'll explain to Laurel."

"Just like that? That's not going to go over big with Louemma."

"Tough."

"I know you don't have to take my advice, Mr. Alan, but you might want to consider not ending their good times so abruptly."

"That's how Laurel ended *our* relationship," he muttered.

"I wouldn't know about that. I do know Miss Louemma is really looking forward to something she and Miss Laurel have planned for this weekend. The other day they collected leaves. Saturday, Miss Laurel's gonna paint heads, arms and legs on construction paper, and Miss Louemma gets to glue on leaf bodies. Plus, your grandmother bought them a junior Scrabble game. She smiled, "We all agreed Rose is going to be so shocked at how good Miss Louemma has learned to spell when she sees her again for tutoring."

"All right. I'll let them have this weekend. But I'll still go over there in the morning and tell Laurel."

LAUREL WAS SURPRISED to see Alan striding across her footbridge. She hadn't seen him in three weeks. Not seeing him had left a dull ache in her chest. But this sudden appearance was worse. She missed him terribly. Missed their walks. Their shared laughter. And dammit, she missed him in her bed. But apparently he'd moved on.

"Daddy! I didn't know you were coming. Guess what! Laurel and I made fresh strawberry sundaes last night. They were so yummy. I wish you could have had one. Can you come for one next time?"

Louemma's happy laughter affected Alan as nothing else could. Forgetting why he was there, he spanned her waist with his hands and lifted her up for a hug. He swung her around twice. "Gosh, it feels like forever since I've seen you, sweet pea. I need a minute to talk to Laurel alone. Let Dog walk you to the Jeep. I'll bring your suitcase and be there before you can say Jack Robinson."

Louemma giggled and called Dog. "That's not true, Daddy. I can say Jack Robinson a hundred times before you get to the Jeep, I bet."

"No way. Let's see."

The minute the girl and dog were out of earshot, Laurel

said, "Are you here to make excuses for the mess your workers are making of Bell Hill?"

"No. Some mess is inevitable. I trust Mountain Builders."

"I don't. I don't know why they have to cut down so many of the big trees."

"Dave Bentley hires local men. They have respect for our environment."

"Like hell. Last week…"

Alan cut her off. "We can't seem to communicate on any level anymore, Laurel. I'm here because after this weekend with Louemma, I want everything to stop but her lessons. No more dinners. No sleepovers."

"Why?" Laurel's face fell.

"She's…getting too attached. The psychiatrist thinks so, as well," he said lamely.

"What? That's not true. Louemma said the doctor in Charleston was happy with her progress."

"I'm not going to argue. She spends more time here than at home. I refuse to compete for my child's affections. I'd end things today, but Birdie says you two have already made plans for the weekend. If you'd rather cancel that, I'll break the news to her." He should probably explain how Emily had manipulated Louemma to divide her love—just so Laurel wouldn't have that stricken look in her eyes. But, he reminded himself, Laurel didn't care about his feelings. He didn't owe her any explanation.

"No. No," she said, her voice strained and close to breaking. "She's so excited about making the leaf people we found in a craft book. She has her heart set on it, Alan. I'm afraid I don't understand what I've done. I love Louemma dearly. But…if her doctor said—how can I object?"

"That's right." Feeling lower than the lowest weasel, Alan left.

Laurel followed his progress, thinking her heart couldn't break again. But it did. Tears slid down her cheeks, and she had to rub them away. She'd always managed to piece her life back together—but maybe not anymore. Since Laurel had never truly believed that Alan was like the other men who'd hurt her, she'd actually started to hope that time might heal their rift. It seemed time had run out.

Seeing Louemma smiling happily at her from the Jeep window made her tears run faster.

CHAPTER FOURTEEN

ALAN DID A POOR JOB of giving Louemma reasons for putting an end to her extra outings at Laurel's.

"I don't *care* what that old doctor thinks, Daddy! I want things to be how they used to be when you liked Laurel."

"Honey, I do like Laurel."

Louemma withdrew and simply stopped talking to her father. By Friday, no one in the house said a civil word to him. To make matters worse, the weather had turned really ugly. A hurricane slammed into South Carolina. Instead of swinging out into the Atlantic as most did once they hit land, this one blew straight through a corner of Tennessee. Now, according to news reports, it was Kentucky's turn to batten down the hatches.

To avoid the flak he was getting at home, Alan worked diligently at the distillery computer all morning. At one o'clock he decided he needed a break. "Hardy, I'm going to run home and grab a snack. Can I bring you back a sandwich?" Alan asked the man, who'd just come into the room, peeling off a rain slicker.

"Great. Thanks," Hardy said. "MacGregor called," he announced. "He let his crew knock off early. Mac says they can't pour concrete in the mud hole developing up the hill. I'm not a happy camper. All we need is another delay. If you hadn't let that Ashline broad screw around for so long, Mac's crew would've already poured the canal. We need those pipes con-

nected to our tanks. Even with Mac's shortcuts, we're looking at mid-October."

Snapping off the computer, Alan stood and faced his manager. "Don't start harping about Laurel again. That's over and
done with. We can hardly control what the weather does. I'm
wondering about the condition of our backup generators. How
long since we had them serviced?"

"A year. Maybe fifteen months. We haven't needed them."

Alan turned up the droning radio he had on. "If this
storm—Josie, they're calling it—doesn't peter out soon, we
may need them."

"Takes two people to fire 'em up for a test. You got time
to help me?"

"Let me run home first and talk Louemma out of going to
Laurel's for the weekend. I gave her permission, but with the
weather as bad it is, I'd rather she stayed home. They can pick
another weekend to do their leaf people."

"You can't just phone the kid?"

"It's complicated, Hardy, but no. Louemma's mad at me."

"Okay. Maybe we should let our workers who have a ways
to drive leave now. Rain's coming down in buckets out there."

"Sure. Dismiss everyone. Between you and me, we can
keep tabs on the gauges. You can bunk at our house tonight
if this storm socks in like the weather reports are predicting.
Of course, it could still blow itself out as most of them do."

"Sounds like a plan. Sort of like old times, when your
granddad and me held the fort all by our lonesome in that
thunderstorm of '83."

Alan let his mind drift back. He would've been Louemma's
age. "I remember, I think. Didn't Windridge lose power for
three days?"

"Yep. The next week was when Jason ordered the generators installed. We've only needed 'em a few times since. That
storm caused Windridge to have the leanest year on record.

Lost a hundred batches of mash and every damn thing in the fermentation room."

"I'm glad these bad storms aren't a yearly fact of life." The men walked out together. Alan rode the elevator to the basement. He was soaked to the skin long before he wheeled his Jeep into the turnaround in front of the house.

Louemma met him at the door. "I'm all packed to go to Laurel's, Daddy. Yuck—you're dripping all over the floor."

"I know. It's awful out there, honeybee. I just came home to say I don't want you going to Laurel's this afternoon. I've gotta grab some food and go straight back to help Hardy test the generators in case we lose power tonight. Ask Nana to phone Laurel and explain. I know she'll understand."

Louemma broke into loud sobs.

"No tears, please," Alan begged. "I know I said this is your last weekend with her." He touched her hair and she pulled away. "Louemma, blame the weather, not me. I promise we'll reschedule for another time when the weather's better. There's a good girl," he said, bending to dry her tears with his damp handkerchief. "Now run along and send Birdie out here. Hardy's waiting for me." Alan straightened, feeling more than a little distressed by her continued tears. But what choice did he have? He blew Louemma a kiss and when Birdie appeared, requested sandwiches, which she threw together in five minutes flat. Then he squished back out in his wet boots.

"Was that your father?" Vestal called as Louemma hobbled up the stairs.

"Yes." The girl burst into tears again. "He has to help Mr. Duff check the dumb old generators. So I can't go stay with Laurel. We won't get to make our leaf people, 'cause the leaves will get all brittle by the time we can reschedule."

"There, there. The generators will come in handy if this storm worsens. But you know what? Just because the men have things to do doesn't mean you need to give up your outing. Birdie's got the weekend off. She's almost ready to leave for Frankfort to see her son and his family. I'm sure if we ask, she'd swing by Laurel's and drop you off. Dry your eyes and let's go ask."

"Sure, I'll take you. Be glad to," Birdie said. "If your suitcase is packed, we can leave right now."

Vestal waved as the two set off. She closed the door against a gust of wind.

LAUREL HAD BRAVED the wind and rain to go check on her pregnant mare. Cinnabar had grown chubby and cantankerous in recent weeks. The vet assured Laurel the mare was healthy and that everything was progressing as it should. Nevertheless, Laurel worried about her, especially in this storm.

Already the level of the creek had risen to the underside of the footbridge. If the rain continued for several more hours, as the TV weatherwoman warned, Laurel knew the vet likely couldn't get here if she needed him.

Hurrying back to her cottage from the corral, Laurel was shocked to see Alan Ridge's housekeeper helping Louemma cross the rain-slick bridge.

"Hey," she called, veering off to intercept her guests. "I assumed your father would cancel our weekend because of the terrible weather, Louemma."

The girl said nothing. Birdie clung to the bridge railing with one hand as she passed Laurel the suitcase with the other. "Miss Vestal said Mr. Alan's tied up at the distillery. I'm off to Frankfort to visit my son. It was no problem for me to bring Louemma. But it's far more treacherous driving than I expected. At times, the rain blew so hard I couldn't see. So I won't stay to chat. You two have fun. I hope you're planning to stay indoors by a warm fire."

"That we are," Laurel replied with a grin. "And Birdie, drive carefully."

She moved closer to Louemma, wrapping half of her jacket around the girl. They watched Birdie turn her small car around and head back the way she'd come. "You know what, kiddo? That doggy pal of yours is such a fair-weather pooch. He stuck his nose out as I was going to check on my horses, but the big wimp turned tail and went back to flop down by the fire."

Louemma gazed solemnly up at Laurel. "I guess I'm a wimp, too. I wish it would stop. I don't like so much rain. And I hate thunder."

"Then let's scoot on inside. I heard a rumble a minute ago, closer than the last one. Inside we'll be snug and cozy. I'm sure this old cabin's weathered worse."

Her quip at least brought a ghost of a smile to the girl's lips. Truthfully, though, Laurel didn't much care for storms of this magnitude, either. Too many times while she was growing up her mother had left her alone and terrified. Yet that was all in the past. Today she was determined to take her mind and Louemma's off conditions they couldn't control.

"I think we should start with hot chocolate." At Louemma's agreement, Laurel fixed them each a mug. She helped the girl sip hers in between working on her weaving project.

"I'm glad you brought my loom down here, Laurel. I only have three more rows and Nana's table runner will be done. I'll give the scarf to Birdie."

"I'll wrap the gifts and put them in a plastic bag. You can bring it home when you leave, and hide it somewhere."

When the runner was finished, Laurel tied off the last row for her. "You did a beautiful job, Louemma."

"I did, didn't I? Now can I make Birdie some leaf people for her refrigerator?"

"Sure." Laurel had set all the supplies they'd need on a card table in the living room. "There's no rush. We have tonight and all day tomorrow."

"You said we'd play Scrabble. And I wanna start weaving a scarf for my dad. Out of that gray-and-black chenille. To go with his black leather jacket. He'll look so cool this winter. Don't you think he'll look cool?" she said, darting a coy glance at Laurel.

"Cool…definitely." Laurel paused, biting her lip. "Honey, we have time to do it all. Will you paint some of the heads and arms on the construction paper? It's easy if you look at the pictures in the book. Oh, come on, try before you refuse. Watch me. Holding a marker isn't much different from holding your loom shuttle."

"But I can't lift my hand up to the card table." Louemma remained adamant. She refused again as thunder pealed overhead. Simultaneously, lightning cracked outside the window, sending bright reflections skittering across the polished living-room floor. Seated on the couch, Louemma slid closer to Laurel.

"I think I'll draw the drapes." Laurel got up and crossed the room to shut out the intensifying storm. Dog sidled over to rub against the child, who shivered on the couch in spite of a crackling fire.

"There's more light in the kitchen," Laurel said. "Shall we move in there?"

Louemma nodded, her eyes wide with fright.

"We're safe in here, honey." Laurel transferred their supplies and soon the corner breakfast nook was littered with drawings.

Getting up, Laurel attached two of the finished sheets to her refrigerator with magnets. "These are great. Even cuter than I expected," she said.

"I'm sad, though. Daddy says this is our last weekend, Laurel. Why are you and him so mad at each other? I liked it better when we were all friends."

Laurel hesitated, and heard gusty wind rattle her windows and doors. "Did you ask him that question?"

Louemma nodded. "He said it's got nothing to do with me. But it does so if we can't do this kinda fun stuff anymore. Besides, it wasn't nice of him to make you cry. He said he didn't, but I saw you the other day when we drove off."

The child looked so aggrieved, the ache in Laurel's heart grew worse. Unless the storm was making her extra edgy. Sometimes the kinetic energy unleashed by an electric storm did affect her mood.

"It's only five o'clock, but it looks like night out," she murmured, cupping her hands to the rain-drenched window so she could see better. Preferring to drop the subject of Alan, she stepped onto the back stoop and flipped on the perimeter lights. Rain slanted first one way, then another. "Let's take a break. I want to check the TV weather channel to see if they've got any idea how soon things will begin calming down."

"When can we eat?"

"I'd planned to warm up some homemade corn chowder I fixed yesterday. Does chowder and bread sound okay for a stormy night?"

"Oh, yummy! Is it worse out now than when Birdie brought me, Laurel? Do you think she'll be okay driving to Frankfort?"

Laurel glanced at her watch. "I'm sure she's there by now. Her son would phone your house if she didn't arrive on time. Your father or Vestal would let us know."

"Daddy and Mr. Duff are testing generators at the warehouse. He doesn't know I came here, Laurel." Louemma lowered her chin and fidgeted. Dog whined and nosed her limp fingers as she whispered, "Daddy said for me to stay home. Nana and Birdie are the ones who let me come, anyway."

"What?" Distracted by a huge clap of thunder, Laurel wheeled away from the window to pin the child with a frown. "Alan doesn't know you're with me?"

Louemma gave a guilty shake of her head. Her gaze remained downcast.

Needing time to mull over the astounding news, Laurel opened the front door and walked out on the windy porch. The perimeter lights mounted on tall poles whipped back and forth. Even with the sporadic light she was able to see that the creek had risen a lot since Louemma and Birdie had crossed the bridge. Curls of angry water slapped the abutments, occasionally washing over the boards. As she watched in morbid fascination, a rather large tree branch floating downstream hit the bridge, and water spewed up and over it like a fountain.

Panic welled unexpectedly in Laurel's throat. She flew back into the house and slammed the door. "Louemma, I want you to listen to me, sweetheart. This has nothing to do with the fact that you and Vestal went behind your dad's back and did something he asked you not to do. The storm is making me a little nervous. I'm afraid the bridge may wash out. Then you and I could be stranded here for who knows how long. I'm going to phone Alan and have him come get you."

Louemma started to cry. Kneeling in front of her, Laurel lifted the girl's chin and said again, "This is a matter of your safety. I love you, Louemma, and I wouldn't want anything I did or didn't do to bring you harm. But no matter how much I care for you, your father loves you more. This is his decision to make. I'll ask for another weekend to take the place of this one, okay?"

The girl sniffled several times but ended up nodding. Laurel rose and immediately went to the phone. She punched in the number from memory. It rang repeatedly until finally Vestal answered. "This is Laurel. Could I speak to Alan? No, no. Louemma's fine. We're, uh, both fine, and having a good time. I just have a question for him. He's still at the distillery? Vestal, you sound out of breath. Is everything all right there?"

Laurel listened as Vestal Ridge explained she'd been digging in the closet for oil lamps. The lights had flickered a few times, she said. And oddly, at that moment, Laurel's did the same. They went out, came on, went out and took longer to come on. "Vestal? I have Alan's cell number. I'm not sure I'll bother him at work, so if I haven't spoken to him by the time you see him, please ask him to give me a call."

"I will, Laurel. He phoned maybe ten minutes ago. He and Hardy will probably be here in the next hour or so to get something to eat. You girls have fun. I'll pass on your message," Vestal promised.

Growing uneasier by the minute, especially when Dog began to pace and whine, Laurel decided she would bother Alan at the distillery. She didn't doubt for a second that his daughter was more important to him than anything, even his business.

"Your dad's still working up at Windridge. I have his cell number programmed into mine. It's in the bedroom in my purse. Will you keep Dog occupied until I get through talking to him, Louemma?"

"Okay. Tell Daddy I'm sorry I cried so hard I made Nana say I could come when he said I hadda stay home."

"Honey, I'm sure he won't be mad at you. Neither Vestal or Birdie had any way of knowing this storm would get so bad."

Rushing, while trying to appear calm, Laurel fled to find her purse. She hadn't used the speed dial feature lately. A million times she'd told herself to dump Alan's number. As her hands shook, she was glad she hadn't. The wind sounded much louder in here, Laurel realized as she waited for the number to dial automatically. But nothing happened. She held her phone under the bedside lamp and discovered she had no service. Weird. There was a cell tower on Bell Hill. The man who'd sold her the phone plan had said so, and Laurel recalled having seen it both times she'd ridden up there.

Alan's phone numbers were on a paper he'd tucked beneath her bedside phone when their relationship was on a more intimate footing. She started to dial his number, but halfway through received the same message. *No service.*

Frustrated, Laurel realized she had no option but to fall back on her own resources. Returning to where she'd left the girl, she developed a plan B.

"Louemma, I can't reach your dad, so I've decided to drive you home myself. You haven't even unpacked. Let me bank the fire, then I'll get your suitcase and we'll go."

"Can't we just stay here?" Louemma begged, her face stark white. "I don't like to go anywhere in a car in bad weather."

Laurel knew the story of the girl's accident. Her mom had gone out driving in a snowstorm, and her car had hit a patch of ice. "Sweetie, I feel strongly about getting you home where you're safe, sound and in your dad's care. I promise to drive very carefully."

Dog paced to the door and back. Laurel made sure the fire in the fireplace wouldn't get out of control while she was gone. Her worry mounted because the shepherd was pawing at the door and whining almost constantly now.

"See?" Laurel said, grabbing Louemma's jacket and her own heavy wool cape. "Dog's telling us that leaving is the right thing to do."

Louemma, clearly still not convinced, stayed close to the shepherd's side. She let Laurel hustle them both onto the porch. They'd descended the first two rain-slick steps when a horrendous crack of thunder, followed by a jagged fork of lightning, terrified them both. The girl began to sob violently and balked at moving another step. Laurel's heart leaped straight into her throat. Two other things occurred, one right after the other, that added to her fears. First the lights went out—everywhere. The house lights and the perimeter floodlamps that lit the way to the footbridge. And then…she couldn't see the footbridge.

God, where was it? A second bolt of lightning danced along a frothing creek, which had been rising less than an hour ago, but had now turned into a raging monster. The glimpse she got showed mud and debris from the construction site up the mountain being tossed into her yard and into the clearing where her pickup sat.

Laurel became aware of another danger. In the corral, her horses screamed above the roaring wind. One of them, probably the gelding, banged at the gate. A rumble farther up the hill sounded ominous, as if trees were being uprooted. *Was that possible?*

At first Laurel thought they should go back inside, where at least they'd be protected from the elements. Strong, gusting wind and raindrops pelted them with increasing force. Yet the tension lodged in her stomach sent an unmistakable warning. The cries of her childhood had honed certain instincts Laurel had learned to heed. Those instincts prodded her now. They told her that for safety's sake, she and Louemma needed to flee. Flee at once.

"Louemma," she said in as normal a voice as she could muster, "I want you to stand right here with Dog. I'm going back inside the cottage for a flashlight and my cell phone. I want to try contacting your dad once again."

"But how can he come get me, or how can you take me home?" Louemma asked shakily. "The bridge is gone, and the creek's so wide. My tutor told me all about floods. She said Kentucky has them."

"Listen to me, sweetie. The worst thing anyone can do in a bad situation is panic. The calmer we stay, the better off we'll be. We have Dog and we have each other."

"But…but…you're going to leave me and Dog here."

"Only for a minute. Please, Louemma. I need you to cooperate."

Although the girl was as pale as death, she clamped her teeth over her bottom lip and bobbed her head up and down.

Inside, Laurel quickly scooped up the big flashlight she always kept beside her bed, and a smaller one from her bureau drawer. Praying the batteries in both would last, she dug her wallet and cell phone from among the contents of her purse, which she dumped out on the bed. Her fingers could hardly grip the phone. She turned it on, but it was as dead as could be. Dashing into the living room, she decided to try Alan's home on the wall phone. She hated to worry Vestal, but on the other hand, if she was hiking downstream with Louemma, she needed to let someone know, someone who could tell Alan her plans.

But now she wasn't getting even a dial tone. Feeling starkly alone in a topsy-turvy world, and perhaps more frightened than she'd ever been—which was saying a lot, because as a kid fright had been a perpetual state for her—Laurel abandoned the dead phone. Any bad storm could knock out electricity and phone lines, she told herself. The cell tower had appeared to be a sturdy bulwark of steel set in solid concrete. The absence of that signal concerned her more.

She ran down her list of choices; they seemed pathetically few. None would be easy, and none would meet favorably with her young charge. Of that Laurel was certain.

The sounds of limbs breaking and trees hitting the ground far up the mountain, and the increase of mud churning in the stream, were two signals Laurel felt she couldn't ignore. And she had Louemma's disability to consider. But if she did nothing, they might both die. She pictured Alan's grief, and that spurred her into action.

Returning to where she'd left the dog and the girl, Laurel tucked the second, smaller flashlight into the child's jacket pocket, with the bulb facing up. Switching it on, she made another snap decision. "I'm going after the horses. I couldn't reach anyone at Windridge. But I feel it's urgent for us to get away from here. Do you understand me, Louemma?"

"No! No, I can't ride a horse! I won't. Mama, no!" the child screamed. "I won't leave Daddy for that man who rides horses. I want my daddy. *Daddy!*"

Dog licked the hysterical girl's face. He actually pressed her tight to the cottage wall, pinning her there with his body. He whined at Laurel, who gaped at the out-of-control child. Dog moved from side to side to avoid Louemma's kicking legs.

"I'm going to take you to your father, hon. Believe me, please." Laurel's heart was horribly wrenched by each of Louemma's strident cries. She didn't understand the girl's babbling. However, her own mission was clear. Telling Dog to stay, Laurel stumbled down the steps. She fought the wind all the way to the corral. Once there, she made short work of saddling both horses. It was obvious that the mare was hampered by her pregnancy, which made tightening the cinch worrisome. And considering Louemma's state of mind, coupled with a lack of strength in her arms, was doubtful she could sit a saddle, even if she was so inclined.

Laurel's mind went blank for a moment. She'd begun to grasp that the cabin might be destroyed. What else should she bring? The weaving Louemma had worked so hard to finish. The loom Laurel had altered for the girl. Hazel's scrapbooks filled with historic weaving patterns. Oh, and the family photo album. The list grew as she led the horses from the corral. Dragging them downhill through the mud, she looped the reins over the porch rail, then ran into the house again. Dashing out, she stuffed the album, the scrapbook, Louemma's project and two shawls they might need once they reached the main highway into tapestry knitting bags. The loom bumped the door casing as she wrestled it onto the porch.

"We're both going to ride Coal Fire," Laurel announced in a loud voice as she lashed the bags and the bulky loom to the saddle of the nervous mare. Cinnabar's eyes rolled wildly. She neighed constantly, jerking hard on her reins.

"You'll sit in front of me," Laurel said, ignoring Lou-emma's protests.

At nine, she was a good-size kid, even though she was on the skinny side. And when she kicked, bawled and slid down the wall, Laurel had no idea how she'd accomplish getting the rigid girl up and into the saddle.

A horrible noise and a shuddering of the cottage stilled the beating of Laurel's heart. In the shivering glow of another lightning flash, they identified the noise. A bulldozer used by Alan's construction crew was tumbling down the narrow mountain gorge as if an unseen hand rolled it end over end in the turbulent flood. There were also sections of metal cross-pieces from the cell tower.

Mudslide! "Louemma, stop fighting. Stop this instant." Laurel bent down, her face close to the girl's. "There's a mudslide from where your dad's men cleared the trees off Bell Hill. We haven't got time for arguments or tears. If we don't go now—" Laurel broke off, not wanting to tell the child they might die. But something in her voice must have conveyed the message. A shaky Louemma struggled to stand. And the moment she did, she threw her body against Laurel's.

Wasting no further time, Laurel called on strength she'd never before possessed. From the top porch step, she mounted Coal Fire, and felt his hindquarters bunch and shift. He badly wanted to run. Having gauged exactly where she needed to po-sition Louemma, Laurel leaned down from the saddle as far as she could stretch. She grasped the girl under her lifeless arms and hauled her up, placing her astride behind the sad-dle horn. It was awkward, holding the reins, steadying an inert Louemma and holding tight to Cinnabar as well. Laurel fo-cused all her energy on one thing—getting downstream to a safe crossing point before the roar of the moving mud, louder now, engulfed them.

AT THE DISTILLERY, Alan and Hardy had completed the test cycle on one of the big turbine generators when the electricity went out. "Give it a minute. Maybe it's only a temporary outage," Alan said as Hardy swore. Both men carried industrial flashlights and now switched them on.

Alan reached for the wall phone in the fermentation room. "Damn. Phones are out, too." He hung up and made his way to a window that overlooked his home. "The outage is widespread. It's black as the ace of spades out there. Hardy, can you fire up the second generator alone? Louemma's scared to death of storms. Birdie has the weekend off, so my daughter's home alone with my grandmother, and Vestal's not up to par after that last bout of pneumonia. I'd like to check on them."

"You'll come straight back? If this power failure lasts very long, we'll have to get both generators going. Since this one ran like a charm during our test, I'm sure the other will, too. If not, we could lose everything in the aging room—everything that's ready to be bottled."

Alan wavered between a need to check on his family and his responsibility as head of Windridge Distillery. They, and all the families who had someone working at Windridge, depended on good bourbon and steady sales for their livelihoods.

"I'll be right back," he promised. "If the electricity is still out when I return, we'll start this generator and test number two."

Hardy walked out with him and lit up a cigarette. Or rather, he tried to. Three matches in a row fizzled out from the rain before he managed to light the cigarette he held between his lips. "Man, this storm's a humdinger," he muttered. "I'm betting that lightning hit the power station. We're pretty high up here, and there's no glow in the direction of town."

"You're right. Well, I'll hurry. I still don't see any glimmer at the house. I thought Vestal would've lit a few lamps by now."

Alan started the Jeep, not liking how the big tires were slipping and sliding on the short drive to the house. He vaulted out and ran up the steps. "Hey!" he yelled, shoving open the front door. It was torn from his hold by a huge gust of wind. "Grandmother, Louemma—where are y'all?" His drawl always grew more noticeable when he was tired. He wondered why no one was answering. Then he remembered how angry Louemma was at him for saying she couldn't go to Laurel's. In all probability, she was sulking in her room.

Kicking off his muddy boots, Alan hurried down the hall in his stocking feet. His powerful flashlight illuminated the full length of the empty corridor.

Vestal emerged suddenly from her room, looking ghostly in the pale yellow light from an old-style lamp she carried. "Alan! Mercy, am I glad to see you. I tried to call you twice, but we've lost phone service here."

"I think phones went out before the lights. Where's Louemma? Is she still mad?"

Vestal floated toward him, outlined by the two lights. "She's at Laurel's, Alan. I thought you knew this was the weekend they had planned."

"What?"

"Louemma said you were busy at the distillery. I thought you couldn't spare the time to drive her to Laurel's. Birdie planned to visit her son, so she dropped Louemma off there on her way out of town."

Alan stomped up and down the hall about ten paces in either direction. He said a few things he wouldn't ordinarily say in front of his grandmother.

"Honestly, Alan. I don't know why you're so upset. Laurel's a responsible young woman. In fact, she phoned."

"When? Why? Was Louemma frightened of the thunder? She always is, and we've had a lot in the last hour."

"Relax. Laurel said they were fine. She told me they were having fun. I didn't detect a shade of worry in her voice. I promised her I'd let you know she had a question for you. She said it was nothing important and she had your cell number if need be."

Alan juggled his flashlight and unclipped the cell phone from his belt. He'd programmed his number into Laurel's phone and vice versa. He punched the first digit and came up with nothing. Frowning, he studied the readout panel. "No service. That's impossible."

"Why? The lights are out and so are our phones."

He glanced up at his grandmother. "Don't you remember authorizing a cell relay tower on top of Bell Hill? It's practically in our backyard." He frowned. "I've been wondering if our authorizing that tower is what started Hazel on the road to filing for the squatter's rights. An effort to protect the land she loved—to keep it unchanged."

"Who cares?" Vestal waved a thin hand. "I've decided it's all water under the bridge, Alan. Hazel's gone, and so are Ted and Jason. I'm happy with the deal you made in court allowing Laurel to live in the cottage. It's time to forgive and forget the past."

"It sure is. But speaking of water under the bridge—considering the amount of rain that's fallen over the last three hours, I'd be surprised if Laurel's bridge isn't underwater. Damn, I don't like not being able to reach her by phone."

"You're worried because Louemma's there?"

"I'd worry even if she wasn't. After Mountain Builders finishes our expansion, I'd intended to talk to Laurel about letting them put in something more permanent than that wooden footbridge."

"The footbridge is so quaint. It adds to the charm of the cottages."

"Quaint counts for squat, Grandmother, if Laurel needs to get out of her place during a bad storm."

Vestal shivered and steadied the lamp with both hands. "Like this one, you mean? I don't know why, I feel chilled suddenly."

Alan shot her a dark glance. "You're worried about having let Louemma go out in this, aren't you?"

"Yes. Oh, just listen! This house is built so sturdily you can rarely hear the wind. But now… It's so loud, Alan."

"This weather isn't fit for man or beast. If you'll be all right here alone, I'll go and help Hardy turn on the second generator. Then I'm going to take a run over to Laurel's. There's a fire road. I should be able to make it over there and back within forty minutes."

"Good. Then we'll all rest easier. I'll be fine. You go, Alan. Bring them here, and I'll use the woodstove to warm up the stew Birdie left so it'll be piping hot about the time you get home."

Alan pressed a kiss to her papery cheek. "Good. I'll send Hardy down here, too." He tugged on his boots and drove as fast as he dared back to the distillery.

Hardy met him at the door. "I don't know what those idiots from Mountain Builders did up the hill, Alan. We've got ourselves one of their John Deere Caterpillars turned upside down in a pool of mud behind our warehouse."

Alan felt as if a fist had slammed into his midsection. "If we've had a mudslide, what's happening on Laurel's side of the hill? You'll have to start the generator alone and round up some guys to sandbag the mash barrels. Louemma's at Laurel's. I've got to go make sure they're okay. By the way, my grandmother's fixing stew. If I don't get back within the hour, I want you to go stay at the house." He left Hardy and raced back to his Jeep.

As Alan roared off through the pouring rain, he imagined his daughter and Laurel floating before him on the foggy mist, and he muttered at them to hang on.

CHAPTER FIFTEEN

MUD SUCKED AT the Jeep's tires, slowing Alan's progress as he turned off the highway onto the fire road. He hadn't thought the storm could possibly get worse, but gale-force winds buffeted his vehicle even under the trees. Alan fought to keep his wheels in the slippery ruts.

His headlights illuminated downed limbs. He crunched over the smaller logs and maneuvered around larger ones—until he came upon a felled tree and realized there was no way around it.

Already soaked to the skin, he climbed out to survey the situation. He had a few tools, including a hatchet, in a toolbox strapped to the back of his Jeep. But it'd take him hours to make a dent in this uprooted hickory.

It meant losing precious minutes, but he hooked a cable around the narrowest part and tried winching the tree aside. After fifteen minutes and two unsuccessful tries that raised the front of his Jeep right out of the mud, he finally succeeded. "Yes!" His triumphant shout disappeared into the wind as he dragged the tree off the road. He resented the time it took to unhook and recoil his cable.

Once the line was tightly rewound, he allowed his mind to skip forward. By now he was virtually certain there'd be no hope of crossing the footbridge, even if it hadn't been washed away. The more he saw of this storm, the greater was his worry for Laurel and his daughter.

Combined with the anxiety was guilt. Laurel had pleaded with him to check the work being done by Mountain Builders. He shouldn't have been so certain they knew best. After all, what about the shortcuts Hardy had mentioned? Alan should've listened to Laurel. If anything happened to her or Louemma because of his stubbornness, he'd never forgive himself. God help him, but he loved them both so much.

The thought rocked him. He'd never told Laurel in so many words how he felt about her. He supposed that was because of those last few years of his marriage. Even after he'd gotten close to Laurel, there'd been a certain unwillingness to risk his heart and soul again.

Man, there was nothing like fear to force a man to see through his stupidity. And there was no way to describe his feelings for Laurel Ashline other than to say that he loved her wholly and completely.

"Damn! Now what?" The Jeep's headlights, slicing through the black night, revealed the hindquarters of four milk cows wandering along the road in front of him.

Once again he had to stop. Monty Calhoun, a neighbor, leased a wedge of land that intersected with the fire road up ahead. Vaulting out, Alan identified Monty's split-rail fence. He followed it and soon found broken rails. A huge limb had dropped from an old oak and flattened the fence.

"Jeez, cows have to be the dumbest creatures on earth." Alan discovered quite by accident that getting them off the road was a simple matter of finding their leader and shooing her through the opening. The others trailed after her, thank God.

He spared only long enough to do a quick job of attaching the slats to the posts again. Once phone service was restored, he'd call Monty and let him know he'd better check this entire fence row.

Ten minutes later, Alan reached a point less than half a mile from the clearing opposite Laurel's cottage. It was a chilling picture, even this far from her place, and even viewed through a rain-spattered windshield. The creek had expanded to twice its normal width, and the boiling, angry water churned with mud. He dared not try to drive any closer.

He climbed out of his vehicle to shine his powerful flashlight up and down the banks of the normally tranquil creek.

Tranquil was the last word anyone would use to describe this frenzied, out-of-control flow. Fear ate away at Alan's gut. Back in his idling Jeep, he wrapped wet, unsteady hands around a steering wheel already slippery with sweat. Leaning his forehead on his white knuckles, he tried to recall every twist and turn the creek made. There were two other points where it might be possible to cross to Laurel's side. But if he guessed wrong, he could be swept downstream himself. Then where would any of them be?

Who would know he was missing? Not Laurel, who didn't realize he was trying to find her. Not Hardy, who was too busy holding down the fort at Windridge. And probably not his grandmother, at least not for hours.

Imagining Laurel, calm though she was, having to deal with a power outage, a panicked kid and God only knew what else, Alan struggled to get a grip on his own fear. At last, he managed to curb it enough to drive some distance downstream, where he hoped to test his latest theory.

Seconds could mean the difference between fording the creek and not being able to cross at all.

Alan hadn't thought ahead about what he'd do if he simply couldn't get to them. He refused to consider the possibility. He'd save them, no matter what it took. He'd swim an ocean if he had to.

LAUREL FELT LOUEMMA'S constant sobbing, plastered as the girl was to the front of her body. She crooned soothing nonsense near the child's ear. "Keep your eye on Dog," she chanted over and over. "If we trust him, Louemma, he'll lead us out of here. If you trust me and stop crying, it'll be easier on Coal Fire. He's surefooted, sweetie, but your sobbing is spooking him. And it's not helping you. Try to relax. Think how glad your daddy will be to see us when we finally get to Windridge."

"But, its dark, and there's thunder," Louemma cried, stirring in Laurel's arms. "And I can't see Dog. He's black and so is the trail. I'm s-scared."

The gelding stumbled. Louemma screeched like a banshee and threw herself hard against Laurel.

For a moment, Laurel saw stars and had difficulty catching her breath. Then Coal Fire reared, and Cinnabar's reins were ripped from her already numb fingers. Or maybe she dropped them in an effort not to unseat herself and Louemma. She saw that the creek lapped onto the trail. Laurel glimpsed water swirling around her horse's fetlocks. Greedy, encroaching waves washed over what was left of their escape route.

Dog, who'd disappeared into a black patch of trees, bounded back to see what was keeping them. Or maybe he'd come to check because Cinnabar had sailed past him, terrified and galloping frantically. The mare took with her everything that remained of Laurel's life—unless, by some quirk of fate, her loom cottage and her home were spared from the mud rushing like a freight train down the hill.

It wasn't until she'd spent several minutes fighting to stay in the saddle that Laurel thought to worry over what might happen to her poor pregnant mare. What if Cinnabar tripped over the dragging reins? Or were they dragging? She vaguely recalled having knotted them before she mounted Coal Fire. But maybe knotting had made things worse. What if the leather strap slipped to the ground and the mare caught a foot in them and went down? She could break a leg.

In the midst of such upheaval, something else—something

unexpected—registered with Laurel. Somehow, Louemma had managed to wind her hands in Coal Fire's long mane. Right now she was holding on for dear life. *It meant Louemma had raised her arms.*

If circumstances had been different, Laurel's heart would be filled with joy. Instead, all she could do was pray that they, and her poor horses, got out of this ordeal alive.

ALAN REACHED A BEND in the river marked by twin poplars, now leaning at a forty-five degree angle in the wind. This outcrop was significant in that it was the first of the two places where he might ford the swollen creek.

Many shallows along the tumbling watercourse fell away into deep sinkholes where he remembered swimming as a kid with friends like Pete Madison. This particular spot and one other didn't have a treacherous silt bottom. Rather, the bottom here sloped gently, boasting a mix of limestone and shale. Just for the hell of it, Alan, Pete and a group of friends used to drive ATVs across the stream on sultry hot summer days. A half mile down on the other side, the boys would strip and swim in one of the deepest holes around. They'd let the sun dry their damp shirts and pants, and then, refreshed, drive to the last point possible to cross back to this side.

Alan had hoped he could cross here now. With the trees marking the sandbar, even in the dark, this was the most easily identifiable crossing. Of course, during summer and in daylight, fording wasn't risky. Tonight, the creek had more than jumped its banks.

Gritting his teeth, Alan eased the front tires of the Jeep into the rushing water. He hadn't gone two feet when cold muddy water lapped over his door and swirled across the floorboards, soaking his feet. Shoving the vehicle into Reverse, he threw an arm over his seat back and hauled ass out of there as fast as he could.

Drenched with sweat, Alan thanked his lucky stars that the Jeep's motor hadn't died and left him stranded. On the other hand, he hadn't even made it to midstream. Now he didn't know whether to drive on down to the next shallow spot, hoping against hope that he'd have better luck. Or should he park and take his chances swimming? That plan continued to claw at the back of his mind. Suddenly, cut logs—a lot of them—bobbed past on frothy waves. Waves that were far from normal for a six-foot-wide, one-foot-deep creek.

A piece of equipment belonging to the construction crew rolled along in the wake of the logs. "Dammit," Alan mumbled. What if he'd decided to swim and he'd encountered that debris? It would've killed him instantly.

His concern for the safety of his daughter and Laurel grew that much more intense.

Wasting no time, he jammed the Jeep's transmission into first, then second, then third gear. Call him crazy, but he wanted to beat the next batch of rubble to the last shallows.

Arriving at what he guessed was the right spot, Alan lamented that he'd now have to travel a mile to Laurel's cottage on foot.

He tested the bank with his front wheels and did his best to tear his eyes from the seething water lit only by his headlamps. Something big hit the back of his Jeep, throwing him sideways. He opened his door, fully prepared to leap out.

The engine coughed, sputtered, coughed again and caught. His tires found purchase on something hard beneath the roiling surface. Keeping slow and steady pressure on the gas pedal, he moved forward. It seemed an eternity, but at last he emerged unscathed on the opposite shore.

Preparing to drive up a trail that really wasn't meant for cars, but which he felt confident his four-wheel-drive Jeep could navigate, he saw what looked like a head bobbing in the creek.

Leaving his Jeep, he climbed onto the hood and shone his

industrial light down from above. His heart stilled as he recognized one of Laurel's horses, apparently swimming, or trying to swim, but looking wild-eyed and tuckered out.

Alan didn't think twice. He kicked off his boots, ripped off his jacket and made a low dive off the bank, aiming to head off the animal. He misjudged how fast the creek was moving, and came up directly in front of the horse. Already scared, the mare snapped her teeth shut on his left arm, in the fleshy part below his shoulder.

Alan flailed out with his good arm. Twice he missed the bridle. Because the pain in his left arm was so great, he was afraid he might lose consciousness and fail in his rescue attempt, after all. Through force of will his next lunge for the trailing reins was successful. His left arm hung nearly useless as he kicked hard with his legs. He was miraculously able to guide the animal to shore some hundred yards downstream from where he'd left his Jeep on a knoll.

The mare managed to get her legs under her. She was able to scrabble out onto a slab of limestone, and both man and horse lunged as quickly as they could up the bank, where they stood stiff-legged, gulping in huge drafts of air. Alan made sure he kept a firm grip on the wet reins as he stumbled back along the shore, with water lapping at their feet. He had barely enough strength to secure the shaking horse to the bumper of his Jeep. Then he fell to his knees and retched until nothing was left of the muddy water in his lungs.

It was after he'd emptied his stomach that Alan realized the mare was saddled. His brain refused to contemplate the implication. Needing something to do, even with one arm hurting like hell and hanging limp, Alan uncinched the saddle. He dumped it, along with a loom and two heavy tapestry bags, straight into the back of his vehicle.

His teeth chattered from the wind striking his drenched clothing. Not knowing what to do next, he debated whether to attempt driving or to mount the horse and ride bareback up the trail. All the while, his eyes strained for any glimpse of other bobbing heads. If the mare was saddled and carrying things that belonged to Laurel, it could only mean she'd been forced to leave her cottage. Alan's chest squeezed in pain.

And what about Louemma? She was scared out of her mind even glimpsing a horse. Had Laurel tried to get his daughter to ride, and she'd somehow fallen? No, Alan refused to consider it.

What eventually decided him, outside of an urgency to do *something,* was the fact that the muddy path in front of him narrowed as it entered a thick copse of beech trees. Alan's love and concern won out over his doubts. And he had plenty of reason, for doubt, including a weary mare and an arm that had begun to bleed and throb.

Uttering a silent prayer that the pregnant horse wasn't as spent as she seemed, he led her to a stump and managed in one try to haul himself aboard her wide back. Without delay, he urged her up the trail.

Deeper in the trees, the wind was less fierce. In places, the ground appeared less muddy. Still, the mare stumbled. Alan patted her steamy wet neck, bent low over her and coaxed her by whispering in her ear. "Help me find Laurel and Louemma, girl. Don't fail me now and I guarantee you all the hay, oats and carrots you and your foal can eat from now through eternity."

To himself, Alan vowed that if he found them safe, there would be no more accusations to do with land, no more worry about alienated affections, no stall tactics of any kind. Laurel Ashline belonged with him. She belonged with Louemma. If she truly couldn't reconcile herself to his profession, then by God he'd dump his shares in Windridge. He'd sell his interests, down to the last red cent.

Perhaps the longest five minutes of his life passed as he sped over familiar land on an unfamiliar horse.

All at once the mare's ears shot forward. She neighed excitedly, and next thing Alan knew, a dog barked somewhere up ahead in the blackness. He reined in abruptly, straining to hear a second bark, hoping against hope that he hadn't imagined it.

Sure enough, a series of deep woofs drifted toward him from farther up the trail. "Dog…Dog!" Alan shouted hoarsely. "Laurel! Laurel, are you out there? It's Alan! Oh, God, can you hear me?" he screamed, redoubling his efforts.

The German shepherd loped into view. Behind him came the sound of a heavier animal pounding along the trail. Branches cracked and broke, and Alan's mount danced right, then left, neighing in confusion.

There was another duller, more ominous rumble that Alan couldn't identify. All at once, a huge dark horse hove into sight, running at breakneck speed. Alan feared the animal would collide with his mare. About to slide off her, he checked himself and grabbed instead for the horse about to thunder past. It took all the strength in his good arm to hold the bigger, heavier gelding.

Laurel saw Alan as Coal Fire reared. She shouted his name. "Alan! I'm so happy to see you! But we have to get off this trail. We're trying to outrun a mudslide," she panted. "We're only moments ahead of it."

"Daddy, Daddy," Louemma screeched. "Laurel promised to find you, and she did! She did."

"Turn," Alan yelled, more than alarmed. "Uphill to your right," he commanded, as old habits clicked into place. Merely verifying that Laurel and Louemma were alive made him happier than he'd ever been.

Laurel didn't question his orders as she might have under other circumstances. Her arms ached horribly from hanging on to Louemma and from gripping the reins on a horse that could falter at any moment.

Using what breath she had left, she whistled for Dog, and hoped he'd hear her and come back. If it hadn't been for him—well, who knew what would've happened to them at the cottage.

The big dog streaked out of the trees and barked wildly at his mistress.

"Keep angling up and left," Alan called insistently. He hated to let go of the gelding's bridle, but with the rocky terrain he had to. They were all breathing hard. It wasn't easy to speak, but he tried to explain anyway "There's a series of caves along a narrow bluff. We'll be safe there if we can find them. Pete, Joe and I used to play there as kids. If the opening hasn't grown over, I think the outer chamber's big enough for us to squeeze inside with the horses."

"Will the mud cover the opening and seal us in?" Laurel shouted as Alan urged them ever higher up the dark, uneven slope.

The severe pain stabbing in his arm stole Alan's ability to answer.

It was Dog who found the entrance. They would never know if he'd stumbled on it by accident, or if he was imbued with some survival instinct that led him to it. Either way, they would always and forever hail him as their hero.

Barking, the mud-spattered dog paced back and forth at the opening. He jumped aside as Laurel and then Alan rode into the dark slash in the hillside. Laurel, first in, startled a hundred or so bats that had probably returned home to wait out the storm.

Wings flapped so near their heads and near the ears of the horses as the bats flew out that the skittish mare bared her teeth and snapped ineffectually at one of the low-flying mammals.

"Ugh, Daddy, it stinks in here," Louemma shrieked. She turned and hid her head in Laurel's chest.

Fumbling for her flashlight, Laurel switched it on. She

played the light over the ceiling and saw they'd apparently displaced all of the cave's former occupants.

Alan slid off the mare. He rushed up to Coal Fire and tumbled Laurel and Louemma out of the saddle and into his arms. He made no apology for his tears. And he couldn't seem to stop stroking first one wet head and then the other with his good hand. Nor could he stop raining kisses over their beloved faces. The arm Cinnabar had bitten hung loose at his side, so Alan could only hug them awkwardly.

It wasn't until Laurel's muffled voice drew his attention to the fact that Louemma had flung her arms around Alan's waist that he realized his daughter was the one hugging him back so tightly.

All their excited talk was cut short as a rush of mud rumbled past the entrance, and they held their breath. It wasn't long before they discovered Alan's predictions had been correct. The roaring, hissing, vibrating river of mud didn't quite rise to the level of the limestone caves.

"Alan, my God, your jacket sleeve is soaked with blood." Laurel felt him wince as she turned away from the cave mouth, accidentally bumping his left arm with her flashlight as she did.

"Horse bite," he muttered, bending to lay his cheek on Louemma's head. And before Laurel got out another word about his injury, he pressed his lips to her soft mouth. Feeling her return his kiss was all Alan needed to revive his flagging spirits. Lifting his head, he scraped back her soaking, stringy hair and smiled into her upturned face. "I don't even know where to begin. How did you get Louemma to ride with you? How come she's able to hug me? Tell me this part's real and not just a dream."

"It's no dream," Laurel assured him, although she mopped at tears she couldn't keep from shedding. "Louemma, sweetie, tell your father what you said back at the cottage when you didn't want to get on Coal Fire. At first, I didn't understand, but as we were trying to outrun the mudslide, I think my brain figured out what you've been holding inside, honey." She propped the big flashlight on a ledge so that it illuminated the chamber.

Louemma's fingers stroked the fur on Dog's head, and she buried her face against her father's waist.

Laurel went down on one knee. She pried the girl's face away. "You need to tell him, okay? Please? You're so brave, I know you can. Remember, we were on the porch?" Laurel knew a little about purging trauma, yet she couldn't bring herself to meet Alan's confused eyes. "Louemma, you mentioned your mom, and…a man. A man who had horses."

"Doug," Alan murmured, his lips thinned.

Louemma nodded. "I 'member. Mama said we hadda go live with that man. He rode horses at the racetrack. We saw Doug lots, and I didn't like him 'cause he kept kissing Mama. That day—the day I got hurt—she made me go. She said I wasn't ever going to see you again, Daddy." Louemma sucked in trembling lips, and tears streamed from her eyes. "I cried and cried. I couldn't stop. Mama turned around and said for me to hush. I know she was mad. Then the car went sideways, and backward, and spinned around and around. And—and she went to heaven to live with Grandpapa Jason. I did it, Daddy. I made her wreck the car. I'm sorry, but I didn't want to leave you forever. I didn't." She threw both arms around Alan and hugged him twice as hard as before.

"Oh, Louemma." Alan sank down next to Laurel, all the while clutching his daughter with his good arm. "You didn't make Mama wreck her car. Her tires hit ice on the road. And there was fog. It was a true accident. Louemma, it *wasn't* your fault. And…I'd never, never have let her take you away from me for good. I'm the one she was trying to hurt by saying that.

Not you. But I promise your mother and I always loved you very much. You were the best thing in our lives, honeybee."

"Are you sure, Daddy?"

"Positive. Absolutely." Alan's eyes lifted to connect with Laurel's. He steeled himself against her pity; after all, his wife had been leaving him for another man. What he saw reflected in her gaze was love and admiration. It gave him hope. Allowed him to say what he hadn't been able to until now.

"Laurel, today I learned there are only two things important to me in this whole world. Louemma and you. Well, and Grandmother, of course. I want—I'd like… Uh, will you—?" He fumbled for the words. His attempt to express his feelings was halted by Dog, who set up a commotion at the cave entrance.

Alan grabbed his flashlight and they all rushed to look. What they saw was Laurel's horse shed sliding by. Horrified, they stared down on the shingled roof. That worrisome sight was followed closely by Laurel's front porch, ripped from its concrete mooring.

Alan slipped an arm around her waist. Cradling her and Louemma tight against him, he said in a gruff voice, "I'm trying—not very successfully—to ask you to be my wife, Laurel. You and Louemma are all that's important to me. Everything—and I mean *everything*—is replaceable. Spinning wheels, looms, cottages, antiques—or my occupation."

Laurel clung to Alan, loving his solidness. Loving his strength. "You can't mean you'd give up Windridge for me," she said. "It's your heritage, and Louemma's."

"Oh, but I do mean it, sweetheart. You have only to say the word and we'll start our lives anew. Provided you can get past my bullheadedness. God, how I've missed you. You tried to get me to go and see what the construction crew had done. If we're assigning blame, then it's mine that you've lost your family treasures."

She leaned her head on his good shoulder. "Treasures are nice, Alan. But all I've ever wanted—ever *really* wanted—is a family to love me. One I could love in return. I feel bad about losing Hazel's scrapbooks of historical patterns, but it's nothing compared to my fear that I might fail you. If I'd let something terrible happen to Louemma... I love her so much, Alan. And I love you."

"When the storm blows out, maybe we can still salvage something from your cottage, Laurel. We've only seen your shed and the porch. Those cottages were built on strong foundations."

"It's okay," she said, placing her fingers over his lips. "Either way, the patterns are lost. I tried to save them by tying them to Cinnabar's saddle. Her saddle's gone. I didn't cinch it very tight because of her pregnancy. I'm just so thankful she made it out alive. I want her to have her foal. Babies equal new beginnings, don't you think?"

"You tied Hazel's scrapbooks to Cinnabar's saddle?" Alan smiled for the first time. "Sweetheart, maybe the patterns are safe. I removed Cinnabar's saddle and tossed it in the back of my Jeep. I noticed a loom and two knitting bags. I never took time to look inside. If my Jeep survives the mudslide, and it might because I parked on a knoll, we might salvage those things." He hugged her, his smile giving way to earnestness. "When we were talking before...were you, uh, saying yes to my question? I mean—"

Laurel grasped his face between her hands. She kissed him hard, smiling through her tears. "Yes, yes, *yes* to everything. Well, almost everything. I won't ask you to give up Windridge. I was such a stubborn fool. I knew I loved you the day I thought I'd lost you. The day you said Louemma couldn't stay at my house anymore."

"I can explain that. Emily tried to make Louemma love her more than she loved me. I imagined it happening all over. You're not like that, Laurel. Forgive me for ever thinking you were."

Louemma gazed at the two adults from her spot on the floor of the cave, where she hunkered down, both arms wrapped tight around Dog.

"Daddy?" she asked when the couple finally emerged from an especially lengthy kiss. "If we're marrying Laurel, does that mean we're marrying Dog, too?"

Startled at first, Alan, his good arm still clamped around Laurel's waist, felt laughter bubbling up. He realized he was being given a second chance to laugh and enjoy life. A chance to love and maybe—someday—add to his family.

"I'm having a hard time picturing Dog in a tuxedo. But you bet we're marrying Laurel, honeybee. And that means accepting everyone in her family. I already promised Cinnabar a warm stall and oats for the rest of her life if she held out long enough to let me find you two. I think my promise goes double for Coal Fire, since he carried you and Laurel out of harm's way. But Dog? I guarantee he'll eat steak from now on. If he hadn't barked at me, we might have passed each other in the darkness."

Louemma used both hands to lever herself up, something she hadn't done since the accident. "When can we leave this stinky old cave? I want to go home. Nana will be worried, I'll bet. And can I call Birdie—oh, and my friends, to tell them I'm getting a new mom. And...can I go back to school, and—"

"And we'll get your dad's arm taken care of," Laurel said, breaking in. "Horse bites can be nasty if they aren't properly treated."

In spite of Louemma's long list, Alan didn't seem in any rush to leave. His primary focus seemed to be kissing Laurel....

She didn't object very strenuously. And neither, really, did Louemma. After all, she was assured of getting the two things she prayed hardest for every night—that Laurel would live with her, Daddy, Nana and Birdie. And that she'd bring Dog.

"Dog," she mumbled, smothering the animal in hugs.

"Some days that start out really, really bad can end okay." She kissed him right on his wet snout.

The shepherd licked her cheek and whined softly in her ear, which Louemma took for total agreement.

EPILOGUE

SPRING HAD AGAIN COME to Ridge City, Kentucky. Laurel's second spring here. This March was better in every way than the previous one, when she'd so recently arrived in the valley, heartsick, scared, yet hoping for a bright future. Even Dennis had moved on. In his last note he said he had a good job and was still sober. And she'd found peace and comfort, she thought as she raised the window to let in the breeze. It carried with it the delighted laughter of her stepdaughter, Louemma, who played tag in the field below with three of her friends and Dog.

As she watched the kids, Alan drove in and climbed out of his red SUV. Smiling, Laurel waved at her husband. His new vehicle was just one of many changes brought about by last September's flood and mudslide, which had destroyed much of Laurel's past and damaged Alan's beloved blue Jeep.

So much had happened since the disaster had forced them to strip away the veneer of their lives to expose what really mattered.

Hearing his footsteps on the stairs, she ran to greet him with a hug. These days they stole these blessed moments alone whenever they could.

"Hi, beautiful." Alan swept her up and swung her around. Laurel always laughed, because he made her feel as young as Louemma.

"You've been to Bell Hill," she said. "So the reforestation is going well?"

He kissed her, set her down, then pulled off his jacket and tossed it over a brass coat tree they'd salvaged from her grandmother's cottage, along with a few looms and Laurel's favorite spinning mule, which had been restored.

"The way they do the planting is a fascinating process, Laurel. Kids from the college forestry program scatter and cover seeds they harvested from the remaining crop of pinecones. You wouldn't believe how much progress they've made."

"Alan," Laurel said pensively. "Are you *positive* you have no regrets about scrapping your business expansion plans?"

"Dissolving the corporation and scaling back to a smaller, more selective distribution of our bourbon is the best thing that ever happened here. Hardy agrees. He's much happier back making bourbon than being general manager. Well," he added with a wink, "that's not altogether the best. Our marriage was the best." He reached out and ran one finger idly overt the gold spinning-wheel pin she wore on her lapel. Alan recalled a time when he doubted he'd ever be in a position to give Laurel that pin, and now she was never without it. He turned her so they could both look out the window. At the kids, and the sun-dappled estate. "Your brilliant idea of opening up Windridge for tours and letting Vestal run them has given my grandmother a new lease on life. Shaved ten years off her age."

"I only suggested something Vestal mentioned on my first visit to Windridge. She's the one who said people were always asking you for private tours." Laurel paused. "So, you don't think all the adjustments she's had to make since we got married have been harder on her than she's willing to admit?" They'd had a small wedding at the house the previous Christmas.

"Are you kidding? Watch her. She's in her element." His laughter vibrated against Laurel's back.

"I have. It's a treat to see her—she really is a natural. I hear her spiel sometimes when she winds up her tours in the showroom downstairs. And she's the one who insisted we display and sell my weavings. I swear, she never lets a tourist leave without buying a scarf, a shawl, place mats or something. But listening to her brag about my work is enough to make me blush."

Alan slid his hands around his wife's waist and rested his temple against hers. "What's most impressive to me is Louemma's three-hundred-and-sixty-degree turnaround. Before the accident, I used to think she was a happy kid. Now she positively glows. I have you to thank, Laurel. You gave me a gift I can never match."

"Oh, I wouldn't say that." She took his hand in hers and flattened it across her belly. "Dr. Fulton said that if all goes well, we can expect a very special family gift by Thanksgiving."

Alan turned her slowly, his face filled with awe, which gave way to the biggest smile. "You…aren't pregnant?"

"I am. Barely. Birdie knew before I did. She said she read it in my eyes. That woman's mountain intuition is uncanny. She's going to claim it's the result of some herb sachet she tucked under our mattress."

Alan whooped for joy and rained kisses all over Laurel's face.

"I know we said we'd wait a year," she said nervously. "How…how do you think Louemma will react? We have a month or so to figure out how to tell her."

"You're worried?" Alan dropped another kiss on her lips. "She'll be the happiest person on earth."

Laurel went very still and slowly reached up to brush her thumbs over Alan's cheekbones. "Louemma can't be the happiest because I am. I'm finally living my dream."

"Me, too," he whispered, turning to press his lips into her palm. "Just the other day, Louemma said, 'If our new life's a dream, I don't ever want to wake up.' I feel the same way."

They stood comfortably entwined until the phone rang, and

the next carload of tourists arrived. As Alan went back to his computer and Laurel to her loom, both knew their love would flourish in this valley; season after season.

*Turn the page for a special treat—a preview of
Roz Denny Fox's first book for American Romance!
We're delighted to present*

TOO MANY BROTHERS,

*coming next month.
It's fast-paced and funny and it features
Roz's trademark warmth.
We guarantee you'll love*

TOO MANY BROTHERS

*from Harlequin American Romance.
Watch for it in September 2004.*

Chapter One

Daphne Malone put down her phone, threw her hands in the air and danced a zany victory dance around her perpetually unmade bed. She'd just been offered a job. Not the greatest in the world, but a start. In the middle of her jazzy dance to a blaring CD, a strand of curly dark hair caught on one of the four posters, bringing her up short. The jolt sobered her. This was real. A job. In a few hours.

She dashed to her cluttered closet, and because Daphne never did anything slowly, she rummaged around frantically until she uncovered an old beach bag. With her free hand she began pawing through costumes she might use today. She couldn't decide, so she tossed in accessories. The bag was already bulging, and she still hadn't settled on a costume. Maybe she'd phone her mom for advice. Calandra Malone had taught both her daughters how to sew at an early age, which was why Daphne had such a splendid array of clown suits.

She grabbed the phone from her nightstand and hopped around, pulling on a pair of clean white jeans while punching in her parents' number. Daphne juggled the cellular between her cheek and shoulder and braided her long hair into a single, more manageable plait.

"Mom? Guess what?" she said the instant Callie Malone answered. "I've got a job at a birthday party this afternoon, over near Commerce. I am so excited!"

Daphne rolled her eyes. "It's *near* East L.A., not in East

L.A. Yes, Mother, I know Kieran says that part of the city isn't safe for a woman alone. But I'm going to the home of someone who's a friend of a friend of the wife of one of Dane's partners. It's a party for ten seven-year-olds. How safe is that…?

"Okay, okay! I'll check in when I get home." Daphne glanced at her watch. "I called to see which outfits you think I should take, but I need to run. Be happy for me, please. It means money, at least, until I get the break I'm really waiting for."

Daphne lowered the receiver at the last possible moment, listening to Callie, who continued to spout dire warnings. She ended with one good suggestion. "Take a variety, Daphne, and see which feels right when you get there. Just…be careful, sweetheart."

Daphne added her favorite clown suits to the bag, all the while wishing her parents and her three older brothers would believe she could take care of herself. After all, she was twenty-six. Granted, Kieran subsidized the apartment, but only until she could get herself established. Meanwhile, why couldn't the lot of them stop hovering? Her sister, Becky, was a year younger and they left *her* alone. Of course, Becky had a solid marriage, a good career and she was already a mom herself. Daphne's jobs had been a disaster up to now, and her love life—well, that didn't bear mentioning.

Lugging the beach bag down to the vintage chartreuse VW Bug that her brother Perry had lovingly restored, Daphne let a perfect sunny fall afternoon rejuvenate her spirits. She was an eternal optimist. She wasn't going to let her mother's undue alarm change that.

Placing the directions to the party on the empty seat, Daphne dropped her sunglasses over her eyes and chugged off along the familiar streets of Culver City—the suburb of L.A. where she'd lived forever.

Like a pro, she cut from the I-10 freeway to the Santa Ana

Freeway, eventually exiting on Atlantic Boulevard. A cop's siren screamed over her new Josh Groban CD. Daphne automatically moved to the right and rolled to a stop. Squinting into the sun out her side window, she watched in amazement as five police cars sped past. Daphne couldn't tell if Kieran was driving one. Her brother did sometimes patrol this area. She hadn't spoken with him since the previous Friday because she'd spent the week baby-sitting their oldest brother's kids. As a rule, she'd know Kieran's schedule. The Malones were a close-knit family in spite of her complaints about their hovering.

Five blocks farther down the road she discovered the police had cordoned off the street she was supposed to turn into. Not familiar with this neighborhood, she wasted time locating an alternate route on a map stored in a side pocket of her car.

The roundabout journey took her down some scuzzy streets. Remembering her mom's lecture, she locked both doors. Thanks to a network of one-way streets, she finally found the one she wanted by making a big *U*. The homes were older, but she was relieved to see they were well-maintained. The one she sought was at the end of a dead-end street. A partially wooded lot bordered it on the left, intersected by trails. Neighbors probably walked their dogs there or jogged through the trees.

Daphne hefted her beach bag, draping it nonchalantly over one shoulder as she checked the house number. She mounted the steps and knocked.

A harried, very pregnant woman opened the door. She introduced herself as April Ross. After exchanging a few words, April led Daphne into a living room that was a mess of floating balloons. "Forgive me, please. The first helium tank I rented didn't work, so I had to take it back. This is Natalie, the birthday girl. Nat, Daphne Malone, our party clown. Honey, will you take Daphne to the guest bedroom so she can change into her costume?"

April finished tying off a balloon and added, "The guest room has a sliding glass door leading out onto the patio, where I've set up for the party. I know you said you'll probably change costumes during your program. I thought it'd be easiest to run back and forth into the house through the slider."

"Sounds perfect. Thanks, April. I'll scoot off and dress so I can help you greet the kids. Or tie balloon bouquets and let you greet them, whatever you prefer. In any case, I'd better hurry. I see a couple of moms bringing kids up the walkway now. I'll just go, get out of your hair." Daphne moved toward the hall.

"Thanks for your offer of help. I'm frazzled and I hate being late," April wailed. "Oh, and Daphne, thanks a million times over for bailing me out on such short notice. Nat had her heart set on a clown to do magic tricks. Like I told you, I booked from an agency, but apparently the receptionist flipped two pages at once on her calendar. Another family got first dibs because they'd phoned first."

"No problem." Daphne grinned. "Tell your friends, in fact. I need all the bookings I can get between now and when I find permanent work in my real field."

Daphne chatted with the birthday girl as they walked down the hall. She loved kids, and often baby-sat her niece and nephew whenever Dane and his wife, Holly, needed her. Natalie Ross was cute and talkative. Before she scampered off, Daphne learned that she wanted her to paint the faces of all the kids attending the party.

So, she'd been right to bring all that stuff. Daphne intended to make this the coolest party ever. Humming happily, she dumped her costumes and face paints across a cheery yellow bedspread. Matching curtains blew gently in the breeze.

She circled the bed and closed the miniblinds. Still feeling exposed, Daphne pulled the lined drape across the glass slider for privacy, leaving the door open for easy access to the patio.

Muted sounds of children's laughter and boisterous shouts drifted through the closed hall door. Daphne kicked off her sandals and skimmed out of her jeans. She had her T-shirt nearly off when a scraping sound at the slider made her swing around.

It'd be impossible to say who was most shocked, Daphne or a scruffy-looking man who stood poised on the balls of his feet as he stealthily shut and locked the glass door. The drape slipped through his fingers, silently closing them in together.

The T-shirt plopped at Daphne's feet. Her throat tightened and her hammering heart battered her ribs. Feeling the stranger's Delft-blue eyes making a thorough examination of her, she grabbed the first clown suit she could reach and covered herself as best she could with the slithery material. She started to scream, but suddenly found her breath driven from her lungs by the agile intruder, who vaulted over the bed in a single bound and clapped a strong hand to her mouth. A no-nonsense pistol caressed her ear before she could force air, let alone a scream, past her numb lips.

Her brother Kieran would've said only a fool would fight against those odds, but Daphne wasn't about to die without putting up a fight. She tried jabbing an elbow into her captor's midriff, but hit rock-hard abs. Next she attempted to disable him by stomping on his foot. Except that she was barefoot and he wore boots, as she quickly discovered. And the more she struggled, the more tenuous became her hold on the clown suit.

"Chill out," he growled, jerking her tighter against his own heaving chest. "Who the hell are you?" he demanded in a gruff stage whisper.

"Mmmf…mmfff," Daphne mumbled against his sweating fingers. He smelled sweaty, anyway, and rough whiskers scraped her neck, although his longer, sun-streaked blond hair was soft where it brushed her cheek. What a funny thing to notice *at a time like this*.

As her initial shock receded, Daphne tried to store her impressions—for the police—supposing she got out of this alive. He was tall. A rangy build, like her brother Perry. She was five-foot-eight; the man was taller. And stronger by far, she was learning. She couldn't budge him, and twisting only tightened his grip on her.

Her legs felt every quiver of his taut muscles hidden under threadbare blue jeans. A once-black sweat-stained T-shirt hugged a muscled torso. Iron-hard biceps indicated her captor probably kept fit working out or doing manual labor.

For all she knew, he could be April Ross's pool guy.

Although probably not. He seemed inordinately interested in what might be happening on the street in front of the house. *Bingo!* How close was the Ross home to the area cordoned off by police? It'd be due east of April's backyard. Quite close. Too close. Daphne began to shake uncontrollably as her mind revolved faster. He could be a hardened criminal. Maybe even a murderer.

That thought came when he forcefully dragged her to the far side of the front window, where he used the barrel of his gun to tip aside the blind. Apparently he didn't like what he saw. He swore ripely under his breath and flattened them both against the wall, fast.

It wasn't that Daphne hadn't heard such language before. Her brothers, Dane, Kieran and Perry, were a firefighter, a cop and a long-haul trucker, respectively. Even though she frequently complained about having too many bossy brothers, oh boy, did she wish any one of them would burst through that door right now. If she ever got out of this predicament, she vowed she'd pay strict attention to every one of her mom's lectures, too.

"Where's April?" her captor asked right beside her ear. "Are you keeping her company because Mike deployed again?" Ever so slowly, he slid his fingers off Daphne's mouth. But as she geared up to bellow for help, he waved the mean-looking pistol in her face. The cry froze on her lips.

"Get dressed," he hissed, sounding almost angry. Her fingers felt all-thumbs, and there was no way Daphne could comply.

Muttering, he gave her a shake and repeated his demand.

Logan Grant found that he was beginning to be affected by the armful of half-naked woman he'd surprised when he slipped in April's back door. At first he was too shocked over seeing anyone—let alone a partially clad anyone—in a room he'd counted on being empty. That, coupled with the fact that he was positive his cover had been blown in a big narcotics buy gone sour, meant Logan wasn't having the best day of his life.

Special Agent Grant had spent six months working his way into a position of power in an organization his agency had been trying to bring down for two years. He'd been minutes from meeting the next big fish in the scummy pond, which would've been another step up the slippery, slimy ladder of crime. Then all hell had broken loose. Cop cars had roared down side streets from all directions. And when push came to shove, Logan had been forced to take sides.

Billy Holt, his superior in the local opium import ring, saw him knock out another ring member and steal a pistol from him. Now Holt had more interest in tracking down Logan than in staying to fight local law enforcement, one or more of whom had to be on the take. Only an insider could've tipped off the cops.

Logan knew too much about the next big shipment due to land on California shores. It made him dangerous to the organization. Dangerous and expendable. Even now, two cars filled with Holt's trusted henchmen were combing the streets, hunting for him.

Under other circumstances, Logan thought he might work up a red-hot interest in this big-eyed, leggy woman—in close proximity to a nice, soft bed. Unfortunately, at the moment, saving his skin and hers took precedence over baser instincts.

He'd come here because his sister's home presented his only chance of escape. Though taller than Mike Ross, Logan thought he could borrow Mike's razor and fit into one of his shirts. Change clothes, use April's cell phone to contact his office, and poof, he'd be scooped up by associates, leaving Holt to wonder how he'd managed to pull a disappearing act.

Things rarely went according to plan in a special agent's life. This day had gone to hell more rapidly than most, however. Billy's goons cruised the streets, alleys and backyards, leaving Logan—what? With a hysterical, nearly nude female threatening to scream her head off, that was what.

To make matters worse, he'd stayed too long. He'd already put everyone in this house in jeopardy. He let loose another stream of colorful invective. Under current circumstances, it was all he could do.

Daphne's addled brain took in his second barked order—get dressed—and that was what she was trying desperately to do, even though it meant peeling the clown suit away from where she had it plastered to her front. Even though it meant revealing her scanty Victoria's Secret finery to a crazed gunman.

She attempted to shake out the material, bend and slide the colorful, baggy jumpsuit over first one leg, then the other. She nearly tripped and fell flat on her face. It wasn't humiliating enough that the gunman caught her. Oh, no. Worse, he zipped the suit all the way to her neck because her fingers were shaking so hard.

"What kind of getup is that?" he asked, eyeing her speculatively.

Fully covered now, Daphne felt a bit steadier. She smoothed back a stubborn curl that had slipped out of her clip and snapped back. "It's a clown suit, you idiot. I'm here to perform at a birthday party. Natalie's. Her name is Natalie.

You, uh, called her mother by name. Are you...ah...a fr-friend of April's?"

Hearing herself squeak, Daphne crossed her arms and grabbed her elbows just to have something solid to hang on to. No one, especially her brothers, would ever believe her if she told them she'd stood here trading niceties with a man holding a gun on her.

Logan noticed her wide, tawny cat eyes fixed on the 9 mm Luger he'd taken from one of Billy Holt's confederates—a much larger and more lethal weapon than the handgun he usually carried, a snub-nosed Smith and Wesson. All things considered, the party clown was holding up well. He figured that most women in her position would either be dissolved in hysterics by now or they'd have fainted.

"So, we're finally making progress," he said. "Dammit, I forgot Nat's birthday. I'll have to make it up to her later. Listen, can I trust you to open the door and call April back here without screaming down the house? I need to talk to her, but I'd rather Natalie didn't see me looking like this."

"I don't think so," Daphne sniffed. "You have one hostage already. I won't be party to helping you get another. Especially not one who's pregnant. What kind of degenerate are you?"

"Hostage?" He grinned then, showing two rows of very white, very even teeth. "I think you've been watching too many cop shows on TV. Just attract April's attention, please. Then sometime, when I'm not so rushed, maybe you and I can sit down over a cold beer and talk about how I'd have done things differently if I really *was* making you my hostage."

Receive a FREE hardcover book from

HARLEQUIN ROMANCE®

in September!

Harlequin Romance celebrates the launch of
the line's new cover design by offering you
this exclusive offer valid only in September,
only in Harlequin Romance.

To receive your
FREE HARDCOVER BOOK
written by bestselling author
Emilie Richards, send us four
proofs of purchase from any
September 2004 Harlequin
Romance books. Further details
and proofs of purchase can be
found in all September 2004
Harlequin Romance books.

*Must be postmarked
no later than October 31.*

**Don't forget to be one of the first
to pick up a copy of the new-look
Harlequin Romance novels in September!**

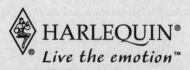